I0685588

GreyLore:
THE DARK
a novel

by
ar grey

ar grey

These stories are fictions; their only reality is their semblance
to our lives.

We aspire to provoke thought, not offense. If anything herein
offends, please forgive us.

"The dark begets the light, cossets and celebrates the light, revels in the light."

ag

Chapter 1.

Tendrils of light stretched languidly from the dark, itself receding not grudgingly but tenderly and lovingly, embracing the wisps of radiance and warmth as it retired under the longed-for crisp, clear dawn. The dark acceded reverently, adoringly, to buttery shades and dreamy, brightening skies now slowly and serenely dissipating the dark's lingering chill.

Slowly, gradually, the faltering thaw enveloping and suffusing the masses encamped and overfilling the streets and sidewalks and alleyways and every cranny and corner of the vast city square and all its surrounds relented to the sunshine's cosseting embrace, now gently cradling the gathered and still gathering mass.

A woman stretched and yawned. A man roused from the residue of dream. A young girl rose and shivered and arched her back in a moment's vision of scintillating grace revealed amid a suffusion of tongues sweeping stale lips and grimy teeth and fetid breath and base scratchings at unshamed fissures of mind and body. Limpid groans and tethered profanities and unapologetic belchings and gruntings scattered themselves amid all manner of trace betrayals, tagging each for who and what they are, and now remains only to fathom why they are here, why they are here now and, simply, why they are.

To the discerning, the languid, placid mood was clearly evolving, slowly and steadily and inexorably transmuting to an imminent, inevitable collapse. A woman snarled irritably. A man swore hard under his breath. A child mewled miserably, and more, still more amid gouged and pocked rumblings, nearby and distant, ever more and still more bitterly submerging the horde under staccato mutterings and festerings over some or other trivial and not-trivial blight and irritant, unaware and not caring to be aware of the what or the how or the why of this descent—let others decide and render it right, right now. Or else.

Gradually, inescapably, the gathering heat of the quietly seething mass suffused the bleary eyes and groping fingers and snarling faces and sunken, well-marred flesh. The growing heat endowed the congregation with a slowly engorging vigor and animation, imbuing the amassed with a barely subdued, feral malevolence ever more visible and audible and palpable, verging ever nearer to rank and effusive, cratered by growls and barks and gruntings and mutterings that progressively punctured its torpor, marking the slowly escalating stirring of this harvest.

Unsheathed violence was suborn as torpid chafing under barely recognized, subliminal reverence to cause greater than these provocations of base and overlong endurance of close air and seething rage, thick and clotting at throats, clutching at every breath. Only the veiled promise of this— their purpose and intent, here and now—held them from exploding into unadorned, unbounded savagery, staying them from savaging throat and eye and body and mind and more.

Words broke through grunt and growl, more hiss and snarl and glare and grimace than cogent and coherent, words lobbed at anyone and everyone and at no one in particular as they in the crowd congealed under dim hope and vague prayer to their purpose. They held themselves above their compulsions, somehow, barely, for what drew them here, now, like this.

Words penetrated, cloying and clawing to be heard, some even legible—'soon' and 'free' exulted—their remnant dissipated and lost amid the din and clutter of sound more noise than word. This was sign and signal revealing the mass as aware, at least subliminally, at least in barest rudiment, awaiting full awakening, coiling, readying to leap.

The people that were massed on the cracked and buckled and pocked streets and walks and stoops and tiny, bedraggled lawns were more wretched and restive and angry than any expectation or full understanding. Quiet, inward seething roiled them, unmistakable to least perception, civility and humanity straining on threshold of rupture, would not long endure, and then—feral madness.

A near-distant clamor from the back office erupted in a raucous laugh that was DeCeeve. The man blustered into the back room nattering away as all peace and quiet collapsed.

Ben Rob couldn't shear eyes from the precipice unfolding in the streets and alleyways below, and only nodded brusquely to DeCeeve as he let DeCeeve drone on, now finding himself languidly floating, distant and immersed in evanescent images suspended before him… a scattering of beautiful, *beauteous* young people interspersed among a sea of imperious murk—sowing seeds, *his* seeds.

He regarded his vision:

They were not simply, merely, beautiful… they were *beauteous*, listing on beatification—endowed of keenest insight, of sharpest discernment, of manner and bearing and presence adorned of demure modesty and thrilling innocence that fully captivated any and all on whom they focused even least attention. And they were his, fully his.

Amid these reminiscences Rob drifted back to Allman and to The Rafford, looming, not threatening but—ominous.

Rob slogged out of reverie, re-took *now*, and compelled himself to look-in-the-eye what he'd abandoned—and what he'd set into motion outside and below him. He could not escape what he'd set to motion as he scanned the scene of the amassed below, its face and effect extending beyond even *his* vision.

'He' rouses to awareness—finds himself suspended in the dark. He exists… formless and timeless in the dark, in the unimaginable dimension of the enduring, unmeasurable dark. The dark exists not as a void but as an indefinable essence—engulfing and subsuming all things, from real and surreal to

illusion and delusion and self-delusion, from the infinitesimal slightest to greater than any possible imaginings.

At first 'he' is aware of nothing—not UNaware but fully aware... of nothing—of neither light nor absence of light nor any attribute of space or time that he could perceive or imagine. He realizes that this absolute, this dark, IS something—which has no identity but is, simply, 'the dark', the words meaningless in and of themselves, there being no words existing by which to define or describe what and where he finds himself... being.

He realizes that in this here and now HE does not exist but for this state of disembodied thought and feeling arising as a vague essence of something, of someone, who does not, could not, otherwise exist. He is, in this sense, very much and singularly alone, part only of the dark.

Now, after an immeasurable transpiration of time—time not in the least measurable in this here and now—a vague, vanishingly feeble glow aspires to timorous existence amid the absolute of this otherwise consuming dark. The dark stretches beyond experience, beyond knowing or imagining—here and now intent on NOT devouring him... or that frailest aura now materializing in this, its earliest, most precarious conception, incarnation.

He—indiscernible singularity rising out of nothing, out of nowhere—is merged into existence and, now, is witness to another conception and birth, this a faintest aura itself now materialized into existence from out of nowhere, from out of nothing.

"How can something arise of nothing?"

His thoughts mingle with the emergence of this newborn essence of faintest aura and so, finally, there exists a here and a now the nature and purpose of which—his own and, now, that of this newfound aura—he cannot begin to fathom.

Chapter 2.

Rob stood shrouded and cosseted in the dark, reflecting on those first days at The Rafford.

"The Rafford...."

The very sound echoed power, derived simply of itself, evoking lightning and rolling thunder, tongues daring to abandon sanctuary and utter the word 'Rafford', the very word chilling him with arrogant, condescending threat—if he dared, whatever he dared.

"The Rafford—of the not-for-the-likes-of-me, lair of the hidden, the secret from the-likes-of-me," and as afterthought, *"the wretched-likes-of-me."*

He wondered it absently, why the image of 'wretched'—base and miserable and vile—sprang to mind, even as the eye of the beholder—his own—held him immobile:

"I suppose we are all, each in our own ways, 'wretched' to some lesser or greater degree."

He silently prided himself on his magnanimous grace, allowing that the 'likes-of-me' are only 'likely all' rather than 'surely all' wretched. He thought on it a moment—then reviled himself his grudging, petty generosity, derived of greed, of transparent aspiration, thoroughly base in itself, that he himself was, must surely be, above the 'likes-of-me.'

Memory wafted through him, a chilling wind, and he tried to put his finger on how, why, some few he'd met those first days at The Rafford had made him feel... alien.

He recalled the morning he'd first seen them strolling across one of The Rafford's vast pedestrian malls in that small, tight grouping of theirs, the hallmark of theirs.

"Not strolling... marching. No—marauding."

They were tramping across The Rafford commons advancing in his direction, their approach provoking a vague, subliminal sense of... *"of what, unease? What else to call it?"*

He couldn't put his finger on exactly what the sight of them inspired in him, *"surely not fear,"* but he understood the 'surely' was shamefully open and exposed.

"Maybe it's more of... dread."

He wondered at the sanctity of such nuance, so needing to shelter pride—*"no, self-esteem"*—and wondered at the what and the why of it, of how we think ourselves or urge ourselves or need ourselves to be, or to *not* be.

"And why such depths of animosity, antipathy, at just the barest glimpse of them?"

He watched them, mesmerized... *"a malevolence inching toward me, not in space or time but in some other dimension of thought and sense, their essence somehow more grim and foreboding than I can even imagine."*

He groped for the words to ply the thoughts, couldn't put his finger on the sense of unease, disquiet, they inspired, and wondered if such sense was only in him and in no one else, and what does *that* tell of?

As they approached he realized it was only one among them who inspired that... *"revulsion, what other word for it?"*

He soon discovered the name of that inspiration: 'The Junior Allman' it was called.

It was a strange name, singular, and Rob wondered what such a person, young man... *"Chimera"*... could be like, who is so named.

Rob observed the small agglomeration approaching, TJ Allman somehow its inspiration, its fulfillment. He could discern, like a taste or scent or feel from some vagary of the group's essence, that TJ Allman, at its center, *was* its center, the center of its gravity and mass and very existence, around which the others agglutinated, to whom the others couldn't resist adhering as from an unfathomable, surreal force of nature, they enveloping him, engulfing and embracing him— the word *"obscenely"* rose to mind—emulating him in every least detail of walk and manner and thought, groveling and ingratiating and oozing around him.

"Promiscuous..." the word *"whores"* edged in the word's wake... *"cultists, mindless acolytes."*

"Idolaters," silence whispered in the dark.

8

The whisper brandished images of what is done in the name of zealotry and the worship of imagined gods and living idols, for which any atrocity is fully justified not just as demanded but as commanded, not just as right but as righteous.

TJ Allman was tall and thin, even gaunt, with a thicket of dark hair flowing loosely above steel eyes but cropped short at back, with chiseled nose, granite chin, vermillion lips. But the eyes... those were his power, something in the eyes, of coldest hardened steel, of calculating indifference callous to anything, to everything, with no room for least humanity, failing any least compassion, decrying any least refuge of the timorous or guileless.

Those feelings were fleeting apparitions come and gone, leaving only the residue of... something, and Rob wondered if everyone felt such or if only he did alone. Such is never talked of, and Rob wondered absently why, wondered if people are even capable of such thought, such *kind* of thought, and had learned long ago not even to broach such talk.

The feelings TJ Allman inspired translated to instant caution and vigilant constraint in dealing with him—*"someone with whom to be very cautious,"* and Rob wondered if 'afraid' was the more correct depiction.

The small crowd, Allman at its center, neared Rob. He hoped he wouldn't attract their notice but knew, somehow portending, that it was hopeless prayer.

"Good say... you're with us this morning, eh?"

Rob recognized the salutation, wondered where he'd heard it before—*"yes... political economics"*—then instantly recaptured vigilance.

He'd noted the words, not the faces behind them, and now turned attention to the faces, focusing on them not as some gelatinous agglomeration but as individuals mired within it.

Rob felt a near-overwhelming urge to ignore them, to simply walk on as if not having heard, but knew without least doubt it was the last thing he should do, only inviting a still deeper, baser intrusion.

"I can't forever evade their kind, and pity that," he thought, wondering if 'tragic that' was the more correct, for all

the atrocities suffered for not being able to just step aside and out of the way. *"They—he—would never allow it."*

Rob forced a politic smile, strained it across his lips, struggled it into his eyes, and felt sure he'd exposed his need to force the smile. Then he relaxed as images of futility welled, why *pretend* to be, why not *be...* and his strained smile transformed to genuine as he relaxed into the inexorable with calm, detached equanimity, surprising even himself.

"Maybe it's just my bigotry, my repugnance of the elite, of the privileged—MY fault, not theirs... or his."

He felt tendrils of shame reach for him, for his dark bodings, as silence whispered in the dark: *"No."*

Other whispers: *"Don't apologize for this of yourself."*

He vaguely wondered if he was evading responsibility, culpability, for so tempting, goading, their bigotry against him, then pushed the thought away... *"now is not the time."*

Silence whispered: *"Then when?"*

Debate simmered in him, then held itself in abeyance, for now.

The silent dialogue ended as it began and Rob understood he need only, simply, steer clear of controversy in this least encounter with TJ Allman. A simple matter. But he knew otherwise, portent assured him.

When invited—*"commanded?"*—to join them on their stroll—*"march?"*—Rob forced himself to smile and join them.

"What else to do? Nothing."

"Plesant," one spoke up, very quiet, offering his introduction.

Rob wondered what lay hidden, or not, within Plesant to have been chastened to such restraint, such reticence, the trace residue of self-esteem struggling mightily to rise up against that withering him. Rob wondered what spark remained alive in him, just barely, to raise esteem to such timorous audacity in the face of... Allman.

Plesant waited for consent to speak further, but none was offered and he screwed-up courage and continued, murmuring haltingly:

"Sometimes they call me... 'Pleaser.'"

10

He colored at that designation, silently confessing his shame, his obeisance to TJ Allman glaringly exposed.

Plesant's manner was genuinely welcoming, but his voice quavered, especially at mention of his nickname, at having been so branded, but better to bring it up himself now than to be derided and having it slung in his face later.

To no one and to everyone, speaking to the air or to Heaven, TJ Allman sneered:

"It's because you're so docile, try so hard to please."

Plesant smiled tightly, struggled for genuine smile, struggled it to eyes as well as to lips, failed miserably.

Rob felt Plesant's struggle to self-effacing, miserable smile, and cringed at sight of it.

"What else to do? Nothing," Rob reviling his own wretched cravenness.

Rob loathed his own helplessness—*"worthlessness"*—in righting Plesant's misery, and struggled to rise up against his own witherings, and wondered how much of himself he revealed in what he did—and did not—say and do in face of this provocation, and would have settled for simply concealing his own worthlessness, or worthiness, aware that sometimes silence is all he should voice.

Allman spoke the way he walked, with effortless and absolute confidence of unrivaled power and full control.

Allman spoke, still to the air and to Heaven, his personal confidants:

"So, Pleaser… where's this boy from? Summarize him."

Plesant cleared his throat, stuttered sounds without meaning, and finally managed:

"So… what did you say your name was? You from around here?"

Rob fought the impulse to answer 'I didn't' and 'no,' and instead answered question for question as put to him, answered as pity for the young man 'Plesant' and as diplomacy to the future, who knows that need.

Rob answered as pleasantly as temper allowed, even more so, testament to Rob's will and control—at least over this, now, of himself, if over nothing and no one more.

"That's more than most, even such as this Allman, could likely do."

Rob understood his was only aspiration to rise above, as he struggled to rise above petty provocation and not-so-petty portent of threat, and felt shamed at his own arrogance, thinking himself better for having this trace residue of self-control.

Rob's replies offered meager fodder to Allman's sarcasm and ascendance. Still, Allman excavated opportunity to goad:

"Ben Rob..." pause, search the air for fodder, found it:

"Been Robbed? Ben—Son of—Robber? Or just plain *Robber*? Yes." Definitive judgment decided on character and reality and so, nickname.

"Well, Robber, at The Rafford you'll need to stay on your toes. But you'll find we're a very tolerant lot here—even to those of you from… State," sneering the word. "I encourage you to apply to me for help when the need arises—and it *will* arise, be sure. I may even get you through your need."

Allman continued without pause, still to the air and to Heaven, now apparently to Plesant, whose smile had withered to pathetic grimace:

"Frankly, I can't imagine why The Rafford bothers. If they *could* be one of us they'd *be* one of us, so why pretend they could." There was no question to it.

Allman cocked his head, just barely, to glimpse Rob's reaction. Seeing Rob expressionless, TJ Allman continued:

" 'State'… 'State school'… isn't that where Blacks and Jews go? And of course those Asian kind. They're all a tricky lot, you know—best watch out for them. They'll steal the answers to the exams, sell 'em to you, then leak the theft and blame you."

Allman stole another glance at Rob searching for a reaction, expectation leering behind steel eyes and granite jaw:

"They do it to cheat you, can't otherwise win."

Plesant's smile dropped to a deadpan smoldering and he stared straight ahead, muscles rigid, struggling to control at least himself, and failing even that.

From Allman:

"Don't pay any attention to Pleaser here. He's one of them. Even if he does squeal and protest he's not... I can tell one when I smell one. You're one of them too, Rob. I can smell it on you. But don't worry. As I said: We're a tolerant lot here at The Rafford."

The others in the small enclave every now and then sniggered and smirked as if on cue, but otherwise kept mouths shut and eyes leveled straight ahead. Rob could smell the fear in them—and struggled to not be clone of Allman's pervasive contempt.

Arriving at one of the lecture halls, the coterie moved to enter. Rob was ecstatic relief: He'd share no classes with them—for now. Debate raged in him, ended grudgingly, and Rob mumbled a parting civility to Allman and his swarm.

Allman breathed a smile to Rob:

"Our fraternity's hosting an open house tonight. Nine. Sharp. *Be* there."

Rob kept walking, no reply to the 'invitation.'

"What else to do? Nothing." And again he cringed at this retreat.

In the receding distance, Rob could hear Plesant's voice softly whining appeal to Allman:

"Excuse, please, sir... being new... he won't understand. I'll call on him and... explain."

Allman didn't deign acknowledge that Plesant even existed, he already listed to non-existence.

Chapter 3.

Ben Rob stood silent in the dark, eyes closed, praying gratitude for the great sheet of glass that was the far wall of the back office, shielding him, holding him back from plunging himself into the dark and into the mass of people teeming the streets and alleyways below.

Distant murmuring ruffled through Rob's meandering thought, then a vulgar, overloud laugh perforated the background drone and snapped Rob back into the here and now.

The laugh tore Rob out of his reverie and left him as raw and bristling as a lover abruptly denied his most urgent craving and greatest need—quiet. Rob instantly recognized the corrosive sound, repulsed less by the sound than by its source.

"The sound hunts for me, rapacious predation stalking me, having at me—and that the least malignance of its source."

DeCeeve exploded into the back room with laughter that fouled the air, pervaded the silence and violated the dark.

Rob struggled to refuse the sound and *him*, but could only cling stonily to staring out the panoramic window at the vast humanity occupying the streets and alleyways below.

DeCeeve slammed the door behind, punctuating his assault, intruding and corrupting the silence, further violating Rob's illusion, self-delusion, of command over the silence and the dark. Rob wondered absently how much of this intrusion was DeCeeve's oblivious disregard and how much was a greater ambition toward that purpose, an intentional corrosion. He thought to accord DeCeeve that measure of intelligence and craftiness as being his intent, but resigned himself to the certainty that DeCeeve was simply too dense and too oblivious of anyone but himself.

DeCeeve sauntered jauntily into the back room in his customary, loud and crass and loathsome self, as ever too narrow to anything more, anything deeper, than himself.

The instant the door slammed shut behind DeCeeve, the din of the front-office dissipated into quiet murmuring, the only residue, the only revelation, DeCeeve had even been there.

Rob grieved his loss, mourned the despoiled quiet and illusion of peace, and desolately groped for how, if ever, he could recover peace in the face of all that lay behind DeCeeve, and imagined he understood:

"Only by deserving it."

Lament wailed triumph over him, pallid exultation of frail, wilted truth: *"Lament glories over me as always, recognizes and gloats over my guilt."*

DeCeeve remained oblivious, unaware and uncaring of having corrupted the atmosphere, such refinement beyond him as he inhaled deep satisfaction under smug self-absorption.

He cocked his head back toward the front office:

"Good people, those," nodding sagely: "But not of the same fabric as I—or you." The last, grudgingly.

DeCeeve smiled broadly, extravagant flaunting of generosity for having included Rob within his own sanctity and then, stepping too close, clapped Rob on the back with force enough to jolt, flourishing a smile of fetid persona in vast self-satisfaction under harlequin grin dangled too near Rob's face.

DeCeeve, in conspiratorial whisper, sneered:

"They're scared, you know."

DeCeeve grinned dimly under high exaltation soaring with arrogance, to deign this secret knowledge to Rob.

DeCeeve continued in hushed revelation:

"You hear it in their voices, see it in their eyes, feel it in the very air they breathe," and again he flashed his smirk as Rob recoiled under the other's grand affectation.

"With good reason," Rob muttered quietly, more to himself, with trace smile the residue of his grimace.

"Good reason?"

DeCeeve exposed simmering, genuine rage:

"Good reason? You watch your mouth, Rob, you with your 'good reason.'"

DeCeeve snarled the words in Rob's face, caught himself, transformed leer to smile of pure treacle, then summoned pretense of sweet calm. He took a moment more— *"to rehearse further abrasions, no doubt,"* Rob thought—then:

"Rob—Rob, Rob... Rob," sneering condescendingly.

Rob bristled, amazed he could restrain himself from smashing the man's teeth—*"as he fully deserves"*—and managed to sustain his silence. Rob couldn't help but hear the condescension suffused in the sound of his name, a feint of long practice by DeCeeve, signaling the finality of his words, the transcendence and rightness and righteousness of his words, fully above any least challenge.

"That's not the way," Rob determined, weakly certain that he was correct in restraining himself from smashing teeth.

DeCeeve continued, satisfied with Rob's silence, taken as servile contrition:

"I've got that President Kurb of theirs right where I want him."

DeCeeve flashed another treacly smile as he clenched air in fist white with force, President Kurb a fly mortally helpless in his grip.

DeCeeve hissed theatrically, eyes drawn, lips vermillion: "And you *know* it," sneering lofty triumph down on Rob.

DeCeeve concluded:

"That bill will finish him—and you *know* it!"

The sound of his words was carnal thrill to him—as Rob recoiled at sight and sound and thought of him.

DeCeeve couldn't help himself, fully in throes of lusting over his dominance, and continued as sage to dim pupil:

"You saw it almost as soon as I did. I know. I saw it in you."

"As if you could see anything of me."

Rob clung to silence—against revulsion of *himself,* he was fully aware of his own guilt, how his own hubris had landed him here, now, like this, with DeCeeve and those like DeCeeve defiling him.

16

"I deserve to be hunted down by his self-righteous arrogance, my own ascendance having brought him here, to this, to befoul me like this."

Rob forbade the sneer working his lips, urging him to self-idolatry, and struggled to revile himself as he fully deserved.

Rob recalled in painstaking detail, undertaking to explain to DeCeeve again and still again, with all foreboding, nimbus words exhorted to empty face and vacant eyes, the ways and means to achieve this perfection of Rob's design:

"Endeavoring to train parrot to words, more sound and noise than sense and reason to DeCeeve and such of his kind."

Rob stopped himself, struggled still again to silence word and look and thought against the onrush of his own arrogance and ascension reaching for him to grip and rip him, reviling him for his own, insidious and loathsome corrosions.

DeCeeve: "That bill will finish him, end of the great political machine that launched President Richard T. Kurb in his once and long-gone landslide victory—and flaming end to his Reality Party. He cannot hope to recover from the backlash coiled and waiting, wet-hot and ready to penetrate him."

Eyes glossing under ethereal revelation, DeCeeve continued, lubricated by the crushing triumph he envisaged:

"That crowd below tells the story: They despise him with passion unsurpassed in Presidential politics. And I…" he sneered a sideways glance at Rob, brimming with barely veiled disdain behind thinnest veneer of credit to Rob… *"we—* spawned that unbridled hate. I… *we"*—sneering another grudging attribution to Rob—"were the architects of the platform that cornered and pinned him, from which he's got no escape!"

Again DeCeeve snatched-up a fistful of air in almighty triumph over Kurb and the Reality Party, eyes turned rapturously heavenward.

Rob recalled, fully silent to word and look:

"I struggled through countless hours melding into weeks and months and years, coaching DeCeeve, to instill in him some least scraps of rudimentary understanding of my

17

scheme. I scripted his every line and tone and look, fully my blueprint from first to last and, now, to the very threshold of ineluctable triumph." Rob cringed at thought of such Pyrrhic 'triumph.'

Rob recalled endless hours exhaustively driving his words into DeCeeve's mouth:

"Kurb is a socialist through and through—he supports ever more unaffordably extravagant benefits to the poor and middle classes. He supports ever greater government regulations that only increase the cost to business and only further constrain job creation. He supports ever more stringent environmental restrictions on oil and gas and coal that only further drive up the cost of energy and of business. He supports ever expanding credits to wasteful green projects..." and on and on: *"Kurb will succeed only in bankrupting our free enterprises! Kurb isn't just FOR big government he IS big government! Kurb isn't just FOR socialism he IS socialism! Kurb is the FACE of socialism—the archenemy of our free markets!"*

Now DeCeeve intoned to Rob, depicting Rob as the ever-dull schoolboy forever needing instruction:

"President Kurb—imminently *ex*-President Kurb—has no way out! He's the aristocrat's President—deigning ever more charity for the people while jobs disappear and welfare becomes not just a *way* of life but *becomes* life. He stands in the way of a new era of *real* freedom and *real* equality. He's the walking dead and he can't even smell the stench of his own rotting corpse!"

DeCeeve punctuated his rapture with a cackle of obscene laughter, gazing heavenward for his just reward. Then, as if of his own thought and word:

"If he vetoes my—*our*— Bill," casting another condescending glance at Rob, "the people's incarnate hate and rage will immolate him, and he and all his women and men will be reduced to ash in the inevitable conflagration!" He flashed an arrogance of dark portent at Rob.

DeCeeve: "If Kurb signs the Liberty Bill the people's jubilation will riot through the streets and through every corridor of every State Capitol and every local ward and every corner of wealth and power and everyone will know *I* have won!"

Now DeCeeve acceded nothing to Rob, Rob not worth the bother of the pretense.

DeCeeve: "Either way… the people will see Kurb as he *is*—the craven, morally bankrupt Harlequin of the old, worn-out, broken down ways. And either way… I've *got* him!"

Again DeCeeve raised eyes to heaven in blissful anticipation of ethereal reward, fully savoring the smile of Goodness he envisioned shining down on him.

Rob stared at DeCeeve, struggled to fully grasp the abhorrence he himself had created.

Rob deliberated silently: *"This… the people have earned."*

Rob deliberated another moment, and reviled himself:

"No. The people don't comprehend the future they're falling to… if they did, DeCeeve and our Liberty Party would have been dead and rotted before we'd ever gotten started."

DeCeeve droned on, but now Rob was lost to him:

"DeCeeve is right… Kurb has already failed, is already finished and done—and cannot be un-done."

Rob meditated in awe: *"How could DeCeeve so thoroughly misunderstand Kurb? How could DeCeeve so fully be subverted by our—my— illusions and dogma?"*

Rob contemplated that enormity:

"Kurb has a solid record of defending the interests of common, ordinary people. He's got a long-established record of straightforward, honest dealings. Kurb's policies have modestly restricted 'free' enterprise so to cushion ordinary people from the worst of this devastating recession—and DeCeeve knows it. How can he so fully deny it… to himself?"

Rob was mystified:

"How could such self-deception ever have spawned? How could DeCeeve be rendered so pliable, so self-deceiving, as to utterly suborn reality to our own political theater? How could DeCeeve be aware and still be so fully un-aware? How can DeCeeve so thoroughly devour our—my—lies?"

"No, not lies—evasions."

Rob felt himself flailing, drowning in the dark, asphyxiated by the weight of his own guilt, fully understanding:

"I'm simply comforting myself, deceiving myself, by constructing such self-deluding, self-idolizing cause between evasion and lie, interring myself within my own deceptions and self-deceptions, to which I'd so willingly, willfully, succumbed."

"Still, I understand the vanishingly small distinction between evasion and lie, despite self-idolatry seducing me into self-deception: Evasion is, by its very nature, intended to deceive—and so is more damning than any simple lie. Evasion is a lie no matter how you explain it or excuse it, no matter how you justify it or disguise it. Or try." So he defiled himself.

Rob heard whispers reviling him in the dark—*"reviling me as I fully deserve."*

The image of Allman rose-up, faced him eye to eye, rejoiced to find Rob finally recognizing his own corruption cajoling him in the dark:

"Deception—for the greater good—reveals the greater truth. You need justify it to no one... least of all to yourself."

Rob's eyes glossed over as recollection overtook him, of days at The Rafford, of ploys undertaken, overtaking of their own, and... *"of Allman—insidious inspiration to a conspiracy of deception and self-deception in the guise of the 'greater good'."*

Rob, challenging Allman: *"Whose 'greater-good'?"*

Allman: *"You would say it doesn't matter—as long as it's yours."*

Rob stood silent in the dark, looking down over the panorama of streets and alleyways below, observing the scene through the vast back office window-wall, lost in the sea of people crowding the streets below, riveted by his recurring nightmare of blissful vision: his beauteous people sowing the seeds of his truths.

'He' finds himself suspended in the dark, sole onlooker in the dark—now witness to a vanishingly dim aura materializing in the dark.

Within that spectral glow a diminutive creature unfurls, finds itself seated on highest perch, and now both figure and perch struggle to rise fully into existence within that impossibly pallid aura, all enveloped in the dark.

Figure and perch and aura scintillate, vacillate between reality and extinction, at times not there at all and wholly enveloped in the otherwise absolute of the dark, and then materializing back into uncertain, precarious existence.

As 'he' observes, he witnesses the dark not as a void but as an all-encompassing creation endowed with inherent vitality of some deeper reality and he... countenanced to awareness and to witness.

'He' is aware that the dark yields to, allows existence of, such thought and feeling as he and, now, this other newly created, newly born, are allowed to experience of this 'here' and of this 'now'. He is aware the dark is only now become newly inhabited, newly inhibited, by these newborn conceptions—his and theirs—even as the 'how' and the 'why' remain inert and unfathomable.

The diminutive figure on its highest perch cosseted within that palest aura all cling to each other, each in its own way sentient, each nestling with and somehow within the other amid the all encompassing, subsuming dark, each subliminally aware that without the dark they have no existence, there can be no existence. Creature and perch and aura depend, each on the other, for anchor and survival—and understand, in turn, that they need the dark and, somehow, the dark needs them every bit as fully.

'He' understands that he is witness to each embarking on its own, and his own, unknown and unknowable destination and purpose, and more—on that of the sustaining, subsuming dark.

Chapter 4.

It was early days at The Rafford and already Ben Rob breathed deeply of the rarified atmosphere, reminiscing to hardly any time ago on thoughts and dreams of the future, of low-hanging fruit awaiting him, stalled and halted in their very creation—*"I only needing to reach up and pluck the future and render it not just possible but inevitable."*

"The Rafford..."

Rob rolled the words over his tongue—*"The Rafford"*—feeling its power as a vague and distant, vulgar craving, all but unimaginable so short a while ago, amazed at such fundamental transformation imbedded in so brief a span of time.

"Unimaginable?"

He mulled that a moment, suddenly understanding:

"Yes, unimaginable—for failing not to aspire but even to imagine aspiring."

Rob considered the enormity of such hardened conditioning, meticulously conditioned to not even *imagine* aspiring to greater futures, imbedded so immanently within us as to be wholly above and beyond reach, unthinkable, even unimaginable.

He considered the depth of such subliminal subversion, such absolute control and conditioning, and staggered under inchoate comprehension—inchoate because:

"Even now, even still, full comprehension of such thorough and effective manipulation is beyond my comprehension—how to imagine a thing beyond all experience, beyond that of anyone I'd ever known or could know?"

At least that much he understood, now.

He drove thought aside, 'now' remaining only to prepare for the day—*"and it's still such early days for me"*—and avoid confrontation.

Images of Allman and Plesant tramped by, and he shuddered under thought of what the year would bring if early days had already brought… this.

But thought exerted will of its own, as he knew it would and too often did, despite his greatest will to *not* succumb.

"Some things are in-your-face uncontainable."

And still more of doubt and self-doubt:

"Why am I even here? State University's good enough, right? That's the place for me: Good, solid reputation for good, solid achievement, a place in which to feel comfortable and safe. A place from which to launch a good, solid, comfortable future."

Rob struggled to convince himself he *preferred* the unpretentiousness of State: *"It's 'me', after all, so much more… me."*

But he knew better. From the very beginning, even before awareness of it, he'd known, somehow had felt, somehow had understood—*"and Goodness only knows how… or why."*

From an elusive wisp of a notion, he'd somehow understood the essence of the contradiction in some primal, guttural way. In the silence and the dark of those years gone by, he'd thought he could ignore those murky, fleeting images of undefined portent and forget the very notion of it, and even forgive the compulsion of it—*"and now, can I?"*

He considered that perception stirring in him.

"I can feel it—The Rafford—welling in me, begin to surge in me… and render me fully, irretrievably woken to my own self-deceit and self-idolatry."

"And shame," whispered in the dark.

"The Rafford, the taste of The Rafford, is now in me, won't ever leave me, and I've got to deal with my contempt for myself, that comes of being suborn to petty ambition and vulgar pride rooted in the greeds of self-idolatry."

Whispers in the dark cajoled and provoked:

"So, State's okay? So, you prefer the good, solid reputation of State, the comfort and safety of State, the prison and life sentence of State, the preserve of the mediocre and the

meek at State? Well to hell with State, to hell with that asylum for timid minds and dull ideas…" as silence whispered in the dark: *"and to hell with you."*

Shame gripped him and shook him, then he shucked-off self-contempt:

"State's a diversion, a ruse. Like a strategy of war, launch feint after feint to divert the meek from the real, defining battles, routing time and energy and aspiration away from the real struggles, from the real front-lines of minds and ideas—and power—that can only be conceived and spawned and fulfilled in the rarified, celestial Raffords of this world."

He deliberated, staggered under the enormity of possibilities:

"I allow myself to uncritically accept a de-facto, second-class status—and allow myself to convince myself that I prefer it. The 1%'s repression and oppression of the 99% are both cause and effect, derived of subtle manipulations and concerted efforts to marginalize and de-legitimize that vast underclass—the 99% that are the poor and the middle classes and the not-lofty-enough-no-matter-how-lofty-you-think-you-are classes of this world. And this subliminal rendering is the reflection of the power and control we give not just grudgingly but willingly and even joyfully to our legislators and executives and judiciary—and this conception renders all other oppressions and repressions, through all history, petty and trifling by comparison, parochial and provincial by comparison."

He understood its essential iteration:

"The ultimate ascendance of the top tier, even above that 1%, is having people like me never reach this awareness, to have people like me farmed-out to the institutions and preserves and labors under which we are subjugated, once and forever and irretrievably subjugated, under the conviction, under the illusion and delusion, that our leaders are right and righteous and represent us and know what's best for us—convincing us to convince ourselves that we are in fact too ignorant and too simple to understand the complexities of this world, and more, that we would be undemocratic even to consider, let alone to aspire to, our vision of real justice. And

so the 99% are confined and constrained by the 1%... and made to believe it is for our own greater good."

He considered:

"We are driven to be convinced of our ignorance and ineptitude and so yield not grudgingly but willingly and even adoringly to the cardinal hubris of the 1%."

Awakening shuddered through him—the sight and sound and feel and taste of *truth*.

"The sound of truth..." and he refused to think any more of it, refused any thought to contradict and discomfit his new-found assurance of that truth, and closed his mind to any other thought, to any least self-doubt, as whispers in the dark taunted:

"How can you, why should you, be different?"

He fought to suppress whispers in the dark:

"How can you possibly know, how could anyone as ordinary as you possibly know, be absolutely sure, of such grand subterfuges? Can 'the sound of truth' swear itself true?"

He fought the near-overwhelming impulse to shrug off this discovery, to abandon this illusion, delusion, as simply the gnawings of imagination, or of paranoia—thinking the 1% capable and guilty of such vast manipulations.

"The notion is near-overwhelming: that I'd already been conditioned to shrug-off any suspicion that the 1% fully manipulates and subjugates the 99%. Even now I feel the need to convince myself I can't possibly be right—and it is that very notion that I've got to resist."

Still he argued with himself:

"How can I know, be absolutely sure, I can distinguish truth from illusion—or paranoia?"

He deliberated:

"I can FEEL the eddies of power around me! I can FEEL the 1%—and most particularly those who control the 1%—inspecting me, surmising me... dismissing me! Or trying to. I can feel their will bearing down on me and on all those like me, down through all of history."

Rob tried to shrug-off delusions of conspiracy... *"but how can I deny what I feel? Their power is gathered around me, engulfing me, driven to devour me and snuff me out, in their craving to bend the future to their will—I can FEEL it! How can I deny what I FEEL?"*

With a final lunge against such extravagant ravings, Rob struggled to sidestep the downward spiral of thought and feeling and, he had to admit to himself, paranoia, and lurched to seize something of serenity, or some least bit of something close to it.

He struggled to turn his mind away, tried to reminisce about the past, about where he'd been, about how he'd gotten to The Rafford—but again the word *'Rafford'* rolled through his mind... *"a palpable presence whose power I just cannot deny despite my every effort to deny it, the word impelling me to confirm the self-doubt and the debased humility inspired and instilled in me through all the years of my life and through all the years of the lives of everyone I'd ever known or could ever possibly know."*

Rob considered the twist of fate that had brought him here, to The Rafford, and understood that it was not, could not be, random chance:

"My grades and my placement on the national exams were high enough to provide an illusion of having a chance at one of 'The Raffords'—but I preferred the modest excellence of State. And so, to State I went. I'd been counseled to consider other universities, marginally more impressive or prestigious, but those were essentially expensive versions of State, with bloated reputations and meritless posturings. But 'The Raffords'—such were never mentioned, or fleetingly and derisively out-of-the-question for the likes of me."

But one thought riveted:

"And I didn't mind! I'd even convinced myself that I actually preferred State! I preferred mediocrity—and wasn't even aware of it! And that's the killer—I was not even aware!"

He resurrected the sound and taste and feel of memory:

"Almost three full years at State and then, one day, out of the blue... a letter. It didn't even have my name on it, just my address and 'dear student.'"

Rob recalled:

"I'd considered that salutation—omitting my name— the appearance of blind chance, of being randomly plucked

from an anonymous sludge of addresses. The scheme was rank… and thoroughly transparent."

He recollected:

"The letter offered an exchange. If I was so inclined and motivated and ambitious, I'd spend a year at a Rafford and a Rafford would spend a year at State—a 'pilot study' by the graduate studies department of one of the Raffords."

Rob re-lived the feel of that letter, the feel of it in his hand, fingers pricking and sparking at the feel of that letter, and had recognized it instantly—*"the feel… of portent."*

"I'd realized even then that at that very moment I had already embarked, I had already been set into motion, before ever taking my first breath of The Rafford."

"I remember such premonitions—what else to call them?—at other times too, at some or other trivial awakening to new realities that were looming, hanging in the air at my face, waiting only for me to pluck them… and I hadn't given those imaginings a second thought."

Rob marveled at the influences exerted all around us by the unseen:

"From the first, I'd understood—they would interview me and test me, craving to know: What could I or anyone like me possibly want of a Rafford or possibly do at a Rafford? I thought it singularly demeaning, transparent posturing, probing me for what I might want of a Rafford. Of course, they wanted not what I wanted but what… they… wanted, whoever 'they' are, hidden and secret deep in their lairs. Of course. What else. Their evasions were a child's game. Their purpose: to assess the peril posed to them by the lesser."

"I understood from the first and so, during the interview process, I clung to sincere demeanor and straight talk and simple reply and I balanced everything they probed, forbidding any slightest smirk or sneer at their grand and manifest, childlike transparency and pretense. But I understood thoroughly: They were delving for any least betrayal that such as I might suspect them… and usurp them."

He recalled realizing:

"They had absolute grip on wealth and power… and were definitively resolute in plumbing the depth of threat that I

and such as I posed or could possibly pose—I and my kind, my class. They were probing, readying, arming—against me and everyone like me."

Rob smiled grimly:

"So I gave them the right answers and lulled their suspicions that I might be even least aware of them or of their purpose. I maneuvered around their suspicions—right enough in the right ways... and wrong enough in the other ways—and revealed to them that I was sincerest sycophant to their vainglory, that I was the embodiment of awed humility of them, my betters. I was extravagant gratitude for the opportunity to genuflect to their supremacy. I was their most humble servant in any and every way possible. I would bend over for them and smile abiding gratitude to them."

"I knew with an absolute certitude that I'd maneuvered them to select me. How did I know? All the while they were dissecting me and inspecting me, what I'd felt with that first touch of their 'invitation' to be interviewed, that pricking and sparking sensation flooding through me at first touch of that letter in my hand, grew ever more intense... and its ends ever more inevitable."

Rob brought himself back to now:

"And now? I've embarked on their study of me, their study in anthropology, like Jane Goodall and her apes—I and my class, primitives in the King's Court under scrutiny by The Royal Academy—studying me and my kind... so that I and my kind could never mount any least resistance, so never able even to image being any least threat."

Rob smiled genuine satisfaction verging on joy:

"And that's fine with me—they won't, can't, imagine it's me studying them."

"But," he had to admit to himself, *"what I really want, what I really intend, is to study 'my' self, my need, my insatiable need—to know my own 'self', so to overcome my own self."*

Rob wondered what he was capable of, of malice, and of what good, of what best of all—*"no matter the cost and damn the cost."*

"That… drives me: To measure my 'self' against theirs, against their 'selves,' and to pit my 'self', my will, against theirs. And that… I can do best not by studying them but by being them."

Whispers in the dark:

"And all you learn will be yours."

Chapter 5.

Ben Rob stood silent in the dark looking out the great window of the back office of the Liberty Spire. He stared down at the great mass of people milling and elbowing amid every crack and crevice and corner of every street and alley below.

A near-distant, musical din of chatter penetrated the silence and the dark, punctured by a singular, overloud, vulgar laugh. Rob bristled at the sound, soiled and corrupted by the sound, battled his urge to storm out the back room and launch himself at the source of that sound, barely managing to stop himself, marveled at his own strength of will stopping him pounding that excoriation, violation, into repugnant memory.

"I haven't yet done what I'd set out to do."

That was rationale and justification and resolve for the otherwise inexcusable refusal to commit harm against that fetid persona and its excreta.

It was simple statement of fact... *"with neither grief nor relief nor any judgment on what I'd set out to do, just aiming to get done what demands implacably to be done."*

DeCeeve exploded into the back room, vaporizing all vestige of quiet, the dark itself corrupted by the sound and him.

DeCeeve inhaled deeply, strutted, smug amid full satisfaction, nodding sagely back toward the front office:

"Good people, those," cocking his head back toward the front office.

"But not of the same stuff as you and I are made of."

Rob denied DeCeeve any least expression of repugnance for this, just one more of DeCeeve's signature condescensions, and DeCeeve not worthy of open revulsion, he beneath even that.

DeCeeve smiled broadly, stepped too close to Rob, clapped Rob on the back with force enough to jolt, and flashed a toothy, photo-shoot smile that exposed self-idolatry nestled in vanity and self-satisfaction. Rob couldn't stop himself drawing back, fully repulsed, and silently cursed himself for this retreat, exposing traces of his revulsion, revealing too much of himself to this harlequin shade.

DeCeeve prattled on, oblivious to nuance:

"They're scared, you know, *should* know," again cocking head back toward the front office.

Silent words flooded Rob as he struggled to tease-out the ones he needed, wanted, would use and, after fleeting hesitation and with grim voice and look, muttered:

"Yes, our people *are* scared—and so am I. And so should *you* be."

"Watch your mouth, Ben Rob," uttered as lofty wisdom to the dull lesser, lord to vassal.

DeCeeve glared threateningly as Rob stared, amazed by DeCeeve's brazen display of ignorance and stupidity and wholly unjustified self-assurance.

"How could he not know to whom he's fully bound and obliged?" It was incredulity more than question.

DeCeeve: "But rest easy, Rob, my people... *you*... have nothing to fear."

He gave Rob a curt nod with a wink and a smile, then drawled:

"That crowd down there is *my* crowd, and don't you forget it. They're down there for *me*, and don't you forget it."

Rob was staggered by DeCeeve's self-delusion.

"How can he so distort why that crowd is down there? He thinks those people are his and give a damn about HIM?"

Rob, aloud: "All the same, with every day and every hour that crowd's getting more restive and volatile. It wouldn't take much to ignite the whole mass to explode in our faces."

DeCeeve: "All we need do is channel their rage and hate right into the White House, straight onto Kurb's doorstep—and *I'll* be sitting pretty, all safe and secure and ready... to lead them to my Promised Land."

With a sneer and wink excreted in Rob's face, DeCeeve added:

"And don't you go worrying your pretty little head, Rob my boy. I'll make sure you're safe. You've got nothing to worry about—as long as you stick with me."

Rob debated lambasting DeCeeve, to drag him down two pegs and more, decided against it, what use, no point—for now—and instead:

"When the amassed down there explode, it'll transmogrify into a mob the likes of which we've never witnessed—and even *you* will be powerless to pacify them. They'll come unhinged and deliver carnage the likes of which we've never seen. Our people in the front office have good reason to be scared. So do I—and so do *you*."

Rob omitted: *"You're just too dense and arrogant to admit it, even to yourself, especially to yourself."*

DeCeeve raised eyes to Heaven in glorious communion with the Heavenly as he pronounced in lofty tones:

"The people that count are fully cosseted in my march to the White House. You'd do well to remember that Rob, and to be fully with me, 200%."

He didn't finish the 'or else'—*"the schoolyard bully"*—leaving Rob to wonder who, what, was behind DeCeeve's self-confidence and arrogance.

Rob regarded DeCeeve for a long moment, struck by the other's self-delusions, and couldn't help but see another's hand behind the words.

"Allman." Of course. Who else.

"Or whoever's behind Allman."

Rob gazed down on the grand vista afforded by the great window of the back office, and recalled first memory of Allman, revulsion filling him. Then memory called to him images of loveliness, of ideals, of all that more than redeemed those of Allman, visions of his beautiful, beauteous people rising to mind... *"stunning to witness, mesmerizing to hear, fully convincing the dowagers and their harrumphing magnate-husbands to bend ear and open pocket-book to their cause, to MY cause—to uplift the downtrodden and the beaten and the bereft, thereby to fully free-up the upper echelons of wealth and power. And oh, how captivating are my beauteous young people,"* eyes glossing-over as he recalled their hallowed earnestness and devotion—to him.

Memory recalled the name, specter, rising from its depths, what need proof, Rob knew, 'it' self-evident to least scrutiny.

"Grotesque harlequin of greed and hate pretending in the name of all that's good," and with that Rob damned not DeCeeve, pawn and toady, but Allman and those behind Allman.

Rob shuddered under all that threatened, under all he could not anticipate or prevent, and turned rage and hate on Allman, proof or not, what need proof under the deafening ring of truth—and fought against revulsion of his own rank hubris.

"The only way to assure the success of my vision is to predict the unpredictable—and stop it before it starts."

"It's already started," whispers in the dark.

Rob fought panic as he felt himself lose control of what he'd started, wrestling against the precarious and perilous realm of the transition he envisaged, amid visions of the disparate futures he was even now creating—subverting, corrupting—by any least misapprehension, miscalculation of that transition.

"If I'm to be the people's shield and paladin, I've got to safeguard them from the very thing I've damned."

'He' is sole witness to a singularity newly emerged of nothing, of nowhere—frailest creature melded into existence, cringing and whimpering atop its highest perch, interred within its vanishingly feeble aura—where an instant before only the dark existed.

He observes this realm of otherwise formless existence through an otherworldly dispassion, mesmerized by the gaunt shade struggling to curl into itself, withdraw into itself, atop highest perch immersed in palest aura—as the dark stretches beyond imagining.

He and frailest creature and highest perch and most pallid aura lurch between existence and extinction, between reality and illusion and self-delusion, in vital battle to rise fully into reality, struggling with dread more than fear—of what lay in wait.

Chapter 6.

The radio clicked-on and the news blared intentionally over-loud, so to break Rob into the day. He woke out of deep sleep, refused the curse perched on his lips, stretched and twisted under the cover of his bedding, then lingered in the warmth of his bed heedless of the need to rise, these extra moments of peace among the too-few pleasures to let slip by.

He listened to radio-headlines of near-overwhelming desolation ravaging the world, the country, the community, the heart and mind… and refused it reaching for him, wondered how to stop it reaching him.

He slogged up, now more fully awake, and prepared for day washing, skidding into jeans and T-shirt under loose-fitting flannel shirt—*"my uniform"*—and swung out the door for his morning run, how else to plunge into the day than by plunging.

"Time is an irreplaceable, irrecoverable benediction."

He wondered if 'benediction' was the right word, wondered if 'burden' was the more honest and faithful.

"After all, I'd rightfully be languishing in bed right now, but for time commanding me."

He understood such miracles, what else to call them:

"Life itself is the one other irretrievable, irrecoverable benediction, fount—burden—of existence. Both time and life need full embracing with the utmost energy and, especially, awareness, if not zeal, drawing us grudgingly into the light."

With deep breath drawn on this first tendril of day, Rob plunged into the dark of earliest dawn.

Most men didn't think her pretty, but she was possessed of power and energy visibly bursting from her, that gripped men and firmly engaged their want, plunging them into need. As if the energy of the sun and stars themselves, by design of her maker's infinite wisdom, lay barely constrained within her, her grace and power coruscated, blinded.

It was early morning, not yet a glimmer of full daylight, and the brown-eyed girl was up and going and already gone, vaulted onto bicycle and sprinting onto path and down the lane and instantly away.

She was aware men ogled her, wanted her, wanted *of* her, to have her... *"for what?"*

She wondered just what it was men wanted of her, knowing her body was the least of her, and why only that of her did they want, how could it be *that*, such infinitesimal trifle of her, which they want, all they want. Thought of it over-brimmed her with revulsion.

"Sheep and dogs and rats and worms they are, always and only in heat and rut and blind hunger for me, not least aware or caring what they are and will likely always be and uncaring in the least for me and for what I am."

The image of them sickened her, so little to them. *So* she denied them her time, her attention, her *self*.

"Even here, at The Rafford..." she paused in mid-thought, lavishing derision and contempt for the men— *"boys"*—of The Rafford... *"vaunted bastion of the best in men and women, tomorrow's elite, cadre of leaders and doers and makers,"* thoughts couched in hate and rage and disdain of them.

Of men, she understood their transparency, their course vanity and venal want, and mourned their substance, thinnest veneer, even here at The Rafford, why expect any more or any better of them here.

She was driven, working her bicycle with impudent speed that would be reckless but for her lightning reflexes and keen awareness of where she was and how she was, too quick to harm anyone too slow or dull to scuttle out of her way.

"Besides, they always scramble out of my way," and she laughed mirthlessly at their clumsiness and simple-mindedness.

"Even the women..." she paused to consider silent words groping to express disdain, contempt, even of the women.

She was vulgarly proud, ashamedly proud, brimming on arrogance, to be more girl than woman, she in jeans and T-shirt under loosely flowing, flannel shirt while others of her kind skittered and pranced in tight or short or billowy skirts in which to whore themselves.

"Yes, I'm proud to be more girl than woman, for having least understanding of women—pale, listless, lifeless homunculi, the crumbs and leavings of humanity, wasting time and life in the gutter of vapid pride and bloated vanity and worthless material-swill no better than the men."

She struggled to constrain her fervid contempt and prayed to always be more girl than woman, determined to do more and be more than vapid prey, so she *willed*.

She screeched and skidded to a stop beside piles of The Sentient, the school paper—*"my paper,"* she prided herself as the one woman... *"no, girl"*... blighting all the others, *"doing more and getting more done than all the others, men and women, combined."* It was not hubris but simple truth.

Her habit was to think and feel and do—without pride or vanity, deriving simple truths from uncolored reality, knowing and not just thinking or hoping, and restraining as best she could from sneering at the vacuous pork of those teeming 'others'... filling precious pages with fluff and stuff and nonsense, all editorial and opinion with scarcely any real news, even now, even with all that was coming alive, to anyone who would see, who would care even to look, at The Rafford.

She marveled they didn't shame themselves into oblivion, *"as they ought,"* wondered if she was being too harsh, too unkind and unfair, and decided even this image of them was too light and lenient with which to measure their failings—*"especially here and especially now, with King and Dean Ivry at center stage, now more than ever."*

As she stooped to gather up The Sentient, keenly aware of young men—*"boys"*—ogling her, as ever and as always, she slim and fit and exploding with energy and life enough to put life itself to shame, if those others were any measure of life.

With visible effort she heaved two stacks of The Sentient into satchels at either side of her rear wheel, they weighing more than she did herself, and cursed herself her weakness, hating weakness—*"especially my own"*—and lamented having only human strength and energy with which to live life, even aware she was her own severest judge and critic.

"But, after all, what is... is," and she accepted base reality, never begrudging reality—*"ever,"* she fully affirmed—except to redouble effort and will to overcome reality as best she could, except to transfigure reality into even more zeal and life.

She was fully aware of the contours of her, her exertions straining her against the fabric of her shirt and jeans, even she all-trying to *not* put on a show, still knowing she was a show displaying herself to the men—*"boys"*—all-gawking, all eyes devouring her, knowing she made them strain in their pants and sad she couldn't un-make that of them. After all: *"Boys are people too, right?"*

She wondered that of them, and understood:

"What is... is," she confronted reality, *"and even still, what else can they be than what they are. And what else can I be than what I am, and even still I wonder how to hide myself from them, but... why hide myself? Still, I try to hide myself—for them, for their sake,"* she thought, *"not for me. No need for me."* And she pitied them their miserable failings.

Two young men—*"boys"*—approached from near distance. She noticed them at once, leapt onto her bicycle and ground into the pedals with all her weight and strength and fast reached speed as they neared, they first jogging, then running full-out as she picked up speed and left them behind, bent and struggling for breath, with hardly strength enough to ogle her one last moment.

She twisted round to watch them recede, shrinking more of them than just their distance, and contemned herself glorying in their smallness, though fully deserving... *"the brutes,"* she sneered, *"dumb sluts,"* she reviled, *"flabby wimps, smart-ass pimps, vulgar and mindless corrosions... even if they did catch me I'd give 'em the hell they deserve and will someday surely get."*

For a brief instant she again wondered if to revile herself her harsh judgments, again considered condemning herself, then reflected that, though maybe too harsh of her, *"still it's not untrue,"* and she relented and forgave herself damnation, assuring herself:

"I'd forthrightly stand and take and fully accept such judgment were it the other way round, they judging me."

For another brief moment she wondered if she was lying to herself about her own personal integrity, and finally shrugged 'who can say,' knowing that only in Heaven could she be judged fairly and rightly, and that would have to wait.

The brown-eyed girl lost herself in wandering thought, her thoughts not letting her be, not yet, as thought of those 'men,' of being used and abused by such as them, haunted:

"They and their kind are so many, too many. They and their kind fill the world with their filth and decay, drowning in their selfish, carnal, pointless minutes and days and lives not least aware they're drowning, preferring to flounder in their oblivion of mediocrity than to struggle to be more than the so-little they are. They and their ilk would have me and those like me work to the bone and reap for them than lift finger and will to do for themselves any least beyond the stupid and worthless and pointless, beyond their self-idolatry and simpering, puerile pleasures. And they are so many, so vastly many!—while I and my kind are vanishingly few and ever fewer still, it seems. And as our burdens weigh ever heavier they wallow, ever fatter, ever more thirsting for more and for still and always more, until I and those like me whither and disappear, leaving them to themselves. And I and those like me are happy leaving them to themselves, just to be away, anywhere away, from them and from the likes of them."

The brown-eyed girl watched them fade out of sight to the nowhere from where they came, and struggled to calm herself and her revulsion of them, struggled back to the glory of the just-rising sun and warming day—and struggled to not revile herself for her arrogance and hubris.

Ben Rob was lost in thought as he ran, that being the greatest that running can offer, that anything of life can offer, being lost and consumed in thought… *"almost,"* whispered from the dark.

Rob hardly saw the pavement at his feet as his mind swirled amid thoughts of a fraternity party, and of thinly veiled threat, and of powers totally alien and elusive to him. He didn't notice the bicycle speeding for him.

The two collided with force enough to catapult her into air and throw him scraping and skittering down the path.

The brown-eyed girl didn't even see what hit her as she hurled head over heels over the handlebars, landing with an audible *thud* on her back beside the runner, she sprawled on the pavement with wind and sense knocked from her, dazed and barely conscious, lying still and silent on the path, he crumpled beside her.

Rob staggered to his feet, then knelt down at her side, staring down at her, for a moment able only to stare down on her, one glimpse of her sending him with quietest voice and softest touch to whisper to her and to stroke her smoothest, sweetest cheek and stare into gently blinking eyes, overfilled with fear and worry and so much more for her.

The brown-eyed girl roused to fuller alertness at his touch and for a moment lay where she was, staring up at him, allowing herself to lounge in that realm for a precious moment. Suddenly she woke fully, scrutinized him with suspicious eyes and set sneer, all of her tensed, readied, she now wondering what had happened, was happening—would happen.

For a moment she lay there watching him staring down at her, how strange that this boy had beaten her to her feet. She closed her eyes a moment to savor the feel of dream, of a boy who'd beaten her to her feet, of a boy she didn't loathe, could admire....

For just that briefest moment she allowed herself, willed herself, to linger in dream—then she recalled herself and scrambled to her feet and stood above him, he still kneeling, and she rallied against him, readied against him, *he* rightfully kneeling at *her* feet now.

Rob stared up at her, then slowly, painfully, stood upright, realizing he was straining to stand fully upright, aware his full height was too little, he being too little and always too little and striving to be less little, rationalizing to convince himself he was tall enough, and enough *is* enough after all.

The brown-eyed girl stood her ground as he rose, she not backing away or least budging from the spot she commanded as he stood, now standing so near, too near and— not near enough.   He wondered that he couldn't help himself standing so near, and still not trying in the least to *not* stand so near—and stare into endless eyes, not able to tear eyes away to see anything more of her. He guessed they all stared at her, every one, men *and* women, always staring at her, and why should he be any different, no better and, surely, less.

Rob felt gripped, possessed, not able to tear eyes from her eyes—from enormous chocolate eyes, infinitely sweet and deep, and then from flowing auburn hair dazzling the sun, paling the sun, at play with sun more than sun at play with her, from smoothest, pink skin, and wondering how soft such skin must be, needing him to stroke her, caress her, love her.

Finally he allowed eyes, couldn't stop eyes, as they strayed down to slender shoulders and to glorious curves of T-shirt under loosely-flowing, flannel-shirt at play with the wind, and then to smallest waist above curving hips, wondering how those jeans felt, being so near her, touching her, caressing her, and his breath heavy at envy of jeans and shirt and wind and sun, she allowing them to play freely with her.

The brown-eyed girl returned his stare as she gauged him, not noticing, or caring, that his eyes strayed as all their eyes strayed:

"Scrawny. No, wiry. Short. No, tall enough, tall enough even if not taller than me… and that enough."

She wondered why she'd added that last thought, felt it needed to be added, felt *he* needed it to be added.

And, she had to admit—strong.

"Yes, there's strength in that body, and…" somehow she knew, without least doubt… *"mind."*

She didn't know why she'd thought that, but knew it to be true, somehow undeniable.

She blushed at that, and couldn't help but blush wondering if *will* was strong in him too, thought it was, hoped it was—*knew*, somehow, it was.

For a fleeting instant she wondered if his will was a match to hers, or if stronger even than hers, and finally managed to quiet her thoughts, it didn't matter:

"Strong is strong enough," she decided.

They stood like that, facing each other like that, eyeing each other, wary and filled with—other thoughts. And feelings.

So much was already between them, more than just quiet wind at play between them. They stood like that for an enduring moment, neither wanting, nor able, to break the silence between them, with warm sun and gentle wind and languidly waving leaves and swaying branches playing with them and all about them, the sun and wind staring down on them, small animals scampering below and flitting above, all watching them, staring, not least afraid of them, somehow aware of who and of what they witnessed here and now.

The two stood their ground, standing so near each other, not able, not willing, to give way to time and space, to gravity and sun, all drawing them nearer, pulling them nearer, they resisting the power of gravity and sun only by dint of strength of will, and uncertain of it's rightness, leaving them wondering why they resisted, wondering all silent even to themselves, why they resisted.

The timeless moment ever-slowly passed and they found themselves mumbling awkward, self-conscious whisperings of apology so powerfully tinged with sweetness, sound and sigh more than words, full with meaning, mumbled to each other, words they didn't yet have for each other, apology mingled with regret of what they didn't understand, they struggling to understand what had happening, was happening, and most of all, would happen.

Finally, they stumbled away and trudged away, each looking back, then looking away, and looking back again, wondering what had just happened.

The brown-eyed girl creaked back onto her bicycle, wondering about dregs and now, somehow, not all dregs, and Rob limping painfully down the path, fraternity and threat now totally eclipsed by this brown-eyed girl and a new world order.

Chapter 7.

Ben Rob stood by the great window of the back office overlooking the teeming of people, amassed and ever-massing below. He stared, silent in the dark, as DeCeeve exploded into the silence and the dark spewing corruptions and corrosion.

From a dark corner of mind Rob was aware of DeCeeve droning on, and didn't care in the least, he, *it*, didn't matter in the least, his dronings or him, as the beginnings of nightmare resurrected and what matter DeCeeve and his dronings aside that.

Thought drifted Rob back, to the beginning, to that first brick in that yellow-brick road to actuation, here and now materialized not of gold but of turgid morass threatening anarchy and insanity. He drifted back to those first days and to those days soon after—and to his beauteous people:

"You, all of you, are become truth and light in the dark. Here and now you, all of you, begin preparing the way, to guide the elite—and the people—as their guiding light, shepherding their way," so he instilled them, installed them, to light the way.

So proud he was of his wondrous young people… *"hardly more than children and vastly more than children, the incarnation of youth and beauty beyond the trivial luster of their physicality, reaching into the realm of ethereal truths. They are beyond compare, beyond imagining, only in reality could such pulchritude exist, not of body but of mind and spirit and energy and passion and, if coached just so—will sway and conform even the most hoary and rigid minds."*

He mouthed their words for them silently as they recited his mantras, imbedding his truths into them, his lips moving soundlessly as he guided them in word and wisdom and will.

"Your brilliance will dazzle and guide that great murk of the self-anointed ascendant as beacons of light in the dark, coruscating through the murk of their pretensions, of their self-delusions of ascendance, as you ignite them—and immolate them."

He left silent his intent, even to his beauteous people:

"That—will surface in its anointed time."

He grappled with his truths—*"THE truth,"* whispered silently in the dark, his arrogance assailing him—and struggled against still more truths silently whispered from the dark:

"You arrogate the self-delusion of your own preeminence as you shroud your blasphemy. You abhor the murk of the elite you champion—they and their ilk and their condescensions of supremacy over you and those like you—as you soil yourself in that very murk."

He considered that 'elite'... *"repressing and oppressing the people, relegating the people to bare subsistence—or worse, to a life-long struggle aspiring unreachably to breach that spare subsistence. The elite bury the people in a realm where the people are scarcely alive, compelled to struggle in unattainable aspiration for what little remains of their lives. The elite raise themselves up by shouldering out and tramping down the people, enriching themselves by denying the people life as it should fully and rightfully be lived, and preen in idolatries of greed, enriching themselves beyond voracity and faith."*

Rob mused contemptuously:

"And what to call that vast elite who plague the people? Less than human, still they are—somehow—human, if only by virtue of their genome. I've got to accept them as human if for no other reason than of simple humanity, theirs—and mine."

Nimbus residue haunted... *"defiling my own vanishing humanity."*

Rob struggled to cleave away the *in*humanity of the elite, how else to see through to the spare remains of their humanity.

How he loathed that elite... *"that subspecies of human, that ilk of pretenders to humanity, who lead us into oppression and repression with their self-adulating, self-idolizing laws, dictating over us as they wallow in their self-appointed, holy rightfulness to so lead us… 'for the good of the people.' The weapons deployed by the elite are a bare half-measure above those deployed by rabid jihadists and fevered zealots—a difference of degree not of kind. The elite unleash not bombs or bullets or blood-lusting bedlam but worse… self-serving 'law-and-order' and lobbyists and patronage purposed to relegate the people to bare and less-than-bare subsistence. The rabid physical violence of self-righteous zealots is at least open and honest under their sanctimony and greed in the name of their 'holy'—while the elite prance and smirk and adorn themselves in subterfuge as they wallow in illusion and self-delusion behind cries proclaiming 'in the name of freedom!' and 'keep the free market free!' amid their demonic greeds and sanctimonies in the name of their own—and no one else's—self-righteous holies."*

The dark played him, teased and taunted and tested him:

"Maybe such laws and oppressions with which the elite afflict the people is the way it should be, exactly as it should be—the people deserving no more and no better."

Rob struggled against such provocations, groped for a measure of dispassion, fought to repel the preoccupations and seductions of hate and rage even as those screamed outrage to his face.

"And only remains: how to evade being dragged under by remorse for co-opting their ways and means as my own."

He brooded in the dark, behind the veil of his own shadow… *"that shadow of hate and seething barely constrained beneath my surface, against which I need all will to forge some semblance of tolerance and forgiveness of the elite, and more, of myself, for my vast failings, as my 'need' bucks and strains against what I should want of compassion for the people."*

Then memory of his beauteous people surged and soothed his bristling hate and rage, re-awakened his lofty ideals for humanity and of what humanity should be, embodied by these youthful radiances, here and now readying to step into the breach and light the way—as whispers from the dark correct: *"No... YOUR way."*

He observed his beauteous young people, revering their brilliance and humanity as they went about their cosmogony... *"overflowing with scintillating dignity and honest humility as they permeate and illuminate the elite. The radiance of my beauteous ignite and transmute that murk from its vast ocean of vanity and venality. My beauteous are perfect for my campaign, ripened to fully penetrate and suffuse and transfigure that murk with my teachings, as the murk wallow oblivious."*

He paled, lamented:

"And so too my beauteous, my innocents, my radiances—every bit unsuspecting," he not daring to dull their radiance with the taint of foreknowledge.

Rob struggled and failed to suppress his trace smile, beaming pride, for his beauteous people, young and alive and full with his teachings. He watched them with greatest pride as doting father over scintillating issue... *"as they artfully navigate the cold dirt and squalid murk of the self-styled great and greater and greatest lords and ladies, those succumbed to pretensions of regal dignity and righteous certitude, preening in the enormity of their reflections, wholly immersed in the fullest, grasping greed of self-adulation reaching to self-idolatry."*

Rob suppressed retching at this image, conjured fully alive and unspeakably loathsome, and compelled his vision away from those inhabiting the murk, of those who are the very fabric of the murk, and compelled himself back to images of his beauteous, wondrous beacons of light—and frantically struggled against his own greeds and transgressions reflected on them.

"My beauteous are glorious, more than words can say, as they sow my seeds of evolution, no—revolution. Artful and sure and infectious they are, transcendent beyond resisting as they conjure the future by transforming casual conversation into their—my—social and political doctrine. My young luminaries are highest art—my art—as they morph less-than-innocent social gatherings into platforms fabricating and

generating the ineluctable flow of history, sowing the history they—I—fashion for that murk and for the people, far into their future. And soon all will know their future by name, by the name—I—put to their future: The Liberty Party."

Rob welled with pride—and struggled to convince himself it was fully deserved and rightfully earned and not the manifestation of his own petty and grasping greed, of his own corruption and self-idolatry—*"just like those of the elite,"* whispered out of silence in the dark.

"I am NOT like THEM!" screamed silent denial praying transcendence over superficial likenesses, praying the semblance was of the very sheerest veneer, without substance—*"none!"* screaming silently under such indictment.

But whisper derided: *"Thou protest too much!"*

He struggled to convince himself he was *not* just another odious manifestation, rendition, of those he reviled, the very substance of the murk, who arrogate their ascendance in the murk, and he struggled... to shun loathing himself.

Silent, even to himself, especially to himself, he wondered how to keep from sweeping aside the veil guarding him from awareness that *he* is the most rotted essence of that murk, he with his greatest intentions to not lead—*mis*lead— himself on the road paved with best intentions.

'He' regards the scene—so dim and distant he is not sure it exists at all except in fevered imaginings. He rises to believe he perceives the scene in actuality: Vanishingly dim glow embracing frailest creature seated on highest perch, all three engulfed by, immersed in, the unimaginable dark—he as witness.

He observes the scene merge more fully into existence, the scene growing ever cautiously larger, brighter—or he ever steadily nearer. He to it or it to him, how to know and why to care when so little seems to matter—when even time and place seem not to matter in the least, and only wonder if any of it matters at all, wondering less IF it matters than HOW it could possibly matter, as he witnesses this birth within the absolute of the dark.

ar grey

    He struggles to understand the least of this 'here' and of this 'now' into which he, and now these newest-born, have been issued—and of what lies in wait.
    Now only awaits the rest.

Chapter 8.

The phone rang.

Rob—limping and straining from yesterday's debacle with a brown-eyed girl and her bicycle, and just back from his morning jog, such of it that he could manage, shambling along as he pushed himself through the run, and only now done with shower and shave, in midst of funneling into his uniform of denim trousers and pocket T-shirt under open flannel shirt, both hanging loose—finally reached for the phone.

He stopped in mid-reach, allowed the phone to ring still longer, thinking... *"let the phone ring, relax, take your time, answer when you're good and ready, when you're fully ready,"* understanding that he'd never be fully ready.

"Whoever it is could wait. Or hang up."

He didn't try silencing the thought, hoping they'd just hang up.

Then dream overwhelmed reality, as it sometimes should:

She steps close, closer, breath at his breath, for them to breathe the same air, to breathe of each other, he and his wondrous girl... his by virtue of her essence, of her intent, that she is his and he hers, and for now just she, here, at his side, siding with him through all things, fidelity to right and truth and Goodness—"and me."

He presses cheek to her, lips to her, she asking that and more without sound, seeing his answer in him as he explains:

"It's not you phoning me, so it's not anything or anyone, nothing and no one, not important in the least, it can wait, whatever 'it' is. Maybe 'it' will hang up."

He turns fully to her, presses close to her, closer, holds her in the enduring moment, his arms wrapping her, holding her close and still closer, fallen to rapture in enormous brown eyes infinitely deep, drawing him in, deep and ever deeper.

The phone rang, insistent, demanding, and finally he woke to the phone—*as she smiles to him, tells him silently, no word needed, "it's okay, I—am here."* He smiled back to her as he lifted the receiver and clung to silence, still lingered in the image of her.

From far away:

"Good say.... Hello? *Hello?*"

Rob instantly recognized Plesant's voice and his peculiar salutation, waited another moment to reply, afraid to wait too long, didn't want to prolong and risk increasing... *"what, trepidation? fear?"* in the other's voice, his own reply risen of pity more than compassion, his kindness struggling against contempt for the poor creature Plesant.

"And for me," he fully understood.

In what he hoped had only a slightest edge of frost, Rob finally reply: "Yes?"

"That you, Rob? This is Plesant."

Rob waited, all silent. After a moment's hesitation, hearing anxiety—*"fear? panic?"*—as a claxon palpable through the silence in the phone, Plesant spoke near-shrilly:

"'Power'—that's our fraternity, you know—is having a get-together. Tonight. Nine. Sharp. It oughta be okay, low-key, oughta be—fun."

The last word was a listless, lifeless afterthought in clear effort to entice—*"ensnare,"* Rob couldn't help but think.

Plesant's desperate plea clambered through the phone, reached for him, roused pathos and pity in Rob even more than repugnance and contempt, for Plesant, for his tone and words and straining edge of panic... *"over a phone call—to me, so fearful of so harmless and powerless a one as me."*

After another moment's silence, without further waiting on a sound from Rob, Plesant rushed on, pleading thick in his voice:

"You'll be there, Rob—right? *Right?*"

Rob waited, didn't know why, reviled himself the game, gouging at excoriation clearly exposed in Plesant's mind and body and life—and still Rob waited, reviling this inexplicable, pedestrian coldness and cruelty, understanding it was not aimed at Plesant and mourning that, just the same, Plesant was target and victim.

Dream, again—*"who are we without our manifold little faults and failings and dreams?"*

He understood:

"Mine may be 'faults and dreams'... but what are those beside the manifold worse and worst of others," images of Allman and all that is Allman's rearing to mind.

Then she drifted in him again:

He turns to her, she at his side, taking his side, always on his side and no one else's, not even her own, as he for her, and she hearing and seeing and knowing him fully and thoroughly and even still—even still!—always with him, on his side, as she looks at him and considers him through enormous brown eyes, filling him with something he cannot understand and aches to fully understand.

"You wonder about me now, for this, my beauteous brown-eyed girl, wondering with tendrils of inchoate contempt dawning for me at this spark of coldness and cruelty in me, for Allman and for Plesant and for all the likes of them and so for all humankind, for the so many just like them, possessed of barely a shred of kindness or humanity. You wonder if I would seek to deny it or defend it, this edge of cruelty I harbor, wondering what moves me, wondering if to abhor me. Beside you I am brute animal and so am innocent, knowing and having known no better, pinned and writhing under the implacable constraint pressed against me by such of humankind as they—and now, too, I am rendered victim to you and to your slightest whim."

Rob inhaled, opened his mouth to plead to her, prodded by her look and feel and breath, hoping, pleading, praying... *"you do not see that and only that of me."*

Plesant continued:

"Rob? You there? *Rob?*"

Escalating desolation struggled to *not* scream at Rob through tiny, distant voice over the phone, clutching for him.

Finally, shame overwhelming contempt, Rob replied:

"I'm here. I won't be there. I'm busy."

ar grey

Almost as afterthought, still in cold monotone, Rob added: "Thank Allman for me, for the invitation," as Rob reviled himself his own cheap entreaty to mollify Allman.

"*Wait!*" frantic urgency filling his voice.

"*Don't hang up*! Rob, *please...* come to the party. It would mean a lot."

He repeated, as if the first didn't quite communicate the urgency of need... "it would mean a—*lot.*"

Confession under utter surrender: "It would mean a lot—to *me.*"

Then, clinging to soiled fragment of self-respect:

"It'll be fun, low key... fun," in desperate measure.

The despair in his voice shivered through Rob, to think what lay behind such abandon to fear and prayer.

"*He doesn't know what else, what more, to say to extract my promise to be there.*" Pity overwhelmed contempt.

Plesant continued, pleading in every word and sound:

"There'll be girls there too, and you'll meet some good people, some nice girls—it'll be... okay," as if Rob needed assurance of what he knew could not be possible.

"Thanks for the invitation. I've got plans. Take it easy..." about to hang up the phone....

"*Wait!* Rob... *wait!* I called to invite you myself, but... *Allman* invited you." As if that said all. As if Rob didn't understand. As if that would make the difference and convince and compel.

"Thank *Allman* for me, for his... invitation. Bye."

"Rob, wait! *Don't hang up!*" voice groveling and beseeching in prayer on bended knee.

Half-a-moment's pause, to regain breath and semblance of calm, and Plesant's desperate plea issued again:

"Wait... look—it's more than just an invitation." As if it needed saying.

"Allman wants *you*... to *be* there. Nine. *Sharp.*"

A fleeting moment's hesitation later: "It's... it's not a request."

Rob heard disembodied, plaintive voice in the phone, the embers of what had once been Plesant:

"Rob, Allman's got a lot of... push... here. When he asks, people do. He can cause a lot of problems, Rob. I mean a *lot* of... problems. Please Rob, don't cross him—what *for*? For *this*? What could it hurt? C'mon. What do you say? Please—nine, tonight. Please. For me." Desperate need, inescapable.

"I don't know, Plesant. As I've said, I've got plans for tonight."

"Break 'em. Please—for *me*. *Please...* for me."

The last was final resignation, everything done that could be done—and everything perched in the balance.

Pity... and disdain mingled with contempt, a form of hate, and Rob relented, a little, enough:

"I'll have to see."

It was all Rob could offer and it was abundantly enough and more than enough for Plesant.

"Great! Fine! Okay! Terrific—see you there tonight! Nine... *sharp*. Please—don't be late. *Please*."

Rob heard, felt, the sigh of reprieve at the other end of the line, then the line went dead.

Sweet dream, cling to it long as you can, Rob holding the receiver for a long moment, deliberating... *as she, all warmth and love and truth, watches and waits, all silent in the dark, all patience with him, for him, holding him close, closer, in the dark, for the here and for the now, nothing but the two of them together in the dark.*

Absently, speaking aloud to himself:

"So. Allman can cause problems. No, he can cause a *lot* of problems. So: How to deal with—it."

Dream, still, again, so grateful for dreams... *he regards the embodiment of love and truth still by his side, and pulls her close, closer, and presses lips to her, to the softness of her, first at neck, then to the sweetness of her lips, then staring silently into vast brown eyes with dreams of falling into her, she all warmth and softness and silence for him, nothing to say so nothing said, just being with him, for him, is enough and more than enough for them both as he, every bit and more, for her.*

The day passed.

Some days pass with grace and gratitude, others just pass, are done, despite all will to be more and to be made more. Sometimes all such days can do, the best they can do, is pass.

Rob arrived back home, near end of another day, restless, unsettled. He hated the feel of 'unsettled.'

Rob hesitated a brief moment, then changed into jeans and open flannel shirt over pocket T-shirt hanging loose and now... time for his run. No matter he'd just had his run that morning, there's always time for a run. When, how else, to think.

He fastened the Velcro bindings of his ankle weights and then stepped into the cool, dusk air, breathing of freedom waiting on him, patience for him in air and sky and fading sun. And no matter the illusion, the feel of it exhilarated him and *that* a most-prized frond.

"Letting me think, away from over-loud stereos and dormitory roommates—that is freedom. And," he reflected gratefully, *"I've got a private room,"* and greatest freedom in that, too.

He understood his great luck at such singular luxury, as almost no other had at The Rafford despite all their entitlements. He understood, too, that it was not luck at all to have been accorded a private room.

"It must be—so is—part of their experiment... observe the transfer student from State in his own little environment," only wonder is where the video camera and microphone were lodged, smiling grimly at his contempt of them, let them watch and listen... *"of my intent, not theirs."*

He cherished this luxury of 'privacy' like no other, as he wondered to what surveillance he was subject.

"No, not quite 'like no other.' There are other luxuries, so many, for which to pray gratitude. I just need bother to, need care to, need will myself to... look and see and fully appreciate."

The evening was beauteous, dusk fading languidly and gratefully into the dark, a few scattered students quietly strolling the paths under gentle breeze and swaying, welcoming leaves and branches, all bathed in indigo skies amid tree-lined lanes with small life scampering and flitting amid the trees.

Serenity washed over him, soothed and calmed him, smiled for him, made him understand his vast wealth, like no other, needing only to see it, to understand and appreciate it:

"How can I not?" thought asked, understood: *"Why then do the overwhelming of us… not?"*

Rob focused his attention on Allman and on the looming 'party.'

"And why the word 'looming'? Why dread?"

Rob settled into his run and into his thoughts, grappling with the feelings roiling him, unsettling him, to understand them, and so himself. He let his mind wander, it needing to wander, to sort things through with will all its own, to see where it goes, where it takes him, he standing-by quietly, patiently.

A thought: *"Regardless of what he is—emergent ferocity of threat, embodiment of defiling contempt—he's a force to reckon with, to be careful about… very careful."*

Another thought: *"I can't let him manipulate me, use me, abuse me."*

And another: *"Still, such a small thing, one evening, a little 'get-together,' what harm… it'll probably be nothing more than a dull gathering leaving a dim memory of an unpleasant evening."*

And finally: *"Besides—it'll save me a little trouble… no, a lot of trouble. That's worth something. I've got enough trouble without that… little as it may be. Still, even a least bit more is more than I need or care to have. Besides, I can handle being a little flexible, even with my principles—I guess."*

The 'I guess' whispered in the dark, wondered where lies the threshold between 'flexibility' and abject surrender.

Chapter 9.

    The near-distant drumbeat of front-office chatter softly ruffled the cosseting dark and the peaceful silence in which Rob basked. He stood by the great window-wall in the back room of the back office of The Liberty Spire, deliberating over the crush of people milling outside and below him. Then DeCeeve's odious laughter pealed out and despoiled sanctuary, desecrated serenity, and the door flew wide to complete Rob's defilement.

    Rob stood apart, tried to stand apart, from DeCeeve and his repugnance, and lost himself again in viewing the massed and amassing overfilling the streets and alleyways below him, more hunger than humanity he again dissolved into that agglomeration, fully riveted by recurrent nightmare of who and of what they were, may be... will be.

    Rob recalled, thought he recalled, wondered if this, now, was recall or something else entirely, something not of memory or of dream but of something else entirely, of some other dimension of the possible, or of the inevitable....

    He strolls The Rafford paths as a disembodied observer, from out of nowhere, from out of nothing, perched outside it all, peering in as a singular audience viewing life and the world, his and theirs, but his pivotal... *"as each of theirs is pivotal in their own small way, each immersed in, submerged by, their own trifling rites and pretensions—so unlike me,"* and again, shame.

    His run done and twilight darkening into night, his feet follow their own path, of themselves, he a simple passenger on feet imbued with will all their own. He doesn't think to wonder at this, natural as natural could be, more than anything in the human realm, here in this rarified, diminished isle of his essence, wholly uncorrupted by the human worlds—as yet.

Twilight transforms and draws imperceptibly into night, then into otherworldly opacity of black beyond night, then into the lightest touch of an impenetrable dark beyond any since creation. He finds himself verged on the precipice of an unknown edge where moonlight and starlight and every smallest strand of light, from dimmest lamppost to shaded dormitory window to distant headlight, has fully extinguished. He is in and of a dark where every slightest trace of light then existing or ever having existed or ever having been least imagined has vanished into a dark beyond any since creation.

"Even the dark needs to have been created," silent whisper in the dark, touching on his own.

He is lost in a dark never before witnessed or imagined but for this singular nightmare/bliss of the dark.

"Everything is part of every other... thing," silent whisper from the dark reaches to him, for him, assuring and reassuring, soothing and comforting and cosseting him amid the unimaginable, absolute dark, beyond all experience, eyes as well shut as open in such absolute of the dark, where even sound and touch are dark, where exist only disembodied thought and sentiment.

He is amazed that he is, somehow, not amazed but is, rather, calm and rational, even imbued with an unassailable impulse to open wide his arms and embrace the face of this inexplicable, unimaginable terror that is this absolute dark. It is all of that—and somehow not that at all but... bliss. How many times is the depth of nightmare revealed to be the seed of transcendence? How to explain the inexplicable? How to least grasp the unimaginable? He does not pretend even to try.

His feet unerringly walk imperceptible trails fully lost in the dark, following indiscernible route to unknowable destination, he wondering only at the extravagant calm filling him within this inexplicable, unimaginable realm.

Whisper in the dark: *"Would that life could always be so, without glare or dissonance or cringing or wailing but only serene, anonymous ambling in emollient silence in the cosseting dark,"* and he dreads not being terrified in this dark, portent filling him, wondering at him, of 'why' and... *"why me?"*

The present rushed him back, stunned and stilled, as silence collapsed around him and he found himself standing, still and again, in the back room wincing under the grating noise spewing out of the loathsome mouth that was its source. DeCeeve's clatter was a gouging, corrosive violation of the cosseting dark that Rob so fervently needed, rending the peace and despoiling the dark with the odious noise of repellent words and repugnant meanings under DeCeeve's leering, heaving eyes.

Rob threw himself back into memory, or dream, or prayer, or something else entirely, contemplating the near/not-near past—or dream, or prayer, or imminent, parlous transition into a future he could not discern....

The car slows to a stop in front of that house, that grand edifice, opulent showplace, palatial extravagance— *"obscenity, abomination, corruption under pretensions of smallest greatness and most-petty aspirations to swarming wealth and power."* He fumed at the image of their—*"no, my"*—assumption to greatness, veiling their—*"no, my"*— vanishing smallness and all that lurks within such vanishing smallness, *"and mine worst of all."*

In the moment's remembered, or imagined, or augured interlude, DeCeeve still droning in the near-distant background, Rob watched the amassed congregating outside and far below him, on display through the grand panoramic window of the back room. Rob floated in reverie of dream, of possibility, of prayer, of 'what' and of 'what if'....

He takes a moment to calm himself, to recall some least slips of tranquil imaginings, and strives for the appearance of calm in silent prayer of ushering-in a new reality:
"No point raging when cold, prosaic reality demands simple calm, behind which to excite—incite—to greatest effect."
He is sickened by this cold, heartless calculation of his.

Several more cars—expansive displays of solid, dignified affluence and overweening, suffusing confidence and overflowing arrogance—slow to a stop behind his, the foremost. So he knows he will be not merely welcomed but jealously fêted by his host.

He smirks invisibly and remains silent under this vision of pretense to greatness and prowess and power within that grand arena. Lurid and garish and scarcely veiled seductions promised all of that to those inside his host's dominion, his own now on the cusp of a far grander illusion.

"But not all is pretense," he knows, understands, *"not of this host… not of mine."*

He wonders how much is grand illusion and how much coldly calculated, unyieldingly inevitable fact.

"Behind these people and their grand homes lies power laid idle, they watching, waiting—for me."

He fights to silence the thought… *"to coerce them— no, shepherd them—as their guard and guide and… lord."*

Shame wells under his own hubris, rivals something still baser—*"greed,"* the whisper clutches, silent in the dark.

Rob forced himself to relent, to abandon ravaging thought, to admit to the truth of his implacable demand to still DeCeeve's repugnant voice, to purge life from that loathsome life, and compelled himself to recognize, beyond all resisting, DeCeeve's need… *"to spout and preen in barest fig-leaf over the little he is and, down deep, knows he is."*

Repelled by sound and sight of DeCeeve, Rob propelled himself back into reverie of past, or imagined past, or future….

He regards the grand edifice that is the home of his hosts, imagines them churning among their honorable guests, and loftily spurns demanding the homage that is his due— thinks is his due, knows is his due, nothing less would do, simple truth demanding they genuflect and abide to him. He turns his back on all of that, for now, and prides himself rising above all of that. For now.

"Lead them gently, that is the way—for now," he knows, sure beyond doubt, rejects wondering how he could be so sure.

He draws himself into himself, huddles inside himself, the need for warmth setting him against a coldness creeping, settling in him, the quiet before the coiling, readying to strike.

He is stillness and silence in the dark, in the town car, beside his beauteous driver. His driver follows his lead, they of his beauteous all follow his lead, as he keeps to absolute stillness and silence, strained to fully understand their need.

"Surround yourself with those of yourself who thoroughly and immanently understand you, are become extensions of you. Only so will you reap," whispered in the dark.

He wonders at the extravagance of hubris—*"founded in and fully of greed"*—and fears his own beyond that of all others.

At invisible sign the driver steps from the car and swiftly—*"efficiently,"* he prides—steps to his door, opens the door, and stands still and silent, waiting, respect verging on veneration in awe-filled eyes and lips and manner, for him, for inspiration and aspiration laden in him.

"Or my imaginings of it."

He shunts the thought aside: *"No time now for any least intrusion of doubt or depredation—or despair."*

He emerges from the town car, absently whispering courage and revelation to his beauteous young driver—young man or young woman, either and both at their appointed times, all-fervent to his calling.

"Now... we begin."

His beauteous young people, filling the town cars trailing immediately behind his, emerge languidly and stream exaltedly into the grand edifice. He feels their thrill, feels their exhilaration trilling through him as they contemplate thought and word and act as await them.

Words rise of themselves and he wonders from what fount of the dark—if from inside him or if from some other source entirely—had the words been conceived, nurtured, borne to fruition, and finally implanted into carnal reality, for his beauteous to utter here, now, they knowing only that he'd breathed into them his words, from somewhere of the dark.

"At long last the time is now. And so... we begin."

From within the grand home, from inside the great bay window of the voluptuous ballroom of the grand edifice that was his host's home, he stares out into the night.

"Everyone who's anyone is here," the vulgarity of the notion repels him.

He admonishes himself for decrying simple truth, meant without hubris—*"truth is truth,"* he opines silently, gratuity to himself, and again wonders how he could know with such finality.

Their words of greeting, of tribute, to him and to his acolytes, gush from the mouths of his sponsors immediately on their arrival, his host near-genuflecting to him and his cortege, his wondrous, beauteous acolytes, each and every one awesome to behold. He knows this, is sure without least shadow of doubt.

He envisions a great, serpentine creature receiving and hailing him and his bounty. The creature displays myriad faces belching and gloating and leering at him from all along its sides. And of them, of this of his host and their lot and their kind: open-armed welcome for him and for his bounty, his dazzling acolytes, and Rob understands their aspirations of him—*"prayers to me"*— though an outsider, an ultimate outsider, a grotesque harlequin of an interloper insinuated among them, *"still I embody their grandest, most fervent prayers."* He wonders of their prayers and of the worthiness of their prayers:

"There is not, cannot be, more worthy prayer than praying to me," and Rob cringes and decries and denies he's ever harbored such thought, let alone intent—*"that such as they genuflect to such as me, and rightfully so, for the riches which I will... all too soon... shower upon them, beyond even their fetid ambitions and fervid imaginations and basest greeds."*

He absently wonders, not as question but as simple, honest musing: *"How can they even think to allow me—me!—*

access to this palatial estate, to the here and now of them."
Silent whispers fill him in their greed, and his.

He knows Allman's roll in this: *"Permission granted
by Allman and the Allman's of this world to this host and to
their ilk, for me and mine to access their loftiness, they milling
and chatting and cavorting in their repulsive profligacy."*

To the silent whisper—*"everyone who's anyone is
here"*—he imagines he sees teeming masses in the dark
outside... *"clothed in the dark, looming only just beyond
perception in the dark, creeping near, nearer, now so very
near, craving to be in, pressing to be in, imminently rupturing
in—even as they are made to feel less than nothing, rendered...
vulgar, dirty, ignorant, stupid, voraciously deserving of nothing
and fully deserving of less even than that."*

He suppresses a smile, refuses to acknowledge
gloating:

*"The very earliest beginnings of the end... THAT, here
and now, at this very moment, on this very spot."*

He struggles to withhold outright laughter at these
harlequin pretenders agglomerated around him and around his
wondrous retinue. These elite fawn for would-be favor,
imagined favor, lusting and supplicating favor, *"MY favor."*

Smiling satisfaction fills him as images conflate:

*"Here and now, Dorothy takes that very first step onto
that singularity, onto that exacting point of the very start of the
yellow-brick-road, its very first beginnings lying here and now
in this 'home' and at this very moment."*

He marvels silently at the countless points of light
igniting the crystal of the grand chandelier suspended above
them... *"so like my wondrous, beauteous people, thoroughly
dazzling and utterly shaming these gathered personages, these
diadems and fineries congealed here and now."*

He observes his marvelous young people under hidden,
near-overwhelming pride:

*"They are scintillating pulchritude sprinkled amid the
pervasive murk, shining amid the roiling sea of murk, risen
high amid the murk, incarnate rainbows radiant and divine
amid the murk, navigating the murk easily and casually,
flowing above the murk with arresting transcendence, their*

dazzling brilliance igniting through eyes and lips and minds thoroughly and irresistibly transfixing—and all beyond least awareness."

He allows not the smallest lapse in his demeanor, presents himself as the most gracious honoree, the model guest-of-honor, privileged to be welcomed into this finest home. He mills and mingles within the murk smiling and flattering and ingratiating—*"and aspiring to eradicate my near-overwhelming gloat over what I am conjuring here, now, on this very spot, at this very moment, in their very midst."*

He smiles at their smug ascendance and haughty airs and superior stares—*"like the fetid breath and stinking sweat of a serpentine execration, of a dead and rotted corpse, they exalting themselves thinking themselves succubus aspiring to seduce my angelic acolytes—and me—but here, now, with no awareness of THEMSELVES rapaciously seduced and fully penetrated."*

He represses boundless loathing of these people, they of the murk, and… smiles. But harbored beneath his glow, beyond reach of the dark inside him, dimmest awareness of the loathing coiled and readied… *"against me."*

He overhears the bleatings and blarings of those milling gauzily about him, revealing mind and heart through eye and lip in smirk and sneer and leer, and understands:

"It's all the same, just exactly the same—for anyone who's someone and for everyone who's no one, all of it is just exactly the same: Suffocation under petty lusts and unmerited ambitions snorted through dismal, leaden eyes filled with vapid, shimmering greed," and shudders to know:

"I and my beauteous people every bit as much," aware his beauteous people are as thoroughly unaware of his intent as those of the murk milling here. He laments its irrefutable truth, as always demanding and commanding, inescapable.

He circulates and drifts amid the roiling murk, a stalking predation… *"intent on wresting each and all of them, and the very tide itself, to my will."*

He overhears stray words, commentaries and mutterings groping for still loftier strata, their imaginings of their own magnificence not nearly rarified enough to suit them, the status quo of their towering ascendance even still not near lofty enough to sate them:

The champagne is 'thin,' the hors d'oeuvres 'stale,' the caviar 'bland,' the petit fours 'dull,' and on and on... as the hundreds of millions and countless more, vastly more, hunger and freeze and wait and hate with rising, uprising rage.

He reviles himself: *"The razor cuts both ways, and more ways than we can know,"* he in its sights, he knows, is sure, but cannot help himself, will not stop himself.

He understands, is sure he understands—and loathes himself for hating both worlds, theirs and his, he with a toehold in each, flailing to understand which he more abhors and by which he deserves to be more abhorred, and which he designates the more abhorred, wondering what it matters, both abhorred.

Thin lament creases his lips in skeletal smile as he determines to—unable to *not*—forge their futures, all their futures, to his will and vision—*"and damn them all, and me most of all."*

Rob struggled to quiet amid DeCeeve's abomination, contemplating memory, or dream, or portent, of all that eludes.

The disembodied 'he' regards the scene haunting the all-embracing dark—gaunt figure cringing on highest perch in vanishingly feeble aura—and wonders if his vision is real or imagined, illusion or self-delusion—or something altogether different, of indefinable measure. There is an elusive oddness about the gaunt creature, seeming to exist somehow as less corporeal even than the rest, to be of a still more indeterminate nature even than the rest.

The gaunt creature seems endowed of life but is not quite 'of' life as he knows it, believes he knows it. In this here and now, he realizes, the creature is of something he cannot fathom, like no other ever created, hardly existing at all, even here and now seated on its highest perch within its vanishingly feeble aura. They—dim aura and highest perch... and gaunt creature above all—list between existence and nonexistence, between memory and illusion and self-delusion, lost.

"Lost... where? In what?" he struggles to understand.

"In the dark," silence whispers, he struggling to fathom its source and to grasp any least of its meaning.

Chapter 10.

Rob finished his evening jog and stood catching his breath outside the door to his dorm, sweat dripping, legs heavy, straining not to cringe over, arrived at the limits of exhaustion.

"That's the point: Expend all strength and energy— and ease into the night satisfied you've done your all to end the day with not one iota of strength and energy wasted. How else to end the day, no other way."

He jolted suddenly alert, glared at his watch, saw... *"nearly nine."*

He forced calm, willed himself to a calm in which to reflect, forbade rushed and frenetic lurching, and went about showering and grooming and preparing at forced leisure and, finally, left for the Power Fraternity, stridently *willing* calm, wondering if the day would ever reach him when calm would rise of its own without the desperate need to muster it, plead for it. He forced himself to steady strides as he walked, struggling against but unable erase dread and foreboding stalking him.

"Now past nine," whispered.

He wondered, despite himself, what reaction awaited his late arrival, forced himself to remember he was only wondering, not worrying. Or dreading.

An ordinary, even friendly voice spoke from behind Rob and broke that *something* that had seized him, insisting he was wondering, not... anything else.

Rob turned. Plesant's smile froze.

"Good say... you're pale as a corpse! You okay, Rob?"

Plesant stared at Rob, searched Rob's eyes probing for that *something* against which insistence strove was cause only for wondering and no cause for... anything else.

After a long moment's pause, in conspiratorial whisper, Plesant hissed: "Someone get to you *already*?"

Plesant's tone and manner woke Rob to his surrounds, to the grey, dynamic tensions imbedded all around him. He searched furtively about him, then relaxed to the sight of an ordinary scene—young people absently milling and laughing and drinking and chatting—and calmed visibly, wondering why he'd needed to search out calm, finally deriding himself his anxieties.

Plesant stared at the bruising studded over Rob's face and arms, nodded to chairs nearby, guided Rob to sit.

Plesant repeated: "Somebody get to you *already?*"

Rob ignored the question, and implication, made no mention of being run-down by a reckless female cyclist, then wondered a moment if it had been reckless—or fully intended.

"No, she'd been at least as battered as I was."

Rob wondered to what lengths Allman—or his sycophant cronies—would go, and refused to believe such of her, his brown-eyed girl, and then wondered why, understood why, exactly why, and cursed himself the burdens and privations of having been born a heterosexual male in this day and this age.

Doubt resurged as Plesant wondered under his breath, not for Rob to hear: "How could it have been arranged—and done—so *fast?*"

Plesant shrugged off the thought and resurrected calm: "Glad you made it, even late," but his suspicious stare lingered.

Rob forced himself to quiet, winked and smiled, appropriated a relaxed and casual manner, and tried for light-hearted:

"Nice little party you've got going here. Just routine little gathering of friends and neighbors, or something... more?"

He hoped his tone didn't betray sarcasm. The party was a extravagance beyond measure, lavish and no doubt a very costly affair, catered by smartly uniformed young people with free-flowing cocktails and liquors and numbingly varied tasties and pastries and treats of every conceivable kind, more than he could imagine, completely beyond his experience. The sight left him repulsed, the decadence repugnant, especially in such times as these.

The guests were dressed in highest fashion, flashing jewels and fineries adorning designer tuxedoes and formal evening gowns flashing deepest décolletage... he alone dressed in ordinary jacket and trousers.

"Intentionally," Rob mused, wondering if paranoia suited him, driven to conclude this was all simply to embarrass him, leaving him wondering why anyone would bother in the least with him, even to embarrass him. But he smiled warmly to Plesant and remained cordial and sociable.

Plesant smiled back weakly, appreciating Rob's lighthearted conciliation of this elaborate circumstance. Plesant was clearly trying to be warm and friendly, meaning to keep the atmosphere light and pleasant for Rob, who noted and appreciated Plesant's kindhearted effort on his behalf, and couldn't help but wonder where and how such generosity had been kindled in Plesant, shelving images of Plesant's sufferings—*"for kindness to have been risen in him."*

He wondered: *"Can those who've never suffered feel compassion?"*

Still, tension behind Plesant's mask was palpable and the unease was growing by the minute. Some *thing* was imminent.

In a moment's quiet, Rob couldn't help but hear silence whisper:

"Had she been... recruited... to run me down? No— she'd been as battered as I was... worse. Still—could it be?"

"Of course it could be," silence whispered.

Doubt lingered and he wondered what he'd felt at her touch, at her look, when he'd first beheld her and she him, after they'd managed to their feet.

"Would this end as just another set of bruises from which to recover, over which I'd have to answer for, to myself—of so much that is so much worse than just physical pain?"

He thought of Allman and his Power Fraternity, the edge of fear creeping near. Then Plesant sidetracked Rob's musings by quietly announcing:

"Tonight we're initiating three new candidates. We do it every semester. Only a vanishingly few are ever accepted."

He added quickly, thick with apology:

"But I'm afraid we don't consider non-Raffords," and as afterthought: "Sorry."

Rob struggled to suppress outright laughter at this revelation, struggled to be diplomatic, and clung to silence.

Plesant continued mildly:

"Tonight's the trial for the new candidates."

To Rob's blank silence, Plesant replied:

"The Power fraternity president—Allman, of course—and his Inner Circle select a quality they consider essential to the character or personality of a brother and..." searching for the right emollient, "test it."

There was an interruption in the flow of Plesant's word and look, a momentary flicker of... something, then Plesant continued as if nothing had come and gone in that instant. It was unmistakable, leaving a heavy residue of... something.

"Regret? Remorse?" Rob wondered, knew he'd find out for himself... *"and likely all too soon."*

With scarcely a pause, Plesant continued:

"I was tried and inducted two semesters ago. 'Charity' was the trial. They didn't tell me that, of course. They don't tell anyone what they're being... 'tried'... for."

That momentary flicker resurged, stronger than before, and Rob wondered what had taken possession of Plesant in that moment.

"Cold hate under almighty effort to overpower it," the thought popped into Rob's mind on seeing Plesant's expression, hearing his tone, feeling his manner, filling every trace of him—then all clicked back as if nothing had happened, nothing at all, in that blink of en eye.

Leaning face near, too near, lips hardly moving, aspiring to words spoken silently, to communicate subliminally, so no risk being overheard, Plesant breathed:

"At least I *think* no one knows. I know *I* didn't... but sometimes I think more goes on here than meets the eye. I don't know if it's imagination—or paranoia—or real. You know, should know, that *I* am not in their 'Inner Circle.' But I think—*know*—a lot more goes on they don't let on about."

A moment's silence, then Plesant continued in hushed whisper:

"My induction was a rough one, as these things go. They never explained just what happened that night. Induction's usually a mind-game, tough but no real harm. At least, that's how it's supposed to look... 'to separate the Powers from the powerless.' But... last semester was another bad one."

Rob saw a dawning awareness in Plesant's eyes that *every* trial was a bad one, no matter how it was spun afterward.

Suddenly, Allman materialized and Plesant was instantly silent as Allman spoke to the air between them:

"Well, Robber... a bit late—but welcome nonetheless."

Rob considered... *"'nonetheless,' not 'just the same.'"*

"Entertaining him, are you Pleasure?" spoken to the air. "Not boring him, I trust? Not talking too much, I trust? Not blithering out of turn, I trust?"

There seemed to Rob more than an edge of threat behind Allman's unsettling quiet and control over Plesant. Allman's serene voice and manner jarring and more unnerving than any overt belligerence or threat. Rob understood it was so intended, *"nothing straightforward from Allman, veiled provocation and contemning insult better suited to him. I expect nothing less, or more, of him."*

Rob had learned long ago that no one, absolutely no one, could or should be trusted—until unequivocally proven worthy of trust.

"And even then, trust has its limits."

After a few tense moments of verbal sparring, more like combat, absorbing Allman's barbs and veiled intimidations, Allman dismissed them both by, simply, turning his back and walking away.

Rob inhaled, about to press Plesant to tell him more of his story, of his suspicions and—abruptly stopped in mid-breath.

Rob couldn't help but stare, transfixed, become stone and silence in mid-sentence.

As quickly, he recovered, tried to recover, prayed to recover so that Plesant—or anyone else—would not notice.

"What power, total and absolute power, noticing such of me would lever over me," Rob cringed, cowered to imagine.

He couldn't help but stare, transfixed by a brown-eyed girl stirring across the great room, stirring in him that beyond anything he'd ever felt or dreamed he could feel. Heart pounding and breath gasping he struggled for calm as he heard himself ask Plesant as if hearing someone else speak, eyes struggling to not be riveted on a brown-eyed girl:

"Tell me, Plesant… about 'charity.'"

He battled to hear Plesant as he saw *her*, stared at her, mesmerized by her, trying to *not* watch her every movement—sitting, smiling, gazing deep in thought—as men swarmed over her, vied to be near her, nearer her, nearest her, none able to tear eyes from her.

So Rob saw her, watched her, prayed to not leer at her, how could he not. From some remote dispassion he understood she was no great beauty—but she was imbued of beauty beyond measure, beyond anything eyes could see or lips could taste, her power captivating beyond reason or resisting.

He watched her, the very air sparkling around her, the air fully alive around her, *for* her and only for *her*, every molecule edging to be near her, nearer her, nearest her, beyond anything even air could ever hope for, and so—*"what hope for me?"*

He couldn't tear eyes from her, from eyes and lips and curve of neck and curves of her, of all of her, and she so quiet now, so very quiet now, even as men buzzed and swarmed and preened and postured and vied for her—*so* he saw her—and she sitting with drink in hand and not a sip drawn, sitting among them, so near them and so vastly distant from them, as a star aside an empty world, she staring into space not seeing or hearing or caring for them, for anything of them, all empty, she lost in private thought and dream of which he could only pray to be a part, even the smallest, most remote part, any at all immeasurably more than he could hope for.

He felt something in him he'd never felt, that maybe—*"maybe she's thinking of me."*

He laughed at himself for his shameless hubris, *"that she might ever be thinking of me."*

Somewhere far away, Plesant's voice droned on, words filtering through vast distance, barely audible, barely discernable, palest sound amid the blinding hue of dream of her.

"Not much to tell, really," Plesant droned—and so began his story.

Dimly heard and distantly understood, Rob didn't even struggle to full attention, lost in dream of his brown-eyed girl.

"Three of us were tried. Two of us... finished. Only I was chosen."

Through densest fog, Rob discerned in Plesant a sense of *something*... of regret at having been chosen—*"or of deep guilt,"* thought struck him, whispered silently from the dark.

Suddenly, a thought interjected, jarred:

"What's... she... doing here?"

He struggled against whispers from the dark:

"Is she some vacuous thigh spreading it for The Power Fraternity, seduced by money, by power, by"—and through overarching revulsion—*"Allman?"*

He couldn't bring himself to believe it of her, understood his fear—of her—if she should be a pernicious, conniving carnivore who must never be trusted—*"never be loved,"* and he fell under at that, crushed and anguished by that.

"She wouldn't be here otherwise," no other conclusion.

"But... I'm here!" hope and prayer resurrected, whispered fervently.

He understood he'd have to... talk... to her. Ask her. Somehow.

A thought struck him, an absolute conviction:

"This is not the place for me to show any least interest in her." He knew it with absolute certainty, beyond least doubt.

Rob forced attention back to Plesant, struggled to keep from glancing back at her, staring after her, noticing she wasn't dressed the way the others were dressed—no cleavage flashing, no hip and thigh splayed in sky-high cleft of flowing gown, no jewels crusting her in grotesque parody of taste and culture.

"Simple, modest, she. What does that speak of?" Hope and prayer suffocated, left him breathless.

Again Rob forced attention back to Plesant and again Rob found himself staring at her, wandering with her, lost again in hope and prayer for her.

"If only I knew her name! If only I knew where she lives, what classes she takes, where she spends her time, what she's interested in, what she likes to do, and..." with gaunt and ghostly dread... *"who with."*

Thought stalked him, haunted him:

"If only I could meet her, talk to her," and unspoken, un-dared, whisper... *"love her."*

He struggled through silence, of all he craved of her, like nothing he'd ever felt, had ever imagined he could feel or could be felt.

Plesant droned on:

"It was really just an... unfortunate... accident."

Distantly, Plesant sounded as if he was excusing his words, speaking them true, true or not, even to himself, especially to himself.

This sparked Rob back to Plesant and to his words.

"Nothing more—I'm sure of it! I'm... sure."

Plesant's voice drifted to silence in its struggle to convince it true.

Rob's musings over a glorious brown-eyed girl, and half-hearing Plesant's ramblings, were abruptly exorcized by a single, thunderous explosion—followed by absolute silence and stillness. The silence devastated, more even than the explosion.

One moment, the crowd was milling, people were sitting and chatting and laughing. The next—all was silent and still.

Rob lurched round, saw:

Four massive figures—shrouded men—materialized, brandishing what looked to be shotguns, one still smoking. Hooded and masked and all in black, with only dark eyes and pale lips exposed, three of them occupied, *took*, the great hall, took possession of each of the three exits—and with it all hope of escape, of survival, but for their pleasure.

The fourth wandered malignantly, mingling with the crowd, closely inspecting first one, then another, then others, flaunting a massive carnality under broad grin in ostentatious display of in-your-face command, impudence beyond dare, with feral virility and boundless empowerment, sneering and leering at anyone with least impulse to resist or shy away, in scathing display of vibrant, lurid thriving, gloriously wallowing in his, her, *its* element, fully and luxuriously on display and at-play, all fun and games, gorging and fully devouring and decadently savoring the dread and terror of every soul.

That one played with his, her—its—weapon, pointing the shotgun at random figures who flailed and trembled before it as 'it' fingered the trigger and vaunted broadest grin and defiling eyes fully displayed and here and now ready with full-finality to end any smallest history of petty life that might dare anything but cower.

He—more likely a 'he' than not—mixed randomly with the crowd of coiffed and adorned and ascendant personages and would-be personages, aiming his shotgun carelessly, wantonly, stepping too close face-to-face, lip to lip, breath-to-breath, *that* an intellectual and spiritual savaging far deeper than any physical assault, and then, to one of the women.

He jabbed his weapon fully into her chest and squeezed the trigger and in barest time aimed up and fired-off an explosion that shattered ears and shuddered everyone there, then barrel lilting and again fully pressed against another chest, or throat, or face.

Those many who'd seemed at first unfazed and confident of ruse and subterfuge as show and bluff, suddenly stiffened with smiles frozen and eyes drawn and fear crawling.

Then the other shotguns waved threateningly, aimed randomly, thundered jarringly, their owners yowling and firing-off still more shattering explosions only barely off chests and throats and faces.

The ogre roaming the crowd then herded the crowd to a close-huddle in a small antechamber, then cleaved three young men from among them—shotguns aimed and ready to claim for heaven and hell whoever happened in the way, or if too slow, or if too anything but instant and exacting obeisance.

The three armed men, those in servitude to the fourth, slipped heavy silk hoods over the three cleaved, would-be initiates. One hesitated for a fleeting moment, was answered by the fourth marauder with a blindingly quick rifle butt slammed into his face, his blood flying, spattering, convincing him and all who witnessed, all who were there, of existential need, and then the hooded, would-be initiate was instant compliance, pressing hand to face to stem streaming blood and stumbling where shoved and now genuflecting as he was shoved, along with the now effusively deferential other two.

All three candidates for Power were instantly marched to and then bodily thrown into a waiting van, one heavily tinted from windows to windshields. With engine roaring and another black-hooded figure displayed in the driver's seat, the van-door slammed shut and tires screamed and pavement smoked and the van careened into the dark.

The instant that followed was all silence and stillness. Rob was first to react, first to reach the spot from where the van was already receding—saw no license plate to reveal anything to anyone, the van careening blindingly into the dark.

Amid the erupting chaos, Rob stepped back and turned to leave—and collided with a very still and very quiet figure standing right behind him, staring straight at him.

Eyes met and Rob froze, mute, staring, fallen into vast brown eyes, nothing else existing in all the world but endless brown-eyes.

Then she smiled and the sun shone even in the dark.

Rob stared at lips and eyes smiling gentle warmth to him, and her spell eased him, erased his emptiness, and he began to raise arms to her, to encircle her, to envelop slender waist harboring un-surprising strength and confidence, to draw her near, instinct not will pressing him, and he blessed instinct with all heart—and managed to stop himself.

"I was gonna head you off at the pass," she with quiet whisper and gentlest smile and breath for him, embarrassed, or shy, but not afraid, almost laughing, but quietly, so to fill, not

defile, maybe afraid to laugh, wanting to laugh, but only—
"together with me," his thoughts dared.

"I thought you were gonna take off after them," she
with trace smile in whisper, eyes rapt, breathing him in.

Struggling for words, he abandoned words, none clever
enough or funny enough, but any would do, if he could find
any.

Rob stuttered and stumbled, felt the ultimate fool,
transcendently clumsy and stupid and anything, everything,
that no young woman would ever like or want in a man and,
finally, warring to subdue frantic struggle for words, she
quieted him with look and breath.

Finally, he to her, in quiet whisper:

"I would've… but… I can't run fast enough."

He tried to smile, felt it freeze awkwardly on his face.

A moment's hesitation later he added clumsily:

"I bet you could've caught 'em, if you had your bike,"
he smiled stupidly with brain-dead leer meant to be warmest
smile, and now eyes downcast under fear haunting where joy
should be.

Awkward, stupid, foolish—then all-joy staring at lips
curling into gentle smile for him as she laughed quietly for
him, dearest gift to him, for him.

Then, she to him in gentlest voice and softest eyes:

"Hey, I'm really sorry about before—I oughta watch
out who I run over," and he saw, somehow, that she was glad
she hadn't said 'whom,' wondering how to be smart but not too
smart, so not to frighten a skittish, gentlest boy.

Then they laughed quietly, a bit forced, and tension
melted just a bit, he struggling against taking gentle hold of
her, she holding back just a bit from him, no thought of more
than just that silence, daring enough only to stare into each
other's eyes, to lips, for a timeless moment.

Suddenly, clarity returned—and Rob knew this was no
place for them to talk, much less be seen together, not here and
not now and definitely not like this.

He stammered: "Let's… should we… do you want
to…."

It was even worse than usual now, stammering and struggling to talk to a woman, to ask a woman, to try to sell himself to a woman:

"I... a piece of meat on the butcher's block to be sized-up, judged: if good enough, or not, if worthy enough, or not, of spending—wasting—an evening's time and attention."

She parted lips, inhaled slowly, about to reply when Allman's voice fouled the air:

"Good say! I'm so glad to see you again... babe!"

Rob watched Allman sidle up to the brown-eyed girl and curl arm around her, squeeze her too hard, press solid lips to pink cheek and softest neck, lingering at neck, then he whisper too loudly:

"You look so *good* tonight, babe—like *always*, Lainy. Let's you and I get away from here, away from losers and their ilk. Let's you and I go upstairs, like *usual*, and we'll... *talk*." snorting obscene smirk in her face.

The last was accompanied by a fleeting glance to Rob, face turned so eyes peeped from behind soft, sweet flesh of neck, lips still pressed, lingering, at softest flesh.

In the blink of an eye Rob mumbled vague apology and turned and sloughed away without a glance back. He didn't hear her far-away voice behind him, didn't hear her fulminant corrosions at that *thing* beside her, didn't see her savagely throw its arm from around her, didn't see her twist its neck under fiercest slap to its face, didn't see her lurch away overfilled with loathing.

Rob didn't notice any of those as he slumped silently away in the dark.

The brown-eyed girl stared after him as he sludged away, hands deep in pockets, shoulders hunched high, head hanging low, shame overflowing him to see her with that *thing*, she whispering silently in the dark to him:

"You gonna just shrivel and die every time some jerk manipulates you into feeling the way he wants you to feel, urges that you feel?"

The words whispered silently from the dark amid rising question and doubt of him, she left battling if or not to stand there and watch him go—as she stood there and watched him go.

Chapter 11.

Ben Rob stood in the silence and the dark contemplating the vista afforded through the vast glass wall of the back office. He viewed the massed and ever-massing multitude outside, far below, reflecting on that gently roiling sea:

"Gentle—for now," silent contemplation of the cathedral for the amassed, awaiting the imminent.

Rob's grim musing, a specter blending with the crowd below, was gently ruffled by a soft, near-distant din rising into awareness from the front office… now a gouging corruption as din transformed to repugnant laugh rotting through the vanquished silence—DeCeeve and his odious laughter fouling the air and despoiling the tendrils of calm and peace within which Rob sought desperate shelter, tenuous respite amid the brewing dark, that vestige now desecrated.

Rob stared down over the multitude below, mute and deaf in the silence and the dark, struggling to suffuse himself of warmth and closeness and all else he imagined would, if Goodness so willed, permeate the great mass of people milling below him. He stroked fingers across the glistening smoothness of that glass threshold—the great glass wall shielding him from all that lay outside, far below him, behind which he recoiled into himself from elements that would gouge him and hollow him out of his truth… then the ineluctable corrosion in the guise of DeCeeve corrupted the silence and the dark.

Rob meditated on distinctions afforded by that great glass wall, distinguishing him from those outside, beneath him:

"Outside and beneath… me."

He was repulsed by intimations of loftiness, his over theirs, wondering—*"if no different and no better… what am I?"*

"And what are they," silent whisper taunted in the dark.

The notion was manifest obscenity, decadence beyond imagining, beyond enduring, pervading the rending attitudes roaming him, hunting him at every juncture of every shade and shadow and least trace of difference among and within every class and category and thought and dream and prayer inhabiting him, taken possession of him.

"How different from them am I, can I possibly be?"

"No different at all. None at all." silence whispered.

Rob's musing collapsed as the door burst open and corruption in the shape of DeCeeve and his vulgar laughter penetrated the silence and the dark within which Rob sheltered, isolated and insulated within an invaluable moment's sanctuary, now mourning having to emerge to this, compelled to this.

DeCeeve's very presence excoriated, his every word repugnant, sneering words through repulsive leer:

"Rob. Rob… Rob… Rob."

The sound abraded, repelled Rob through every fiber of thought and prayer:

"What had I done—will I do—for this to be deserved."

Sound drifted into background as Rob allowed, abetted, thought to wall off the words, to route chafing, grating sound to pass through him untouched and unheard but for a distant trill of shroud. Still, despite all will, words penetrated him, engulfed him, sparking a torrent of crackling thought to hurl him back….

It is a seeming trifle, this small caravan of gleaming town cars with their heavily tinted windows now slowly, languidly, pulling up to the house—"'home,' if you could ever call such a monstrosity 'home'," he muses—*lurid ostentation of one among the murk of that great, grand elite, "my patrons for this evening's banquet, for this fund-raiser, for this, my cause."*

He wonders about seeming trivialities, of all that seems trifling and is not.

Thought haunted Rob and he wondered if to be shamed or restored to renewed vigor by such restive thoughts anticipating: *"this, less politics than subterfuge,"* leaving him wondering if politics can ever be more than venal subterfuge.

Rob prided himself on being fully honest—with himself:

"How honest can people be—with themselves—when all is contrived self-delusion steeped in the arrogance of greed?"

He considered:

"Indoctrination—that is what we're here for, what we're here to do. After all, what is political discourse? Honest and open debate of issues and perspectives?"

He laughed *silence* to himself, struggled against whispers to keep from laughing aloud:

"As practiced in the here and now, political discourse is nothing, less than nothing, but evasion and distortion—and outright lie. Our political 'discourse' is nothing less than propaganda—misinformation and disinformation—intended to indoctrinate, pure and simple. Dupe and scam the undecided and deride and demonize any and all who oppose for any least reason. What else possible when 'news' is subordinated to the profit of producers and sponsors."

Silent whisper gloated as he battled to *not* gloat:

"The triumph of my beauteous young people, even now only just embarked in creation, even now only just on threshold of disseminating their—my!—truths among this murk, speaks for itself without need to gloat. There is no need or reason, ever, to gloat. Even in greatest pride and joy there is no place for gloat. After all, my triumph could as easily be usurped by a still more squalid cause, and but for the Grace...."

Rob silenced further thought, not daring even to consider what, but for that very Grace, he could be suffering and yet might—*"will,"* he shuddered—suffer, feeling its certainty stare him in the eye, face him down.

"It takes but one demagogue—" the 'me' remaining cosseted in silence, aware it's 'me' only *this* time.

Thought drove him, remorseless, unrelenting:

"Who am I to arrogate that singularity, that Almighty Grace is mine and only mine, for me and only for me and for no one else ever or ever possible—as my rapacious kindred spirits have through the ages marauded and defiled and continue still to voraciously scheme in their overarching greed and pretense of 'for the people' in grotesque, leering pantomime of perfidy—against ourselves more even than against our lesser... and anyone not exactingly of our mind is necessarily our lesser."

Silent whisper maligned him pitilessly:

"We assail under the banner of Almighty Goodness with ostentatious pretensions of piety that assures, guarantees, we are the fully-deserving, the fully and only righteously deserving."

Rob suppressed an unbridled repugnance of those vast others of his kind... almost as much as for himself.

Silent whisper marched-on heedless of his sensibilities, damn his sensibilities:

"Once I am ensconced in the hearts of the great murk, of that grand elite, with my disciples milling and chatting and flirting amid that sea of murk—of matrons and dowagers and patriarchs and codgers, murk by virtue of being colorless and lifeless and full with themselves and their dark greeds—I will nestle-in to watch the flowering of my gratification, through my beauteous acolytes, embarking on this, my dazzling prologue."

"My beauteous, young and vibrant and brilliant and resourceful and replete with glib wit and well-honed discourse, are resplendent jewels scattered amid the murk, amid the horde of the elite, some few now gathered here, and soon-not-nearly-soon-enough, my bounty will be gathered amid such societies across the entire spectrum of the electorate."

"And we—I—will transcend."

Rob refused the urgings of his hands to rub together in rapacious anticipation amid near-crushing guilt and shame and struggle to *not* gloat.

'He,' and the three—gaunt creature on highest perch ensconced within faded aura—drift nearer, insidiously and

relentlessly nearer, 'he' to them or they to him, he as easily floating toward them as they to him, all drifting along imperceptible route to unknowable destination in the absolute of the dark, singular beyond experience anywhere, ever.

'He' wonders how he remains mute and calm amid this profound inexplicable as he looks up from impossibly near and regards the diminutive creature just the other side of shadow.

'He' watches the creature as it is compelled— powerless to resist unknowable command impelling it—to stretch tremulous fingers toward that infinitely diaphanous veneer of shadow enfolded between them and 'he' poised just outside, all four themselves engulfed in the absolute of the dark.

'He' witnesses the diminutive creature snatch arm, hand, fingers frantically back from the edge of that vermillion shadowland, jerking back, trembling and mewling piteously in renewed struggle to shrivel still further into itself and bury itself still deeper into that highest perch and fade still further into that cosseting, dimmest aura.

The creature cowers piteously as it stares unseeing into the absolute of the dark stretching past imagining, beyond the far side of that vermillion borderland, that vanishingly thin margin of shadow where dream and prayer descend into ineluctable revelation.

The piteous creature is impelled, cannot resist, and cranes neck to peer unseeing into the great dark, cringing under the outpouring less of haunting fear than of torrential, preternatural dread of what lay in wait.

Chapter 12.

Rob trudged through the dark, head slung low, shoulders hunched high, arms buried deep in pockets, lips stirring silent rage.

"Impotent bullock, spineless troll..." on and on, reviling everyone, everything, fully understanding:

"It's me I damn."

He lived and re-lived the scene, ever more shrill in memory and mind, ever more inescapable, until frenetic howling sets to rip him apart and then—silence.

For a moment Rob silenced thought, or thought silenced him, then rage resurged, still and again, on who, what, controlled... *"I my rage, or my rage me."*

The scene re-lived, again, still and *again*... facing Allman—and the brown-eyed girl.

Amid resurged abhorrence and galvanized loathing, he... just... stopped:

"It's not Allman filling me to this."

For a moment he thought sure it was the girl unleashing this.

"But... no."

He forced himself to honesty—the last refuge and final resting place of the self-idolater.

"When all else fails, resort to honesty—with yourself."

He could still recognize truth staring him in the eye:

"It's me I revile, cowed and helpless under her, under pointless, powerless submission to her and to what—I—had let be... by not speaking out, by not exorcising my outrage, by not saying something, anything."

He considered:

"Anything's better than nothing."

He deliberated, wavered:

"Sometimes. Maybe—No."

He reflected for a long moment, thought to launch again into self-loathing, stopped, no point, and somehow willed himself to swallow rage and outrage and acid, self-contempt.

"Better silence than impotent flailing, what point that."

Thought raged… *"what I could have said, should have said—should have done!"*

Thought and revulsion battered him:

"The weak passively accept the history into which they are born, the strong forge their own… and how I despise weakness—especially my own."

Rob recalled his thoughts and feelings, images raging in him, and flung himself into bed, all rage and hate, intent on summoning sleep to soothe and pacify, to blot out memory, to drive thought and feeling into the discarded past, to stanch ravings and scar the rotted wound. But despite all will he succeeded only in still more self-loathing under still higher rage tossing and roiling and turning and writhing him until finally he bolted upright in barely stifled scream under clenched teeth and balled fists and finally… he surrendered to misery and flung himself out of bed, tore-on his clothes, and stormed out the door and into the dark.

He raged along the path his feet chose gradually feeling the cool night air reaching into him, begin to calm him, then he stood aside himself in silent challenge to himself as the dark corners of mind whispered him awake to himself—and ever slowly shame and self-revulsion ebbed, and ignited nerve quieted, and then only remorse endured, with lingering struggle to rationalize, justify, explain, excuse, and maybe forgive.

"You're only human!"

But revulsion of himself resurged to denounce him, sneering contempt full for him:

"'You're only human'—the last refuge of enlightened absolution, the best and last recourse to those like me, of vast and manifold flaws and failings."

"Still, I'd be consumed and spent if I couldn't forgive myself my human failings, at least to some smallest measure."

He had to, so he did, what choice, no choice.

Rob didn't notice or track where his steps took him—*"even my feet usurp control, I not able to control even my own feet,"* and again he struggled to contain outrage clawing him.

He found himself at an exhausted truce, he and his thoughts, and then he looked up—and found himself at the Power Fraternity pushing open the door, mystified by how or why he was there pushing open the door.

Plesant looked up from being alone and sprang instantly to Rob's side, hurriedly grabbing an offering of cup and coffee and holding it up to him, obeisance to Rob, near genuflecting—oblation for the events of earlier that night.

Plesant studiously forced calm, took a languidly fevered sip of coffee, and with pretended cheeriness mock-scolded:

"Ben, where you been? I've been looking all over for you! Hope our gun-toting 'kidnappers' didn't scare you off."

Rob watched Plesant trace quotes, fingers waggling in air at the word 'kidnappers,' afraid the inflection in his voice would fail to communicate the scene as having been purely performance art, for the sake of the initiates.

Rob laughed invisibly at pretense and play, Plesant's about the earlier commotion, his own of his brown-eyed girl—and of Allman. He fought to downplay his own petty failings as trivial, invisibly shaking his head at the turmoil gnawing him, intent on devouring him—*"when all I need is a bit of time and distance and simple patience, for myself, to set matters to perspective, trivial in the scheme of existence"*—hoping it into triviality, huge as it seemed then and silently still certain it would remain so no matter how he rationalized and trivialized its truth.

"Truth is truth, after all," silence whispered against any thought of transmuting truth into anything else or anything less.

Plesant continued, euphemizing the drama, pretensions less to teacher than as preacher to slack-jawed child:

"Those 'abductors'"—fingers waggling again—"were play-acting, playing their part in the 'trial,' the test for those three candidates."

Rob understood that Plesant invoked this imagery less as attempt to rationalize than to illuminate, and he stared at Plesant as he struggled to not stare—at poor clod under profound misunderstanding of this reality.

He wondered if Plesant wasn't *mis*-understanding but *dis*-understanding—*"fully intent, aware or not, on denying the truth to himself, deceiving and deluding himself by portraying—to himself—such dehumanizing corrosion as a lofty trial, mis- or dis-apprehending such base and demeaning 'play' as just a well-meant offering to the privileged, as just an enviable and laudable forum for self-discovery."*

Plesant's oblivious self-deception was vastly repellent.

Rob considered… and doubted any real harm would come to the three candidates, but was equally sure mortal harm very likely could.

"The perpetrators are no doubt roaring with laughter, secret in a shadow of the dark, caring not in the least what harm might breach the three candidates—and likely wallowing in images of their greatest harm. Anything short of murder could easily devolve against the perpetrators—and all-likely that too—and who would know and who would care and who would lift smallest finger for their redemption, that of the perpetrators or of the victims."

Rob absently wondered:

"Privilege and power are without borderlands… except when breaching another's, more powerful or more privileged—and otherwise nothing at all to stop them."

Rob shuddered at the supernal underpinnings of such reality as Plesant continued without pause, excitement building, mouth motoring in advance of thinking:

"And guess what—you won't believe your luck!"

Rob felt a presence behind him as Plesant suddenly lost all animation and abruptly coiled tight and clamped shut, overfilled with panic and… *"dread,"* the only word for what Rob saw, felt, in Plesant, *"dread more even than fear."*

In quietest tone and meekest look, Plesant muttered:

"Guess I've got a big mouth, huh," and no question to it.

From behind Rob:

87

"No guessing. You do. But everyone knows it. Don't they, Robber."

Rob turned to see Allman's sneer.

"Even *Robber* here knows you've got a big mouth, don't you, Robber."

Allman's smile was embodiment of derision and scorn.

Rob clung to silence, what else.

To Rob's silence:

"You're too kind, Robber—the true mark of the impotent and impoverished."

Allman spoke to air, listing toward Plesant with a smirk, talking to Rob through Plesant:

"You'd have made an apt candidate for our Brotherhood, *Robber*, at one of our trials awhile back."

Allman regarded Plesant:

"You remember that one, don't you, Pleasure. 'Charity,' we called it, didn't we, Pleasure."

Allman turned to Rob, inspected him up to down, then stared him eye to eye:

"It's a favorite subject of mine you know, the illusion we call 'charity.'"

To Rob's persistent silence, Allman continued:

"Charity—intentional kindness..." near-chortling at such fantasy.

Allman—stepping between Plesant and Rob, back fully to Plesant, no longer relevant, no longer existing—addressed Rob directly, his stare boring into Rob to penetrate him, or try:

"Tell me, Robber—*is* there such a thing as 'intentional kindness'?"

"Finally, a straightforward question"—and thought immediately shifted:

"Straightforward—from Allman? What does he mean by 'intentional' charity?"

Images of the privileged and moneyed sprang to mind... *"preening and strutting behind award and tribute for extravagant munificence, vast bestowments even still paltry to their exalted profusion, charity given not as second-thought but as side-show of intent... to bask in the envy of the lesser, to wallow in horded accolade and, above all, to engineer."*

88

Silence whispered, to temper Rob in his full-willed animosity—*"jealousy?"*—to diminish and defame:

"Still and all, the potential for vast good works behind their voluptuous gifts renders trivial even their basest motivations," so Rob reviled himself his arrogance, caring to sneer at even the most posing, self-serving—*"self-adulating, self-idolizing"*—benefactors. Then instantly, again and still more, self-repugnance surged to abase him for damning the smallness that is, all likely, simply beyond them, simply beyond their awareness and will, wondering—*"if I were in their shoes..."*—awareness resurging to be ever grateful:

"But for the Grace of Goodness, there go I"—praying he'd never be challenged by such wealth and privilege, fear brimming to think, to know:

"I am no better—and likely far worse."

Rob understood Allman well enough to know he never posed simple, straightforward questions, and again Rob surrendered to the sanctuary of silence, *"where else sanctuary."*

To Rob's persistent silence, Allman launched himself in a feint of all-mild, quietly-reasonable, sunny discourse belying pugnacious, provocative words in quiet tones:

"People like you bristle with smug, self-righteous good intention. People like you reek of vapid, self-adulating generosity full with 'kind' intentions. Don't you, Rob."

Allman dropped the emphasis on his pejorative 'Robber' and shifted to issuing mockingly gentle words behind scant cosmetic of bland, solicitous smile—under eyes anything but. He inspected Rob closely for any trace defiance, or cowing, and smiled-wide at sight of both facing him straight on, naked and exposed.

But Allman granted, grudgingly and silent to eye and lip:

"This Robber is a courageous poser, staring me down, staring me eye-to-eye, daring to stand up to me."

Something in Allman's eyes flickered, just then, for a briefest moment, and Rob couldn't help but wonder:

"Is there something of apology in those eyes, something of kindness, of warmth and even of brotherhood, latent in those eyes?"

Rob deliberated, slightly awed at thought of such notion occupying Allman. Then that look in Allman's eyes vanished, come and gone as if never having been, and Rob wondered, *"had that impression been an illusion perpetrated on me BY me... or had that been a genuine spark of quiet, exalted humanity?"*

Rob couldn't be sure and was left to wonder, to struggle in the balance of his own bigotries—*"to balance my harsh realism and dull cynicism with my blind hope and charitable—or ingenuous—credulity. Which is truth and which deception... and which self-deception?"*

Rob pondered:

"FROM what depths TO what depths do such as Allman and his rarified ilk exert their power? Do the 'lesser' and the 'lofty' each labor under their own need—to follow, or be followed? Are the lesser, both the innocent and the not-innocent, simply unable to contain their awe and veneration of towering personalities, of demagogues and despots, and follow them... like sheep? Do the lofty, the likes of Allman, draw-in the lesser by strength of will and tentacles of power... like spider to fly caught in its web? Or is something entirely-other at work, something more mystical, of a covert, learned skill or native power... like snake mesmerizing mouse?"

Rob wondered if he'd just imagined that sense of... something—of comradeship, of fellowship, of *something* in Allman—reaching out to him, trying to reach out to him, even crying out to him, *for* him... *"now gone, gone as if never having been."*

Rob shook his head lightly, wondered where lies the vermillion borderland between insight and imagination, between illusion and self-delusion:

"They are not for now, such questions," and he pushed further thought of it out of his mind, for now.

As suddenly as it had started, so it ended, and Allman's cold, hard, calculating persona was reborn, reclaimed eyes and lips and manner and all of him, and Allman transformed back to himself—and turned his back and walked away.

Plesant stood quietly staring at Allman's back, the look of daunted wonder filling him, gaping his mouth. Finally, after an over-long moment, Plesant spoke in subdued voice and tone:

"I thought for sure he'd tell you. I don't think it matters now…" and in hushed voice, unable to contain revelation to himself, still staring after Allman's ghostly remains, Plesant murmured incredulously:

"We're lucky to have gotten off so easy."

Plesant muttered the words more to himself than to Rob, mystified by such magnanimous offering from Allman, sparing still more of Allman's excoriation and defilement, leaving Rob wondering just what Plesant meant and who had been so lucky, Plesant or he, himself.

Then Plesant continued, still in hushed tones:

"I don't think it's ever been done before—Allman wants you to undergo 'trial.' He wants you to be a Power brother." Awe lived in those words, at such singular precedent.

Rob, too, couldn't help but stare at Allman's ghostly remains, haunting the air in which he'd been standing:

"No—he only wants me to try."

Chapter 13.

Rob stared down over the milling sea of people displayed through the vast back office window-wall, fully immersed in the dark, fully suffused of silence, fully relishing the moment's transcendent peace. Then fleas and tics and lice and worms and snakes and rats and all manner of vilest corrosions swarmed and crawled and crept and writhed, penetrating him, violating him, excoriating flesh and mind and spirit screaming, craving, to shatter him—exploded out of the silence and the dark in the specter that was DeCeeve, his laughter spewing out of sneering mouth and corrupting mind and decaying spirit all too-near Rob's own—*"too near my own shape of it, unlike his only by shade of grey, we, all of us, are grey, of some shade or other, after all"*—replete with DeCeeve's signature harlequin leer derived of loftiest, self-endowed immensity of Almighty hallowed, hollow blessedness.

DeCeeve droned-on in rancid decay of mind and spirit as Rob turned away, impelled to show his back, compelled by images of Allman and all that is Allman's in glorious corrosions... *"so like DeCeeve's,"* as memory catapulted:

The Power Fraternity 'event' was the pretense of a light-hearted gathering of friends and lovers, a pretense of no stress and no pressure—a friendly little get-together. Allman, through placid eyes and smiling face, launched thinly veiled contempt rankly exposed in feint of softest voice and kindest eyes, illusion and pretense to mild and quiet and reasonable and cordial.

Rob recalled Allman pontificating through word and eye directed kindly at Rob, and he wondered if Allman was baiting and taunting—or simply, now, for reasons known only to him, the embodiment of earnest, honest sincerity elaborating to his point. Allman, in gentlest tones:

"People are left to suffer the shallow kindnesses of great and greatest intentions, don't you think so, Rob?"

Allman had abandoned his derisory 'Robber,' leaving Rob to deliberate under brewing suspicion that braced him alert to the subterfuges of the other's character. To Rob's silence, Allman continued, Rob grateful for the refuge afforded by silence... *"my last and only refuge,"* as images of the brown-eyed girl rose to him, offered him a still greater refuge.

The sound of Allman returned Rob to the here and now as Allman spoke, with measured tone:

"We all aspire to fill ourselves with paternal and fraternal kindnesses, with most well-meant intentions, aspiring to be always true and honest and pure, don't we Rob."

Still only silence from Rob, awaiting inevitable finale to farce, even as thoughts reproached him for his cynicism. Allman continued airily, now injecting measured tones of taunt and dare scarcely sheltered behind vermillion shadow of halcyon words:

"Of course you know what I'm talking about—our communal sanctimony about honesty and truthfulness, that last a distinct entity in itself."

"Here it is," Rob anticipated, welcomed this unveiling, awareness dawning to the terminus of this flow but still unable—*"unwilling,"* for some dark, Goodness-knows motive, he realized—to channel the flow of talk away from its now inevitable conclusion, he himself now fully allowing and abetting that flow, now of *his* doing, not Allman's, as Allman continued mildly:

"Not that you'd do anything like it yourself, of course—lie, that is. Lies are like sex, you know—or don't," through wry smile and condescending eyes, "something you hear about, read about, watch other people do, it being tolerable for the other guy but not for you, a bit dirty and so not for you, beneath you, you above all that, right?"

Not waiting for reply, recognizing Rob's blank, noncommittal stare, watching Rob struggle to calm appearance if not to calm itself against the rising vitriol, Allman continued:

"I bet you don't lie. I bet you *are* lily white. I bet you think it's vile and contemptible and beneath you ever to lie. Lies are so akin to sex, aren't they... you'd never lower yourself to actually doing it, would you?"

No reply, so: "Would you?"

To Rob's silence Allman roared, half-howled:

"*Would* you, Robber?"

The din of ambient conversation abruptly froze silent as all eyes turned, transformed into mute and motionless voyeurs awaiting *something* from Allman, something special, something of spectacle, something worth their wait and their stares.

Mesmerized by Allman's rising heat, feeling the glares around him pressing-in on him, Rob answered—*"what else to do? Nothing"*—with vague notions as to why he chose *this* in reply, fully aware of falling straight into Allman's game:

"No. I don't lie." It was a lie, of course.

Rob wasn't sure why he'd uttered those words, lied, here and now, of all places and times, maybe begging the question:

"Who does not, has not, and will not ever lie, when even Goodness lies, recognizes the need to lie, must need to lie?"

Rob recalled a Biblical lesson from earliest childhood—*"lie... out of overarching need to preserve relationships, so delicate and friable and needful, so very needing beyond superficial pronouncements of hurtful truths...."*

From Rob: "There are lies and then there are... lies."

Knowing better than to continue but not able to stop himself, feeling himself hurled into the pit even as he wondered why he so willfully obliged Allman to hurl him into the abyss, Rob couldn't help himself as he continued:

"Only needed is: How to know the difference between lies and... *lies*—the first rarely avoidable, the second rarely forgivable."

At this early juncture of debate—*"argument, battle, will versus will in estranged battle for integrity, for... supremacy,"* Rob smiled secretly at this bounteous overabundance of drama he was provoking—Rob already anticipating losing the battle.

"Allman's sure to win, must inevitably win—and gloat and sneer and condescend with smug ascendance at 'The Raffords' overcoming their lesser of State, of those like Rob."

Rob studied Allman, studied his eyes, lips, manner, and recognized in Allman... *"regret, my reply heralding inevitable victory too easily won, filling him with disappointment for being robbed of this opportunity to fully relish triumph over a grudgingly worthy adversary."*

And, too, Rob saw that Allman, underneath it all, recognized Rob as a grudgingly worthy adversary—*"though who can say why, what he sees of me."* Rob was genuinely at a loss to imagine what smallest virtue Allman could possibly see of him.

Then Rob wondered about his assessment, his insights of Allman—*"no, sophistry... in the guise of insight,"* deprecating himself for lauding himself over being honest with himself.

Rob dismissed the thought that he could perceive Allman's regret at 'too easy a victory,' and disavowed his perception that Allman thought more highly of Rob than Rob did of himself.

"It's all imagination, no reality to it," and Rob set to wonder what lay between imagination and reality, and how to distinguish the two when their shadowlands encroach and meld and so are rendered indistinguishable.

"Still... Allman is searching for something, as if for answer to some question the answer to which I harbor, hoping the answer will somehow leach out of me and suffuse into him—answers to questions... of kindness, of compassion, of insights he believes do not, cannot possibly, exist."

Rob was suddenly flooded with pity for Allman.

"Allman's always and ever needing to be superior, needing to be in absolute command and in absolute control with no least place for any glimmer of wavering or weakness or blunder or apology or regret, not for a moment, always racing to crush any betrayal of his world and of his ascendance— caged beast ensnared in a cage of his own creation."

Rob shuddered under silent whisper of lament, it struggling to convince him that such imagined insight is outside and beyond Allman—*"who am I to think I can contravene to uplift and deliver him, let alone fathom him."*

For a fleeting moment an expression of... disappointment... colored Allman's face, then vanished as if never having been, and the familiar leer and contempt returned to fill him, he now grinning knowingly:

"Of course you lie, Robber. We all lie and cannot help but lie, consciously and willfully. You put the lie to your very denial."

To Allman's smug face, Rob paused, all silent, considering what, how, to reply, this being important, telling, to be communicated with just the right look and tone and word.

Allowing the pause, Allman finally interjected, now with marginally kinder eyes and tone, preaching kindly, softly:

"The worst kind of deception is *self*-deception."

Despite seeing the inevitable conclusion and Allman's inexorable victory in this little game, Rob replied quietly, aware he was allowing himself, abetting himself, as fodder to Allman's bloated, gloating hubris:

"Well, sometimes I withhold the truth. That's not lying."

Allman replied, check-mate quietly flaunted in eyes:

"Withholding truth *is* a lie, is *intended* to lie, its purposed to distort, to mislead, to deceive. *That* is truth, no matter how you couch or veil or evade or deny. Or try."

Rob contemplated resorting to tired clichéd argument, heard answers and rejoinders in his head, anticipated their inevitable conclusion:

Rob: *"It's the intent that matters: Lies are intended to deceive—for the liar's gain. White-lies and half-truths and withheld-truths are intended to spare the victim pain—whoever the victim."*

Allman: *"Sparing the victim? You mean sparing the liar, sparing the liar's pain, sparing the liar from telling painful truths—both kinds of lie are for the betterment of the liar, both are for the liar's sanctity and sanctimony, both are for the liar's pride and exaltation, both are for the liar's pretensions and self-deceptions of owning a loftier purity. If not for being profoundly terrifying—the 'innocent' liar's holier-than-thou pretense of supernal enlightenment—it would be laugh-out-loud self-idolatry. You and those like you play at deceit so casually and so thoughtlessly—spouting your transcendent pieties as if possessing the entirety of ethereal righteousness—that you are all the more terrifyingly contemptible, all the more filled with the vilest corrosions of deceptions and self-deceptions."*

The argument played-out in Rob's thoughts in the blink of an eye and, so, with hardly a pause, Rob turned to Allman and looked him straight in the eye, and quietly, simply:

"You're right, Allman. You're absolutely right."

Rob meant his words sincerely, absolutely. Allman *was* right, absolutely right.

Rob regarded Allman—and for a moment saw him in a different light. Allman seemed illuminated, seemed suddenly elevated, seemed beyond the world of petty jealousies and rivalries. He saw Allman as if for the first time, as if Allman's genuine self was only now revealed, endowed with deepest understanding and most incisive, honest discernment.

"He sees past—through—our social veils behind which we are suborn to our dogmas and greeds, complicit in the expedience under which we willfully blind ourselves. We take our deceits casually, deceptively—self-deceptively—and delude ourselves of our own motivations, exploiting and awaiting being exploited by our own vapid illusions and delusions, by our own deceptions and self-deceptions."

For the briefest moment it seemed to Rob that Allman's demeanor had transformed, that Allman accepted him now as an equal rather than as the inferior, subordinated rival— the enemy. It seemed to Rob that Allman now radiated some intense, new emotion that had been exhaustively constrained and suffocated and atrophied and finally expunged through a life so-learned and so-ingrained, and now he thirsted for something… like this, an authentic brotherhood beyond and *other* than the trite and not-so-trite deceptions and self-deceptions rife within the Power-brotherhood pretenses and those of their kind.

But like a vague mist, come and gone and now not sure it had ever really been, the illusion, self-delusion, vaporized and now only remaining was a vague memory of… something, of something half-forgotten, and now—gone, as if never having been.

'He,' the disembodied 'he,' watches the gaunt creature seated on its highest perch within its cosseting, palest aura. 'He' watches it stretch fingertips toward the vermillion shadowland, the borderland cleaving its universe of feeblest aura from the disembodied 'his' universe of the absolute of the dark waiting just beyond, just out of reach.

'He' observes the frail creature peer out and reach, and reach, and finally surrender its try at grasping hold or catching sight of who, what, lay in wait in the dark only just beyond the vermillion shadowland. It seems to lament being refused by that vague and indeterminate… thing… lurking in wait in the absolute of the dark, just beyond his reach.

The creature again raises tremulous fingertips, ever haltingly, toward that borderland, inching body, arm, hand, fingertips ever nearer, ever timorously and ever guardedly nearer, and nearer still, until fingertips are leveled a breath from that vermillion shadowland. Under surging effort its fingertips breach that final, vanishingly thin gulf of irreducible quality and quantity of space/time separating it from that vermillion shadowland, and from the dark awaiting just for it, just beyond.

It stretches, reaches… again collapses in a lament of failure. And now 'he' reaches, extends fingertips in the absolute of the dark just outside that vermillion shadowland. 'He' reaches near, nearer, near as he can—and watches the gaunt creature try again, stretching fingertips vanishingly near his own.

The creature cranes neck to peer into the absolute of the dark waiting just beyond the vermillion borderland.

'He' cranes neck to peer into that vanishingly faded aura just beyond the very same vermillion shadowland.

Then pale creature screams through shadow lips and gaping eyes, suddenly seized and irresistibly drawn. 'He' watches the gaunt creature soundlessly scream just as now 'he' screams, is seized, flails wildly within the absolute of the dark just beyond the vermillion shadowland.

'He' cringes, screams soundlessly, peers out—and finds HE is seated on that highest perch within that faded aura.

He feels the aura's earnest try to console, to comfort— and mourns the aura's loss, feels the aura's lament for its vanishingly feeble consolation, for its near nothingness of comfort, wrenchingly impotent as shield and paladin against the absolute of the dark awaiting just beyond the vermillion borderland, caging him on highest perch and faded aura.

Chapter 14.

Rob walked as he always walked—books tucked under one arm, head hung low, shoulders hunched high, hands buried deep in pockets. He'd once considered how he appeared—to others as well as to himself, as he'd appear to himself if he saw himself walking so—and struggled if to and how to decide if it mattered in the least, and decided it did not, vaguely dismissing the notion out-of-hand, nothing for it anyway, nothing he cared to do about it anyway, how and what people thought of him and the ways of him, of how he walked or of anything of him, were all too far outside him to worry over:

"Should I do or think or feel or believe just because someone might catch me at it, because someone might think something, anything, of it—of me—because of it, good or bad? They can all go to Hell."

He'd convinced himself of the rightness of feeling so, and that he really meant it, no exceptions. Still, he wondered if he had what it takes—of strength of will, of independence, of simple ignorance and childlike heedlessness of consequence, of true grit—to harbor such lofty convictions.

He wondered: *"Would I rather conform to the ambient crowd and surrender myself to their intrusions and judgments? Should I obsess and perseverate over what they might think or say or do? Such threat renders the vast morass obeisant to the least whim and command of the mob—should I be that?"*

He understood: *"It's easy to reject, even revile, what you know little about. What do I know of true grit, of rising above—or of falling below—my simple and petty self-immersions?"*

And vaguely: *"Heedless, or willfully ignorant, of vast disdain and even hate and outrage directed at me, for my unblinking and unfettered thoughtlessness and heedlessness of the consequences of their contempt—is that what I aspire to?"*

He reviled himself his self-delusions and impurities, thinking himself better for clinging to his petty self-immersions.

Rob thought back to Plesant's words:

"I don't think it's ever been done before—Allman wants you to undergo 'trial.' He wants you to be a Power brother."

Plesant's voice had been fully awed at such singular precedent, and Rob remembered staring at Allman's back as Allman sauntered loftily away, imputing understanding: *"He doesn't want me to be a Power brother, he only wants me to try—failure and shame assured."*

Rob lost himself in reverie as *her* image faced him, eye-to-eye, breath-to-breath, he struggling for breath, lingering over her, lost in her eyes, in her lips, in everything of her, in wondering of her, and suddenly… aware of fear of her.

He faced her in memory, held her close, all eyes to her, whispering to her lips:

"If I seem cold and distant, it's for fear of you. How can I explain such fear, risking to seem, and be, shriveled and shrunken in your eyes?"

Rob could only shudder under unfathomable faith:

"But I know you'll… understand."

He wondered at this supernal esteem of her, edging to reverence:

"How could I justify such lofty expectation of you, of anyone?"

He wondered how such extravagant esteem could ever be fulfilled, and pitied her, and himself, for such unreachable expectation, so setting her, anyone, to certain failure.

Rob strolled along the path, hardly anyone about, and recalled:

"Today is rally-day, the day of the student strike, a one-day, all-day boycott of class, for the display… solidarity with one of our own." He resisted thinking 'one of *their* own.'

He recalled Panther King's impending expulsion and the rousing student passions—spearheaded by The Power Fraternity proclamation:

"King is hostage to and victim of the inimical provocations and persecutions of our administration, led by Dean Ivry, deploying King's grades as pretense and ploy for King's imminent expulsion."

The article, written in The Sentient, the school's flagship paper, went on:

"Panther King challenges the status quo of the entrenched bureaucracy. He challenges the oppression of the student body by the arrogant leadership of Dean Ivry. King challenges the insularity and elitism of the academic discourse and content and decries the spare diversity of The Rafford—of ideas and ideals more even than of the corporeal."

"King may have had an occasional lapse in a grade or two," the narrative went, "but Dean Ivry would dismiss and reject him out-of-hand rather than work with him and uplift him, and elevate the complexion of The Rafford itself. King's activist dissent, not his grades, convict him and sentence him."

"The issue goes further as the cries rise up: clear and simple bigotry—less racial than economic and, most decisively, social and class bigotry!"

The word was hammered home endlessly, relentlessly:

"*Bigotry!*"

So the Power Fraternity brotherhood characterized the administration's posture toward Panther King.

Rob suspected, or realized:

"All this turmoil is simply meant to rouse passions, anyone's and everyone's, never mind whether for or against, justified or not. Agitate and incite, provoke and inspire—hate and rage and outrage. Such is the nature of politics and the media, where even ravenous religious zealotry is hardly more than a weak and distant pulse, a parody of pretense, fallen under the staunch, underlying authenticity of political dogma, expansively fueled by the media."

Rob confirmed silently, swore silently:

"Politics is not all-local but all-personal, steeped in personal integrity—and its screaming absence. Harbored in the greeds of each polarity wallow the provocations to hate and rage and outrage."

102

Rob struggled to imagine the 'why' of the Panther King and Dean Ivry uproar:

"Why generate such intensity of passion? Why stir the students so virulently? For what gain?" and, suddenly aware: *"For whose?"*

Inevitably: *"How can this possibly advantage Allman?"*

Rob reviled himself his certainty, not even questioning that certitude, and didn't wonder that this turmoil would end in blood, only wondering how much—and whose.

Once again Rob rebuked himself for his bigotries against Allman and the likes of Allman, but couldn't stop himself or help himself, the truth of it, *"the likely truth of it,"* self-evident:

"I despise the fetid arrogance and rancid hubris and unflinching, rapacious greed of even the palest rendition of all that is Allman's."

How could he not revile himself, subordinating Allman's greed to his own, deluding himself that… *"my greeds are noble and righteous."*

Rob had read the articles, had heard the arguments:

"King is too arrogant and extremist and disruptive, agitating for 'we the students!' to have more sway—even *veto* authority—over our curriculum, over course content and contour, over who will elect and how to select the instructors and professors and administrators, over the mode and manner of testing and grading, seeking to usurp our legitimate leaders."

" 'We the students!' have earned and deserve a greater voice—a *controlling* voice—in The Rafford. It is for *us* to override the indoctrinations of misinformation and disinformation by which we-the-students are led and misled, manipulated and controlled, here and now and through all our futures, wherever that leads and misleads us."

Rob was aware of whispers:

"King is subversive, converting too many to his way of seeing, thinking, believing—the 'cult of King'—and for *that* he's got to be silenced."

Vague whispers penetrated, of how he'll be derailed, with intimations of 'soon.'

103

"The whispers," Rob reflected, *"are rife with feral speculation of the role played by Allman and his Power Fraternity, whispered to have some dark leverage over Dean Ivry on behalf of King—passionately refuted by Allman and his marionettes, who angelically forswear all but the most upright and forthright debate."*

Rob concluded: *"Allman spouts emollient words of denial to curry the image of being the champion 'of the people for the people' as he's anything but, sowing seeds of subversion and intimidation and betrayal of King's future— and theirs."*

Through his revulsion, Rob couldn't help but admire Allman.

Rob had heard the arguments and counter-arguments, and was deeply sympathetic to King, but deplored and condemned the means to that end—*"ever-growing crowds whipped into ever-escalating frenzy that will inevitably accelerate into...."*

Rob paused, imagined Allman's hand at work, wondered to what extreme Allman would propel them... *"having strangers materialize atop platforms sprung-up out of nowhere—and stationed up beside King—on seemingly spontaneous gatherings. Interlopers materialize and exhort the ever-gathering crowds to fight for King whenever and wherever and however, anytime and anywhere King appeared, appealing to the crowds for King's emancipation, for fair and honest judgment of him."*

"And sometimes these strangers were imbedded among the students crowding-in to see and hear King. Sometimes these strangers would hoot and howl and rile the crowd for their righteous affirmation and full-throttled support of King. Sometimes those strangers whispered softly, or spoke plainly aloud, or screamed-out shrilly—to provoke and incite in support of King. And sometimes those strangers would just mill about, scanning the audience, monitoring and photographing."

"But to what end?"

The question mystified Rob, redolent of *intent*, of sinister workings veiled from him.

"And now: feral support for King is commanded while simple, quiet sympathy is forcefully reviled and righteously damned... and disinterest and apathy are transmogrified into mortal sins betraying the 'we the students' canon."

It was early evening and students were few and widely scattered as Rob meandered the paths that led by the great oak—*"or is it sycamore?"* absently wondering and shamed that he didn't know, somehow sure he should, wondering why he should:

"How can I, born and raised a city boy, trees rarer there than potholes here?"

Rob suddenly blundered into a crowd tramping noisily, boisterously, along the Rafford Commons, waving placards, shouting slogans, yelling profanities... and lobbing stones in the general direction of passers-by who didn't instantly join-in.

Rob was sure he understood them:

"These ragtag collections of students... and outsiders... milling toward The Rafford administration building are more than just delving into the fashion of the moment, the lemming-thing to do—they're devolving. Their cause is now de rigueur—compulsory, no longer subject to choice—they descended into barbarity."

"So much for the doctrines of freedom and diversity of thought," his frown was a miserable press of lips.

"Activism and extremism, in support of mob rule and anarchy, are no longer just expected but are ordained and commanded."

Rob bristled at this oppressive populism, at such compulsions... *"where freedom to think and feel and judge for oneself are reviled and damned."*

He felt fully righteous—and shamed to be so smugly self-righteous:

"How different am I from them?" knowing he'd just as soon compel them to his own thinking, feeling, believing... *"and to hell with them if they dare anything less."*

Rob veered clear of the growing crowd trammeling some small distance from him, maneuvering casually away so not to attract their notice, finally reached the knoll with that incredible oak—*"sycamore?"*—always ready to embrace and shelter him, eager to shade and comfort him under enfolding insignificance, away from the crowd.

"And populism be damned," Rob avowed silently.

He applied himself to his work... *"they dole out lots of work here—to keep us in line, to keep our noses to the grindstone, to keep our hearts and minds labored and encumbered, without time for thinking or feeling, or politics."*

He smiled, imagining the perfect solution to the greatest upheavals savaging the world: *"Just enroll every anarchist and revolutionary and terrorist into college or grad school or med school or law school— and keep 'em so busy they'd have no time for hate and rage and outrage."*

He laughed silently at this transcendent scheme as he glanced up and noticed a far-away figure staring him down. He/she/it was glowering at him from among the gathered protesters a small distance downhill from him.

"Even at this distance I can feel the protesters raging, wrenching themselves out of calm reason and fair judgment. No room for such trivialities amid righteous rage."

He watched others among the crowd, fingers pointed in his direction, faces contorted in furious debate, gestures limned of rage and outrage aimed and slung at him with killing glares. Then he saw them hunting for rocks and sticks and anything with which to implement their hate, their lips snarling, their arms in frenzied gestures.

Rob wasn't sure if he saw or only imagined he saw all that, and readied to stand and walk away, rush away—run with all he had. He wondered if he should, or not, and judged to stay, defend this vanishingly small realm of rational disinterest and calm reason.

With heart pounding and breath catching he forced himself to root to the spot, to sit there and stand his ground against tyranny imminently making for him as that first of them, who'd been staring him down, put arms and hands up against the others to dissuade their intent, impending violence, and to persuade them with unyielding words, barely credible, *'put it down, just... put... it... down!"* and imagined he saw that one judging if and how to make for him as the others grudgingly abandoned their sticks and stones. He admired the power of that one… *"the power to sway a rabid mob,"* a truly remarkable, even heroic feat.

"Sure enough…" to his complete un-surprise, *"that one is separating from the others and is tramping, marching, up the hill toward me, struggling to suppress rage and outrage, intent on intruding and contemning and savaging me in my little swathe of peaceful sanctuary."*

Rob felt sure that one intended not violence but impassioned argument, and tried to imagine the workings of the mind in that one even now storming up the hill at him, for him, and he wondered:

"What harm could I pose? I'm a peaceful scene—harmlessly sitting under a sheltering tree, alone with my thoughts. What harm in me? What possible provocation could I be, sitting here in my near distance?"

Imagination failed him and he could only wonder what thought and emotion powered that one heading up that hill straight for him.

Again he wondered if to walk off, or run, or stay and face unbending hate and rage heading for him. Then, too late: *"It… is almost on me."*

He suddenly realized the figure coming for him was not an 'it' but a 'she' rising toward him and, watching her resolute movements, glimpsed *her* perspective, witnessed *her* thoughts and passion… *"that coldly indifferent traitor-to-the-cause sitting smug and satisfied under his little tree. How would YOU like to be the one witch-hunted out of The Rafford?"*

He watched her reach near… slim, not tall, flowing brown hair, snug-jeans under white T-shirt under loose flannel shirt flowing in the breeze… *"the breeze at play with her, closest intimate of hers, loving her as no one could, ever."*

He was struck by her:

"So contradictory," thought whispered, *"her appearance and manner, appealing and repellent all at once."*

Such contrasts unnerved him, rendered judgment precarious, *"what should I think of her?"*

He mused at her mode of dress, *"comfortable, anonymous—like mine. No social or political statement or label to her clothes, or of her."* She was a violation of his creed.

"But there's something about her..." and he realized she roused him, then braced against her imminent onslaught.

She stormed up the hill with head bent, shoulders hunched, hands deep in pockets, staring at the ground at her feet, her long brown hair streaming rivulets around her... *"seeming not to notice me even now, about to stumble over me sitting here with book in hand."*

She didn't look up as she reached him but only took deep breath and began to lash him:

"What're you *sitting* here for? Get up and *march* with us! What's *wrong* with you? Can't you *think*, don't you *feel*?"

It was command to subordinate as she turned and pointed finger back at the column, mob, of marchers down the hill behind her. She jabbed finger into the near-distance, at the marchers down the hill, to add force to her words, to compel her force into him.

For a moment Rob stared at her, instantly recognizing her, and suddenly had to fight for breath and calm and reason for her, then struggled to voice for her. The battle finally won after an overlong instant, he replied as smoothly and quietly as floundering calm could allow, in softest voice he could mine, eyes riveted on hers:

"I'm not... part... of that, but... thanks anyway," breathed through quiet stammering.

He felt thoroughly the fool, how to be politic when all impulse was to lash right back—*"and rush up, take her...."*

He wondered at the savagery of passion, all silent until suddenly raging, and prayed hers to be too.

At the sound of his voice, more than at his tone or words, she glanced up—and eyes and manner transformed.

A moment more—to grapple with countless understandings and apprehensions and still more countless choices of eyes, lips, posture, words, tone—and then she... just... stopped.

She stared at him for a long moment, then averted eyes, not able to look at him, had to avert eyes and stare at the ground at her feet, and finally mumbling something quiet, something of vague apology, and turned back down the hill, eyes riveted on the ground at her feet.

"She'd hardly looked at me, hardly noticed me..." but just the same, he was sure she'd noticed him.

He watched her go, stared after her as she trudged away, couldn't tear eyes from her as she flowed away, searing her into memory and already savoring the memory of her, even here, like this, for that fleeting moment of her when their eyes met.

He couldn't relinquish the vision of her eyes and for a fleeting instant readied to run after her, to chase her down... *"to grab her and hold her and cling to her..."* then he breathed deeply, managed to shove impulse and thought and image of her from his mind:

"What could she possibly want with me anyway."

Chapter 15.

The back room of the back office, imbedded in the heights of the great Liberty Spire, was bathed in the dark, all comfort and shield for Rob as he stood silent witness to the scene outside the vast panoramic window, overlooking the roiling masses outside and below him... *"below, not beneath, me,"* he reminded himself, shamed he had to remind himself.

Rob pushed away the near-distant din imposed by front office chatter, refused the provocation of DeCeeve and his repugnant laughter, recognizable anywhere, loathsome always and everywhere, as images drifted him back:

They were more than stunning, they were beatific.

Theirs was not just a physical presence, awing of itself, but the embodiment of articulate intelligence, of energy and idealism and starkly pellucid rationality, radiating shards of dazzling brilliance—*"as the sun itself,"* Rob exulted—streaming from them, *of* them, shining glory down on all who witnessed, streaming from within them in founts of highest transcendence.

"Who would not be thoroughly swayed?"

He was witness to their unrivaled majesty... *"how can I not preen and gloat,"* absolving himself of his struggle to *not* preen and gloat, cringing to think and feel the absolute truth of it, without least hubris, and redoubling his struggle to sway himself into simple, disingenuous truth about himself:

"I am just like, and unlike, any of the murk gathered here, there is no place for pride," struggling to deny anything more exalted of himself than of anyone else here, *"all of us paled before the exalted transcendence of my beatific disciples."*

He fought to not stare, how could he not stare, at the unrivaled grace and charm and covert skill—*"their truest art,"*

Rob smiled secretly—of his youthful radiances, his acolytes, each drawing the raptured attention of every one of that murk, of that elite, extracting willing and ardent avowal to airy conversation imbued of subtle—and not—dogma and doctrine:

".... It was horrid, simply horrid!"

The alluring ingénue mesmerized the hoary grandees with a deepest décolletage and freest-flowing skirt barely and only just affording decency, seeming hardly more than little girl inserted among them, swaying with just the right lilt of voice and eye and lip and hip, of just the right measure of demure sway of bared shoulder and back and thigh, of just the right innocence in wide-eyed gaze reaching deep into the eyes and hearts and depths of rapt men of age and station and presence and power, drawing them in, candle to moth—*"spider to fly, no: snake to rat,"* Rob wrestling to prize himself free of the downward spiral of analogy and analogue describing *himself.*

Rob smiled secretly as his virtuous young disciple ignited fervid assent and impassioned support from the wizened plutocrats and kleptocrats clustered around her with more need and greed even than want, clinging to her every sound and glance and gesture and barest movement.

Another of Rob's cortege mesmerized that host, horde, in continuing narrative:

"Those poor little children had no means of escape, trapped and pinioned and helpless as they were in their tiny suites..." as she pressed herself into herself, dreamily groping herself as she groped for words, holding herself close, closer, before resuming... "as their hovels were wanting of heat and water and food and decency..." holding herself with eyes downcast in demure abandonment under tumescent forces pressing-in on her from all sides, overpowering her, leaving her near-supine and needful as she held herself and continued breathlessly... "and what could they *do*? How could that poor baby *survive*?"

The dowager-men maneuvered near, nearer, slavering to be nearer, pressing close, closer, urging themselves to her, teeming and swarming and pressing to penetrate her with their primal need, each envisaging her fully abandoned to them in her desperate *need*.

"And, you know..." another of the beatitude continued, impassioned and vulnerable and needful... "I actually feel a bit, just a bit, and maybe more than just a bit..." under artful sigh and blush and sway of hip and thigh in desperate need... "I actually feel..." she paused half a heartbeat... "*responsible* for that poor little baby, that tiny, desolate creature, so helpless and so *needing*."

Secret eyes and lips and tongues and hands and all else of them, of this murk, of this elite, of these men of power and station and weight, held subtle and not-subtle gropings through eyes and smiles, self-deluded as wanting only to soothe and reassure and comfort vulnerable youngest, ethereal beauty... behind which preyed all-ardent greed for her through fevered urgings for her.

Another vision of beauty continued for a nearby clutch of patriarchs, their forlorn need of her radiating with fully righteous pity and piety as each of that murk prayed *he* is whom she wants, needs, must have, to warm her and comfort her through her need, through her hardship and turgid need in face of all that assails innocence and youth, thoughts hardly veiled... *"how could I deny her, withhold from her my... comforts?"*

So, beatitude continued:

"I do *feel* for them so terribly..." she too in masterful feint of hands to self, drawing herself into herself in demure affectation of overwhelming helplessness and need... "and I do so *want* for them, for those poor, tiny souls caught and helpless and needing..." with all eyes penetrating her deeply, fully, again and still again, each and every one of those ascendant with all eyes penetrating her to their fullest... "in a world so fraught and bristling with cold and cruel and callous disregard of them and of their desperate need. How could so frail and fragile a creature of Heaven as that poor little baby possibly survive?"

Another vision of wonder and grace and beatitude cast wide-eyes piercing each and every harrumphing aristocrat of wealth and power and station, they surrounding her, engulfing her, she supine less to their compassion than to their passion, her mastery veiled behind artful word and tone and swaying hip and thigh, presenting herself as fully supine and helpless and open to the wizened men but only to *one* among them, artfully coy to each and every single one of them.

Rob struggled to keep from pealing into outright laughter, to keep sparkling eyes and consuming arrogance and grasping ego silenced at this vision of the future being forged here and now, invisible to all, even to his beatitude, here and now delivering *his* ordained future for them all, and revealing no trace outward sign of the depth of his revulsion... of himself, for all he was, for all he conjured here and now.

Next, Rob battled broadest gleam and widest grin as he surveilled his scintillating young men, disseminating *his* word and *his* truth through their mouths and past their lips. And again all the same and just the same, now the dowager-*women* mesmerized by alluring, enthralling young men as compelling to this murk of women as to their counterpart men.

"Imagine their need..." breathed one among the strikingly handsome, vital young men, he as all his cohort of the fabric of beatitude, piercing the dowagers with eye and lip and sway and more:

"Their landlord had repeatedly expressed ravenous interest in that innocent flower—she hardly more than a child!—and of course not just for himself but for all his 'associates'! Of course she and her good father absolutely rejected, adamantly spurned, the landlord's advances and entreaties and demand. But as their dinners shrank from meager to none, as their heat dwindled from cold to ice, as that poor, unfortunate father lay exhausted and spent after inhumanly long hours of arduous work for vanishingly small reward, she, in all her flowering innocence and need and sacrifice, in witness to the devastations visited on her father and on her forlorn brothers and sisters, stole into the night... and this courageous young flower, full in her budding womanhood, pure as driven snow, under all love and innocence and virtue for her dearest family, surrendered herself and all of herself and all of her *future* fully into the hands of that sinister, vulgar lord and gave of herself to his cohort and to *all* his cohort in cheapest, most tawdry, most reprehensible and shameful exchange. For father and brothers and sisters there is no room for shame aside greatest, most dire *need*."

The alluring young man drew himself into himself, cringed into himself with tear in eye as dowagers melted around him, engulfing and fully devouring him with eye and thought and heat and need, swelling themselves in rivalry for him, stroking him and holding him and assuring him of their most faithful, undying devotion and full, breathless support.

"And none among the murk, nor among my beatitude, in all their countless numbers none are aware or can even imagine the inexorable future into which they would be— are being! —vaulted, of which they would be— are! —the vanguard of my new world order."

Rob ambled amid the murk, amid that elite, in pretense of cordial mingling, while ever-closely attending to the near-silent whispers of conspiracy disseminated by his beatitude as they suffused and infused the murk. His supernal creatures waxed gratitude with angelic eyes upturned to Heaven, then downturned in diffidence of all-demure piety and sanctity, for the unfettered, ardent support sworn to them by that host:

"Of course, all *we* need do is provide some smallest modicum of funding for such innocents—for that sacrificing waif and for those like her, and for her long-suffering father and for those like him, and for her wastrel mother and for her helpless little brothers and sisters and for all those like them— to educate them and train them and then gainfully employ them in whatever manner suits us best, *we* their generous, giving, most-enlightened patrons."

And with all sincerity and piety:

"And of course we will pay them some small remittance as a living-allowance while we educate and train them—some smallest stipend to support them while we educate and train them. And as they work off their due, market forces should and must set their wage—of course under exemption to the minimum wage: How in good conscience can there be a minimum wage for such altruism? What socialist propaganda that, needing to mandate a minimum wage for such generosity? And of course, for their own sake, for their own health and self-esteem and well-being, we will, we must, accept from them repayment of the cost of their education and training and living-allowance—allowing them a most generous time in which to amortize their debt to us, of course levying their accrued interest costs."

And more, in downcast eyes and angelic voice:

"And we will employ them and empower them to extract *themselves* from the morass into which they'd buried themselves, into which they'd dug *themselves*. And what pride they'd know, lifting *themselves* up by their bootstraps. *So* we shall deliver them—with the blessing of Goodness Herself!"

The beatitude swam amid their pronouncements and the murk smiled practiced smiles bathed in long-practiced lusts and glories and greeds—as Rob drowned in the repugnance of his own creation.

'He,' enfolded and entombed in the absolute of the dark, is drawn into need and craving that prey within the vanishing aura. He observes the gaunt creature on highest perch within that faded aura as it stretches fingertips slowly, tentatively, toward the vermillion shadowland separating its realm from his.

'He' stretches fingertips in the dark, tremulously, tentatively, toward that vermillion borderland, that shadowland separating him from that gaunt creature on highest perch bathed in dimmest, faded aura.

'He' and gaunt creature stretch fingers, near touching, only shadowland separating his fingertips from those of the gaunt creature on highest perch within faded aura.

'He' is suddenly gripped, subsumed, by overwhelming panic as fingers, hand, arm are seized and torn into shadowland.

Gaunt creature shrieks and howls as fingers, hand, arm are suddenly gripped and torn into shadowland.

'He' issues silent scream, finds he cannot scream, cannot utter least sound above the silent wail of the faded aura within which he is now and abruptly engulfed, the cosseting aura now surrendering all pretense at consoling and

comforting and cosseting, now fallen to its own secret needs and urgings as it recoils from what lurks in the absolute of the dark waiting, resting patient, just beyond in the dark.

'He' arches back, and still further back, from that vermillion shadowland, that infinitely sheer borderland between faded aura and the absolute of the dark poised just beyond—and finds that HE is seated on highest perch within vanishing aura.

He screams silent scream to find himself in so familiar a setting, on highest perch in near-faded aura—and how can this be, having only just been safely harbored, observing from the sanctuary of silence and serenity fully enfolded in the dark?

He stares down, gapes at arm and hand and fingers as they stare back, glaring mutely, rendered to shattered bone and torn flesh, and he grieves from outside himself, pleading all silent prayer in need to know:

"Why?" and "Why Me?"

He wonders why need and craving warrant such requite, then regards himself again, sees he is whole, sees that nothing of him, not arm nor hand nor fingers, is rendered—yet—and shudders under what is and what remains to be.

Chapter 16.

Rob woke to earliest morning sun only just breaching the vermillion shadowland of the dark. He inhaled deeply of the morning, as deeply as morning allows, fully cherishing this anticipation, these impending moments of strolling to class through *this* morning's realm, through *this* distinct stillness and silence and peace, each unique of itself, for as long as it lasts.

He heard, in the near-distance of roaming mind, a quiet rustling behind him, a quiet voice calling, and dismissed both as random perturbation of thought and dream, and kept himself to himself though parched for some smallest more.

"Hey," in quietest, softest sound.

Her voice reached for him ever gently, tender caress to lightly slumbering emotion, felt more than heard somewhere beyond awareness, reaching into cosseting dream.

The sound of her, sweetest of all sound, drew him from one reverie to immerse him in another, infinitely more welcome.

He stopped in his tracks for her, suddenly aware it was for her, as he would at the slightest of her, and dreamt she'd do every bit as much for him... then felt gentle fingers stretch to him, lay gentle hold of him, softest of any touch, her touch shuddering through him and turning him to face her, he wandering and lost in the power of her smallest touch.

She paused for a long moment, lost in his eyes as he in hers, his eyes holding her all quiet until finally she broke the spell and spoke velvet tones barely above smallest whisper:

"About... yesterday," she paused, lost to proceed, exhorting remnant courage, and whispered: "I'm... I'm sorry."

He wandered in her eyes, she pleading his pardon in eyes trailing off to another 'I'm... sorry,' and she turning away, unable to withstand his eyes.

She held silent and still then, as if that word, cosseted in those eyes and in that voice—*'sorry'*—held all meaning, spoke all of her and still more needed to un-say and un-do of all she'd said and done the day before.

He watched her eyes, her lips, the shape of her, and felt the depth of her regret, limned there for him, just and only for him, and he wandered in dream that she could feel anything for him, let alone this for him, and thoughts strayed into the sudden bounty of the morning, only in reality could such abundance exist, beyond imagining.

His mind emptied of words and thought, and he could only beseech understanding of why here and why now, why like this with her, all other sense and wit stolen away.

Suddenly desperate for her not to mistake silence for coldness, he began stammering, something, anything, no idea of what—and she silenced him, quieted him, comforted him with healing words in softest voice full with understanding.

Her eyes to the ground at his feet:

"I know I sounded... ratty... yesterday. I'm... sorry," again lingering in the quiet of that word, 'sorry,' so little, so much.

She'd said it again, to be sure he understood her, that *she* was apologizing to *him*... knowing full well he should be apologizing to her—for his indifference, yesterday, to what she so clearly prized, why else march, why else storm up a hill to belabor a solitary specter who should be doing so vastly more than sitting there watching. She wasn't sure why she was even apologizing, only feeling the need of it somehow commanding her.

Suddenly shy, she couldn't look him in the eye and stared at the ground at his feet, adding forlornly:

"I didn't... mean... anything by it. I'm... sorry."

Again that softly lingering word, when had she ever uttered it before now, and she'd never been shy before now and why now and why here, with... this.

She'd said it so softly he didn't actually hear her words but saw them on her lips and in her eyes.

"It's... okay," in equally gentle sound.

He said the words ever slowly, drawing-out words and sound for as long as he could, to stretch time, struggling to stretch time for her.

They both stood like that, still and mute, staring at the ground at their feet, each not daring to look at the other and risk breaching the fineness of the moment, until finally she whispered:

"Well I… I guess I ought to… go," but she didn't move a breath from him.

Suddenly roused to understanding, Rob blurted:

"Hey," quiet, nervous, "feel like a bite of…" and quickly added, "coffee?" and felt the fool, well deserved.

Heart pounding, breath gasping, he struggled to look up, to look at her, to… and didn't know to what of her. Finally, he managed to look up, to watch her, to stare at her.

She looked up too, then, and saw him stare at her:

"I… I can't… I've got class now. I'm already late.…"

She left her answer hanging in the air, more to say, not said, and she quick-turned to walk away, head down, shoulders hunched, hands buried deep in pockets. Then, with a half-turn and renewed life and now all loud for him, to be sure he heard:

"But there's gonna be another march tonight… six o'clock… by the library. Maybe… maybe I'll see you there." He recognized the tone, wondered if he recognized her tone:

"Not question but… hope?" thought dared to whisper.

Then she turned and slogged away… *"to class,"* he murmured to himself, disappointed that he'd been willing, even anxious, to skip class for her—but she not for him.

He battled himself, had thought sure she'd have a warmest 'yes!' to him, and not turn him down flat like this.

"What does that say of me? What does that tell of me… of my sense and of my judgment and of my… worth?"

He felt crushed and abandoned, less even by her than by himself, by his own judgment:

"How can my judgment let me down so thoroughly?"

And reviling himself still more:

"How can I trust my judgment if I can't even trust my judgment of HER? And how can I trust anything of myself if I can't even trust my judgment?"

And in forlorn abandon:

"Who can I trust, in what can I trust, if I can't even trust myself?"

He found himself hurtled back into the image of her with Allman.

"Allman—of all people, Allman!—wrapping himself around her...."

Thoughts and images of them, of *her*, so thoroughly repulsed him he had to cut-off thought, cut-off feeling, feeling still more foolish and still more shrunken and still more humiliated by his stupidity, by his starry-eyed foolishness, more even than by her so-easy and so-ready dismissal of him.

He vilified himself... *"for dreaming dreams that live only in children's stories and neurotic glories, for dreaming not dream but nightmare."*

He'd thought himself past that, above that, and fought the cry in him that such understanding always inflicts, feeling himself lessened, feeling himself breaking, splintering, now fighting to keep at least partly whole, wondering which rendition of him would win, likely had already won.

He couldn't escape the conviction, not daring to verge it on knowing, that she'd felt more than just trite apology and a vague... something... for him, then wondered:

"How much of life is... and how much is just imagined, just pointless and senseless and hopeless?"

He warred against himself, against self-contempt and shame, understanding one thing, honesty winning out:

"I want to see her, be with her, and"—to his greatest surprise—*"even despite Allman wrapping her."*

He wondered at that, never before even least considering that of a girl, of any girl, even of such a girl, if with the likes Allman.

"Guilt by association," thought contemned, reviled.

"No—damned by association," silent whisper intoned.

Then he cursed himself for even thinking of damning her, and cursed himself again and more, for not.

Chapter 17.

The din of front-office chatter violated the quiet of the back room, despoiling the sanctities of memory and serenity. Then smarmy, loathsome laughter penetrated the residues of peace as DeCeeve threw open the door and further violated Rob.

DeCeeve laughed and droned as Rob watched the man's eyes and lips on fully ludicrous, repugnant display:

"He's not remotely aware, least cares, that my attention is on his eyes and lips and on the sound and noise of him, not on his words. What words could he have, of sense and meaning, so lost in his petty conceits and self-delusions, so lost in his own small mind and self."

Then Rob choked back repugnance—of himself:

"This is the man I will render as the next President."

Rob strained to hear words amid DeCeeve's noise:

"I don't have to tell you, Rob, where I've got President Kurb—a dream come true, a damn lucky dream come true!" smiling repulsive gloat, leer hanging in eye and lip and every shard of him.

Rob smiled sickly to himself:

"Luck? DeCeeve thinks 'luck' is pushing that bill through committee and both Houses? And THIS is whom I'll get elected to succeed President Kurb?"

Self-revulsion near overwhelmed, but for thought of the greater good salving him, behind which lurked silent whisper:

"How great must the 'greater good' be to heal this?"

Then Rob's attention flickered, and he was thrown back to The Rafford.

The evening breeze was wonderfully cool and extravagantly soothing, the perfect setting for dreams drifting by, beckoning and commanding Rob to render them carnal.

For an instant dream gripped him—of a brown-eyed girl walking alongside him, their shoulders gently brushing, her hand in his, holding his, holding him.

Rob closed eyes and wallowed in wistful supplication… as that grand house approached, he to it or it to him, who can know as nightmare tore him from divine reverie and hurtled him into this succubus of *his* rendering, as his beauteous ingénues flowed and flowered amid the murk of the elite—disseminating the seed of his dream.

Rob swept grandly into the pretentious splendor that was the grand home of one among his host, and meandered amid the murk of the elite gathered there for him and for his acolytes, he near-invisible beside his sublime disciples, they allowing him to invisibly observe and listen-in on his beatific splendors.

From one alluring, dazzling young woman:

"And what could the poor man *do*? He was already working three jobs and still struggling to put food on the table and heat in that tiny bedsit of an apartment that was all he could manage, what with his wife gone, dead, without health insurance her medical costs were definitively out of reach, she killed by illness and by too much work and too much need and too much of everything but peace and security and medicine. And what of his little girl and her tiny baby? What *could* he do but surrender to his landlord and to those pimps and pushers"—and to the collective gasp of her audience she blushed evocatively pink in virtuoso performance, Rob's imprimatur—"to what *could* he resort but to kneel and genuflect to those butchers? Of course he started muling drugs and whoring his precious little girl—for the *sake* of his precious little girl and for her tiny, precious baby! What else could he *do*?"

Rob watched hoary, bejeweled gentlemen snug up to this beatific radiance, repugnantly pressing themselves against his enthralling, childlike ingénue as she mimed supernal compassion before her rapt audience of grey-templed bastions of power and position and posing, now softly moaning and panting and wheezing to her every word and movement and blush as she breathed and swayed and touched herself in parody of straining need and demure, vulnerable compassion.

Wandering a small distance, he listened-in with barely concealed pride to the quiet conversation, conversion, of others of the ascendant elite already fallen to the invocations of still others of his alluring young acolytes, presenting themselves as seductively wide-eyed children supplicating and proselytizing their elders and betters.

From one wide-eyed young man, hardly more than breathless little boy:

"And what could he *do*? Why, he could borrow the principle with which to educate himself and with which to find employment, real and meaningful employment—meaningful to *us*, of course, to whom else?—and borrow the cost of housing and clothing and feeding that innocent little jewel, his little girl, and her tiny baby. And as he works of course he would fully recompense *us* and be thrilled to fully recompense *us* as the least he could do to honor his debt to us, his benefactors."

The ingénu continued under slightest smile, to arouse complicit assent to this newly-disclosed stratagem:

"And this widower/father/grand-father/mule would most happily repay us fully—with interest, of course—for all our costs of time and material and money with which we will furnish him. And of course he would be honored and most grateful to be so empowered, to be able to amortize the price of this fabulous opportunity that *we* afford him, and fully amortize his debt to *us* over however much time he may require—at interest rates *we* determine, of course. And he would be overjoyed to have *us* garnish his wages to satisfy this privileged obligation. And of course there would be *no* minimum wage—what ludicrous nonsense, mandating what only *we*, the free-market, could rightfully determine. Who else could be burdened or bothered with that encumbrance? And he would be overjoyed to welcome *us* into his home and into his family, *we* having provided him such opportunity—of course under contractual strictures *we* exact, to optimize *our* profitability for this offal of fabulous opportunity. Who but *we* could provide him and such as him with this fabulous, most generous, most altruistic opportunity?"

"Think of the incalculable rewards *we* would glean from the countless vast whom we would sanctify with our magnanimity!"—and, as afterthought, as still further enticement and inducement, the beauteous young speaker added: "Think of *our* reward and think of *our* esteem in providing him and such as him with such magnanimous, sumptuous opportunity, afforded only by *our* vastly generous succor, chastely benefiting him and his little girl and her tiny baby. And remember *our* reward, even beyond our gratification and fulfillment, multiplied by their countless numbers, all fully and righteously owed to *us*! And never forget his little girl and, in the years to come, *her* little girl and think of all *they* would owe us and would gratefully repay us in whatever coin best suits them—and *us*!"

Rob roamed the murk, model guest of honor, smiling cordially here, chatting airily there, admiring this of that and that of this, all while steeling eyes against revelation of his contempt of their haughty airs and superior stares—*"suffused of the fetid breath and stinking sweat of their foul and imminently rotting corpses, still animate even in the throes of their demise,"* and smiling fawningly as he lubricated them to their future—and fully reviling himself.

'He' finds himself seated on highest perch amid vanishingly pale aura bounded by vermillion borderland, as the dark patiently waits just beyond reach. Now 'he' strains to something new looming at him, the far-off din of voices rising to claim him amid a savaged, destitute quiet, issuing claim to his very existence within the fevered imaginings of realities and illusions and self-delusions—and those of the multitudes wailing and raging for him and at him in massed chorus.

Voices rise higher, higher, endowed with the feel more than the sound not of simple bleating and pleading but of outrage and demand, of scream and wail beyond command, of their most urgent need beyond even his portent.

He struggles to apprehend, cannot fathom that greatest need eluding him, crying out for him, just and only for him.

Voices rage in their impenetrable need, he not simply witnessing and hearing but feeling their need within the fabric of sound shuddering under the ineluctable command, now as always grappling to fathom: "Why?" and "Why me?"

Chapter 18.

Six pm and the sun was still blazing, suspended immobile, indecently high above the horizon, oblivious of dazzled eye and sweated brow.

"And what to do? Nothing. Suffer it—accept it and regale it, the vast and manifold bad and good of it."

He wondered if all things possess this dichotomy, all he need do is choose to believe it and so transform all things into the unity of good needful of the bad, intertwined lovers as only the fiction of true love allows, each incomplete without the other.

Rob trudged along to the Rafford Commons stepping absently onto one, then another, of the myriad paths hardly aware of where his feet bore him, letting them decide, willingly or not—*"one way or the other, one as good as any other"*— and his feet decided, unsure if he could sway them even had he tried, thoughts brooding him of a brown-eyed girl he might, or might never, sway—*"as if I could sway anyone of anything."*

He was startled to alertness by a small crowd gathered on the Commons, now finding himself immersed in them, gripped among them, realizing he'd more than half expected this—*"time and place being what they are."*

He wondered why he, or his feet, had willed himself here, the last place he'd ever willfully bring himself, then realized, of course—*"but for my brown-eyed girl."*

He turned the word over in his mind—*"my"*— wondering what it could possibly mean.

"Nothing of this world has ever been, or will ever be, 'mine.'"

At a small distance from himself he argued with himself:

"Time and place can only be what they are… resolutely true to their nature, indifferent to, and callous of, my wants and needs."

"Isn't everyone and everything always true to itself?"

He wondered it abstractly of Allman, on rare occasion spying in him a glimmer of compassion in odd, unguarded moments, and wondered if it need always be true—*"he, at moments, seeming so other than his nature. Or is THAT his nature, seeming one way while being, at heart, very much else?"*

He wondered if that dichotomy ruled Allman, oppressed and suffered him. He doubted any such thing of him, but the doubt was now just as resolutely planted… *"that maybe yes, all that he showed of himself was just that, show."*

Those of the crowd, not yet mob, were clearly of Panther King's following, milling about and barking slogans, followed by shouts of 'amen' and 'right on' at the end of all their slogans.

"Six o'clock," he studied his watch, wondered if his watch was complicit in rendering her the lie, *"she said she'd be here"*… and he only now came alive to how he ached to see her.

A small pack of speakers stood on the platform overlooking the brewing crowd, one among them now stepping to the microphone, tall and lanky and with full-sphere of close-cropped hair accented by dark aviator sunglasses somehow endowing him with a vaguely sinister, menacing look. Another man stood nearby, this with neat crew cut and goatee framing Benjamin Franklin glasses… *"the scholarly image, counterpoint to the image taken by the speaker's appearance of raw, guttural power."*

They sported long robes, and shirts etched with a deep V, revealing well-muscled, hairy chests, both topped with a fez.

Rob smiled at the pretense:

"The subterfuge of image, of a challenging impudence, of disputing them at one's peril, to underscore their point and demonstrate how threatening their difference—any difference—can be to the norms of the Rafford and, personally, to those of Dean Ivry. They intend to expose the rest of us,

those not firmly committed to them and to the Cause that was Panther King, any 'other' being but tools of the entrenched elite. They edge on verge of threat, posing as the new and the different and the righteous, to cower the administration, contending that Panther King's scarce poor grades are pretense levered against him, retribution for his defiance."

He considered that: *"But who can rightfully deny or affirm the validity of that pretense, of King's poor grades, aside from the administration itself?"*

Rob didn't doubt the stench of politics, and more—something vague and sinister, veiled and prowling—behind the administration's vow to expel Panther King... *"in the name of academic integrity, for 'the greater good.'"*

"The very notion of 'the greater good' is rank with the stench of politics—and hypocrisy: on the one hand inviting me here to The Rafford, I so un-like them in my way, while intent on expelling Panther King, he so un-like them in his."

Rob didn't doubt that neither he nor Panther King were much like the rest of The Rafford—*"the Rafford Ascendant."*

Rob caught himself spouting cliché, realized he was already stained with Panther-King-thought, spouting the same ideas down to the very words they and the likes of them even now are deploying on the podium above him. He wondered if not just his words but his *thoughts* had been hijacked, if his very *feelings* were being transmuted, by the Panther King rhetoric—and judged that, still, his thoughts were his own, then wondered if even *that* thought had been implanted from outside him.

Rob shrugged away thought as he scanned the audience, but thought intruded of its own:

"Rich and privileged, every one, assenting in the name of fashion and fun, for appearance and display, not one daring to be out of step with the 'de rigueur' vogue—neither optional nor voluntary but exactingly obligatory, demanded by and for their pretense to the social status of spiritual loftiness and enlightenment."

Rob scanned the audience again:

"Sons and daughters, every one, of the entrenched business and political noterati, glitterati—the children of the

elite. And here they are, on full display, preening to condemn the system and the policies that had catapulted their elders—and them—to the heights of power and control, that feed and clothe and nourish and cosset and elevate them, that swaddle them so impregnably within the heights of their own subterfuge, of their self-proclaimed, fully-deserved, self-righteous ascendance."

Thought took him, swept him up:

"So far removed is this elite from any least knowing or conceiving—how thoroughly spared they are from the base struggles of everyday life, here and now simply hungering for the adventure afforded them of 'life.' What do they know or care of 'life', entranced as they are by the promise—the romance—of everyday life, knowing and caring nothing of its real stench, of the real hunger and the real threat of the gutter. This, here and now, they conceive as some idyllic romance the substance of which they know nothing about and of which they actively grope to know nothing about, as they stand here and now with their wide-eyes tight-shut while affirming the ideals spouted here."

"This elite determines to loftily expound on the issues heated here—as 'the help' serve them tea and biscuits behind hidden, secret revulsion of them. And this elite openly sneak their weeds and their powders, penetrating themselves and each other with their needles and themselves, glorifying themselves behind blissful ignorance and transcendent denial, wallowing in their decadence, entranced by the romance and adventure of 'the struggle,' knowing nothing of the stench and threat and reality of that struggle. This elite is hardly more than a putrefying carcass, shockingly-close kin to their lesser, much as they deny it to themselves—THAT reality lying in wait for them just over the horizon, as the elite crow over how many jobs their trickle-down largess hands down to the people… how many chauffeurs and maids and pool-boys and boat-builders and personal-servicers they feed and clothe by virtue of their generosity in employing—exploiting—the lesser."

Rob jarred alert as the speaker finished triumphantly, looking over the crowd now bursting to applause and cheers and hoots and whistles of fervent approval and unbending support.

Rob absently wondered about the truth of it, of any of it: *"Did Panther King fail the school—or did the school fail Panther King?"*

He was sure, not knowing or caring how he could be so sure:

"There's more to this than grades. Long-entrenched values are being questioned, doubted, challenged— threatened... with the stench of blood in the air."

Rob lost himself in silent murmuring about appearance and reality, about values and virtues, about what's fair and who judges fairness and who *should* judge—and wandered from the crowd, head bent in thought, hands deep in pockets, meandering and lost in thought as feet commanded steps.

Suddenly—stillness.

Rob stopped in his tracks, suddenly straining on the absolutes of stillness and silence, and looked up. The strain of the overarching change swept through him—of the sudden, crushing stillness and silence. Even through his fugue, how could he not have noticed.

Rob halted in mid-stride, listed to that stillness, to the feel of that silence—the tension, the coldness, beyond anything commanded by wind or weather, of something rising, of hate and rage and outrage rousing, waking, of which to be exactingly careful... and deeply afraid.

He'd never experienced anything even remotely like this, but the feel of it was inescapable, engulfing, devouring, rooting him and set to bury him.

Through some primal instinct he *knew* to stand perfectly still, to show no least trace of fear or regret, a stalked animal, skulking prey—knowing instinctively to stand his ground so not to be rousted into exposing himself to predation prowling him, circling him, closing on him.

Slowly he pivoted, turned, faced predation full-on.

Rob stared at a crowd of seething faces, all eyes on him.

He knew, again from some inscrutable, primal fount, to face this enemy eye-to-eye, to not flinch or back away an inch, to swell large before them, to take his stand undaunted, uncowed—*"or the bloodletting begins right here, right now—with me."*

Then he turned away, ever slow, and heard directed straight at his back, out of bullhorn from the podium:

"You *dare* turn your back? You dare turn your back on *us*, on our good and just *cause*?"

Pointing middle finger at Rob, the speaker intoned with fulminating, righteous rage:

"*Complacency* is the threat! *You* are the threat—the greatest, most fulminant threat! *You*! Yes, *you!*" jabbing middle finger at Rob, standing his ground a near-distance away.

"*You* turn *your* back on justice! *You* turn *your* back... and walk out on justice—but Panther King *cannot* and *we* cannot! *You* turn *your* back but *we... will... not!*"

The crowd susurrated up to a feral growl that pitched into a crescendo of howling that Rob could *feel* cascading up from the ground and through his spine.

Sporadic curses broke through, rising into unsheathing hate and unbridling rage. The man on the podium thrust his middle finger at Rob bellowing:

"You can't *just* walk away! You can't *just* turn your back!"

Then, as Rob knew it would be, it was:

"If you're not *with* us you're *against* us!"

"That worn-out threat and lament," as he'd known it would be.

"There is *no* middle ground! Every silence in the face of elitism *is* elitism! Every back turned on exploitation *is* exploitation! Every mind closed to oppression *is* oppression! You *can't* just turn your back! You *can't* just walk away!"

The orator finished with his hand raised up and then with knife-edge violently chopped down—as across Rob's neck.

The crowd began to move. Flowing slowly at first, a massive slug taking first painstaking slither toward him, the mob slowly gathered speed, exuding nearer. Words lent heat and fire to the amassed thing and its pace gradually quickened, flowed more freely at him, transmogrifying fully into a mob with all of which a mob is endowed of mindless hate and mounting rage and, finally, untethered outrage—as Rob stood his ground and faced them down, rooted to the spot by a wholly encompassing fascination of a suddenly discovered, altogether novel malevolence abruptly materialized in-his-face.

"*I've got to stand up to this mob and face it down, stare it down eye-to-eye, quash its whetted craving which only a still-greater will could cow and subdue,*" silent whisper presaged.

Even as he thought it he knew it was hopeless, worse than useless. The impulse to run welled in him, threatened to overwhelm him—but he held his ground aware *that* is his only chance.

"*Stand my ground and face them down—and suffer them face-to-face, eye-to-eye,*" with scant hope, he knew, as the crowd surged at him.

Then, of sudden and inexplicable impulse, he coiled into himself and hurled himself into that mob—and was devoured by the gaping maw of that heart of darkness.

In embers of fading awareness he recalled thinking how... *irritating...* this all was, "*to end like this, with the likes of them, here and now, like this.*"

From a vast distance the soundless *pop* of dim flashes lit the dark—and wonder what it could be slowly roused him.

"*What could it mean, this far-distant flashing? Like no lightning ever existed, here and now keeping its distance from me, keeping ever distant.*"

He wondered it through fugue, wondering if he should wish it nearer or dread it reaching nearer, wondering how he should know and for which he should pray.

Then sound... "*no, words,*" he dimly realized.

Laconic sounds—"*no, words,*" he reminded himself—immeasurably lethargic, sluggish and over-lazy, too calm and too quiet, without least urgency, ambled at him in the dark.

Rob opened eyes slowly, painfully, as sound transformed to word:

"There, now. Easy, now. That's enough, now. Ease up, now. Enough of that, now."

So laconic the sounds, wonder if of dream or nightmare.

Rob wondered why everything was 'now' and why the sound of it was so soft and quiet, as if the speaker wasn't sure *that* is what he meant or wanted, 'now' rather than 'soon,' or 'later,' if ever.

Eyes wide, at first only to the absolute dark, all light drained not just from sight but from mind too, and then gradually, ever slowly, dim light etched into eye and mind as sporadic flashes of light blinded here and there, now and again.

The languid voice sounded again, droning, ever-slow, so casual, without least urgency or demand… 'enough, now' and 'break it up, now'—not *expecting* any least attention be paid to softest voice and most sluggish demand.

Amid the isolated, slothful words sporadic flashes of light insisted, persisted, in-between, maybe because-of, those words—and he caught sight of distant eye and vermillion lip mouthing laconic, undemanding words through slyest smile.

Slowly, ever gradually, Allman made his way to the ground where Rob lay sprawled. And slowly, ever gradually, trailing too-close behind, wielding camera with flash—dim features of his brown-eyed girl.

And still and again he reviled himself thinking her 'his.'

All Rob could clearly understand were thoughts disembodied from mind:

"How had they managed to maneuver me here, to this?"

Silent whisper defiled him, thinking her 'his,' as conclusion tore through him. Then, very gradually, the predation of all-encompassing rage… eased.

Slowly, very gradually, hate and rage and blinding outrage smoldered to dull embers, and—revile it and resent it—he understood the enormity he owed Allman, both the good and the bad of it… *"or the goodness and the evil of it."*

Very gradually, ever slowly, other voices rose to awareness echoing Allman's very tone, and Rob dully marveled that those voices aped even the tone of Allman's voice.

"But if not for Allman," thought played at him, *"I'd not have needed this rescue."*

But the *just* in him argued back in silent whisper:

"Until you know without shadow of doubt he is, in fact, your savior."

And Rob swore at the silent whispers in him, listed on damning those whispers but unable to mobilize the will—until sure without shadow of doubt.

Chapter 19.

Ben Rob stood by the vast window-wall of the back office, at the pinnacle of the Liberty Spire, silent in the dark, mesmerized by the scene of chattel, charnel come alive, languorously churning and milling on the streets and alleyways below… waiting.

"For what?"

Rob knew without doubt they could not articulate just what they waited *for* but knew, equally without doubt, that each and every one of them was aware of waiting on some imminent transformation—only of what and to what remained cloaked to them.

"And to me," he lamented, under roiling visions portending just exactly what they waited on.

Then silence erupted into raucous laughter as DeCeeve burst-in to desecrate the silence and the dark, throwing Rob into memory, or illusion, as the two battled for ownership of him….

Rob stepped unhurriedly into the great foyer of the grand home and luxuriantly eased himself into the heart of the gathering, mesmerized now by those beauteous creatures *he* had installed here, for this, for their meaning and purpose. He struggled against his eyes, suppressed lustrous pride of them.

"It's an awful story, magnificently *awful*—but true in every detail!"

The striking young man held the gaze of each and every matron crowding him, the audacious among them pressing into him, stroking and caressing him, some secretly molesting him, and he—smooth and articulate and soaring far above their base posturings and fondlings, having been exactingly practiced and desensitized and inured to all of it.

Rob exulted over the fruition of the countless months of assiduous rehearsals of just such scenes, played out precisely as this, thoughts filling him of replicating such scenes across the country and into every campus and salon and living room of everyone who's anyone, thoroughly ingraining and disseminating *his* convictions first into the hearts and minds—*"and souls,"* silence whispered in the dark—of his beauteous troupe and from them into what residue of hearts and minds—*"and souls,"* silent whisper compelled—yet inhabited his host.

"And how must I and such as I, and *you*," ingénu gazing crestfallen into the eyes of each and every matron hanging on his every word and movement, "respond to such?"

The mesmerizing acolyte paused, gazed soulfully into the eyes of each and every harridan, moistened his lips with a breathy moan just *so*, and continued:

"As a thinking and *feeling*"—hands clasped to heart, slipping down to loins, cringing every slightly toward the nearest of the matrons with stricken, heartfelt gaze focused first on flaunted cleavage, then on thirsting lips, finally to craving eyes—"member of our social order I cannot help but accept some measure of personal responsibility... of *guilt*... for such heinous transgressions of basic, human dignity as that poor little flower of a child—giving of herself to her father's bosses and landlords and all his other oppressors, giving in to them just *so*, to keep a tattered roof over their heads and bare morsels in their mouths and threadbare scraps on their backs."

He paused a moment, cast a breathless look to each, lingered on breast and lip and eye, then continued:

"Two and three jobs were not nearly enough to provide the least that decency should provide a family... and need transforms to demand, always and everywhere, for momentary sanctuary and fleeting respite in a few grains of powder and a smallest dip of needle stolen out of his forced trafficking—what else is he to *do*? Knowing he'd already compromised himself and sacrificed himself to see his family through so they might scavenge meager scraps of food and warmth and life in some least semblance of decency and dignity. What is *he* to *that*? And no one need know and all he need do is deny it—to himself—and so he buys and sells and does whatever to and for whomever, so to sustain him and his family, so to impart some meager succor for his children, however he can, as best he can—and that so little, too little. And so what else could the poor flower of his little girl do, be still and silent when *she* could make all the difference and even be his deliverer?"

A long moment's soulful pause, then:

"And as a vibrant, feeling member of our class how can I not feel the shadow of... responsibility and... *guilt* over such shattered lives and dreams?"

His indrawn gasp of lament was mirrored by each and every doyenne and, from the most ascendant of the matriarchs, a bit more austere than the rest, a bit more haughty:

"Oh no, of course not, my dear boy! Oh my dear, dear young boy you *cannot* in *any* sense, not even in the *remotest* way at all, hold yourself responsible for *all* the misfortunes of *all* the less... uhhhm... *fortunate*... members of the public, of the common people of this, our great society! How *can* you?"

Gazing soulfully into her eyes, enveloping her hands in his, bringing them gently to his heart, tenderly kneading and caressing them:

"We must all, as a society, share in the horrific tragedy of such stories and take our measure of culpability in this sad and tragic state of... *affairs*."

With that word he drew-in a breath and watched as she closed eyes and visibly pinked, sighing and breathing heavily.

Then he coo'd softly, lips a breath from hers:

"Still... there must be something, some least *thing* we could do, might be able to do, *should* do, to uhhhm... to *relieve* their, uhhhm their... *embarrassment* and her, uhhhm... *shame*—if only to salve *our* responsibility and our, uhhhm... *obligation*." He remained all-watchful of breast and lip and eye, imprisoning her in rapturous anticipation, as his well-practiced pauses and gropings for words penetrated her.

The matrons 'tut-tutted' denial to this resplendent young man and his overtures to their responsibility and need to relieve and soothe such torment and suffering among the lessers of their great society and, precisely on-cue, a rival matron rose breathily:

"Oh yes, my *dear* young boy, yes!"

That one held him now to *her* bosom, clasped his hands in *hers* now, intoning with deep solemnity:

"Of *course* we will involve ourselves and intervene in such horrid circumstance. After all: *Noblesse oblige*—it is our responsibility, our *duty,* to uplift and succor the lessers among us. After all, it is *de rigueur*—necessary and expected and even *required* of us—is it not? Of *course* it is! And you *know* you can count on *us*—on *me*," pressing his hands more fully to her bosom, "to be your most enthusiastic, *fullest* supporter in *every* way!" smiling knowingly, rapacity starkly unveiled in darkest eyes.

The young man gazed into old-woman eyes with steadfast strength and youthful vigor and Rob laughed, all silent, to witness hoary matrons blush and sigh heavily and peer salaciously up through downcast eyes, struggling to stammer:

"My *dearest* young boy, your concern for such poor and helpless creatures touches me *deeply*," as she clasped his hands fully in hers and pressed them deeply between pendulous breasts: "I feel in my heart just as *you* do! I *assure* you, such poor and helpless creatures *will* be comforted—my foundation *has* always and *will* always give *most* generously to *all* the very *best* charities and social causes. What more can one do? Don't torment yourself—allow *me* to uhhhm... *comfort* you... in your compassion, in your, in... *our*... terribly dire straits," as she pressed herself more fully into him in crass and lurid facsimile of immersing him within her warmth and comfort.

And from all his beauteous disciples the same and more.

Rob envisioned such scenes played across every venue in every context at every pretext, and smiled.

'He' lists nearer the vermillion borderland hearing outcries of greatest need rising out to him, reaching out for him, for him and only for HIM, and lurches back and tears back onto his highest perch in the fading, vanishing aura.

'He' cannot but return, impelled to list into that vermillion shadowland from where the multitudes cry out their

need to him, for him and only for HIM, and from his highest perch, bathed in vanishingly faded aura, he reaches out and finally breaches this, his vermillion shadowland—and cries-out as arm and hand and fingers are torn and shorn, his ragged flesh flailing, screaming.

From outside himself he hears himself cry out:

"Why?" and "Why me?" through endless echo in faded aura the sound of vast multitudes reaches for him, ever dim and distant as they cry out for him from within their shadowland, and now he suddenly comes aware to its true nature:

"Not cries—screams!"

Chapter 20.

Rob peered through the dark and glimpsed a shadow reaching at his throat, gripping, crushing—*"Allman's hand!"*—and woke sweated and breathless to realize that, for all his time lost in the dark, he'd thought himself alone. And now:

"What other shadows, who else's shadow, roams the dark unseen?"

Rob woke more fully—to flashes of light in eerie depiction of surreal movement amid echoes in the dark, the light illuminating nothing, witnessed only as bursts of silent brilliance popping in the dark, and of sounds revealing nothing, overheard as guttural noise in the dark, churning, molesting. Both soundless flashes and empty noises approached, slowly nearer, nearer....

Gradually, in slow-moving kaleidoscopic sight and sound, the first merged to faces gaping down at him as the second transformed to voices and then to one singular voice above the others, above the so many clamoring others, and in languid dream discordant sound melted into words:

"Okay, now." And: "enough, now." And: "break it up, now," in laconic apathy.

The voice was strangely languid, overtly soft and quiet and sluggish, of drawl but nonetheless commanding—not simply expecting but commanding obeisance even through slothful voice and tone and measure, just so, measure for measure, receiving exactingly commensurate obedience and nothing more—or less. And just so, those of the mob relinquished Rob in slow and languid indifference—in deference to command, rigorously measured to command. Rob was awed, overwhelmed and daunted, at the profound depth and fidelity of such servitude.

"And," Rob was sure, *"they are so commanded to allow this degradation to continue, for me to bear it longer, for them to ease only marginally and that only for now, so to let this abuse and humiliation linger—and, as promise for their pleasure, of more and still more for untold times more and for no reason than simply for more. And how could they— anyone—find joy and pleasure in such, and no doubt this, to Allman, is small spectacle… to flaunt not just command over them but obeisance of them, to place on sumptuous and vulgar display absolute command down to the very tone of voice and twist of lip of master to exactingly-trained worms, rats, dogs, monkeys that people this herd."*

Rob stirred, barely half-conscious, wondering if his were coherent deliberations or ramblings of nightmare transgressing threshold of awareness, and then gradually woke a bit more fully to place and time and circumstance amid gently quiet murmurings of command couched within sporadic flashes of silent light exploding on him.

Rob woke still more fully to Allman and to his voice and realized he was hearing command issued laconically to end this assault—and there: the brown-eyed girl stood over him with camera in hand and flash in his face.

"How had he—they—maneuvered me here, to this?"

He paused in mid-thought and through silently wailed lament witnessed his brown-eyed girl standing over him with camera in hand and only now fully woke to her regard of him—*"contempt of me"*—proclaimed through flashes of light… *"and only that for me."*

Gradually, through slowly resurgent awareness and reason, rage eased and, grudgingly, so too of hate and resentment. He understood the enormity he owed Allman, both the good and the bad of it or, more exactly, the good and the evil of it.

He understood that Allman had rescued him, and cursed the debt but understood:

"But for Allman I'd have no debt."

Then another voice in him urged:

"Until you know for sure, he is in fact, now, your savior." And Rob cursed that voice—and thanked it.

"How can I not practice what I preach—should preach?" and he cursed the repugnant burden and price of *so* preaching.

"And why only I struggling to rise above… and no one else," with no question to it, even understanding that he is *not* alone in such as this, could not possibly be alone under such trial and hardship, impossible as it is, just now, to imagine.

Rob staggered and stumbled up to his feet, wavered— and found himself standing face-to-face with his brown-eyed girl, again cursing himself for thinking her 'his.'

He staggered, and eased himself back to the ground… *"so she can't watch me fall flat on my face,"* and just as he knew it would be, so it was: she setting camera to eye and finger to shutter release, ready to snap another shot.

Suddenly—she stopped.

Rob watched her drop her arm, camera in hand, saw her transfigured by sudden shock of understanding, of recognition, first of Rob, then of the circumstance in which she found him—and herself—and he saw in her eyes that she was stunned to what they'd been maneuvered and, he understood: *"to what SHE'D been maneuvered."*

In that instant of recognition—she witness to it all, here and now in her face—Rob understood, saw it in her eyes and on her lips and through her every movement… and felt all that he'd felt for his brown-eyed girl resurge, rouse fully alive… then flounder, submerge, drown.

She stared at Rob for a long instant, found no words, suddenly couldn't look him in the eye, could only stare at the ground at her feet.

Behind her, Allman stood grinning widely, reveling in the scene, and:

"What has Allman to do with her—and what does that make of her?"

He remembered starting out, scant time ago, checking his watch and wondering… *'It's six o'clock'*… wondering if his watch was complicit in rendering her the lie that, *'she'd be here at six.'*

He'd realized only then how much he wanted her to be here, and how much he'd wanted to be here *with her.*

142

"And so, here I am—with her."

Rob could only stare as Allman reached across and curled a slithering arm around his brown-eyed girl and pull her tightly to him. Rob watched her eyes, vast brown eyes that held so much… *"and holds nothing, not the least, for me."*

Rob saw her staring, watching him recoil in witness to Allman's arm wrap her, embrace her—and watched him tear eyes from her, stagger to his feet, sway half-a-moment, and stumble away without a glance back. Again.

As she watched Rob slog away she was consumed by the explosion of revulsion at this repulsive, bilious slug coiling her, and now flung repulsive tentacle from around her, would have torn it from its shoulder and thrown it to the ground and ground it to the dirt from which it had risen, had she the power.

Rob saw none of that, saw none of the brown-eyed girl's savage ferocity as she shoved Allman's arm and Allman himself violently from her, heard none of her shrieks of contempt and revulsion of him, saw none of her desiccating abhorrence of him in answer to the satisfied leer flaunted in her face, would have clawed-out his eyes had that been her way.

Rob slogged numbly away, desperate to hide his pain from his brown-eyed girl even more than from himself, and only defiling profanity for himself for how he could still, even now, think her 'his' brown-eyed girl, staggering under the power such creatures as she have over such creatures as he.

"And now," understanding the essence of it, *"I'm branded 'elitist' and 'oppressor'—'arch-enemy'—for having ambled away and seeming to side with Dean Ivry over Panther King, for seeming to favor Panther King's expulsion despite all reality. Who cares about reality when appearance dictates."*

And still worse:

"What now of my brown-eyed—whore," reaching definitive conclusion of her, and mourning her deeply, mourning for her even more than for himself.

He trudged along the path his feet chose, hearing, thinking he heard, swore he heard, jeers and cat-calls and all manner of derision and revulsion and defilement and threat hurled at him from not-far corners of mind and voice—

"inhuman voices," he contemned, *"howling animals,"* and lamented slandering animals so foully.

As he stumbled along he suddenly came aware to new silence in the dark… *"listening for me, hearing me thoroughly mystified by how I so profoundly misjudged her, so wrongly allowed my thoughts and feelings to so fully cloud and distort my vision and perception, to so absolutely confuse and delude and betray myself. I'd understood Allman in a heartbeat—why not her?"* Of course he understood why not her.

Then memory stirred and he suddenly remembered her name, how Allman had called her: *"Lainy,"* and he lamented and mourned the sound *'Lainy.'*

Thought churned of its own, fully contemptuous of him:

"Or am I even now misjudging her—judging from bruised ego and glimpse of Allman's oily triumph?"

Thought battled thought in swirls of chaos, in turmoil of rousing doubt about judgment and perception and powers of reason, of distinguishing truth from lie and reality from appearance, of struggling to understand misapprehension and deception from *self*-deception.

"I've always trusted my judgment deciphering character and intention, assessing—judging—people through and past what they say and do to what they ARE. I used to be so sure—and now I'm sure of nothing. Some may let others judge for them but I can't, won't—and now? If I cannot trust myself, who and what can I trust? To what and to whom can I turn? On what can I depend?"

"On nothing and on no one," silence taunted, tested.

Fear, then panic, blossomed, stalked Rob, and he found himself adrift in a timeless, boundless existence where nothing had meaning, where truth and deception mingled inseparable, indistinguishable, rendered meaningless abstractions swabbed on some canvass interred within nightmare.

He began to doubt his perceptions, to wonder what was real and what imagined, what illusion and what delusion and what *self*-delusion as panic welled in him and submerged him, drowned him.

Then the sweetest sound—the voice of a young girl laughing, joyful, beyond any sound in reality—sang out to him in the dark, sweet and gentle and warm and loving and faithful and trusting—and the sweet, gentle sound of her dissipated all panic and all trace of fear and doubt. The sound of her reached for him, held him and cherished him and adored him and loved him, and that sweetest, loveliest of all sound sang out for him, sang ever gently for him:

"Stop," silence whispered her song for him in the dark. *"Just... stop."*

Ever gently, ever tenderly, her voice reached for him and caressed him and calmed him and settled him and soothed him and suffused him and he... simply... stopped.

Within that supernal sweetness a renewed stillness found him—and he found himself outside his apartment door.

As newly returned from an arduous and tortured odyssey, Rob found himself quieted, rested, even hopeful. The torrent of oppression had receded, faded, now gone and only distant memory of... *something*... importuning, and even that now fading, now gone. And *now* was only for silence in the dark.

Chapter 21.

The silence and the dark soothed immeasurably, and Rob cherished the dark, palliating and quieting beyond all else, under veneration of small cost and priceless value of such peace, even as such peace ensnared him in bitter corrosions for any cause that might least portend gouging such peace in the dark.

And, fulfilling portent, the silence and the dark collapsed as DeCeeve stormed into the back office and corrupted space and time with his base, vulgar laugh as he threw open the door ignorant of—or oblivious to or, more likely, contemptuous of—peace in the dark.

DeCeeve cared nothing of the sudden quieting of front office chatter the moment he'd stepped through the door, not noticing—likely not caring to notice or, more likely, taking long-practiced care to *not* notice—the sudden quieting of voices from the front office, quiet voices of subversion, but to him alone.

DeCeeve bludgeoned into Rob's awareness, clawed him first peripherally and then full-on with eye and lip and noise of himself, violating the straining quiet to which Rob struggled, as he stared out the vast window-wall overlooking the mass of people shouldering each other in the streets and alleyways and every bedraggled lawn and every spare inch below him.

Elbow sharply jabbing Rob in the rib, DeCeeve whispered conspiratorially:

"They're scared, you know," nodding down to the mass gathered outside, beneath him.

No reaction, so DeCeeve, with pitched emphasis:

"They're *scared*!" with vigorous affirmation of bobbing chin and squinting eye glorying in pontificating to his lesser.

Then, to silence, with a jerk of the head back toward the front office, as if whispering sagacity:

"And *they're* scared too, scared witless of that crowd below us—*beneath* us," with effort to sly, secret wink and nod.

Rob forced himself a nod in agreement, anything to shut him up and to recover, as best he could, of what spare tranquility remained to him, if any, in the face of all that was DeCeeve.

Oblivious, or indifferent, or contemptuous, DeCeeve:

"With our vow to give the people what they want—of work, and of opportunities derived of work, and of stimulating the economy to untether the rich to create still more work—those in the front office are petrified the people down there," head jerking down to the mobs below, "will seize the moment and fire up our revolution right here, right now—and run them off and snatch away their diamond-studded rings and their platinum watches and their gold-encrusted pens and tear into their gated communities and plunder their fine homes and their wide-screen TVs and fancy electronics and *do* their wives and daughters right in front of them, on their very beds and couches and carpets and kitchen tables."

DeCeeve arched back and raised eyes to Heaven in blissful anticipation of crowning achievement—"and *that's* when I'll usher-in the *my* wave, The New Wave—and mollify them with my look and sound and word..." and still more of repulsive, gloating leer... "before I—*we*," another odious wink of gratuity, "impose martial law."

Rob strained to hear the ovation filling DeCeeve's imagination, *"what vanishingly little there is of it."*

In the back of mind Rob wondered whose words DeCeeve parroted, implanted by some shrouded guru.

"The words are so like..." and he wrestled to call back familiar-sounding words whispered long ago, in hidden corners, *"and no doubt my Liberty Party has been deeply and fully penetrated by Quislings reporting, but—to whom?"*

Rob didn't wonder to whom, knew to whom, was sure he knew, *"all but sure—Allman,"* who else, even as he defiled himself his certitude... *"without smallest shred of proof."*

Rob considered:

"Somewhere out there Allman's wearing his smug leer—but it will end as I will it."

Rob resolved it be so… "and so it will be, just exactly so"—and ignored silent whispers in the dark auguring of what *will* be, regardless of Rob's greatest ambition and intent, as images reared….

Rob milled among that murk, the elite, overseeing his troop of beauteous people, his vanguard, observing and gauging their quiet manner and sermon as the elite preened and postured and pressed too-close around them—and reviled himself his base and manifold bigotries.

"How different am I from this murk? I would as they, and more, preen and strut in self-deception, that I deserve transcendence…" as portent, in horrific imagery, shrouded.

Rob forced attention back to his beauteous vanguard, observed and heard, now to one stunning young woman:

"As preeminent members of our society, we owe it to *ourselves* to uplift these poor, pitiable creatures that scrimp and save and strain to feed themselves and their families. They don't need to make-do with old CR-TVs and cordless phones and desktop computers. We can, we *will*, uplift them with *our* goods and with *our* services—and with our credit. We must, we *will*, raise them up to a standard better than they have— with the easiest of terms," under alluring wink and nod, "to repay their debt to us. Of course they can't live nearly as *we* do, still they can live better than they do—as our interests flourish…" and with quiet denouement: "… for the good of the people."

The exquisite young woman gazed rapturously heavenward as she coo'd with breathless, hungry lip and eye at the grey-templed men of wealth and stature and station hanging and harrumphing on her every word with eyes riveted on her décolletage and thighs and all else of her exposed to them as she continued angelically:

"We must invest in ourselves and legislate to reach this lofty goal, most laudable mission, of uplifting our fellow Americans… for their greater good," forswearing silent whisper taunting… *"for YOUR greater good."*

And, too, all-attention to the alluring, beauteous young man as he struck the pose of supplicant pleading to the wise, transcendence of his audience of sallow-faced, jewel be-dripped matrons, all to a woman fervently nodding enthusiastic support and succor fully eyeing his chest and buttocks and all else of him they could expose by imagining.

And each of his beauteous disciples supplicated and inveighed for their audience to… "prepare the foundations for a populace better able and more willing to bring *our* factories and *our* businesses to heights of productivity and profitability and authority and control as never before witnessed."

And in breathless triumph:

"We can, we *will*, reap rewards beyond any we've yet known or can even imagine!"

Rob witnessed his beauteous creations weave their spells and he strained to silence imminent, triumphant joy as this ascendant audience fell completely under their enchantment—*"as cascade of action and reaction reach fruition—and rend."*

Rob edged nearer the most auspicious of that elite, spoke treacle-voiced in softest edge:

"And, of course, as you are well aware, the Supreme Court has now blessed our rightful privilege and more, our *obligation*, to buy our elected officials with their pronouncement of unlimited campaign contributions—*that* now ordained to us," as Rob struggled to *not* gloat and swagger.

The dimming glow of failing aura presses him against the threshold of his vermillion borderland, the shadowland where all things imaginable are within reach—if.

'He' feels the light fading, seated there on his highest perch, and wonders what the inevitable dark will usher in, cause to be. He stares down at his arm, hand, fingers—shorn to the bone of flesh with scant, bare fragments clinging, flailing, screaming. He wonders what he deserves, wonders why he suffers so little when he deserves so much more, far more, of suffering and of misery than that with which he's been so far

awarded, his award for contriving others' anguish, the least of which shears some others' arms, hands, fingers to be carved free of flesh, stripped to bone with barest remnant clinging, screaming, and wonders:

"What have those others done to deserve their rewards of desolation, of this, of here, of now, all of it MY doing."

"Why is my despair so pallid and hidden?"

He understands that most ask 'Why so much?' as he asks 'Why so little?' of despair, incalculable as his remains, understanding portent hidden in this too, and cringes under what such portent avows him.

He wonders this, the true price of his covetousness, as far off din flares louder, or nearer, and wonders why such outcry rises to flood him here, now, like this. What explains this privation crying out to him, crying out for him, reaching for him, in this vermillion shadowland of imminent portent? The far away stirring seems shorn of hope and he realizes, comes fully aware: "Who am I, what am I, to be spared any least of this?" and girds against the inevitable of what might—will— be.

He shifts, lists into this threshold of his vermillion shadowland, borderland between the extinguishing aura and the absolute of the dark unrelentingly encroaching, and is intently silent against dimmest shadow of outcry, ever distant, ever nearing, of gently pounding surf whispering portent, leaving him to wonder, "portent... to what?"

He lists on his highest perch, draws onto the verge of his vermillion shadowland, readies to peer into shadowland, and understands the same awaits thought and spirit as had awaited, rewarded, arm and hand and fingers. He resigns himself:

"What need I of thought and spirit here, now, for this?"

So armed he girds, peers into, must and cannot but peer into, his vermillion shadowland.

Chapter 22.

Dim light rose up from the dark, mirroring Rob, empty of warmth, empty of color, empty of everything more than faintest vestige of aura.

"And why not? Why should I deserve anything more."

Waking to every dimension of misery from last night, aching and straining through every bone and joint, he recalled his beating at the hand of the mob last night.

"No... at the hand of Allman," he thought, no, was sure without slightest list to self-contempt for such unproved denunciation—cardinal sin any other day, but not today and not in the least fading his certitude.

To that Rob paused, considered why *this* to compromise him, and wondered at feeling no self-reproach, no self-contempt, for this breach, and wondered what this tells of him—*"rising to highest standard when convenient... and only when convenient."*

He fought near-overwhelming urge to snug deeper between sheet and blanket and so compel sleep to aid and abet escape, the best escape, abandoning all—*"myself not least"*—to surrender to soft warmth of cozy bed and halcyon fugue of sleep, to erase what lay in wait for him on waking, on rising, on stepping out that forsaken door.

"What is a scant few more of minutes, hours, days—a lifetime—in which to linger and recoup in softest warmth? When else, where else, such rarified, opulent luxury?"

He breathed deeply as he strained after quiet, after calm, wondering why those so elusive now when never so wanting before. Thought of the brown-eyed girl edged and elbowed to hatchet him into full awareness and Rob renewed all-effort to search after calm and quiet, realized its abject failure, and finally surrendered to demand of reality and dressed and girded and stepped into the dark.

"*What would I do, where would I be, without my morning run to dissipate rage and hate? And regret.*"

With that small comfort he dove into the dark and into the cold morning air and down the path and into the wood.

But even against full-will, mind works, and now Rob contemplated, unable to dissipate what raged:

"*Is it really against my full-will that my mind works and broods and rages?*"

Another thought, from another part of him:

"*Maybe that's how my mind's supposed to work.*"

He considered, gave up, caved to the inevitable:

"*I deserve a day off—after last night.*"

"*Who says—me? What do I know of what and who does or does not deserve of time off, or of respite, hospice, for what slights I suffer? Who says for what, and for how slight, and for when, and for how long?*"

"*Come on—one day, just... one... day—who could deny me one day?*"

"*Who are you to deign a day of Holiday? For surviving a mob's—or Allman's—assault?*" and hidden—"*or hers?*"

"*Come on, one day—can you begrudge me one day?*"

"*The future is deigned, and is so, one day at a time. And if this day why not another, and then another, and then countless others every time some or other sycophant dreg to the mindless cavorts with you or antagonizes or shames or bloodies you—or bashes your head in or breaks your neck or leaves you comatose and paralyzed in a ditch in the dark?*"

"*So you're telling me I cannot, must not, ever take a day off, even one day, for any least respite?*"

Silent whispers in the dark:

"*No—everyone deserves a shade of time in which to renew calm, in which to resurrect something of calm, to reflect, to search out understanding, to claim something more of this existence than intractable, abject suffering. Only—when? For what? And who's to judge?*"

Finally, he shrugged, resigned to not even a question:

"*Who can know.*"

Even as he ran, memory hounded, of words spouted from atop a platform with almighty, self-righteous sanctimony, aimed at him:

"If YOU are not with us, YOU are AGAINST us!... the face of indifference is YOUR face!... the elitist oppressor is YOU... the enemy is YOU!"

Then... Rob woke. He woke re-born, *feeling* more than seeing a new light, a thing starkly new in the dark:

"Something new, here and now, for better AND worse, waiting, imminent."

He felt a stirring in the dark, felt it come alive... a tension, an apprehension, and too, an excitement, an exhilaration, as on threshold of some pristine, unprecedented origin lying in wait for him, subliminally stirring, awakening just beyond the narrowed confines of his awareness in this tiny, *tiny* world... *"and it's for me, just and only for me."*

He could not free himself from that delusion, from that sensation... *"just and only for me."* But what, eluded.

He heard a softest, ethereal rhapsody calling to him.

He'd recognize the sound of her voice anywhere, and didn't know if to be darkly enraged or supernally uplifted, reeling... *"what to think, what to do—what to feel?"*

Doubt skittered through him, electrified him, screamed at him, and he found himself suddenly breathless and exhausted... *"from my run, what else?"*... and slowed to a walk wondering how it would look to her, how she'd take it, what she'd make of it—he, slowing up, stopping, for her.

"I'll ignore her and walk on. I'll stop in my tracks and turn on her, face her down...."

But time eluded him as he heard sweetest, quietest, most gentle voice:

"I... I brought you... something...."

Ethereal sound of her trailed to silence, even with more to say, he could hear it in her but here, now, to him—only that to say.

Rob took a few more steps more, his feet, not he, taking those steps, he not having least idea what to do, what was right to do. Then his feet stopped, planted him where he was.

He didn't speak, wondered if to turn and face her, look her in the eye... or stand still and silent with back to her, defiant even as thought ranged furiously for what to say, what to do, in unrelenting war less over her than over himself.

"I'm... sorry," in softest, sweetest voice for him.

Her voice was warm sun and soothing breeze and softest caress for him, that in the sound of her, all he could hear and feel of her... *"filled with remorse?"*, he struggling to silence ardent need and prayer in him that she is... *"filled with need of me."*

He heard so much in that sound and craved to hear so much more, even as he reviled himself his prayer.

He shook himself awake from imaginings, from relentless war in him, and paused now to listen, to imagine he could be sure of what he heard in her... *"some overarching trace of lament?"* and wondered what is real and what imagined.

"Here"—in softest, gentlest voice, so much in a word, as she held out her hand, lightly gripping the paper.

Rob debated through raging and, finally, turned and faced her. He stared her in the eye wondering what he'd see there of her, and of himself.

"Here."

She breathed the word again, paused again, now with outstretched arm holding for him a scrap of newsprint. He couldn't tear eyes from her eyes, couldn't take so much as a glance at what she proffered.

"Please... take it. Please... read it," a cry in her voice, he heard, thought he heard, prayed he heard.

The sound was softest caress of gentlest breath, more wonderful than anything he'd ever felt or heard, was ever felt or heard by anyone, anywhere, and now she couldn't look him in the eye, could only turn eyes away to stare at the ground at her feet, arm outstretched, soft, delicate fingers barely touching a thin fold of newsprint held out for him.

The silence was long, she waiting for him to speak as he hunted words to say, scouring himself for words to say.

To his silence, she finally spoke:

"It... wasn't how it... *looks*," in lost and urgent voice.

154

"She sounds like I feel," and again he wondered what is real and what imagined.

Still silent, staring at her downcast eyes, he groped for what to say, do, *feel* as he watched tears fill her as she lowered her arm and turned her back and trudged away, not seeing him struggle for words and raging at himself as he struggled for words, staring at her back as he struggled for words… and she just walked away, and he just let her walk away.

The day passed as *she* had… in miserable, slow labor.

He kept waiting for… something, with no clue for what.

No papers yet, no photos yet—and already Rob could feel contempt stare him down at his approach, words rushed to whisper as he neared, catching glimpse of words as he passed, harsh and excoriating, muttered too loudly at his back from those who'd once had only stony silence for him, and now stony silence from those who'd once had kind words for him.

The next day promised the same. Rob woke to the dark weighing on his every move, every thought, and he reviled himself for *still* grieving for a kind word and a gentle touch from his brown-eyed girl—and how could he even think her 'his' brown-eyed girl.

His run long done, he lumbered to class. He caught sight of a copy of The Sentient as it swept by him in the wind, someone had glanced at it and had carelessly, thoughtlessly cast it aside.

"What do these people think of, what is the environment to such as them, they above such paltry trivialities," even as he reviled himself his contempt of them.

Rob stooped and picked it up, not to read but to honor the environment, even with fingers shaking and heart racing for who knew why of portent.

The front page was splattered with photos of Dean Ivry and Panther King, the lead article telling of their bitter story, the latest twist and turn of the still-evolving saga etched in exacting detail, in as disinterested a staging as any public information could be, far beyond anything of commercial or even publicly funded media's pretensions, artifice.

He scanned the page irritably and then, presaging what he'd see, turned the page.

He turned the page and saw his eyes staring back at him. He'd never thought to be spared that but, somehow, for some reason, had thought she'd spare him that.

"What was I thinking," not question but lament at his own foolishness, *"to imagine she might feel for me, have any least thought for me, to spare me."*

"Why should she care in the least for me, what am I to her—nothing and less than nothing, a story for a news clipping, to ignite still more contempt for me, to hawk her papers... just like all the rest of them."

He let the paper drop from his fingers and watched it waft away on the wind, *"maybe it'll be seen by still others—for them to revile me too."* What of the 'environment' beside this.

Suddenly, a maelstrom of thought and emotion savaged him as he heard a voice behind him, still as ever softest, gentlest, sweetest sound, *"and why still that for her?"* he lamented.

She spoke ever quietly, ever gently, *"with a trace tear in her voice?"* and again, still, reviling himself his wan prayer, still there, even now, even with this.

"Wait. Please... *wait.*"

He heard his own lament in her voice.

Rob froze, stood his ground, still and silent, what is there to say, do—*"nothing."*

He waited and finally, to her enduring silence, he turned to face her. The look in her eyes staggered him and he fell back a half-step at all he saw in her eyes. Her eyes locked on his and she stepped near, nearer, a breath from him—so he couldn't shut her, or himself, from her, so he *had* to hear her and, maybe, if she could will him to, listen.

"It's not how it *looks!*"

Supplication and demand interlocked, she stepping still closer, a whisper from his lips, her lips a breath from his, so he would breathe her in and have to breathe her in and she him.

She spoke with a cry in her voice, so he knew to listen.

He stared into her eyes and breathed of her and despite all will found himself struggling against near-overwhelming urge, command, *need*—to take her and hold her and press her still closer and be with her, just *be* with her.

As quickly as the spell had been so it was broken and he backed away a half-step, about to turn and walk away, this time for good, when something... changed, something *happened* in her... and she exploded in a rage of fury and she grabbed him by the shirt and pulled him still closer and screamed in his face as he half-struggled to turn away and not for a moment able to turn away:

"*Face* me! *Listen* to me!"

She screamed the words between tears streaming down her face and... turned and walked away.

Suddenly, reborn to life, he woke to her and rushed to her and grabbed her and pulled her around and forced her to face him, and forced himself to face her.

He gripped her arms and held her tight and in hoarse whisper, his breath at her lips:

"*Why?*"

And immediately:

"Why *Allman?*"

He'd shocked himself, realized for the first time what lay behind his hurt, having nothing to do with his photo or the paper.

He held her for the space of a small eternity, his lips at hers, his breath at hers, wanting nothing but to render the moment eternal, terrified of her answer, panicked at the imminence of her answer, this precious uncertainty so far more than any possible answer he could conceive from her.

She froze at the sound of his words, stunned at understanding their meaning, and screamed in answer:

"What? *What?*"

Incredulity blanketed her face, left her powerless except to stammer again: "*What*??"

She pushed him away and then other expressions flooded her as she felt him loosen his grip to let her push him away when he should have clung to her and held her and not ever let her push her away.

She reached for him and gripped his shirt and with all strength dragged him to a stack of thin newspapers standing nearby and tore up the top paper and thrust it wildly in his face, jamming it full in his face—then caught herself and let the paper slip down and away. With eyes aflame, glaring him full in the eye, she rammed the paper to his chest and screamed: *"Read it!"*

Hesitating only long enough to recover himself, Rob was obeisance itself, how could he not be, here, like this, and took the paper, turned the pages to his photo staring up at him, and read the caption beneath his photo: *"Who* is the Enemy?"

He looked up to see her watching him intensely, scrutinizing his reaction, then read:

> *Who* is the enemy?
>
> Behind accusation reeking of ignorance and stupidity and bigotry the self-righteous fight their fight.
>
> Against whom and against what and with what weapons and tactics are non-issues to those who strike any easy target within reach, deserving or not, guilty or not.
>
> When do you judge not by fact and reason but by convenience and caprice? When is an audience converted to a mob and the speaker to a heretic preaching against his own gospel? When does the fight against oppression *become* oppression?
>
> That 'when' was last night—on the Commons.
>
> No man is emptier of bigotry than whose picture is staring you in the face here and now as you read this. Yet he stands accused of being The Enemy, accused, tried, and *convicted*—by a mob and its heretic!
>
> I can only thank Goodness Herself for the cowardice that filled the mob and held it rooted just barely short... of *murder*!
>
> The only offense this man committed was to turn away from a mob being preached to and incited by its heretic to judge and hate with no

more truth and justice than the twisted word of its preacher!

The only offense this man committed was to demand scrutinizing the truth *for himself* and to demand reserving judge for *himself*!

The only offense this man committed was to reject mob rule, reject mob deaf and dumb and blind bigotries, and undertake his *own*, independent, rational judgment with dispassion and disinterest—as every thinking, feeling member of our social order must—to exercise his *own* judgment!

It is not he but the mob and every member of that mob who are guilty! *They* are guilty of the elitism and of the oppression they contemn! *They and their preacher* are The Enemy! They brand as 'elitist' anyone who demands free and independent thought and brand as 'oppressor' anyone who dares defy their own ignorance and blindness and bigotry!

The man pictured here is not our enemy but our Guardian, deserving our deepest respect and our most profound gratitude! The *mob* and its *preacher* deserve our contempt and our damnation. And whoever you are: I love and respect what you stand for—and so I love and respect *you*.

If you learn anything from your studies at The Rafford, learn to recognize and revere the values that make us great. Learn to recognize the values that will make us great again—and refuse any lesser standard.

The article went on, but Rob stopped reading. He looked up to his brown girl and breathed infinite gratitude to think her—to *know* her—*his* brown-eyed girl. Or hope it.

But a thought struck him, rooted him to the ground, to that spot: *"How perfect is perfect-enough? How near to perfection has she got to be?"*

He stood immobile, watching her, scrutinizing her, gauging her even as she returned his stare eye to eye. Then he blurted, without meaning to but *having* to, not able to stop himself:

"I can't let my feelings for you blur the truth, distort reality, contort my judgment."

She stared at him uncomprehendingly as he launched into the residue of his rage and jealousy, confronting her with the manifest, palpable truth of it:

"You wrote all this to soothe your conscience. You lured me straight into Allman's snare, capitalized on the popular mood, galvanized that mob... just to take photo of their savagery—another feather on your cap—and when their violence turned feral it was more than your delicate, sanctimonious sensitivities could bear, more than your conscience and vanity could countenance. So you soothed yourself and indulged yourself and groveled to your sanctimony and suckled your vanity and wrote these words to stage them for me now, a feint of remorse and repentance—to ransom those words for my forgiveness and gratitude. First you betray me, then you betray your readers, and now you betray *yourself*—to soothe your conscience and salve your petty, selfish vanities."

No sooner had he articulated his fear and terror as accusation and condemnation than he cursed himself for having done so, for having lost himself, for having lost self-control and lost rational, dispassionate judgment—and now profoundly, inextricably regretted having spoken his words aloud, cursed himself and reviled himself for having given voice to thought and anguish and fear.

"What right have I to hurl allegation without reasonable, reasoned, least chance to refute my suspicions and fears... not nearly enough for the right to utter such calumny, especially to her, to such as her."

He understood it was especially to *her* he'd said those things and *had* to say those things—would never have to anyone else.

So he realized: *"That's how much she means to me."*

His last thought struck him as his brown-eyed girl stared him in the eye, struck mute and blind by his assault, under such savage onslaught, and all he could do was watch her struggle to understand what he was telling her—of *her*.

"And what it tells—of me," he shuddered to read of her.

The brown-eyed girl stared at him more wide-eyed and horrified with each word he threw at her. Her lips trembled and her eyes brimmed but she refused outright her lips' demand to cry-out loud and her tears' demand to flood from her eyes.

Such was her will.

She rasped through harsh whisper between sobs and gasps, her breathlessness impudent to her command, refusing her will to suppress it:

"How *dare* you? How dare you *assume*?"

Under her glare and tone he staggered back and so she witnessed her power to move him—and to move herself, too. She pressed on:

"How dare you *judge* me like that? You know what I wrote is unadulterated *truth*! You *know* it *is*!"

She urged to add: *"I—know it's true!"* but couldn't find it in herself to lionize him still further, here, now, like this, in the midst of… this.

She struggled to understand him, to ferret out what lay beneath this reaction of his, struggled to calm herself, to wrest herself to dispassionate reason, to semblance of clarity, but the turmoil he'd stirred in her put such thought and effort beyond her reach.

She scolded him and berated him and her voice trembled and her eyes brimmed and finally one, especially audacious tear rose up and betrayed her and rolled languorously down her cheek, flaunting its power over her and exposing her—to him.

Rob stood back for just an instant as he watched her pain, *felt* her pain—and realized his blunder, realized his enormously shameful blunder.

It was simple, really—and he fervently prayed she'd forgive him his vast ignorance and thoughtlessness and profound, boundless stupidity.

Suddenly she broke into a convulsion of miserable sobbing, transformed to child overwhelmed by the harshness and cruelty of everyday life, of feelings which she'd never experienced, had never before faced, for which she was simply not prepared.

But she understood his transgression. It was very simple.

He was, simply, wrong. He had, simply, misjudged her. Anyone can be wrong—*"but wrong... like this?"*

"Yes," she knew, even through her misery, *"yes, even like this—just like this."*

And beneath that she understood, because she understood *him*, as thought and feeling flooded her:

"He'd misjudged me because he's too afraid to believe me, to believe in me—to love me."

She knew, *felt* it of him, without trace doubt.

Thought flooded him, wondering how she could have been so sure of him as to write what she'd written of him.

"How could she possibly know?"

There was only one way she could know.

Then, sudden thought immolated him and he couldn't help but blurt out the essence of it:

"But how can you be with *Allman*? Of all people—how can you be with *Allman*?"

She stared at him for a long moment, stared him full in the eye, and suddenly filled with understanding:

"How can I be with—*Allman*? Why am I *with* Allman?"

She stood back, pulled a half-step back, understanding dawning. Fire ignited her eyes to flame as her lips stretched to grim snarl still somehow clinging to silence, then:

"Who said I'm *with* him? Who said I'm with *him*? How can you think I'm *with*—him? Who—*what*—do you think I *am*?"

Her rage swelled and she glared at him, about to rush at him, about to claw his face and gouge his eyes... that he should think *she* could possibly be with *Allman*.

Then... she stopped.

She stood glaring silently, fire raging her and still, somehow, held herself motionless and silent as scant tears struggled out her eyes, her will finally relenting, surrendering.

She drew in a breath, managed near-silent whisper:

"I am who I am and you know—*know*—who I *am*!"

But too, she understood him, now more than ever, so much more than before, and managed to stammer in near-silent whisper:

"That's *trust*. That's what trust *is*," and she meant not trust of her but trust of *himself*, to judge with clarity and reality.

She knew she'd have to earn his trust and so, would, even as tears filled her and streamed down her.

Then all came clear and he rushed to her and held her and pressed her close and closer and touched cheek to her and looked her in the eye and brought lips and breath to her and kissed her and kissed her tears away and covered her face with ever-gentle, softest lips to cheek and then to lips and then to the sweetness of her neck and buried his face in her neck and squeezed her still tighter as he breathed half-heard words:

"I'm—*sorry*, I'm so… *sorry*! I never meant to make you cry! I never meant to judge you and never, not *ever*, meant to hurt you and make you cry and I can't stand to see you cry and never, not *ever*, because of me or for me!"

He held her tight and squeezed her tighter and covered her with kisses, softest, gentlest, most desperate kisses to heal her and heal all he'd caused and heal all the hurt she might ever have as he blurted between softest lips to her:

"This is my fault, all my fault and never, not ever, yours and don't cry, please don't cry, I can't stand to see you cry!"

And then he found her lips and first gently and then with crushing *need* covered her with passion he'd never known existed and never known *could* exist.

Then he felt her return everything he felt for her, and finally and too soon, ever too soon, they eased, and eased apart, just a breath apart, and held each other and finally looked into each other's eyes and couldn't stop themselves and again pressed themselves to each other for another timeless moment.

Suddenly she pulled away, gently but firmly away, and stared into his eyes and let him watch *panic* fill her eyes and overwhelm her—and she turned and hurried away, head down and shoulders hunched and hands buried deep in her pockets.

Chaos filled him as she pulled away, as she stared at him another long moment and then turned away and hurried away—as he stood and watched her go, stood and let her go.

He watched her hurry away helpless to do more than watch her rush away, feeling something for which he had no words, about which he had no idea what to do. Then he looked up at the sky and watched the grey deepen slowly into the dark—and warm him and amaze him how a moment could change the world.

Chapter 23.

Ben Rob stared out the panoramic window-wall of the back office, staring down at the mass crowding the streets and alleys and every inch of space below. Then the distant din of the front office penetrated and disgorged into the dark, stripping away his focus, tipping him away to revulsion of DeCeeve and his raucous, obnoxious laughter, piercing him and impaling him despite all will and greatest effort to transcend.

Then memory tore back, repossessed:

Around him the students thought and talked only of Panther King and his *threat*—to Dean Ivry, to his administration, to the *status quo* of their traditional, established lines of control and authority and entitlement, and to the oppression and repression exercised and exhorted and excoriated over them.

With the Rafford Board about to meet, protest in defense of King or, rather, in defiance of Dean Ivry, stretched to rupture.

Rob sat silent in the classroom, his well-worn wont, as the others quietly and not-quietly scorned and depredated him, their ascendant arrogance not deigning to lower themselves to understand, or even try to understand, what they imagined was, what they twisted into being, Rob's degraded insularity and self-absorption.

"Taking Allman's lead, no doubt," and Rob instantly denounced himself still again for unproven cause, *"unproven... but all too certain,"* still and again reviling himself for unfairly debasing Allman, and now justly debasing himself.

When debate ignited around him, he clung to silence.

"Cling to stone and silence. Know to evade sordid provocation. Ignore petty controversy and confrontation. Stone

and silence are higher, more laudable goals in dealings with such as Allman. Descending into their morass leads only to being denounced and reviled and confirmed an insular outsider, self-absorbed and base and vulgar, a commoner simply not up to their self-acclaimed Rafford standard—no matter that gutted standard, what do they know of standards."

Rob was mystified by how laconic and casual a leadership Allman exercised over the others, possessing so eerie and so total command over them, *"they according him mystical stature as their führer, their guru, their divinity,"* so he judged and, still again, so he reviled himself for unproven judgment.

"It's more than terrifying that I am almost certainly right about their obeisance to Allman—they seemingly mature and educated and intelligent young women and men, the 'cream' of our great society's crop, effortlessly and fluently and thoughtlessly degrading themselves, willingly and willfully rendering themselves subordinate and subservient, thoroughly usurped of rationally considered, independent thought and judgment. If this is the best our country can offer for our salvation..." he couldn't finish the thought, couldn't face its implications and ravagings, as images of the Supreme Court shoved into view as examples of the pathetic and reprehensible 'cream' of our social order... *"stripping away the rights of workers to collective bargaining, subverting healthcare protections in favor of industry lobbyist lucre, blessing the moneyed elite and their unconstrained political 'contributions' and effectively silencing the voice of ordinary people, and...."*

Rob struggled to silence thought as he stared eye-to-eye into the heart of darkness, images screaming... *"of relentless corrosions of the rights of ordinary people, leading to ever more gaping inequality, presaging the people's escalating outrage, inexorable ripening into blood-soaked confrontation, leading straight into stifling repression as the hallowed trumpet their hollow ascendance... and insurrection obliterates their social order, they blind to the peril they themselves elaborate."*

In Rob's memory, Allman's ice and command breached Rob's surging lamentation:

166

"The *real* problem," Allman pronounced, assuming the unchallengeable and unassailable directorate of the classroom debate, "dulling those like Dean Ivry is their having been born and bred and thoroughly conditioned to act and think and *feel* justifiably superior and rightfully ascendant—and it's become not only acceptable but expected and fashionable and *needful*, in too many circles, to so present and comport themselves, or to compel others to do so for them, in their name. If *you* were raised in a prevailing atmosphere of elitism and entitlement *you'd* think just the same, wouldn't you Robber? *Wouldn't* you... *Robber*."

All now fell to stony silence, all now scrutinizing Rob in full expectation—only *of what* remaining, they knowing near nothing of inevitable consequence cascading from its source.

Rob couldn't help but admire Allman's consummate art and artifice, contorting and perverting 'elitism' into meaning not Allman and all that is Allman's... *"but me and all that is 'mine,' whatever 'me and mine' can possibly mean, conflating Dean Ivry with me, of all people. Allman's skill and artifice are stunning."*

Rob nearly laughed aloud at such a ridiculous notion so readily and eagerly accepted, unexamined and unchallenged, by the body politic represented here and now, in this very classroom.

To Rob's silence, Allman continued his provocation, edging ever more to abrasive and corrosive and contemptuous:

"The *real* problem..." glaring down on Rob, who studiously, tenaciously, clutched at silence, struggling mightily to *not* be roused by barking dog, "is with today's youth. They sit silent in their seats like good little gophers and puppies and pussies and slugs and maggots, clinging tenaciously with all they are to appear blind and deaf and mute in the face of their own neutering. Don't you agree... *Robber*?"

Rob struggled to silence, to constrain racing heart and gasping breath and rising rage, to transcend petty provocation of barking dog, what point, what use, with such as him and his.

Rob had known, had fully anticipated, Allman would bait him, urge to provoke him, to excise him from the peace of quiet reflection. But as taunt and challenge and defilement

167

edged ever coarser, ever more deprecating and challenging, Rob's fervent will to silence weakened, finally collapsed, and he wondered how he could remain silent and above such base fray, then doubted he should, then *knew* he should not—and reviled himself for subscribing to such blasphemy as to bark back at barking dog.

"Some things can't be, must not be, avoided or overlooked and so... must be confronted," and Rob lamented the sacristies of choice and possibility, of compulsion and need, and wondered about manifest contradiction:

"Fighting for peace—fucking for chastity? Into which am I descending?" he fully understanding the incompetence of that analogy and the confinements of blind dogma, the first a genuine need, the second a farcical deception, and wondered how to know the difference, and how to illuminate that difference to an assemblage not un*able* but fully un*willing* to discern any difference at all.

"But right here, right now—it makes no difference," and he lamented having to surrender-up his resistance against doing battle where clear reason is not a tenable weapon.

Rob waited another moment, to magnify for the others in the room the level of this intrusion into and corrosion of his quiet contemplation. He wanted them to understand that *Allman* was the inciter here, not he... then realized they wouldn't understand, wouldn't notice, didn't care—*"don't dare to care."*

Rob opened mouth to speak, mouth half-open to speak, as Allman bloviated his pronouncements again, cutting Rob off with practiced ease and perfect timing:

"Aren't *you* and those like *you* the problem, Robber? Aren't the millions of just-like-you's—petty, greedy, small-minded, self-absorbed, future-bureaucrats and autocrats—the *real* problem?"

With gradually escalating pitch and fervor, Allman continued his simmering rant with expert polish:

"It's *you* and such as *you*, with your self-serving, self-righteous, money-grubbing, malicious self-idolatry who are the problem! *You* and those like *you*, with your vast bigotries and boundless jealousies who, by your silence, rise against Panther

King and all that he and those like him stand for—demanding a least fair chance of honest opportunity. And *you* and those like *you*—with all your *being*—seek to deny him and those like him even the most *niggardly* chance to transcend what they are born to. And anyone not spouting *your* racist and oppressive ideologies could go straight to Hell!"

Allman, with eyes glaring and neck veins bulging and hands clenched in fists of rage in masterful performance:

"*You* and *yours* are the problem!"

As Allman was climaxing he stepped steadily and provocatively nearer and ever nearer Rob until he stood over Rob glowering down and facing him eye-to-eye, breath-to-breath, spittle in face with middle-finger pointed a hair's breadth from Rob's eye.

And still Rob clung to silence, thought seething as he shut his mouth and deliberated, will over wont:

"All this—a show! All this for the others to hear and see and cringe and cower of least challenging all that is Allman's, deafened and blinded and cowed to his outrageous slander and hypocrisy, praying gratitude to Goodness it is not they being so reviled and diminished and demonized."

Rob forced himself still and silent, fought himself to calm—and slowly, ever gently, brushed Allman's finger aside.

The room drew deathly silent as Rob kept the room grindingly, hauntingly silent, keeping the silence alive and only now, finally, speaking:

"Take care, Allman, not to lead your flock astray and over the cliff as you point your finger at me and away from the *real* fault and fallacy. You need point your middle finger in a different direction and maybe not everyone here appreciates that or sees it as clearly as I do and as you should. Keep in mind that maybe, just maybe, you don't see the question clearly yourself."

Rob hesitated for the briefest moment, to be sure of his tone and look and manner but before anyone took his silence as wavering and cowering and surrender, and spoke quietly, calmly, mastering every look and tone and movement, speaking ever softly, ever gently:

"You've got to isolate and... scrutinize... your values."

Rob chose his words with infinite care, understanding that the right words impart worlds of meaning and insight and power—*"to anyone with any least interest to insight,"* and Rob shuddered invisibly at such vanishingly small likelihood, understanding:

"He'd rather cause to incite than offer insight."

Rob continued, the embodiment of quiet calm, before Allman could, with his grand spectacle, disrupt and corrupt Rob's chain of logic and deliberation:

"You've got to... prioritize... your values, reorder the primacies of your values... clearly reason out and understand your urgencies... understand and delineate your *highest* priorities so you don't... *super*ordinate... your biases and self-interests above simple, honest truth."

Awkwardly to start, as Rob spoke confidence gathered, gained stronger, more resolute voice:

"You're confusing the issues," Rob instructed, aiming for erudite illumination.

Rob paused a half-breath, looked Allman in the eye, to signal this was not vanity he was speaking but dispassionate reflection and cogent deliberation, then continued:

"You accuse me of being small-minded, of being a racist, of being an arrogant and grasping elitist, because you see me as standing against anyone who's not just like me. But you don't see the *issues* as I see them, as they *need* to be seen... and you prove your own arrogance and bigotries with your wild accusations and with your stony silence on the *real* matter: the *issues*."

Rob paused a moment, to let what he'd said steep into the audience—the other students now rigidly silent and straining to hear, Rob wondering how genuinely they *cared* to hear—and made no pretense to himself that this intercourse could be anything but a show, a performance... *"for my personal safety, possibly even for my life, knowing better than to underestimate Allman or to underestimate the ready-servility of this all too readily-violent audience."*

170

Now quiet again, so his audience had to struggle to hear and so strain to *listen*, Rob continued softly:

"I aspire to honesty and to honest debate. I work hard to think independently. I endeavor to enlist the integrity of open minds and to discriminate against anyone and everyone who does not share *those* values. For me there *is* no race, there *is* no religion, there *is* no partisanship—there is only the fight against misinformation and disinformation, against bigotry, against closed minds and small minds and those who mindlessly follow closed, small minds...."

Rob was about to add 'like yours' but decided his own well-being deserved a higher priority than Allman's trifling humiliation, *"what good poking stick at rat and rattlesnake."*

Rob absently wondered if 'rat' and 'snake' were the nearest to Allman's character, 'jackal' and 'weasel' flashing to mind, then Rob laid to rest distracting thought as the image of a crouching tiger instinctively coalesced.

But Rob's nature moderated instinct:

"Misguided vessel of the elite," intruded to mind, Rob silently deliberating how Allman's tactics and strategy advanced the agenda of that elite certain that, somehow, they did.

Rob hesitated at that last and in a half-heartbeat's internal debate, if or not to go toe to toe with Allman *personally*, decided:

"Yes. What choice? I've got to attack him, the best defense, after all... what choice but to speak painful truths?"

Then Rob decided against descending to such tactics, fully comprehending that slighting Allman would reflect back on himself with incalculably greater magnitude, and besides:

"What pain can I possibly inflict on Allman? Do brutes suffer such pain? Reality and truth always win out in the end, as they've got to"—even recognizing the emptiness of such naïve myth and fantasy—*"even as truth too-often glances harmlessly off the likes of Allman,"* and Rob kept silent, especially to himself, under the certain eventuality of Allman's reprisal, all-likely inflicting far more harm to him than he can ever inflict—*"or would ever care to inflict,"* silence whispered—against Allman.

Rob fully understood the futility of trying to, or expecting to, win over Allman at Allman's own game, and now settled for such small comforts as silence, *"even those infinitely more than none,"* silence assured:

"Respect reality and simple truths," small comforts in the face of Allman and all that is Allman's.

The look of triumph burst from Allman's eyes as he pounced, making not the least pretense to having listened, submerging and contorting reality with self-proclaimed triumph, the trademark of his ilk... *"proclaim victory loudly enough and it will be believed."*

"So!" Allman ejaculated, eyes glowing, lips gloating, all but slavering:

"So you *admit* your bigotries as you damn all those not 'privileged' enough to hold your values and think your thoughts. You damn all values that are not *your* values and you deceive *yourself* even as you crave to deceive *us*!"

Triumph exalted, exuding out of Allman as he strutted and pranced in his splendor. Then he continued:

"Just because others hold values different from yours, you damn their values and you damn *them*! And *you* condemn *me* as close-minded and small-minded! *So* you reveal yourself and expose yourself as the bigot that you in fact *are*!"

Fury raged in Rob, bucked at the limits of control, needing all Rob's to control his outrage at such disfigurement of manifest truth. But Rob understood, and understanding brought calm:

"There are times when unbridled rage should be waged and loosed on one's implacable enemy. But those times are very few and best chosen very carefully—or we'd all rage all the time at anyone and everyone for any least confrontation. And this," he concluded, *"is not that time. Choose your battles and choose them carefully,"* he counseled himself, and so Rob chose and demurred, forced apology out of his mouth.

Voice quaking with rage, he prayed—wondering why *that* word edged-up to awareness—for his voice to not be taken as weakness, or worse: fear. So he replied with a quiet intensity that stilled the air even through quavering voice:

"I'm no racist, as most anyone would use the word. I am, simply, neutral—about Panther King, about Dean Ivry, about their issues—until I have the facts from *both* sides. I don't know about his grades, I don't know about the threat he manifests, and I don't know about the threat Ivry embodies, to him or to us."

And pointedly staring Allman eye-to-eye, Rob added: "And neither do you."

A moment's hesitation, before Allman could muster a rejoinder, Rob added:

"You're arguing *your* interests, not Panther King's, not the students'… and not The Rafford's."

Allman now resorted to calm, quiet sound, expecting it be taken as *fact* and so, incontrovertible:

"You're just an elitist, ignorant, stupid racist. All one need do, all anyone need do, is read the Rafford Sentient."

"Repeated often enough and with enough conviction and righteous certitude—and any lie is rendered truth."

Rob understood this gospel and understood that The Sentient corroborated *his* version of truth—but that version will be read and *mis*read under the bias of Allman's truth, under the bias he'd injected into the minds and expectations of its readers.

"Too many see what they want to see, believe what they want to believe, and worse: what Allman believes and what Allman wants to believe—and damn the truth."

Rob understood simple truths.

To Allman's demonizing, Rob had no further words. He watched Allman, scrutinized his eyes, wondered what there was to read of Allman in his eyes, thought he saw a glimmer of piety, even of compassion, for Rob as worthy adversary thoroughly beaten and crushed.

Rob tried one more time:

"I'm only demanding truth—from both sides—is all."

Allman, now all soft and gentle—*"possibly out of pity for a worthy adversary's shameful defeat"*—concluded:

"*We* know the truth—only bigots don't, won't, see it."

Surrendering to the impasse, recognizing the futility of argument, Rob finally muttered quietly:

"The question, then, is one of truth, of reality: You say *you* know the truth. I say I—*and you*—do not. Who's right? Who can *know* who's right?"

Answering just as Rob expected, Allman played to his rapt audience as he grandly pronounced to his audience:

"Ben Rob and those like Ben Rob are simply too ignorant and too simple-minded and simpering to discern the manifest rightness and justice of Panther King's cause."

Allman paused, allowed his proclamation to penetrate:

"*I* know who's right. It is all very clear and simple: *I*— am right and *you*, Ben Rob—are wrong. It's as simple as that."

Rob opened his mouth to speak, wondered what he could possibly say and, mouth open, was interrupted by an aggressive, swaggering young woman's voice:

"That's exactly the kind of answer I'd expect out of the likes of you."

They all recognized Alex Sander's voice, the professor for whom they'd all been sitting, waiting. Their regard for her was manifest—the classroom, jam-packed with young idolaters, raptly waited on her, would sit there and await her for as long as she cared to let them sit there and wait. Even those who'd as soon storm and vandalize the administration building and defile the Dean and anyone and everyone not loudly set against him—sat there, ever patient, in adoring adulation.

Such was their regard for her.

'He' inches forward and then—first forehead, then nose, now eyes and mouth and ears, and finally the rest of him—penetrates and falls fully into that threshold of his vermillion shadowland.

For a moment he is frozen under sight and sound overwhelming him, then he gasps and suddenly, violently lurches back, claws frantically back from that brink, from that palest rendition of the dark awaiting him just beyond that vermillion shadowland, even as he feels himself irresistibly drawn further.

He lurches back, throws himself back, cradles into himself on the near side of his vermillion shadowland, needing *to recover from that sheerest glimpse of portent foreshadowed in his vermillion borderland.*

He'd glimpsed a finest, most gossamer-impression of the dark—and found it darker even than the absolute of the dark listing on the far side of his vermillion shadowland, and here, now, faces repudiation of the harbored notion that nothing is or can ever be darker than the absolute of the dark beyond this ever-thinnest, ever reediest confine of his vermillion shadowland.

Now he focuses himself, centers himself simply on breathing, on primal struggle for breath, to resurrect calm and clarity out of this nightmare glimpse of portent, of incomprehensible ravages haunting possibilities.

If lasting for moments or through ages, he does not know, cannot care. Time, as he understands it, as he thinks he understands it, crawls and creeps or sweeps and savages of its own cravings, of its own volition and urgency, laconic or furtive or fully sped, under fleeting leisure or under greatest frenzy and ferocity—under what he has witnessed:

Teeming, surging, wave after wave of skeletal faces imbued with blinded sockets impregnated above jaws riveted into silent screams mired in wailing and weeping....

"No," suddenly aware:

"Not weeping—screaming."

Chapter 24.

The Rafford was a beautiful, lonely place for Rob, now finding him steeped in reverie, awash in thoughts of his brown-eyed girl—thought and dream now finding him laboring to not think of her and to not think her *his* brown-eyed girl, she not descending to him, and he not to her, for reasons neither could clearly fathom, something about judgments and untested fears.

"After all, who am I to expect, or demand, anything of anyone."

Days dragged slowly by and the nights more slowly still, crawling by second after second as he tossed and turned and lay submerged in thought, afraid even to dream, afraid for what dreams may bring of understanding the who and the what of him, the so little of him.

Rage slowly simmered down to anger, then to a sense of betrayal, then to a simple lament that he'd no reason to expect, or deserve, more, not from her, not from anyone or anything... *"who am I to deserve anything of anyone."*

Suborn as he was, doubt reigned and ravaged—of Lainy, of Allman, and above all, of the two of them, lacerating him with relentless, unalloyed simmering fugue of despondence.

As so often at such times, and ever more it seemed, Rob found himself strolling aimlessly across The Rafford Commons, feet randomly, or not, following the heavily wooded paths leading anywhere and nowhere, the cool evening breeze a least salve to what burned in him.

He contemplated his restiveness:

"Not rage at Lainy, she just an actor, or being acting upon," struggling to turn from thoughts—*'acted IN'*—and returning to spare hopefulness, *"maybe blinding me to something more innocent, or at least a bit more innocent... and not rage at Allman, he just a mindless, soulless maw."*

He considered:

"I'm relegating Allman to nothing more than a mindless, soulless husk—a body-function, a need—and nothing else, nothing more."

He realized he was listing to the same with Lainy, *"why should she be elevated to more—or to anything at all."*

"No," silent whisper dragged him to acknowledge.

"I'm not raging at inanimate objects ignorant of anything more than their least, most-superficial, urgings, ravaging with and ravaged by their greed to dominate and control, or decadence in needing to be controlled."

He understood:

"I should be raging where my rage ought to be—at myself—for flailing in pathetic immobility, impotent paralysis."

He sharply halted thought… *"what's the point? No point, none at all,"* he understood. *"Let it go."*

Brooding thought rebuked and defiled him:

"And to think I used to pride myself in my self-control, in my rational dispassion, and sneer and belittle 'lesser minds' that struggle with their urges and needs—exactly as I am now."

He laughed mirthlessly at extravagant hubris and self-delusion. Then, from the dark, silent whisper:

"So the world—you—have got to suffer: to understand the essence of greed, to unleash all resistance to it, to liberate full rebellion against it, to wage fullest strivings against all who engender it and wallow and thrive and glory in it. In this and to this were you born."

He shuddered under the weight of such burden, affliction, anointed to rise above his own greeds and to raise others above theirs, above their flourishing, ravenous greeds, and how needful that and how impossible that.

Rob walked as he usually walked—hands buried deep in pockets, shoulders hunched to neck, eyes fixed to the ground at his feet, blind to the path on which his feet took him—and now absently wondering what he'd say to *'my'* girl, laughing soundlessly at himself, deriding and maligning himself for when, *"not if,"* he'd inevitably see her again, be inescapably cornered into facing her again, not 'if' but only when and how.

He felt his heart pound, wondered why, what should set heart to that, then looked up and saw that his feet had taken him to the Student Union building, the central watering-hole for the wildlife of Rafford students. He fought indecision—stay or turn away, walk away, look the fool for having stepped into and, seeing the crowds in heated talk, flee before... *"before what?"*

He ambled, as casually and unobtrusively as he could, to a stack of *The Rafford Sentient*, the school newspaper— having to fight images of hate steeped against him in deep-set eyes jammed all around him, all over him, their fists and feet held barely in check under the outrage limning their eyes, hardly contained, all but pounding and tearing at him in white-knuckled, spider-fingered hate, needing least excuse and no excuse, none at all, no further reason at all, to batter and claw and crush, lusting to break him, to have full at him under darkening skies and penetrating hate, the stench of his near-panicked outrage reeking far greater than any pheromone.

"What right have they?" haunted and taunted as they stoked their embers against him, he yearning to quite them before they launch themselves unconstrained at him, they submerged by greed and lust for blood, any blood, but his most exceptionally, they contriving themselves as endowed, supernal entities above and apart from any civilized constraint, apart and above their uncontained vanity and dissipated humanity.

But then, furtively scanning his surrounds, he realized no one was paying least attention to him, the air not afire against him as he'd fully expected, and so he meekly slipped out a copy of The Sentient and buried eyes and thought to the print.

He struggled to look and feel calm, the last eluding his most strident effort, he flipping through the pages until he found what he searched for, the editorial with *her* name undersigned, titled: "Of Credibility."

He read:

Some say everything's relative.
No. It is not.

Especially it is not when applied, as some try, to our social and political ideals. Of course I'm talking about *our* ideals, the ones even now trammeled under bitter accusation and blind allegation.

Yes, some things *are* relative: 'hot' and 'cold' have little meaning outside their relative perspective, outside our own, individual points of view. But it is just plain wrong when people apply that kind of thinking to values like 'good' and 'bad' and 'right' and 'wrong.'

Some things *are* grey, shades of grey not clearly good *or* bad, neither clearly right *or* wrong. And sometimes it *is* hard to be sure just what is good and just what is not—but do not twist one into the other no matter how hard you want, or try.

Listen to Dean Ivry and you'd think Panther King was a feckless anarchist, a violent nihilist out to destroy our standards and our values. Listen to Panther King and you'd think Ivry's an elitist reactionary oppressing free-thinkers and anyone and everyone who even least challenges some fascistic Rafford ideal, some imaginary ideal *we* are supposed to embody.

Whatever substance there is to the rage and debate is more murk than clear and more hype than real—when what's real and what's not are confused and contrived and you cannot 'discriminate' just by looking or listening or feeling or thinking. Where is 'truth' when all you have is spin and distortion, misinformation and disinformation?

King tells us to fight the oppression leveled against us by those who control the standard—*Ivry's* standard. Ivry tells us to fight the oppression contrived by those who corrupt 'our' standards. And both sides grope within the chaos and confusion that only further opacify reality and truth, themselves murk even in the best of times and even from the most honest and honored vendors. Sensationalists and exclusionists only further the absurdist absolutes of inflammatory accusation, shedding little of the light and sowing only more of the dark.

But you, *my readers*, just as seemingly all The Rafford, opacify the murk worst of all—by not thinking and not feeling and not judging *for yourselves*! And if you allow others to think and feel and judge *for* you—then you most fully deserve *their* judgment and have no ground to protest or revile when that judgment violates you and all you hold most dear.

Ivry says, plain and simple, that King's failed The Rafford standard and that King is just dissembling, clouding the truth behind protest and allegation.

King says The Rafford standard is *Ivry's* standard that pays simple homage to old, worn-out formulas of the old, worn-out elites purposefully deigned to purge and expunge anyone and everyone who least exerts to raise that standard through free and independent thought—free of obsolete, hoary politics and independent of elitist dogmas that have so long subjugated the thought and sensibility of the common, ordinary woman and man. The elites sow their own order and wreak their own standard and establish their own ascendancy throughout our social order, thoroughly saturating us with the rightness and righteousness of their supremacy—so say King's camp.

And meanwhile I—and vanishingly few others— fight to penetrate this murk. We've gone to both camps and tried to discern the facts beyond the rhetoric, to present to you objective and dispassionate truth and reality as fully as we are humanly able—for *you* to judge for *yourselves*.

And what have I found? *Neither* side brings or least tries to bring light to this morass and neither side is able or willing to clarify the issues and articulate just exactly where each stands.

And if I, and those vanishingly few who see as I see, cannot bring light to the dark, who can? If honest talk and fair hearing fail here at The Rafford—where else, what else, *who else* must it fail?

And you, my readers, *dare* defile and brutalize one among us who stands against this murk and refuses to be bullied or seduced or subverted by one extreme or the other?

The hearings begin next week and I challenge you, all of you, to rigorously consider: Will reality and truth be rendered as twisted and opaque then as they are here and now?

And worse—*we* will not be allowed to attend! And still *worse*—we will have *no voice* in what *they* decide!

If anything should rouse us it is not the courage of that one among us who would stand against such farce on *both* sides—it is the farce *itself!* And *you*, all of *you*, my readers, allow this disgrace and condone this charade by your passive acceptance of *this* stats quo and *so* you tolerate and consent and collaborate and thereby deserve this travesty.

We depend on 'the system' of free and honest debate to protect us—by keeping us honestly truthfully and fully informed. When dissembling and distortion and connivance debase full and honest debate we are—*all of us*—oppressed!

Do *not* revile and brutalize those rarified among us—especially that singular one among us—who stand for free and independent thought and judgment. Celebrate and laud him!

Rob read the editorial, read it again, and was struck by how so like his own voice it was written, as if he'd written it himself. He stared down at the name appended at the end of the editorial: *Lainy*—and how odd she'd used only her given name and how so much like her he was, shying from hoary tradition, challenging stultifying convention.

Then:

An infinitely soft voice broke the silence engulfing him, close and closer behind him, shy and hesitant, even afraid:

"What... do you think of it?"

He *felt* more than heard her words, they reaching into him like tendrils of the silent whispers of his own thought.

Recognition was instant, of course, twinned with fulminating fear of turning and still greater fear of *not* turning—to face her.

"Who am I to turn and face her, or to think I even deserve to turn and face her?"

He turned. How could he not.

"Who am I to not turn?"

Their eyes met and for a long instant both stood staring at each other, delving into each other's eyes, then both abruptly lowered eyes in perfect synchrony, each not able to look the other in the eye.

She spoke first, to the floor at her feet:

"After I wrote it I thought how much like *you* the article was, like *your* way of thinking—and it made me remember... you."

Her lips barely moved, her voice scarcely above silence, her eyes fixed on the tiling on the floor, not able to look up, not able to look him in the eye, afraid of the look in his eye.

He wondered how she could know his thoughts... but she was right, of course. Of course she was right, how could he ever doubt her, not for a moment could he ever doubt her.

She continued:

"That night they... *hurt* you..." and more to say, unsaid.

He heard the cry in her voice, felt it in himself, for her, as she breathed the word, not able to hear herself say the word: hurt.

He watched her, stared at her long after she'd finished, couldn't help but stare and keep staring through the silence, at softest eyes and sweetest lips seeing and speaking to the ground at her feet, the feel and sound of her voice the softest, gentlest sound ever uttered.

Finally, she looked up and looked him full in the eye and he felt more than saw her eyes and her lips softly creased in half-smile, half-dread, aching him to touch her, how could he not touch her, how could he not hold her tight with lips and breath to her.

Of power he did not know existed or could exist he stepped near, nearer, touched chest to breast with breath to breath and with infinite tenderness brought lips just barely to her for just a briefest moment, then he leaned back, just a little, just *so*, just enough to watch her and still be near enough to breathe her breath, to breathe-in her sweetness, and to settle in her eyes.

So they lost themselves.

Chapter 25.

Ben Rob stood by the panoramic window-wall of the back office staring down at the massive crowds deluging the streets and alleys and every corner of every space below. Then DeCeeve's raucous, repulsive laughter exploded around him, despoiling the silence, fouling the dark, and despite all will Rob submerged into loathing.

Then memory intruded and seized:

"That's exactly the kind of answer I'd expect from you."

They all recognized Alex Sander's voice, the professor for whom they'd been waiting, their regard for her such that they jam-packed the classroom and waited on her for however long she willed them to wait.

Silent whispers from the dark:

"Those who'd as soon storm and vandalize and violate the administration building... and anyone found there... here and now sit sweetly and patiently waiting on her, ever submissive and adoring. Such is their hypocrisy and such is their regard for Alex Sander, justified or not—who cares about justice when vogue dominates, lords as singular preeminence."

Alex Sander swept into the classroom as Allman argued that *he* understood the right and the wrong of the 'Panther King v Ivry' sensationalism, he contending that:

"Ben Rob and the likes of Ben Rob are too childishly naïve, too ignorant—or dim—to discern the manifest rightness and justice of Panther King's cause."

Allman stood imperiously pontificating:

"*I* know who's right and *I* know who's wrong," speaking to the air, not deigning to regard Rob directly: "*I* am right and *you*, Robber—are wrong. Simple as that."

To that, as Alex Sander sauntered into the room:

"That's exactly the posture I'd expect from such as you."

She meant less from Allman than from such as him, from such of his *kind*—"*of pretender to hegemony, of strutting under titles such as 'TJ' Allman, 'The' Junior Allman, no one daring ever, not ever, to call him 'Junior.' What pretense, even if so named by preening parents. So was he reared and so did he regard himself and to such was he fully and thoroughly subscribed,*" thought brooded in Rob, "*and exactly so understood by Alex Sander,*" Rob thought, adulating himself for such thinking while silently reviling himself for such self-righteous thinking, even as the dark whispered to him:

"*What do you know of Alex Sander and of what thoughts and feelings fill her,*" whispered to Rob, he grudgingly grateful to the dark, whispering truth to him, to face him eye-to-eye.

"*How well can you know what another, any other, thinks and feels in their heart of hearts,*" Rob realizing *that* holds true all too well for himself... and for others too, all to well:

"*I understand self-idolatry and self-delusion at least that much... how effectively and how thoroughly we delude ourselves that we are more and more right and more righteous than the other, than any other, far more than we've earned or deserve.*"

Alex Sander addressed the class at large:

"If you cannot deliver an intelligent response... keep your mouths *shut*—and don't expose your ignorances and your stupidities and your... selves," lowering her gaze to Allman's delicate regions... "with sordid theatrics."

With that, Allman reddened ever faintly and quietly retook his seat, almost meekly, stunning the onlookers and still further burnishing Alex Sander's consummate primacy.

She paused to inspect the faces now of *her* audience, at least for this moment no longer Allman's. She didn't care even to wonder if her eyes revealed to them her thoughts of them:

"*So torn is their fealty between Allman's will and mine, they reflect only vacant stares, not able—not daring,*" Alex Sander concluded—"*to judge for themselves even this blanket pronouncement with which I judge them, which should come as no surprise or news to them: that they've got to think and to think clearly—for themselves. That they've got to articulate... for themselves... the justice and the rightness of every single thing they do, think, and feel is a child's lesson, one that should not be—but in all likelihood is—shockingly new and alien to them, not just of this particular spectacle here and now playing out in this classroom but of that evolving in The Rafford and in our social order at large, and the very same for every judgment and choice they encounter and render throughout their vacant, un-considered little lives."*

Rob silently remarked on Alex Sander's own condescension, on her own arrogance, she not shying in the least to so judge and belittle those here and now in her charge, entrusted to her care.

Now, to Rob:

"I suppose you, Rob, are sitting there with mouth shut and voice silenced deliberating on some oh-so-clever rejoinder. And I've no doubt you think to stammer-out your own justice on what I am telling you and the rest of you," eyes scanning the classroom, looking each and every one of them straight in the eye, "how you *should* respond to Allman and to such as Allman: 'your values are just that—*your* values... not right, not wrong, not good, not bad, just *your* values.' To which Allman would undoubtedly argue: 'My values *are* good, *are* right, are the *only* good and the *only* right values possible, how else could I—or *anyone*—judge right from wrong and good from bad except by virtue of *my* values?' And this brings us to the only possible conclusion."

Alex Sander paused, less for theatrics than to allow vacant minds behind vacant stares time to translate sound to word, transmit word to brain, flail at understanding, grope after alternative responses, and finally formulate some likely knee-jerk, unconsidered reply.

But.... no response.

Alex Sander paused for a still longer moment to search her audience, as revulsion crawled through her. Finally:

"So—*what* is the question to settle this point?"

Still no answer.

Allman and Rob had answers, she fully knew, but they refused her, waited on her—*"afraid,"* whispered silently, *"of my small, acrid rejoinders, mine always on the ready to impugn fragile little egos. How simple to instill fear and awe in smallest minds."*

She shuddered under the weight of how simply, how easily, she could instill doubt and trepidation, a half-step shy of abject terror.

She would refuse the two this platform anyway or, rather, would refuse *Allman* this platform, aware that Rob would instantly rise to any bait and to any baiting of Allman's without least effort from her but would, otherwise, cling to silence.

Then the dark whispered a still bleaker thought for this enduring silence from her class, still more shattering:

"What potential lies herein—of power to etch certitudes into these enfeebled, emptied little minds. What potential have I, here and now, to carve into these simple little minds MY thoughts and MY intent, to suborn them to MY manifesto."

Alex Sander wondered if her influence—not her will— on these squalid minds was a match for Allman's and resisted underestimating his hegemony over his contemporaries. She shuddered invisibly at such thought and for a moment drew herself into herself under skulking, corrosive thought:

"I'm here not to bend them to MY will but to bend them to their OWN," shaken by their precarious, perilous shallowness.

She finally broke their frightening silence with acrid voice:

"I shudder at the pliable, vulnerable future being here and now formulated and represented"—words *'sadly'* and *'pathetically'* lingered in silent revulsion—"by you: the blind and vacuous elite."

She stunned them alert suddenly slamming hands on table and bellowing jarring demand:

"WHO IS TO JUDGE?"

She eyed each and every one of her audience, watching them jump at her sudden roaring, searching for meaningful thought behind blank stares—*"keeping silent not for want of reason but for want of command: How would—Allman—expect, demand, they answer."*

She considered this assumption, argued with herself:

"How can I know my contempt is justified?" lamenting only that, just the same, she knew. And to *this* arrogance, her only repose was assuring herself that, even still:

"I don't, not with absolute certainty, think I know it," and small comfort that, even still and with absolute certainty, knowing.

What frightened her more than the silence of the class was Allman's—and Rob's—silence.

"Allman keeps silent to reveal his defectors, to scrutinize the class and to reveal who among them is fully his minion, fully sycophantic, adhering mindlessly to his tenets—and who will betray his tenets and so, him."

And with ambiguous sentiment, strongly suspecting this truth:

"Rob keeps silent to reveal—me."

Then she *screamed* in fabricated display of unbridled rage, to capture not just their attention but their deliberation:

"YOU are to judge! Each and every one of *YOU* must judge—for YOURSELVES!"

Silence was absolute under her glare of revulsion, having to speak the self-evident to these ascendant 'elite.'

She glanced at Allman as he opened mouth to speak, scowled invisibly to think what *he'd* say to this.

"NO."

Allman pronounced the word in becalmed, stentorian voice, taking careful measure of voice and sound to appear reasoned and dispassionate.

"I—am to judge."

Again, the instant's silence was absolute.

Before anyone could react, before even Alex Sander could react, Rob slammed book to table and shot-out with calm certitude every bit as commanding:

"Then we're *all* damned."

Rob scanned the room, revulsion prancing in his eyes at this silence, at this repulsively supine reaction to Allman's proclamation… *"allowed so casually, so easily, so willingly— and of all places, here at The Rafford,"* with palpable loathing.

Allman turned to Rob, about to utter some or other scourge and defilement, was cut-off as Alex Sander interjected:

"All right. All *right*!"

Alex Sander was absolute, definitive command.

"I can see we've reached an impasse, an irrevocable dichotomy which no amount of debate will settle, and so," she paused to scan the classroom, "we'll put it to a vote."

"You two," nod to Allman and to Rob, "have made yourselves clear—so sit *still* and keep your mouths *shut*."

Turning to the remainder:

"So—who should judge right from wrong, good from bad, truth from subterfuge from outright lie: Should we entrust ourselves to the judgment of a select *one* among us?"

Alex Sander waited, stared each student eye-to-eye, her trademark, decreeing participation of each and every one, no shirking *this*.

Stony, non-expression met her.

She watched several of her students furtively glance toward Allman, ever cautious—*"ever afraid,"* she didn't doubt, thought she knew, was sure she knew—and first one, then another, then a small handful of others raised faltering hands.

Under Allman's impassive, vigilant gaze, several more, then near-universal, hands rose in assent.

She watched Rob's reaction to this allegiance, betrayal:

"What's going through his head, now?" she wondered.

She scrutinized Rob, eyes, lips, his every movement:

"Sadness? Regret? Rage? Dread? No—fear," she concluded.

"And likely in that progression, as thoughts pierce him with what, exactly, this portends. But," she saw in his eyes, *"there's no surprise, none at all—and fear not for himself but for…"* and she kept silent, even to herself, just what fear pricked him.

"And with that show of hands, Allman proves his point: He—is to judge. He IS the judge, the one and only true and righteous judge."

189

The implications of the vote shook even her.

Rob studied Alex Sander for what betrayed of her thoughts:

"Sadness? No—despair," then wondered if that was not her reaction but his.

Under Allman's eye, and witnessing the vote and the voters, Rob declaimed:

"This should have been a *secret* ballot. *This* is why we have secret ballots."

To Alex Sander's expression, critical of him for having disrupted the order of her classroom—*"but sympathetic to me, even pitying me, for that avowal"*—Rob wondered if she thought his thoughts:

"Would the vote have gone any differently even so? Do the very walls harbor eyes and ears and whispers with which to witness and betray?"

Rob doubted it would have made any difference at all—*"sycophants imbedded, imprinted, to feel and think and act as their lord and master exacts."*

Alex Sander, finished with them for now, uttered a final decree:

"Remember the result of this little exercise—when you study our next semester's seminar: The Social Economics of 1930's Germany."

To that, Allman spoke, fully assured and ascendant:

"We've got to trust our selected leaders. We've got to trust in their sound and valid judgments. We've got to entrust them and warrant them to the fullest: to judge for our greater and greatest good—anything less devolves into chaos and moral corruption."

Rob remained silent to that provocation:

"He talks Democracy and speaks Autocracy."

Witnessing the fervor in Allman's eyes, Rob was seized by his own whispers in the dark:

"But I'll be damned if that autocracy will be his."

'He' sits on his high pew in vanishing aura with face drawn ever nearer the threshold of that ethereal shadowland,

190

that vermillion borderland between the fading aura and the absolute of the dark, for now held in abeyance just beyond that vanishingly thin veneer of shadowland.

He reels under memory of that unbearable glimpse of that moment before: of skeletal orbs impaled above shadow lips not weeping but screaming, all silent, within their vermillion shadowland.

Now he finds himself irresistibly drawn into that vermillion shadowland, grappled and compelled inward.

It is for him and only for him, this shadowland, and he understands that he is impelled to witness again, still and always again, of that remnant of blinded orbs impaled in skeletal faces above silent, vermillion lips undulating amid wave after wave of shadow-flesh shredded and shorn, with each still somehow clinging, screaming, to skeletal remains of finger, hand, arm, face—and he wonders to where pain flees to leave him here, now, like this, in the face of this, beyond imagining, of a churning, writhing sea of skeletal eyes blindly glaring, indicting through soundless screaming… that, his due.

The shadowland, sheerest borderland suspended between him and the awaiting dark, beckons and cajoles and whines and pleads… and now commands, demands—and who is he to resist such seduction, such command. So again he peers into that vermillion shadowland, to glimpse again of what will—or not—lie in wait for him, and not just for him but for all of the 'other,' as the absolute of the dark lies patiently in wait.

Chapter 26.

Lainy and Rob lived side-by-side, arm in arm, hands interlocked whenever together, whenever possible, vanishingly scant moments passing when they could be and were not—this inevitable once Lainy had extracted Rob from his obsessive misgivings and misapprehension about her and Allman:

"There is *no* 'relationship' between Allman and me. There never was and never will be, not *any* 'relationship' between him and me. None. Ever," definitive finality in breath and eye.

She thought to add: *"Is that what you think of me... that—I—would be with the likes of Allman?"* but thought better than to defile her Ben Rob by diminishing his judgments, *"especially of me, especially if he feels for me even the least of what I feel for him,"* and all silent, *"more than words can say."*

To his look of lingering lament, seeing his need for still more convincing and reassuring, Lainy added:

"Not *ever*," and she gripped him and held him and pressed into him cheek to cheek and breath to breath to so assure and *re*assure him, absolutely and definitively and without smallest shadow of least shadow of doubt, and would as often as he needed, he overwhelmed by urgent need to be just so wholly assured and reassured, she wondering:

"What—at whose hand—had he suffered to have such need."

To Rob's persistent tension she impressed truth *into* him, filled it in him, and at long last he seemed fully convinced and he began to relax, relent, and so, finally, fully allow himself *her*.

The days and the weeks passed—and the King issue saturated ever-more into student life, at every classroom discussion and at every casual exchange, every discourse inevitably and unavoidably drew to King and to his impending expulsion.

"Panther King has failed The Rafford, has corrupted the Rafford standard!" Read one headline—not Lainy's.

And, no:

"Dean Ivry has failed The Rafford students, has refused to update and modernize the Rafford standard to fit the times and to fit those borne outside the paradigm of rarified wealth and ever-escalating privilege and overarching power and control that suffuse, endow, the elite!" So ran another headline, also not Lainy's.

Lainy had made her position patently unmistakable:

"Only *evidence* can conscript us—and *that* is in crying need."

Discourse grew to heated debate. Heated debate morphed to confrontation. Then to threat. Then to imminent, seething violence.

Ever more and ever more stridently, speakers materialized, leapt onto chairs that quickly evolved into tables, then podiums, then rugged, purpose-built platforms. Hands cupped around mouths morphed to megaphones and then to microphones booming through amped-up loudspeakers. Spirited debate transfigured incrementally into ever-more shrill excoriation, then to condemnation, then to damnation, then to call to action—"peaceful, of course," went empty rhetoric, hardly even afterthought.

To the casual observer all this evolved naturally, spontaneously. But to Rob and to Lainy there was enough to lead thoughts to conspiracy:

"Someone's going to a *lot* of trouble to cause… trouble. To *foment*."

Lainy and Rob each thought it, whispering their suspicions, suppositions—always somehow leading to Allman.

"But—*why*? What *for*?"

Answers escaped them both.

"Why would a group as reactionary as Allman's support King? You'd think he'd support the *status quo*, the elitist Ivry. And why so *militant* in favor of King?"

That was the only word either could contrive to describe the slow and inexorable descent of the debate.

Rob and Lainy clung tightly to each other, glad to have each other to hold onto in the face of the all too self-evident, impending violence, and mystified only that no one else remarked on it or even seemed to notice—*"and where, aside me, are the journalists?"*

Lainy and Ben tried to shrug off the notion of conspiracy—between Allman and the media—as a product of their loathing of Allman and his faction, and to that of their own cynicism... "maybe even paranoia." But they dismissed *that* self-doubt after least reflection, and conjectured still more... *"of some veiled complicity between Allman... and Ivry."*

"But... there's more to it, there's got to be more to it."
Each felt it.
"Something... deeper."

They felt their suspicions heightening, congealing, with each passing day, leaving them wondering if they saw conspiracy where only natural evolution might well be at work—"at *play*," each thought, as cat 'playing' with mouse, only... "who is cat and who mouse?"

Then Rob began dreaming nightmare, night after night only more nightmare—but as his nightmares never envisaged threat to Lainy, he dismissed them out of hand. At first.

In the first such dream, King rasped: *"I'm a walking dead man!"*

Another night, another nightmare, King denouncing:
"You—betrayed me!"

Rob strained to apprehend whom King accused, certain King had not accused him, or Lainy, as King's voice echoed slowly to silence in the dark... *"you betrayed me, you, you...."*

Dark dreaming transmogrified into still darker nightmare, King anguishing:
"You, my most-trusted... turned on me!"

In nightmare, King turned to Rob and to Lainy, stared them in the eye, bleating despair:
"To where, to whom, can I turn now?"

Panther King cried out those words to Rob in nightmare, pleading and mewling through whispered laboring under the enormity of such betrayal:

"You... tried and convicted and sentenced me—to living death!" as Rob struggled to fathom: *"Who is King damning? Who? Who?"*

Rob beseeched understanding, certain King was not, could not be, declaiming him... or Lainy, "that just not possible!" he was resolutely certain.

Panther King's voice echoed through Rob's nightmares, never fully nestling into silence even on waking, the look and sound of King resonating through every waking moment in quiet whisper beneath the scream of nightmare.

Rob struggled to understand such a paradox as '*living death,*' envisioning King in the throes of unrelenting, endless *dying*, where only death could halt such affliction and *that* ever imminent, ever ongoing—never consummated.

Nightmare filled Rob, again and still and again, now Rob nightmaring his own voice rasping, bewailing:

"The PEOPLE are the power—who possesses the PEOPLE possesses supremacy, unbreachable preeminence."

Rob submerged in nightmare, mystified:

"For what and to whom is such dream portent?"

He tossed-off his nightmares as the by-product of a restless, agitated mind, not surprising amid such restive times.

One late twilight, Rob woke from reverie to mindfulness finding himself amid a crowd churning into mob, realizing:

"My feet must have taken me here after my evening run," again blaming feet for leading him astray of their own volition, disdainful and contemptuous of him.

Rob craned neck searching for Lainy.

"She'd said she'd be here, said she'd meet me here by the giant Sycamore where we'd first met," where he now stood.

"I hate crowds too," sound of softest, sweetest harmony. "Our brains must be simmering in the same stew," with softest, sweetest touch and warmest, gentlest smile for him.

Her voice was the sun, palpable light, of sweetness touched by something even greater still, of more than he could describe or even imagine, the sound and feel of her infusing him.

Then, announced in commanding voice over booming speakers:

"I am pleased and gratified to announce to you here, now, the full and uncompromising support for King by *the* preeminent TJ ALLMAN and his *Power Fraternity*!"

That to rousing ovation.

Lainy, to Rob:

"You know, I've been asking around: No one knows or admits to knowing *why* Allman's supporting King. They all say the same thing. In fact, they same the *same* thing in the exact *same* words: 'It's the right thing, he stands for the right cause, for the common man—and woman.'"

Her expression betrayed her contempt:

"Everyone I interviewed forced themselves to add 'and woman' as a grudging rigor, as an odious addition compelled on them, to be politic... and exactingly so—to the word and tone—just the kind of taint I'd expect from Allman."

"His stench pervades the crowd," steeped in them both.

Lainy worked up a smile, then, for Rob, whispering sweetness to him:

"They always add that when they realize they're talking to *me*," with sweetest laugh in her eyes and voice for him, holding him closer as he held her close, her eyes laughing with his in symphony.

She laughed her words quietly for Rob, knowing how he loved the sound of her laugh, she never shying from whatever he loved, knowing whenever she smiled her eyes and voice for him, always and only for him, he'd step close and still closer and stare into her eyes and press gentlest lips to her and breathe her in and press close and still closer, she never tiring of that of him, wanting always to feel of him and *so* to always remember him and to never, ever, allow herself to forget—not the memory but the *feel* of him—and she made him *know* that of her.

"And you know," she glanced quickly around her, scanning everyone standing nearby:

"I checked those old photos and thought back to the words I'd heard sprouting out of them, from Allman and from those standing with Allman and from all those with the Power Fraternity, his sycophants, zombies, and…" she paused, drew nearer, breathed intently: "all the speakers here, every one, through their every word and tone, every single one—are *Allman's* people. Every one."

The edge of conspiracy reared as Rob stared into Lainy eyes and whispered her thoughts to her:

"This whole thing, this whole King versus Ivry thing— is *Allman's*."

"Yes," Lainy affirmed, then deliberated, adding:

"And when I broach the subject of *why* Allman had taken up King's cause, beyond their platitudes of 'the right thing to do' and 'for just cause'—they refuse any further comment and refuse any more questioning, as if they're— *afraid*."

Eyes staring onto air, Lainy breathed: "But what, exactly, they're afraid *of*… eludes."

Both understood:

"The Rafford… the Rafford *Fraternity*… has a lot of power behind it, has a lot of *people* behind it, has *Allman* behind it, he the embodiment of The Rafford 'standard.'"

They were quiet then and, finally, looked to each other and smiled for each other and laughed softly, self-consciously, aware of how they sounded even to each other, even to themselves, and were quiet for a long moment as they drifted to other thoughts and to other feelings and then walked, hand in hand as always, not able to tear eyes from each other, as always.

Chapter 27.

Ben Rob stared out the great window overlooking the vast crowd gathered and still gathering below, milling and simmering outside and below him—until the corrosion of DeCeeve's laugh tore through the reverie of what awaited them, awaited *him.*

Then memory subverted even that corrosion....

"I see we've reached a pivotal impasse which no debate can settle. So," Alex Sander scanned the classroom, "put it to a vote."

"You two," to Allman and Rob, "made yourselves perfectly clear, so sit still and keep your mouths shut."

Neither let slip any expression to reveal their thoughts to this directive, contempt from the one, grievance from the other.

Turning to the class, Alex Sander decreed they commit:

"Should we each judge for ourselves—or should one, select, judge for us?"

Alex Sander took her time, stared each of her students in the eye, her signature trademark, demanding participation from each and every one of them, no shirking this, *that* her domain and demand.

The vanishingly few who, even after furtive glances to Allman, had raised hands to vote for individual judgment then, as at some subliminal *something* of Allman, near-uniformly dropped their hands. And then, the rarified few hands remaining upheld wavered, veered to submission, and also dropped their hands.

Allman resurrected, voice quiet and *still* commanding:

"Of *course* we rely on the select among us—*that* is why they are the *select*."

Alex Sander spoke to the clutter on her desk, hardly able to look her students in the eye, visibly shamed of them, of their cowed submission and, now, their silence:

"I've had all I can take of this, you're free to go. You're... *dismissed*," and with a wave of a hand blithely dismissed them all from mind, an unprecedented display where always before she'd have been attentive to their every look and sound and movement and now, simply, dismissive of them.

Without looking up:

"Not you two. You two—stay," master to mongrels.

Everyone knew to whom she spoke, Alex Sander reflecting:

"And they're taken aback, inwardly shocked by my quiet condescension, ordering TJ Allman about, of all people, like chattel—'stay'... master to mongrel dog. 'Rob, of course, deserving just that and nothing more'—according to the vacant little minds of those even now scurrying out the door... 'before she takes into her head to stay—to spay—us all.'"

Alex Sander allowed a small, still smile to steal across her face... *"in quiet display of pleasure plying and suborning 'The Great' Allman"*—wondering absently why his initials were 'TJ' rather than 'TG', *"no doubt reflecting something of his parentage,"* then dismissed that thought too, along with the other students.

Allman and Rob lingered by her desk, she committing all attention to the clutter on her desk, pointedly ignoring the two, waiting out their reaction, expecting, knowing, their reaction.

Rob sat casually on a desk nearby... *"silent and watchful, patient and predictable."*

"And Allman... pacing, of course, measuring footsteps to crack pointedly, to resonate against the wood flooring in flamboyant display of irritation, no, contempt, of me—also all too predictably," sneering hardly-hidden disdain of them both.

Finally, Alex Sander set pen to desk and looked up.

She was young, a student herself—in the post-graduate program of The Rafford... *"the cream of the elite,"* rewarding herself a generous measure of ascendance.

Her sharp, dark eyes punctuated her breathtaking beauty. Her thick, dark hair form-fitted to her head, helmeted centurion craving battle, mane densely flowing to the nape of her neck, enclosing her ears, encasing forehead with hardly a space above delicate brows. Her body was trim and fit, without doubt fit, under barely constrained, casual sensuality.

Now she faced *this*—these two... *"forgetting themselves and their place as sessile mollusks rooted to their castes, subverted by and subservient to their castes."*

Her students were the subjects of her doctoral thesis, *"evolving"*—and she couldn't help but think them *'devolving'*—*"before my eyes,"* thought whipped her as her eyes glazed in reflective pondering of these two base animals, setting herself to study them thoroughly and definitively.

She jarred herself back to the here and now—*"to these two antipodes, lingered here before me, beneath me, at my command"*—absently wondering how, not if, she was set apart from them—*"here and now under MY command, I fully controlling in this here and now, as they calculate how fully, or not, to simper before me, beneath me."*

She wondered about these two, so disparate and still so stultifyingly alike—*"with me, as evolved as any human could be or has ever been, working here to deconstruct them, especially that one, the decisively antagonistic one, that 'TJ' Allman poser, blusterer."*

She smiled absently as she stared up at them, looking down on them, not caring in the least to shield her thoughts from them, even had they the skill to discern her—*"or the boldness,"* another thought behind her smile, *"to penetrate my inner self... I allowing myself to smile down on them and deride their infantile façades and puerile pretentions, especially of the one even now pacing before me, strutting for me. But as for the other, the deathly silent... what to make of him?"*

She wondered momentarily about that other one, *"with deadpan expression and studied silence... an axe to grind? Fear? Worry? No... something else,"* and she smiled a bit more broadly, *"something else entirely, something I can't quite put my finger on—yet,"* remarking at the elusiveness of what lay behind that one's expression and deportment, *"a rare challenge."*

Alex Sander was fully apprised and alerted to Allman's role in the Panther King affair... *"as fully as anyone could be who isn't Allman himself. On first judgment, these two are as different as two people could be... but, no: two sides of the same coin."*

"Somehow, I am removed from this Ben Rob character even more than from Allman," and she momentarily wondered if she should lament that suspicion—*"no, fact"*—and decided: *"No, it's Ben Rob's to lament."*

Speaking to the air, referring to them both:

"You need to behave according to your rank and station as schoolboys in my classroom. You need temper your tender sensitivities, your outraged sensibilities, your prurient machismo," with that she cast a brief, revealing glance below their waists, each in turn, "and leave your puerile wants and obsessions in the gutter where they belong. You need to curb the tantrum of the brat."

She spoke to neither and to both—but both accepted that she spoke to Rob. He was silent, nodded curtly, and stood his ground... *"not having been dismissed,"* she, smiling silently.

Allman, meanwhile, affected a pose of supercilious disdain and contempt of this and of *her* that none could miss.

Alex Sander threw Allman a leer of unmistakable revulsion in turn, her loathing flauntingly displayed.

Rob wondered at her unapologetic candor, exposing herself so heedlessly, baring herself so easily, so needlessly and carelessly, compromising the impartial judgment he thought, knew, she ought have, need have.

Now clearly to Allman, seizing him in her glare:

"And *you* need to better grasp where *you* belong—before you antagonize and inflame and alienate too many of your betters and find that *you* are trampled in the gutter where you may well belong and where you yet may well find yourself."

Rob stood by, listening, observing.

Allman stopped his pacing, turned to confront Alex Sander, stepped close beside her, she still seated at her desk, her eyes now level with his belt, leaving her eyes to peer bellow his belt.

"No, Alex."

Allman spoke softly, addressing her in the familiar, disdainful of *her* place and position.

"It's I who'll trample you and the likes of you, and it's you and the likes of you who yet may well find yourselves in the gutter looking up to *me* with your lips slavering below my belt."

With that he placed a condescending palm squarely to the back of her head, slipped fingers indelicately around to her cheek, then down the front of her neck, pausing just above the parted buttons of her blouse as she sat motionless, eyes lingering below his belt. He bent, then, and caressed her knee, then higher, then still higher.

To his fly, she spoke softly:

"You Ivies think you're so hot," no question to it, her breath edging heavier in indistinct reflection of contempt. Or want.

"You Ivies think you're world shakers, newsmakers, grindhouse takers—but you're just panting after *girl*, good for laughing at and stepping on, too afraid to really confront calm deliberation and reasoned intellect, too limp to handle a real woman."

She glanced up—and saw Allman staring down on her.

Allman lingered his stare on her eyes and lips—*"he fully aware and willful, or fully succumbed to her,"* those *Rob's* wandering thoughts.

Then Allman stared further down, pressing eyes to the curves of her, to where her softness was double-pressed against her blouse, to where the fabric of her blouse fawned on her, stretched ever-thin for her, clung fully taut to her, to where she'd commanded her blouse to open a spare glimpse of her, for him, and for other men, and women too.

Now Allman's stare slipped further down, eyes clinging to her, ensnared by thighs and flouncy little skirt—*"enough and more than enough to ensnare anyone and*

202

everyone," those too, Rob's thoughts, seeing in Allman imaginings of her, his eyes displaying her to him in every trace movement.

Alex Sander watched Allman stare at her—*"so dull, so... common,"* those *her* thoughts—watching him not able to tear eyes from her, from the rise and fall of her, he now captive to intimate dance with her, he feeling himself so intimate, now, with her blouse and her skirt, his eyes dancing closest tango with her, she reddening ever slightly, to see it of him, his sweat glistening, his breath and *he* drawing hard....

She smiled a modest, secret smile up at him—*"no, not secret... feigned and hidden, brazen and unrepentant,"* those *Rob's* thoughts as he watched the pair, *"obscenity posing as challenge of wills, she smiling at the fullness she prided herself in revealing of him, he feeling that, needing that of her."*

Rob watched the spectacle: her cheeks pinking, her breath quickening, her tongue licking trace moisture at her lips in feigned—*"or genuine,"* Rob's fleeting thought—want of him, as she stared at the fullness of him below his belt, Rob feeling wholly betrayed as Allman turned and shot a leer at him with curled snarl on lip in answer to her dismissal of him and of his sensuality and of his influence and power over anyone, over everyone... *"and over her, too,"* Rob thought, wondered.

Then Allman abruptly turned his back and sauntered casually, grandly, out the door—he dismissing *her.*

Alex Sander glared at Allman's back as he ambled away, then regarded Rob, saw him staring her down, then saw him with eyes only for the floor at his feet.

She saw him staring at the floor... *"to hide the betrayal he feels."*

She recognized the look instantly, rage swelling her.

She knew he needed her to feel embarrassed for that consort with Allman but, on regarding him, realized he needed her to feel not embarrassment but *shame.* Instead she felt anger, nearing rage, at his impudent assumptions and infantile standards, at his childish jealousy and adolescent disenchantment—and at her own incipient urgings, betraying her so widely. She could not deny, not to him and not to *herself,* harboring no small trace of all he needed her to feel, of shame and self-depredation for her coarse humanity.

Alex Sander understood that, from conception, such proclivities were thoroughly immanent and prided herself... *"that I've outgrown, risen above, such common expectations and standards,"* fully aware of deluding herself.

Then—she softened, recognized his youthful innocence, simple morality, childlike emotion:

"Disappointed in me for betraying my sex, and more—my essence. What he imagines as my exalted dogma and majestic orthodoxy is more than just his illusion or my defilement. How can he face such unfathomable disillusion, I of all people—held to highest standard and most stringent esteem by his idealism and no fault of mine—forcing him to face such brutality of everyday life, in his face, here and now, like this."

She felt overpowering grief for him... *"and for myself, too, he having corrupted—and I corrupting—his image of idyllic perfection, deception of highest morality, of the highest order."*

She pictured him battling against this transition, could *feel* his struggle—*"suddenly, here and now, thrust in his face, he confronting existential war to retain innocence and... rightness. He battles to remain stolid, even if cloaked and cosseted within his idealized universe, simplest of universes, of simple and glaringly manifest good and bad, of self-evident and unblemished right and wrong, of blazingly clear decency and of its polar opposite, which words like 'indecency' cannot begin to portray, reach its depths. Such is—was—his world, such is the world out of which he'd been suddenly and unalterably disgorged, from which he'd been irretrievably abandoned—by me."*

She mourned her role in this, and lamented that she mourned for herself more than for him, and couldn't even say why.

"He isn't ready to leave his soft, familiar world of simple absolutes and imagined assurances and deluded certitudes, of infantile blacks-and-whites without least shade of grey or even any conception of grey, where everyone wholeheartedly agrees and adheres to his hue of innocence. He

isn't ready for a world of cold and sharp, of harsh and hard, of blurred and dim and dismal, of shaded rites and rules, ruled not by lofty ideals of love and hope but by base passions mired in lust and greed and grasping ambition, contrived less of laudable ambition than of base, self-idolatry. Ours is a jagged, cutting landscape where his had been an illusion of softness and warmth, not of sex but of only the most sincere lovemaking. Our reality is of sensuous become sexual, of soft and pink rendered grotesque indecency and strutting decadence, of innocent caress transformed to rapacious assault, of simple affection yielded up and abandoned to lust and jealousy, of guilt and lament without least remorse, of love succumbed to hate breeding dark and darkest intent."

"He deserves to, needs to, lose his illusions… but not here and not now and not by me. Better to learn gently and kindly, to waken to it only when fully ready or, at least, ready enough. Still, better here and now by me than at some other time or with some other eye set against him, some intimate who might well brandish such awareness with gleeful joy and unalloyed malice. I, at least, am simple truth."

Rob felt all that Alex Sander saw in him, and listed to shame, child caught in act of what he is too old for, too grown-up for… sucking thumb, clinging to blanky, struggling against needful sleep after the always too-long and always too-corrosive day. He felt so much the child, so much the helpless victim of everyday callous and pointless churnings that serve no higher purpose than their own soiled and squalid satisfactions.

"What place I, in such a world?"

Rob observed Alex Sander for one moment more, then smiled sadly down to her, *for* her, realizing: *"She's been forced to abandon her own cosseting world of academic detachment, forced all too near-ago, and is still struggling to grapple and recover."*

Rob gathered his books and sulked slowly away.

"She judges my world by hers…" and felt bereft for her, pitying her the far distant descent of her world.

Rob wondered what, of Allman, Alex Sander had yielded to… and what she'd yielded up. He raged to be held at the fringe of it, just beyond understanding it, even within easy reach of it, and still wondering what, exactly, '*it*' could be, of weakness and of surrender.

Ambivalence toward Allman bewildered Rob, that Allman had somehow wrested *something* today, and deliberated on how he was connected to—disconnected from—Allman, and what and how, exactly, Allman had won.

"He is, in one sense, a fervent rival, a bitterest antagonist, even a mortal enemy. And in another, maybe more real sense, he is—my guide."

Rob pondered miserably:

"There is in him some trace of... something, a sort of integrity... behind his twisted self-adulation, a sort of... honor, he bowing to the age-old tenet of survival—not of who is fit but of who possesses the guile to be most fit. His is a simple canon, the simplest: Those who can, lead. Those who can't must, simply, submit and follow... and genuflect."

Rob contemplated this judgment, struggled to discern:

"Is my corrosive judgment of Allman tainted, risen simply of myself, of my own myopic, selfish interests? Or is my new-found, measured judgment—respect—genuinely risen out of objective truth and plain, simple reality? Or am I, simply like the rest, fallen to his mesmerizing taint?"

He wondered how to know the difference and who could judge the difference, who can step outside his—or her—shades of self-interest.

"Can simple truth rise of self-adulation when, in truth, we lie most effectively to ourselves?"

"Can we believe most fervently—while totally blind to the justice of believing the opposite?"

"And—as for a horrifically forlorn brother—how can I not feel compassion and brotherhood for Allman, wandered so far down the wrong path and not least aware how far he'd strayed, likely irretrievably?"

Rob could only lament, and mourn.

'He' is seated on his high pew bathed in failing aura, braced against what awaits. He leans forward and again

traverses eyes and face into that ethereal shadowland, that vermillion borderland, that threshold separating the failing aura and the absolute of the dark waiting just beyond.

Sound, as of pounding surf, and stench, as of rancid flesh, assault him and he cautiously opens eyes and squints out... over a vast sea of roiling, undulating, blinded orbs imbedded above vermillion lips impaled within skeletal faces silently screaming in wave upon wave of overarching need.

The orbs are suffused of cries and wails, all silent, a sea of shrieking, soundless outcry amid the relentless ebb and flow of their number, like pounding surf, pulling away, flowing nearer, away, steadily nearer, an undulating sea of shade on shade within shadow on shadow of vast weepings and prayers, clawing to have and to have at, drawing ever nearer, pulling timorously back, then still nearer, a sea woven of dread more than fear only barely, tenuously, holding back before its full onrush. It flows nearer, then back, then still nearer, abject fear in the form of boiling sea moldering beneath unyielding defiance, slowly nearer, backing away, and then with gathered strength in raging despair urged forward still, then fallen back a bit, just a bit, in wave on wave of dread and grudge and hate despising and loathing, pulling minutely back and then drawing near and nearer and still nearer, raging nearer under ever rising weeping and screaming, he struggling to apprehend any least intimation of "Why?" and "Why ME?"

Chapter 28.

Dawn eased into the dark, gently prodding Lainy and Rob awake. Grudgingly, after prolonging their resistance, they slipped apart and lay quietly lingering in each other's eyes and lips against the abrasions of another onrush of day, patience even now stretched thin waiting on the re-emergence of the dark, so to settle back to here, to this.

They woke before they needed to wake so to hold each other and whisper, always more of each other to discover.

Lainy talked her politics, of the elite and of their disdain and contempt for any and every other. Rob rose to her whispers with heightening words in escalating revulsion:

"What kind of society have we got—where people idolize themselves flaunting their gold-plated Lamborghinis and their million dollar motor homes and their multimillion dollar estates while passersby laud and celebrate and adulate them… for their *decadence*. How could such of the depraved dissolute stare into the mirror and look themselves in the eye and preen in their vanity while vast numbers of ordinary workers are paid less than living wages and they and their families struggle to barely survive and too many cannot even house and feed and educate themselves and their children. And all that even as self-righteous elitists wallow in smug, self-righteous hypocrisy professing themselves Goodness-fearing."

"What kind of society have we got where so many of our leaders fervidly scream and wail and despise and condemn the vanishingly few who campaign on behalf of the poor and the old and the powerless… who have no one to defend them or campaign for them? And all that even as elitists adulate and idolize and genuflect to themselves and each other while christening themselves Goodness-fearing."

"These elitists scream-out 'Liberty!' as reason and cause to roll back gun control—knowing full well *they* are not targets on *their* streets or in *their* children's classrooms. They scream 'drill baby drill'—knowing full well *they* won't suffer the ravages of the dirty air and the dirty water in *their* neighborhoods. They defile health insurance reform and call it 'healthcare' reform—knowing full well *they* don't need to worry about health insurance or healthcare, able to buy whatever care they care to have whenever and however they care to have it. They squander vast fortunes—pocket change to them—lobbying unendingly to suborn duly passed laws, holding the people hostage because the laws benefit not them but people in need."

"The elite despise and deride and defile and decry as 'socialism' any program helping the poor and the old and the long suffering—and do it *in the name of Goodness*! Such heights of arrogance and hubris and self-idolatry reach beyond mortal hypocrisy into blasphemy and sacrilege as they preen and strut in pretense and fraud of being Goodness-fearing!"

Rob struggled to contain consuming rage:

"The face of evil masquerades as piety, its rapacious greed cloaked as Goodness-fearing, its unconstrained and unashamed, grasping covetousness and self-idolatry haunts and depredates in the name of 'free enterprise' and in the name of *Goodness*! The hypocrisy and blasphemy of the elite stalk and hunt down and rapaciously slaughter the defenseless in the name of Goodness and Righteousness!"

Lainy waited, knowing he needed to exhaust this fount of himself, and when finally spent she enfolded him and held him and whispered quietude and soothed his passion and eased his outrage, even if only in the slightest, gruesome reality otherwise unperturbed:

"Not since Jeremiah has there been such greed and conceit and blindness and hypocrisy, and against it *we* do all we can, what so-little we can," Lainy whispered fervently as she held him and embraced him, not hearing his thought:

"All we can... and all we will," as other whispers, silent and brooding, simmered in the dark, hovered in the recesses... *"of my authentically righteous rage."*

And within each, for the other: *"Under his fervent whisper and softest touch, how could I not wholly love him?"*

and: *"Under her passion and compassion, how could I not fully love her?"*

So they clung to each other and soothed each other and resolved to mend the world until, finally, they smiled and laughed at their own arrogance and grace.

They rose and dressed and walked to class hand in hand, arm in arm, touching in small ways and all ways possible, then Rob raised the specter of Allman again, to glimpse of Lainy:

Rob began: "Allman wants me to undergo trial for the Power Fraternity..." to this simple statement he felt Lainy tense, felt her grip tighten on him, belying her silence, revealing her, even before he finished with... "tonight."

He turned eyes to watch her, to see the sun in her, all light and warmth in her—and the dark, too, of vast unknowns filling her. But under his words he could no longer feel the light but only the dark in her, only the grim, the dread, the fear.

"Ben, no... please—*no*," deepest intensity in quiet whisper.

Her voice revealed her, of what he'd never felt of her, never this of her. He froze to the sound of her.

She stopped him in his tracks, turned him to face her fully, and Rob felt the dread and fear in her, and felt in himself a depth of pain and misery in *her* beyond anything he could possibly feel for himself.

She spoke with a voice he'd never felt in her before:

"Ben." So much in the breath of a word.

She paused to gather her thoughts and words to precisely penetrate him, to fully convey herself into him:

"Ben, Allman's—dangerous."

Not enough:

"Ben...."

She turned his face to hers, to fully look her in the eye, and placed gentle hands on his cheeks to force him to see her and to hear her, so to fill him with her fear:

"Allman's more than just dangerous, he's..." searching for the right word, the exact word... "a *sociopath*."

She struggled to reach into him, to force *understanding* into him, but his reply spoke softly, through his own struggle to wrest reason out of her passion:

"I can't hide and cower from the likes of Allman. I've got to confront such... *things*... as Allman. I've got to confront and resist his kind and their simple, common brutalities. He can't hurt me, not *really*. He can't afford to. He risks too much bringing that kind of focus on himself with predation of an outsider. He can't do me real *harm*."

Lainy spoke through the edge of panic:

"Allman's not just dangerous—he's... *irrational*. He is not of sound mind. He is a feral, rapacious *minion* thirsting for blood, anyone's, everyone's, anything and everything to get his way—and he's got every vantage to fully get his way and to fully get away with it untouched, unblemished, and appearing righteous and pristine."

Neither spoke for long moments. They stood breath to breath, gazing into eyes, riveted by eyes and, slowly, eyes settled shut and lips drew near and they calmed and held each other and settled into each other to think, to feel, to fathom their way through this, such impasse singular, and they'd see each other through this too. Somehow.

"Ben—there've been stories. I don't know how true or if at all, if only just talk—about things he's done, things he's done to people, things he's done that are... inhumanly *horrifying*."

"This, from a woman who doesn't frighten," implanted itself in Rob more deeply than any dread ever had or could.

Lainy didn't know what other words to use, 'horrifying' and 'minion,' as Lucifer incarnate, were all that came to mind to convey some smallest sense of who, of *what*, Allman is, is capable of.

Lainy continued:

"Sometimes Allman and I would talk—just *talk*..." emphasized to subvert any trace residue of doubt or jealousy still lingering in Rob... "and whenever talk drifted to you, something comes over him, something in him changes, in his voice, in his *eyes*! And he never says your name, never least hints it's *you* that occupies him, obsesses... possesses... him,

211

thoroughly saturates him. I can't put my finger on it—like he sees you as some kind of *existential* threat, a preternatural rival he can't allow in his... *dominion....*"

That last word lingered, to envisage a world rigidly subverted to his sway, and with that word she flourished her hand in a sweeping gesture that encompassed the entire spectrum of time and place, beyond anything and everything of The Rafford, beyond existence itself.

Rob's eyes riveted on Lainy's, an ice-cold look in his eyes, edged with lunatic hate and rage... and she understood, and pressed hands firmly to his cheeks and glared into his eyes and so assured and reassured him, still and again and always again:

"Ben! You *know*... there's never been *anything* between Allman and me. Never! *Anything!*" and in resigned certitude: "How could there be, you know that could never be, not ever," and in final conviction: "You *know* me—you *know* it of me."

She knew his weakness, *this* his weakness... anything to do with her was his weakness, especially this and such as this—not with the likes of *Allman*. She might be close, even intimate, with any one... but not ever with Allman or with the likes of Allman. And she'd shield him and protect him and cosset him in every way and all ways... for him to have no doubt *at all* of her, of who and what she is, and never, not ever, with the likes of Allman.

She saw him settle, calm, and only then continued:

"You know—*know*—I loathe Allman, detest him with all my heart. And don't tell me 'thou protests too much' because you know me and so *know* its truth. And you know it of me not out of some misplaced hurt but out of understanding *him*, out of understanding the who and the what of him, of *it*— and never *that* of me."

Lainy made clear her perception of Allman as a *thing*—an odious minion, to abhor, to wholly revile.

Now in bland, conversational tones, in a narrative of the simple past, she spoke quietly:

"When I'd first met Allman, I don't know why but I thought I—loved—him. Or rather, that I could. But the very moment after that first moment—I *understood* him."

She took a quick breath to finish her words before he'd a chance to misapprehend, and calmly continued:

"I understood that what I'd first mistaken in him as confidence, as self-assurance, as power exuding of him, was in fact a vast arrogance and impudence, an immeasurably callous disregard, a boundless, condescending contempt and repugnance and disdain of all lesser beings—and *everyone* is a lesser being to him."

At his look, she forged on:

"I *love* those qualities—of confidence, of will, of self-control—and thought I saw them in him. But instantly, with him, I knew I was wrong, just plain wrong. And just as instantly—with *you*—I knew I was right, and knowing you only confirmed unshakably that I am right."

"He's less than nothing to me and, except for that very first instant of self-delusion, he's always been beneath even my contempt. And know *this*: He'll do anything he can to get at you, to undermine you, to hurt you—to destroy you—any and every way he can, even sewing seeds against us, against me."

To that she feverishly added:

"And that's something I can *never* let happen, would do anything and everything in my power to stop from happening."

She looked at him again:

"And I know—*know*—you feel the same for me."

Rob took her in his arms and held her close and breathed of her and prayed to never let her go. But even in the midst of that hold he was edged with doubt, derived of the confidence he did not have… *"of which she is fully aware and despite which, or because of which she—maybe—loves me."*

She felt it in him, in his touch and in his eyes and in his breath, and understood:

"In what can he believe—in me? And if not in me in whom, in what, can he believe—in anything, ever? Better he trust even in me than in—nothing. I am at least as good to trust as nothing, and time will prove me more, infinitely more."

She vowed it and affirmed it and would make him *know* it without any smallest trace of doubt.

They walked, then, in silence, and each treasured every moment of silence between them.

As they strolled, thought churned him:

"To spend our lives like this, hand in hand, arm in arm, always together—is that so much to want, too much to ask?"

He wondered it, understood the impossibility of it, and wondered if that should fade him or strengthen him, embitter him or fill him with joy beyond any he could know—*"of the enormities beyond my simple want, need, of her hand in mine, and this here and this now is infinite Blessing just in itself."*

Finally, she spoke—in cold, harsh whisper. She looked him in the eye, commanded his absolute attention:

"Please, Ben, for *me*, Ben—talk to Plesant, before...."

She couldn't finish the thought and simply added: "Ask him about John. Make him *show* you John. Please—for me."

With that she abruptly turned and walked away. School work and class work called to her and she turned and walked away... head bent, eyes to ground, shoulders hunched, hands buried deep in pockets, for least respite from dread for her Rob.

Of course he'd talk to Plesant. Of course he'd make Plesant show him:

"She asks, I do, of course I do, just as she asks, would do anything, everything, just as she asks," and he chilled at her power over him.

"What else, nothing else, everything else—for her."

Then he walked off... head bent, eyes to ground, shoulders hunched, hands buried deep in pockets.

Chapter 29.

Rob stood in the dark of the back room within the heights of the Liberty Spire, contemplating the massive crowd gathered and ever-gathering below, as DeCeeve burst onto silence, corrupting the dark, crowing over all he was:

"Don't you worry, Rob. You stick with me and I'll take care of you, I'll take good care of you. Don't you worry, Rob—I'll take *good* care of you."

Threat permeated the sound of his words, and again Rob found himself drifting in memory….

Long past twilight found Rob wandering the footpaths of The Rafford, hour on hour amid dim streetlamps and shaded windows and starless, moonless murk of cloud. He ambled as his feet took him, taking him where they willed him—this time, as at many times, to the student center.

As always, especially of late, someone or other was standing on a table reviling the establishment in general and Dean Ivry in particular. The man stood on a makeshift platform high before a gathered crowd. That it was now well past midnight was meaningless at The Rafford, *"as at any university campus,"* Rob imagined, having experienced only the one other, *"the lesser,"* as he imagined, knew, as many of those here thought of those there.

The speaker was dressed in what he imagined was 'ordinary' garb, *"working-man's—and woman's—garb,"* he corrected himself, *"to render himself 'of the people,' and 'of the working classes' and not of the elite, as those gathered here, in fact, are—to remind them where their allegiance lies, should lie, so to lend legitimacy and authority and sincerity and truth to his words of support for Panther King, show being so much more than substance, tone and voice so much more than word and meaning,"* he lamented, knew, certain without doubt no matter the contradictions, no matter the self-righteous, supercilious denials of those in these hordes.

"The book IS judged by its cover and the men—and women—ARE judged by their clothes, and by their clothiers."

He wondered how, if, it could be otherwise—*"the image we see and the tone we hear being so much more than what is and, so, who cares what is."*

The 'common-man' persona underscored the striking contrast of the speaker from his audience and, Rob noticed, even those common-garb clothes were designer labels—*"to highlight not their difference but their commonality,"* Rob understood, *"to demonstrate what little differentiates them from him and how just as easily they could be him, with his attitudes, and so should feel solidarity with him. The incongruity is no doubt lost to the hordes gathering across The Rafford these days."*

Rob saw through the pretense—*"just another 'show,' just a photo-op with which, by which, to seduce and enthrall and subvert his audience,"* and again Rob wondered how much is real and how much just imagined, their thoughts of the speaker, his of them, that they could so easily and so readily be suborn.

The speaker lashed out at the audience, at those standing before him right then, right there in front of him:

"Arm-chair bigots—*that* is what you are! Knowing it or not, admitting it or not, to *yourselves*, that... is... what... you... *are!*"

He ended with an uplifted gaze to Heaven—*"for Heaven to witness the scintillating, self-evident truth, so help him Goodness,"* Rob sneered, all silent at art and artifice, *"he scintillating right here, right now, as the personification of Goodness herself standing here, right in front of us, in the guise of this man."*

The speaker stood tall above the crowd lashing out electrically against... "the casual and subtle and thoughtless, mindless, expressions of elitism and oppression on display every day, everywhere—the most corrosive and dangerous of all: your 'arm-chair bigotry.' You know *exactly* what I mean— the kind of bigotry that's so subtle, so subliminal, that its *absence* is blindly, unthinkingly assumed, taken for granted, accepted as not bigotry at all, not in the least, as you vehemently protest: 'Not I!'"

He scanned his audience piercing each and every one with an accusatory eye, to resurrect the long-dead or deep-buried notion that they not only could be but in fact *are* 'arm-chair bigots,' the most dangerous, the most corrupted and corrupting, the most corrosive of all.

"You sit in your fine homes listening to your fine stereos and tune-in to your fine TVs and you all know, just *know*, how wonderful it is for the common, ordinary folk—all those 'other' folk—to be allowed to shine your shoes and weed your gardens and drive your cars and cook your food and serve your hors d'oeuvre and collect your garbage and fill your factory floors and *service* your fine CEOs and business owners and Congressmen and Congresswomen with anything and everything they got to service you *with*—and you think to yourself: 'How wonderful for all you common folk that you got such fine people as us and ours running the world for you, cause thanks to all us fine people you ordinary folk got jobs and can work—and work—and *work*!'"

Pause, glare every one in the eye, continue:

"And those great people, those great leaders of yours… they take all that we ordinary folk can give, and they take and they take and they keep *on* taking, more than we ordinary folk can possibly give, and those fine folk then go and tell us and sell us: 'ohhh how lucky you all are that you got such fine people as *us* leading you, making *our* country great, fixing it so *you* don't live in no third world backwater where you can lie in the streets and die in the streets… of disease, of starvation, of greed and shame and hate! It's *we* who keep *you*, all you ordinary folk, from those mean streets!' THAT is what you and yours tell us and sell us and for which we sell our *souls*!"

Again the speaker assumed the art-house pose, knowing and wise, piercing every eye in the crowd:

"But," he continued smoothly, solemnly, "where they *really* get us—is in our *schools*!"

Rob noticed the shift—*"and the power in that shift."*

He glanced around, scanned the audience, to see if others in the audience, any others, noticed that shift.

"Now it's 'they' who are out to get 'us', out to keep 'us' down. He, now, is one of 'us' and 'we,' now, are not 'them,' not one of 'them.' Not anymore."

The speaker pressed on... *"he, now, in solidarity with his audience, now he and 'we' are comrades-in-arms, fighting the good fight together."*

The speaker proclaimed to his newly minted acolytes:

"That is where and when they get us—while we're young, while we're innocent, while we don't know any better, while we still trust and still believe that... 'if we work hard enough, tirelessly and to the bone, we *can* move ahead and we *can* get more and we can *be* more!'"

He eyed his audience with consummate artistry, and continued:

"They put down our simple speech and our modest values and our forlorn hopes—and our *minds*! And our *lives*! And even when they're not saying it they're still *saying* it: 'Remember your place! Remember where you live and how you live 'cause that's the only way you *ever* gonna live!' And they don't never tell us: 'Cause that's the only way we ever gonna *let* you live!" Rob heard and understood the speaker's cantillation and slang, *"and now we are rendered 'of the common people,'"* in mirthless derision.

As the speaker paused, Rob remarked at his descent into the vernacular... *"into a more down-market speech, in consummate command of his audience, in progressive subversion of his audience—probably having learned his art here at The Rafford,"* and Rob smiled secret certitude of his commonality with the speaker, *"same goals, but his strategy is... sure to fail."*

The speaker cried out:

"But it's all different, makes all the difference—if your children go to the right schools, meet the right people, learn to *bend over* low enough at the right time to the right people!"

"And too soon we know that mama, dear mama, is *not* lying when she tells us to forget about getting up in the world, forget about getting somewhere in the world, forget about getting somewhere better and more righteous than just work and more work—and fear and shame and more of the *same*! She's not lying… she's just wrong. Dead wrong."

In quietude, now:

"We *can* be more—but she don't know it 'cause she's been pushed down and tramped down and crushed down *too long*."

The speaker's eyes pierced the crowd:

"We *can* live better, we *can* do better—and by Goodness we *will*! We'll damn well *get* our share of those same opportunities, of those same quality schools, of those same high-flying jobs that *they* got! And we start *right here, right now*—with Panther King and Dean Ivry! Who the *hell* says King's failing The Rafford when it's The Rafford—*Dean Ivry!*—failing *King*! And Ivry's failing King 'cause King's *ideas* are different and 'cause *King* is different! The Rafford—*Dean Ivry*—is pushing King down and pushing King out, all fired-up to *destroy* King—for daring to question Ivry and his values and his authority and his power and his *legitimacy*!"

The speaker lowered his tone to conspiratorial whisper:

"And anyone who says different is *not with us*. And anyone who's not with us is *against* us. And anyone who's against us is the *enemy*. We deserve our fair share and make no mistake: We are fighting not just for our fair share but for our very *lives* and for the lives of our *children* and *their* children!"

Rob scanned the audience, saw only blank stare and blank thought in answer to the words. He looked again, and vaguely wondered why it was that so many in the audience looked… familiar. Then he spotted the man staring at him.

The man was tall and lithe, dressed in the same 'workman' masquerade—pretense—as the speaker. The man stared at Rob and, seeing Rob notice him, pressed lips together and, with the slightest nod, signaled he'd been observing Rob all along.

The man then turned to the speaker and in loud voice: "Right on, brother. Right *on*!" with a sprinkling of other voices scattered through the crowd repeating the mantra… "right on, *brother*!"

The speaker continued, re-energized:

"I'm not talking the arm-chair bigotry of race of the 50's and 60's, I'm talking *today's* bigotry, something worse, a *lot* worse, the *worst of all*—'cause it cuts us off from each other and it cuts us off from our *selves*! Today's bigotry cuts right through us 'cause they've got *us* believing: We're not smart enough! We don't know enough! We're just not *good* enough to be… to *ever* be, to ever *hope* to be… the equal of the elite. Who are we even to imagine or pretend we *can* be?"

And in hushed intensity:

"Who are we even to *pray* to be."

The speaker paused, scanned his audience, Rob wondering what he was searching for.

"Looking for approval? Not from THIS audience. Looking for understanding? Not form THIS audience. This audience adulates itself, only THEY are the best and the brightest."

Rob shuddered at the thought:

"THIS—the best and brightest?"

A shiver ran through him, at such image.

"So they think, so they adulate themselves into thinking, drenched and entrenched in their self-idolizing mantras. The thought of them having an 'open-mind' is so wildly fantastic it's beyond imagining."

The speaker continued working the crowd:

"These 'arm-chair bigots' fully believe, are fully and absolutely convinced, they got what they got and are where they are plainly and simply by their own effort and their own talent and their own will and by their fully deserved, Goodness-given grace—and if we want what they got we damn well better earn it and we damn well better *deserve* it! 'This is *America!*' they tell us!"

Sprinkling of tepid approbation.

"And these 'arm-chair bigots' talk down to us and pontificate to us: 'Don't whine to *me* that you're undereducated and underpaid and underappreciated!' And these 'arm-chair bigots' sneer down on us and dismiss us in their self-idolatry: 'Don't whimper at *me* that you're poor and hungry and cold— go tell your mommas and go tell your daddies to spend their money on schools and books and training, not on booze and horses and whores!'"

"These 'arm-chair bigots' will swear to you: 'It's a free country—don't damn *me* if *you* can't or won't work harder or better or smarter than you do! Don't you lash out at *me* if *you* are too this or too that or too anything and everything to raise yourselves up!' That's what these arm-chair-bigots tell us and that's what these arm-chair-bigots want us to believe and to believe *without question*!"

The speaker abruptly sank into deafening silence, and not a whisper from the audience. Rob couldn't tell if the speaker was pleased or incensed at this unnerving silence.

Rob wondered what of portent is held in such silence.

The audience suddenly jolted as the speaker *screamed*:

"*That's* what arm-chair-bigots tell us! That's what arm-chair bigots want us to think and *believe*—to believe deep-down that they're right, that we *are* too this and we *are* too that and we *are* too anything and too everything to deserve any more or any better!"

Then in tiny whisper, willing the audience to crane neck:

"And it's so easy, so damn easy, to say it and think it and *believe* it. And it's so profoundly treacherous because it's so profoundly insidious—you could say it and think it and believe it so comfortably, so naturally—so righteously."

Rarified outcry of 'right on, brother.'

"Those arm-chair-bigots corrode us and corrupt us to the very core of who and what we are. Opportunity? Yeah, we got that—opportunity to be cold and hungry and dirt-poor all our lives without least hope of lifting ourselves up and out of who and what and where we are and are made to be and are born to be—by *their* hand. And make no mistake: Those of us who do 'make it' do so only by the patronage and whim of their slaveholders and bondholders and executive pimps and 'mentors.' We live in the land of opportunity—opportunity for us to be undereducated and underpaid and reminded that we're remanded to ever being helpless and hopeless and crushed all our lives. And *they* got opportunity—to take ours from us!"

A scant smattering of applause, limp and feeble.

"Sure we're free to work, if we can find a job—but that job won't feed and clothe and educate us or our children! Sure we're free to work… and work and work more and work harder and still and always harder, but… for what? For more of nothing and for more of the same? They call it work but I call it what it *is*: theft—of the hours of our days, of the years of our lives, of all our *lives*! For generation on generation we lost our days and our years and our *lives* working and slaving—and now we're losing our *hope*! And when *that's* gone all we're left is the *fight*!"

He paused half-a-moment, glared down on his audience:

"America—the land of opportunity? Sure it is—for the rich to get richer and for the poor to get poorer and to lose the little and the nothing we've got! But our privations and our sufferings are drawing ever nearer their final end. Soon and not-soon-enough the whole system will come crashing down, buckling and collapsing under the weight of *their* greed and *their* grasping and *their* oppression. And they, all of they-the-elite, will fall farthest and hardest and *we* won't be there to work for them and to slave for them and to bend over for them and to catch them or cushion them as they fall because *that* is what they've reaped and *that* is their righteous reward! Their elitism and their repression stalk *them* closest and hardest of all!"

Rob scanned the audience through limp and distant scattering of applause and again wondered how it could be, why it should be, that so many in the audience seemed… familiar. Then he caught sight of that man who'd been studying him, edging near.

The speaker started up again:

"And they cut us down by calling us not poor but 'deprived,' not powerless but 'victimized,' not garbage-men but 'sanitation engineers.' As if re-naming us fixes us—and they pat themselves and each other on the back and adulate themselves and each other and think themselves grand and lofty as they convince themselves and each other that *that* makes us believe we are 'accepted' and so—if we work hard and harder and still and always *harder* till we work our lives and hopes away—we will, someday, 'make it.' But the pay is the same and the hours are the same and the *dead ends* are all the same, just and always... exactly... the *same*!"

Distant hoot of 'right on, brother' near-lost in silence.

"So how do we win our share—our *due*? By taking up and accommodating the elitist deception? Look out, brothers and sisters! We can learn to talk and act and think the same—but we cannot, we *must* not, ever let ourselves *be* the same! Too many people like us, people just like us, who manage to get close to that elitist dream, allow themselves to get sucked-in by their new-found, hard-won mirage of wealth and power and lose themselves in arrogance. And cause they don't want to lose all they've managed to scrounge—they *flaunt* it... but keeping themselves 'in' means keeping the rest of us *out*! The slaves think themselves masters—but they're still *slaves*! They *think* 'now we're of the elite!'—but they'll never *be* the elite. They're a pretense, an illusion, a *self-delusion*, for display purposes *only*—and even that only for such place and time as the *real* elite allow us!"

Silence.

"And to that I say: Don't let the seduction of wealth and place and power grip us and rip us from who we are and where we're from! You *must not* let them tear us apart... less from each other than from our *selves*!"

The speaker again scanned his audience, then:

"It's only by the power of mind, of our own *will*, that we can prevent ourselves from betraying our people and our cause and our *selves*—even if that means some of us will lose that illusion of wealth and place and power. We've got to plunge into the inferno of our own *selves* and rage inside our *selves*—so to willingly and zealously sacrifice our *selves* if we're ever to free our *selves* and so our *people*. Only so can we ever create a society that's truly whole and truly healed—one with *real* justice and *real* equality... for *every* one!"

To a smattering of applause, he scanned his audience again, then proclaimed:

"It's *you*, all of *you*, who stand to lose most—because none of *you* know how much wealth and power you have—and how much you *don't*, how much is only the crumbs that the *real* elite condescend to begrudge you. And those crumbs hang by a finest thread should you, any of you, least offend your masters and overlords. Look carefully behind you and aside you and you'll find the whips and clubs and chains of *your* overlords upraised, poised and ready to strike *you* down!"

Scattered applause, sparse and tentative and hesitant, worse than no applause, rose from those few familiar faces in the crowd—and suddenly Rob realized why they looked familiar:

"They're from The Power Fraternity!"

Realization stunned.

"Why are they here? Why are they applauding this, applauding him? To what end?"

They were applauding, but their applause was small and scattered, hollow and distant, and Rob wondered:

"Maybe that's why they're here, to render faint praise, backhanded praise, to render the speaker and his words tepid support that'll translate into wholly unwelcome."

Still, Rob wondered why they should be here at all—*"to what end?"*

He deliberated:

"They're the ones with the wealth and power—or the semblance, the facsimile, of it. Why should they make a show, even a weak, backhanded show, of supporting these revolutionary wannabe's? Or rather, why should they be directed, commanded, to appear here and to applaud their scant approval here, now—for this?"

He considered: *"For still more of that semblance of wealth and power?"*

Rob wondered just what was really happening here, then noticed that man again—right beside him now, turned and facing him now, trying to steal his attention, staring him in the eye.

Of some motive he couldn't fathom, stirring deep in him, Rob turned eyes up to the speaker on the table and began to applaud, then whistle, then hoot and yell extravagant solidarity and approval. He applauded still more vigorously, with still louder shouts and raves of approval and ascent, and soon—a few others in the audience joined in, then a few more,

224

then still more until a riot of applause and approval rained down on the speaker, whose face showed visible relief as he scanned the audience with an approving eye—*"and assuming the image of righteous redemption."*

Rob closed his eyes sensing *something*, a feel to the air of *something* engendered here, now and only *now*, finally, getting underway. He struggled to fathom that *sense* and where it originated, then realized its font:

"It's in... me."

Rob had no idea how or why or why 'me' or what 'it' is, nor what to do about such sensation... as a cauldron simmering, ready to boil over, of something imminently readying, but—*"what? For what?"*

Then he realized:

"That... is why I'm applauding," as if that answered anything.

Palms uplifted in air, Rob suddenly held them motionless and... stopped.

Rob stood motionless, reached with every sense for that *something* stirring in him, something *needing* in him, of him—with no idea what or why.

Rob suddenly realized the man standing beside him, trying to look him in the eye, was speaking.

From far away, Rob wakened to that other's voice speaking to him:

"Hey man, you there? You okay? You together, man?"

Rob turned to the man and nodded a curt *'sure, I'm fine,'* wondering how long the other had been speaking, trying to reach him, to look him in the eye, as Rob's attention was gripped by... *something*.

"How come you're staring into space like that? How come you held up on your clapping like that?"

Rob clung to silence, shrugged 'who knows?'

The man's eyes reflected a mix of anger and esteem:

"*You* got the people going here, man! If not for you and my man up there," nodding to the speaker, still on the table, still wallowing in noisy approval and applause, "would be starin' at a crowd of dead and nothin'. *You* roused 'em, man.

225

You turned shit to gold—so how come you just stopped your clapping?"

The man eyed Rob as at some laboratory curiosity, as at some contradictory impossibility.

Rob reflected a moment, whether to or not to engage the man, and finally shrugged shoulders and replied, looking his interrogator straight in the eye, wondering why the man looked so familiar:

"I was applauding the *show*."

Rob wondered if the man could, or not, understand the implication, decided not, and elaborated:

"The performance was high art, a sure-fire gold-medal winner for performance art." Then another shrug expressed 'well, you asked,' with the codicil: 'don't ask if you don't want the answer.'

The man looked stricken, then scowled genuine hurt.

"Don't, my man—don't talk like that! Didn't you hear the man? Didn't you *listen*? You're no empty-headed son-of-a-don, are you man? Or are you? Didn't you listen to his words, hear his *meaning*?"

Rob concealed rising irritation, anger, and clung to silence, why provoke needlessly, then wondered:

"Provoke—what?"

Rob replied:

"I listened all right. I heard all right. And it's all bullshit, it's all a crock."

With that Rob shrugged shoulders again, to say: 'well, you asked.'

Rob turned away half-expecting a blow to the back of his head: *"People don't like being told that their highest, most righteous gospel truths are a crock, especially when they are and when they know they are."*

Rob deliberated for a fleeting instant, wondered if he was being fair, decided he was, and strolled leisurely away, *"let him strike me down, see if I care."*

The man stared at Rob's back long moments after Rob had walked out of sight and, suddenly, came alive. The man flew down the path chasing after Rob, muttering to himself:

"Damn—'*who* is the enemy?'"

He stopped dead in his tracks, thought pounding:

"Who the hell *is* the enemy?"

Then he redoubled his effort to catch up with his defiant critic.

The man wondered it as never before. Once so complacently sure that he knew exactly who and what and when and where his enemies were, now… didn't. *So* he came to life sprinting headlong down the path after the man who had, simply, turned his back and walked away.

Catching up to the recalcitrant critic, the man voiced:

"Hey—what, exactly, did you mean by: 'His message is a crock of shit'?"

Rob stopped, turned to face the challenge half-afraid the wrong reply would land him a fist in the face and broken teeth or jaw, but calmed himself and grappled his anger, growing rage, and struggled to settle himself, to reason with himself, that the man confronting him was just asking a simple question, no threat intended or implied—he hoped.

Rob: "The speaker's whole point was that some 'elite' consider ordinary, regular people as their personal slaves, to work their businesses for as little to nothing as possible and for nothing at all, if possible—if not for the laws proscribing anything less than minimum wage. That is sadly, firmly and grimly all too true, of course. Anyone who says otherwise is himself full of crap, either woefully ignorant or a downright fool or worse, a deaf and blind bigot. But to say the elite are just parasites, just a scourge, is plain bullshit, empty rhetoric, raw emotion intended to inflame, with no substance to it. It's the same tired, old racist rant—in reverse—aimed squarely at his audience, to inflame them against the administration and against Ivry. It's just plain-old, tired-old political bullshit, unfounded partisan crap."

The man looked stricken, not angry—*hurt*.

"No! No, my man, *no!*"

He continued, resolute:

"It *is* true that some rarified few among the elite honestly DO usher-in vast progress and even vaster opportunity… but *they* are vanishingly few while the overwhelming majority of the elite are parasites and vermin infesting that progress and that opportunity with empty claims to being of that elite, their true calling only scam and self-idolatry."

The man turned full face to Rob:

"You speak through a lifetime having been manipulated and trained to narrow thinking through subtle and implacable doctrine designed by a system to do just that! You've got to open your eyes, man. You've got to open your mind to see reality, to really *see* what's going on, what's all around you! Don't let a lifetime's establishment-preachings close your mind to what *is*. Think with your *own* thoughts, not through those implanted in you by the established elite! They gut our brains and amputate our minds and graft *their* thoughts into us! The elites *are* wealthy and they *are* powerful and they *do* wash the minds of men—and women... and *children*, from before they're even born! The elite implant their corrosions and deceptions into our minds so that we not only cannot see but cannot remember or recognize or even imagine the truth staring us in the face! They use words like 'common' and 'ordinary' and 'vulgar' and 'simple' and a thousand other words and thoughts to implant and firmly root the notion that everyday people are good only for being used and abused and put down and thrown out, to be debased and oppressed if they're not one of the elite. Even ordinary, common people use those words—to describe *themselves*! So profoundly indoctrinated are we that we don't even recognize when we demean and damn our *selves*. We have, are given, no other words to describe our *selves*! That's how profoundly oppressed we are and we do not even know it and cannot even recognize it—especially those of us who are convinced beyond shadow of doubt that 'it's all just bullshit without shred of substance to it.'"

The man saw a wavering in Rob's eyes, recognized its earliest renderings beginning to stir, saw Rob challenge himself to see in just that light, outside the constraints of a lifetime's indoctrination, and continued:

"But what if I'm right? What *then*? You've got to open your *own* eyes, think your *own* thoughts—I can't do that for you. You've got to do that for yourself—for your *self*—and only *you* can do that."

Rob searched the other's eyes and saw, was sure he saw, the glimmer of genuine honesty, of a sublime sincerity—*"a deeply true believer"*—and didn't know what to say, what even to think, he having thought, been convinced, that he did look truth unwaveringly in the eye.

The man's words echoed through his mind:

"Open your eyes! See what is! See—for your SELF!"

Rob struggled amid thoughts reeling, of truths raging in fiercest battle against appearances and duplicities, and finally surrendered the struggle as a new wave of thought and feeling—of *prescience*—washed over him, whispered to him, roused him in all silence:

"Only living it, will they understand."

The words whispered fiercely to him, gripped him and held him, and he struggled to understand of what, from where, those words reached for him, aware only of the dark, waiting.

Rob stared into this true believer's eyes, scrutinized those eyes, then the man said simply:

"Name's King. Panther King. I'm talking from long experience. You cannot—must not—allow yourself to surrender to your indoctrinations, to be swept away blind and helpless without least *trying* to rise above what you think you know and pretend to know and convince yourself you know, certain without shadow of doubt. It is your responsibility, more—your *obligation*—to discern truth staring you in the face, threatening you with all you know, facing you squarely eye to eye."

Pleading filled King's look and sound with desperate urgency:

"You've got to judge, best you can, for *yourself*, for your *self*. Even if you're not sure, even if you risk showing yourself stupid or ignorant or just plain wrong, you've got at least to *try* to see through to truth and always—always—judge for your *self*! As if your life depends on it—cause it does."

Rob considered, but contempt pushed through, egged him on and gripped him even as he clung to silence:

"When the world is obsessed with nothing but itself, genuflects to nothing and to no one but itself, do—I—have to

229

be different? Do—I—have to be better? When will be my turn to indulge my 'self,' to wallow in nothing more than MY self?"

Rob felt dirtied even to ask such questions of himself:

"Who am I to indulge myself when so few can."

King whispered a beseeching plea:

"Ben: Open your *mind*." No surprise the man knew his name.

A long moment of silence endured and finally, even grudgingly, Rob intoned:

"Where do we start."

Rob uttered the words through the dark's whispering:

"They understand only by living it."

Rob wondered what the words meant, here and now, in this, but felt sure without least doubt the words would immerse him in their meaning all too soon.

The two ambled down the path in quiet, lively chatter, their voices droning softly, fading gradually to silence in the dark.

'He' lists from atop his perch into the threshold of his vermillion borderland, that gossamer shadowland verging between the fading aura still immersing him and the absolute of the dark reaching out for him, looming for him just beyond his shadowland. He leans, stretches, cranes neck, lists just so, and finally allows himself to fall into his vermillion shadowland.

He falls into his shadowland. He straightens himself, peers across shadowland—witnesses a vast, undulating sea ebbing and flowing, nearer, back, then nearer still.

He stares, slowly discerns... a sea of blinded orbs above silenced lips imbedded in skeletal faces, ebbing and flowing, nearer, then back, then nearer still, flowing ever-gradually nearer, reaching ever nearer, horror poised only just beyond reach, only just beyond apprehending, ebbing and flowing, ever-nearer, undulating in a realm suffused of indecipherable murmurings and inscrutable visions of barely held rage and outrage suffused of unbounded hate.

The sea calls to him, for him and only for him, reaching out for him as he strains to fathom meaning and direction and purpose amid shadows in the dark, amid shadow in shadow of weeping and wailing and howling prayer suffused of pleas and screams and outcries raving and craving at him, for him, clawing to have and to have at.

He gropes after understanding, struggles to discern sense shadowing and foreshadowing sense, each blinded orb riveted above silent scream imbedded in skeletal face.

He reaches to apprehend meaning shrouded in shadow and, here, now, confronts soundless prayer, and finally surrenders ambition and abandons asking much less knowing:

"Why?" and still more urgent: "Why me?"

Haunted, he comes aware at least of this: "Some needs are beyond understanding, are beyond even awareness."

Chapter 30.

Rob deliberated on the moments, themselves seeming only moments ago, when Lainy and he had walked arm-in-arm, hand-in-hand, always touching in every little way possible, he wondering if living *this* all his life was so much to ask, too much to want, such a simple want—*"need?"*—reflected in the vermillion borderland between want and need.

He contemplated living life like this—arm-in-arm, hand-in-hand, with her, always:

"After all: She's mine—and I'm hers."

He nearly burst out laughing, hearing himself silently cry-out such child's prayer, wondering at the impossibility of knowing such a life, understanding the impossibility of it, wondering it all the same, *"asking so much, wanting too much."*

He recalled breath and heartbeat at her words:

"Please, Ben. For *me*, Ben: Talk to Plesant. Ask him… about John. Make him show you. Please—for me."

How could he refuse her simple want, smallest need.

"Of course I'll talk to Plesant. Of course I'll make him show me." He didn't add: *"Anything, everything—for you,"* that alive in eyes and voice. He hadn't spoken those last words, hadn't needed to, she already knew.

So, Rob and Plesant stepped into the Hospital, found the floor they wanted, rode the elevator in silence. The strict rule of 'one visitor at any time' held Rob in the waiting room while Plesant visited with the unsuccessful Power Fraternity candidate, John.

Rob sat mulling what Plesant had earlier told of John:

"His assignment was 'charity'—and it did something to him, triggered, must have triggered, some… underlying… something…" Plesant's voice drifting away, fading to silence.

"Plesant emphasized the word 'underlying,' as if what had happened to John should not have happened—and then he'd mumbled the word over, over ad nauseam under his breath, the thought seizing him, gripping him in prayer for it to be true, for it to be the reason for what had happened to John."

"These things don't happen, they just don't *happen*," rambled whisperings from Plesant, ever quiet, nearest silence, again and still again, limning Rob's need… to know what had happened to John that night.

Thoughts fought one another:

"Had something simply gone wrong—or had something been made to go wrong?"

Rob recalled Lainy whisper, soft and intent in his ear, as if the air itself would overhear and expose them both, risk to them both, her words enfolding Rob in prayer:

"It wasn't even in the papers…" she began, paused for breath, calm, then continued:

"I talked to everyone who was there that night—no one would breathe a word of it. Plesant was there that night, must have been there that night, *was* there that night—he wouldn't breathe a word of it either. But he was there that night, must've heard it all, seen it all himself, no matter his evasions and denials and lies."

Her hushed whisper filled Rob with foreboding… *"for her to speak like that, guarded and shrouded like that, even when thoroughly secreted within our anonymity, her mind looking over her shoulder like that."*

She continued, deathly quiet:

"I can't be sure but I'm *sure*: Allman engineered it. He must have, for it to have happened like it did."

Rob reflected back, recalled:

"She wouldn't tell me but she made me swear: 'See it—him—for yourself, what happened to John that night.'"

Rob lost himself in the overarching power of her quiet.

Rob fretted still more when he saw Plesant finally return from his visit with John, hands buried deep in pockets, eyes worn, drawn to the floor and he shuffling as if drained, pathetic and foreboding to witness.

Rob sat silently, waited on Plesant to break the silence, *"from out of his far-away eyes, from out of deep-shaken eyes, from eyes nowhere near ready to look me in the eye let alone for him to speak of it—of him—calmly or coherently."*

Still no words from Plesant as an orderly appeared and led Rob down a long, crisp-white corridor with firmly shut, crisp-white doors stamped into either side, each with a tiny porthole riveted into the metal of the door, at face height. The orderly laboriously unlocked the door at the farthest reaches of the corridor and cautiously, with painful slowness and studied exactitude, cracked the door open just wide enough to let Rob slip past. The orderly remained standing where he was, just beyond the door as he secured the door behind Rob.

A surreal scene greeted Rob, of crisp-white walls, ceiling, floor, sheets, pillow-case, all gleaming white, the sheets lying full-form and sterile on a hospital bed outlining the form of what Rob realized was a young man, hardly more than boy, with head and tiny eyes poking out, eyes staring fixedly up at the ceiling, eyes fully captive, not least glancing away, and Rob not able to resist the impulse as he too glanced up at the ceiling, what could so assiduously imprison those eyes.

Then sound—*"no, voice,"* Rob realized, hardly recognizing the sound for what it was—began in softest whisper even as eyes evinced no slightest change from full-fixed stare up at crisp-white ceiling.

Rob approached, had to impel himself to approach, daunted and unwilling to draw nearer, to look-in-the-eye the man-sized, porcelain figurine sheathed beneath crisp white bed sheet. Rob drew nearer the phantasm, bent ear to lips to hear near-silent words breathed to him, ready instantly to jump clear if *need* rose up, his own smallest amid the other's gaping.

The mannequin voice was patently calm, held under well articulated, clear and coherent, deathly quiet sound.

"Hardly the stuff of such compelling precaution," Rob decided, glimpsing bindings fastening both wrists to bedframe, guessed at ankles too, wondering *"what risk, he?"* with misgivings about the caretakers more than of the care taken.

Rob listed toward the far-away voice whispered under eyes staring fixedly up at crisp-white ceiling... and so began the telling of a past that gripped more tightly than nightmare:

"They arrived, no... descended... on us with fluid, graceful movements, so lovely to look upon from that small distance."

His eyes shifted, caught and held Rob's for a fleeting instant—*"searching for something, something eluding him, for some indeterminate sign of... fathoming?"* how to describe eyes beyond description—as eyes instantly reverted back to cosseting, crisp-white ceiling:

"One of them came straight at me—straight *for* me."

He articulated the 'for' to make clear his meaning, eyes now not for an instant straying from his one safe-harbor, his last and only vestige of reassurance and sanctuary, inhabited in crisp-white ceiling, comforting as nothing had, as no one would.

John paused overlong, Rob wondering if he himself had been to fault, wondering if anything more would be forthcoming as John held words and images in abeyance. Then something softened, relented, and laden images flowed in torrential whisper straining to be heard—*"to be fathomed"*—credible or not:

"As she neared, her grotesque ugliness magnified repellently and I saw of her with greater clarity through her every half-step nearer."

Rob wondered at John's wording, seeing '*of* her', Rob wondering what more 'of' her John saw than simply her manifest, corporeal ugliness reaching him under renewed clarity with every half-step nearer. Images steeped Rob... of shadow phantasms haunting John out of the erstwhile comforting dark, phantasms cloaking her and cloaked within her, shielding her and shielded by her, of darkest odium lurking within her, suffusing her, radiating within and radiating out 'of' her, emanated out *by* her, *that* stalking nearer, closing-in....

Rob shook himself free of nightmare vision and riveted attention back on John, shuddering inside himself at something glimpsed, something indecipherable, unfathomable, as John continued under fraught breath:

"She wore an alluring gown of incredibly gossamer lightness that cleaved to her, more *of* her than clothing her. And she moved with a preternatural grace and sensuality that defies description. No ordinary woman, she, but—what?"

In near ghostly whisper:

"As she neared, her grotesque repugnance magnified into a still more horrific patchwork: Dark-set eyes under thick, brutish brow; coated tongue sweeping rope-thick lips cracked and chafed and glinting with spit reflecting the dim light of the ballroom into which we'd all been herded and implanted; the skin of her face studded with coarse, dark stubble pocking down to her neck; her face the dull, red-brick sculpting of a punched-out boxer or derelict boozer, with eschars marring and carving her face into a still more execrable nightmare of demonic lore."

Rob bent nearer, haunted by John's moribund whisper, mesmerized by shuddering vision presented full in his face.

After a long moment of staring up at crisp-white, cosseting ceiling, John visibly calmed until, of a sudden renewed life, he turned eyes to Rob and exploded in frantic writhing and bucking against his stolid strictures, he glaring up at Rob, staring him square in the eye, throwing Rob flinching back and away—*"from what?"* Rob wondering what in John might leap out to seize him.

Rob stared transfixed as John drew breath and let loose a scream that staggered Rob still further back, skin crawling, limbs trammeled, less at John's otherworldly-shriek than at witnessing those eyes staring out from the irrevocable dark in which only such terror is roused.

With furious, desperate effort John tore eyes back to cosseting assurance of crisp-white ceiling, from nowhere else could any least comfort and assurance be afforded than from that crisp-white ceiling.

Rob imagined he understood: *"Behavior modification—associate calm and control with crisp-white ceiling"*—and realized he could not possibly understand nor least imagine what could root John back to coherence under such darkness, no smallest delusion of sanctuary retrievable even within crisp, white ceiling.

John gasped, breathed, finally continued weakly:

"The assignment was 'charity,' after all."

John searched Rob's eyes, craved smallest glimmer of forgiveness, some least token of charity, found only revulsion.

John sighed long, miserable lament, continued softly, eyes riveted again onto crisp, white ceiling:

"I determined to be charitable, more even than humanly possible. What else to do? Nothing else to do."

He paused another moment grasping after satisfaction with memory of his great effort, conjuring-up a self-anointed triumph at having been 'more charitable than humanly possible,' then shuddering under its niggling comfort, no comfort at all in such pretense of self-adornment, and breathed deeply, girding himself to continue:

"She approached and from that near distance I could see she was gloriously repulsive and devolving extravagantly more so with each step nearer. But I resolutely set myself to exert my all to warm 'hello' and cordial 'great to meet you' with which I determined to empower my voice in all-genuine sincerity and eyes fully to match, unwavering in offering up to her more amity and geniality than humanly possible."

With that, John looked up, stared into Rob's eyes, splayed a cowed, pleading smile beseeching credence and understanding and, seeing mirrored in Rob's face only his own defiled repudiation of that truth, cringed back to silence.

Finally, under the urging need to vent some smallest measure of crushing anguish, he continued to plead his cause:

"Now I had only to await this 'Queen of Charity' to formally present herself to me, to my empty, vile nothingness."

"But as this hulking specter approached, I saw her eyes: large, wistful, magnificent eyes, darkest, shining eyes. And she, in her clinging gown, she too was magnificent, moving in sensuous and alluring and provocative elegance sheathed in smoothest, clinging silk as if apportioned of innocence itself, as to life itself, hidden somewhere, somehow, beneath her looming bulk... and if I could only focus all eyes and prize every sense on those two images of her, of eyes and grace, and fully expunge every other aspect of her—'of *it,*' I couldn't help but think, fought against—I thought sure I'd get through this however dimly I understood just what, exactly, 'it' was."

Suddenly John lurched under twisted lip and eye and Rob flinched back, watched John trying and failing to calm under images of that she-creature's face, and he let loose *scream*:

"My assignment was '*charity*'! What more could I do?"

John writhed and bucked and strained at his bindings, launched himself against his bindings, and Rob fell back farther still, praying John was fully bound.

John stared unseeing as he writhed and screamed against his constraint, Rob imagining he could hear John's thoughts:

"What more could I DO?"... 'nothing,' the most and all he could do.

For that horrific, beauteous wraith, with every intent to 'charity,' John fought with all strength and will against his restraint, no other course possible, no other conceivable, what more could he possibly do.

"My assignment was 'charity,' so I was charitable, more even than humanly possibly."

Rob wondered what John could possibly mean by having been 'charitable, more even than humanly possible,' as he watched John's eyes flare under demons frolicking in his eyes.

"I was punctiliously kind, minutely attentive, and smiled and found laughter at empty banter and emptier chatter—but could not blot-out images of demons in her eyes, dancing and strutting and fornicating in her eyes, flaunting themselves in her eyes."

Rob shuddered at a vision of some demonic homunculus reflected to John through those repulsively beauteous eyes, of revelation witnessed in those eyes. Then repugnance and odium and reek of prancing demons dissipated and dissolved as Rob watched John staring up to crisp-white ceiling, praying up to Heaven in that crisp-white ceiling.

"She came straight at me, straight *for* me, and sat so close beside me I felt the heat of her thigh at my thigh as she pressed herself to me. She moved with a lithe, feline grace, feminine and chaste, arranging her flowing gown with its deep décolletage delicately about her as she pressed herself to me and ever gently brushed hand and fingers first at my knee, then higher, to my thigh, then higher still as she first gently, then not gently, stroked me and held me and gripped me. And I tried so mightily to *not* shy away from her, to *not* back away from her, trying as almightily as I could to show 'charity' as she chatted and laughed and bent artfully to engage me and cajole me and seduce me."

"And I? I responded as only a perfect gentleman would. I was, honestly and truly, even roused a bit, just some tiny iota, by the softness and warmth of her, even under her touch. I drew all attention fully to her, above all else, even through her otherworldly, horrific agency. After all, who am I to look down on her, on paltry, squalid beauty—I less than nothing, less than contemptible, fully odious myself?"

Rob took pause, labored under that image, reflected on his own monumental failings, rearing to obscenity in full view, flaunting themselves in his face, reflecting: *"How could I not disinter at least some trace grace and compassion for those vanishingly few less endowed even than I?"*

Rob was torn from his moment's reverie by John's tremulous shuddering:

"Then," John shivering under memory, "she took hold of my hands, vice-grip hands—large and rough and coarse and hard—and she clamped those hands over mine and I forced myself not just to allow her—knowing full well I little could have resisted her—but to focus all-eyes and all-attention on *her*, on her eyes and on her grace, and try almightily to *not* focus on the dark stubble of her cheeks and on the course hairs of her chest revealed obscenely and repugnantly in deep décolletage but to rivet all attention on alluring, limpid eyes full with compassion and sincerity and want, and to focus all attention to her grace, alluringly beckoning me even through her repugnance. So I entrusted her with my hands and plumbed every depth of charity I could unearth in me to proffer her my hands with grace and gratitude as I fought against stiffening and drawing back and straining against the revulsion retching in me as she clamped my hands and imprisoned me in her hands."

He trembled, then suddenly arched his back and writhed and bucked and struggled and fell to horrific *scream* boring through eye and lip reaching through Rob in desolate plea:

"*I was charitable*! As Goodness is my witness *I was charitable*! Beyond human faculty *I was charitable*! What more do they want? What in all Hell did they *want*? What more could I have done? What more could I DO?"

He stared wildly, blind to who and what and where he was, until finally, with agonizing slowness, he fought himself back to bare semblance of calm, leaving Rob to wonder who 'they' were, who 'they' could possibly be.

John slowly calmed, finally asked, tenuously becalmed and gentle, staring back to Heaven in crisp-white ceiling:

"Could she feel my revulsion? Would that be so hard to feel? Could she feel the depth of my abhorrence? Would she need more than shallowest skill to that? Could she feel some trace intimation from the strain in my voice or the look in my eye or the stiffness filling me? Did something of *me* betray me?"

John stared Rob eye-to-eye in silent plea to understanding and forgiveness rendered patent in his eyes.

Rob watched John turn, stare into air, to see her in the air, and watched him stir mewling not of rage or of hate but of sadness and regret for *her*—and Rob saw John as supernal, with such for her, with compassion and kindness and understanding for *her*, after that of her.

John continued, struggling to a quiet, matter-of-fact tone even as he winced and cringed under renewed vision of the dark, of guttural threat:

"Then something in her... shifted, transfigured."

John lifted eyes to Heaven imbedded in crisp-white ceiling, re-living demon-homunculi chortling and prancing and cavorting and finally splitting from Heaven and descending down to him and *he* transforming, arching and straining and rendered under visions of minions splaying him and exposing him and penetrating him again, again, on, on... he screaming and bucking against resolute bindings and, finally spent, breathed whispered defeat, routed fully debased:

"What had been a casual touch to my knee worked higher, to my thigh, then up, between my legs. What had been tender, innocent touch, natural as could be under all innocence and warmth, transformed to cloying-groping between my legs."

He paused a moment, relived the moment, *screamed*:

"She waged *hands* on me and the pain and the shame and the horror of *her* filled me and I lost all will and couldn't stop and couldn't help myself and I drew back and I struggled back and I fought her and fought against her and fought hard, harder, and still harder…."

John stared into Rob pleading understanding in forlorn, surrendered lament:

"Then she gripped me and threw me down with inhuman power, beyond human strength, and I was crushed to the floor, splattered under her, under her power and under her weight and under *her* in surreal sound and light and shadow…" he suddenly turned to Rob, *screamed*:

"What's real and what imagined if *that* was real?"

He beseeched Rob with burning eyes pleading to know:

"What's delusion and what truth? Was I steeped in nightmare, clamped in demon's grip? Was it sham and delusion or truth and *judgment*?"

John stared into Rob with pleading eyes and all Rob could do was stare back, stare *through* John, afraid to look at John and afraid to *not* look, afraid his eyes were all that kept John whole, afraid a glance away would shatter and fell John to shards, afraid any least sound or least slip would damn John to a bottomless chasm at the edge of which he was only barely clinging, afraid one slightest misstep would cast John irretrievably beyond that most-tenuous ledge, cast him beyond any least help and hope.

John continued, hardly breathing, voice frail, eyes felled:

"I struggled to assure and re-assure myself that she was just teasing me, just testing me, just reaching to know me, to know of my 'charity' and *so* I struggled to calm myself and to

241

resurrect stillness in me and to cling to some smallest measure of control, some least measure of *self*-control—but I couldn't. I couldn't take any more of it and finally I just couldn't *stand* any more of it!"

He suddenly launched into a horrific scream, pleading:

"I *tried* to be calm! I *tried* to be kind! I tried to be the personification, the *essence*, of 'charity!' I *tried*! I did so *try*!"

He arched his back and *screamed* and slowly, finally, fell to soft-whining whisper:

"I shifted in my seat ever slightly, ever gently, *ever* lightly—how did she even notice? How could she notice?"

And in forlorn breath: "She noticed."

Rob watched John tremble under nightmare vision of images gripping his eyes in sightless terror and Rob felt *need* fill him for this tortured wraith:

"Then it happened and it all happened so fast! I wasn't *kind* enough, wasn't *charitable* enough, wasn't *good* enough!"

His eyes gyrated in frantic effort to cast off the vision:

"In less than half-a-heartbeat she threw herself on me and hurled me to the floor and mounted me and lilted back and loosed an animal howl and there in her eyes I saw the *Beast* prancing and dancing and howling in her eyes as she mounted me and pounded me, thrusting her yowling *into* me as she threw back her head and bayed up to Heaven and whored me and tore me and gloated *all over* me!"

John clawed frantic little arcs with fingers strained against bindings as vision reclaimed him and *screamed* in him:

"She rammed claws through my chest and tore down my belly and rent between my legs then heaved me up and slammed me down and leapt on me and straddled me and raised eyes to Heaven in bliss of supernal joy with howling animal-laughter in glorious plea for more and still more as she stripped me down and exposed me to the hooting and cawing of every minion gawping and dancing around me there, standing over me and watching me and getting off around me, she showing me fully to everyone there and oh how she *gloried* in my pain and in my shame and then did as she'd done and exposed herself to everyone there as she flipped me over rag-doll in her claws, and then all hot and hard on me and then

242

ramming *into* me and right there and right then she took me and took me and *took* me again and again and still more and again as I lay there and took it and took it and *took* it again and again and still and always more and *again*!"

Under wild eyes John loosed a horrific *scream* as he lurched against his bindings pleading for understanding and forgiveness, over and again and still over and again until finally he froze in unearthly silence and deadly stillness, drawn and spent, staring Rob in the eye—and Rob found himself smothered in the leering faces of the gathered crowd crammed above and all around John, they staring him down, laughing and yowling and cavorting and prancing with demon eyes urging to have *their* turn at him.

Rob woke from his moment's fugue to John's feral scream in guttural voice under surrendered eyes, bucking and wailing in frenzied outcry now turned at Rob:

"*You! You're* the demon's toy! I'll take *you* as my prize and rend *you* through your eyes and have *you* taste my pride and *to Hell* with your clarity and *to Hell* with your charity!"

Rob watched John arch and stiffen, flesh to stone, and shuddered to know: *"He is lost... and wholly alone."*

Rob stared at the thing called 'John' and shuddered to know *this* made Allman gloat.

Rob stared at screaming eyes living and re-living a moment's past, never outliving that past, never living outside that past. Rob watched John's eyes and saw demons prancing and dancing to leering crowds, as John twisted and *screamed*:

"I'll haunt you with my eyes and stalk you for your lies—and take YOU as my prize!"

Rob watched John's eyes... saw a young boy crying and straining and writhing and *screaming*—as men in crisp-white uniforms rushed in and crowded in with needle unsheathed, miming silent words above curdling screams how they'd make him right as they stabbed him with their needle and assured him with their lies:

"It's all right, you'll be all right," with no hint of what would be right or could ever be right, or when.

Rob was ushered out and hurried out to John's screams:

"*I'll find you!* You'll *never* get away! *You'll never get your way!*"

Rob was rushed back to the waiting room—to Plesant.

One glance revealed Rob to Plesant and Plesant cringed and shrank and shriveled as Rob stared and couldn't help but stare at this *thing* seated here in front of him—that saw it happen and let it happen and let it be hidden and let it stay hidden... with silent prayer for just reward of prodigal impunity.

Rob stared at Plesant knowing Plesant understood the depth of sin he'd committed in his silence. Rob stared at Plesant and saw not a man but an apparition cowed and shamed and deserving more and always more of the same. Rob stared at the thing called 'Plesant' to burn into memory and so to learn and refuse, so to wholly repudiate, the sight and sound and smell and taste and every sense of all that was Plesant, of all he had made of himself. Rob stared at the cringing form of Plesant and couldn't *but* stare, unable to understand or even imagine the likes of that cringing form, praying to never understand.

Plesant dared a glance to Rob, glimpsed a fleeing shadow and all that lay there, and bleated:

"Don't you understand? Can't you *understand*? There was nothing I could *do*! Don't you see? There was *nothing* I could *do*!"

His pleas grew wilder and shriller with each breath until nothing was left of him but whispered scream and distant prayer groping out of shame-scarred eyes, shame-carved eyes, all there was of his eyes.

/

Lainy held Rob in her arms, placed palm to cheek and turned him to look her square in the eye, struggling to keep calm, embattled for quiet tone to voice and eye:

"What you heard, *saw*, of John was only the slip of the inferno, the smallest glimmer of all that is Allman's."

244

She paused to fortify tenuous calm:

"It's amazing what peers out from beneath conceits and hubris and greeds and lusts when those overtake judgment and caution and simple, plain sense, when those in thrall to such needs and urgings—as those of the Power Fraternity—succumb to their greeds and to the likes of Allman, as their urgings drive them under hope and prayer with highest aspiration to just, simply… get into your pants."

She paused half-a-heartbeat at that:

"Not that they ever did… get into my pants, that is… but they tried, oh Goodness knows they urged to, with all their *want* they urged to, driven by their greeds and needs to get into my pants—exposing their naked complicity and odious selves."

Not enough, she judged, and so repeated with intensity that left no smallest place for *any* doubt:

"Not that they *ever* did…" feeling the need for it, in Rob: *"To assure and re-assure him, always and ever, unremittingly, that I am risen to his need, such failings, this need in him, to be absolutely, doubtlessly sure of me, such need lurking even in the best of us,"* and so she assured him and re-assured him, never once skimping on his need:

"Not that they *ever* did. Not ever," and she grabbed him and held him and so, still, assured and re-assured him, understanding him as thoroughly as anyone can ever be understood. Then, only then, she continued:

"But their whispers in the dark, no, dim light…" scrutinizing him, piercing his eyes as she spoke… "what they whispered, all-quiet under fear of being overheard, and under their ambition… to get into my pants"—pausing, watching his eyes, vigilant to see her assurance echoed and affirmed in his eyes and only then, seeing it there, continuing: "they, the minions of The Power Fraternity, whispered of stories that could in no way have been just stories."

She pulled him nearer, pressed lips to him in her need of him, then continued:

"I heard stories of what, in the depths of their most urgent need, people will submit to, *will* themselves into doing despite their greatest aversion, willingly and even *eagerly*, anything, everything, to feed and shelter and keep alive those most dear to them, those they most love: One story tells of a small clan from a destitute village somewhere in the far Southlands, who submitted."

"They were seduced into building an enclosure, a warehouse, constructed *by* them and *for* them—like digging your own grave. In it they were to be interred... in a hermetically sealed concrete block fifty feet wide, a hundred feet long, barely five feet tall. What did they know of such internment, no, *interment*, as that to which they were willingly, *eagerly*, submitting?"

Lainy paused at that incomprehensibility, tried to see it in the air, that need of theirs, such need that caused them to so abject themselves, and she trembled and shuddered under its decay, finally forced herself out from under that vision, and continued:

"He was testing them, testing the limits of them, the far limits of their endurance, of human endurance, using the 50% lethal dose as his limits, that dose being the ever diminishing resources of life: titrating the oxygen ever gradually down, the carbon dioxide ever slowly up, the heat and water vapor incrementally higher, varying the dose of privation until half expired—their LD_{50}—and their sufferings recorded in their moans and cries and outcries, half with their last breath, controlled with exacting scientific precision as to shame Mengele for being too cosseting of his victims, no, 'willing subjects,' they having been made willing by Allman, and by their need, no, by *his* need... for them to suffer and die for his cause... and nothing for them or theirs."

She turned to her Ben and pressed lips to his cheek, to his neck, and finally rested cheek at neck, whispering:

"Different only in degree, not in kind, to what the elites world-over scheme and perpetrate, perpetuate, on their vast unrepresented, undefended lesser. Witness it of any State anywhere, everywhere, no matter its wealth or sham of liberty, in the vast avarice of its wealthiest... to disempower and diminish and undermine and crush their lesser, to seal the unassailable perpetuity of their own supremacy to the heights and beyond, beyond anything and everything imaginable of... greed."

Lainy tore herself back from images of such odium, and pressed on:

"And from there to other and still other enclaves of privation, in other forms of execrable duress: loan sharking, tenancies, servitudes, taxations, and wages—below even subsistence—through oppressions of every stripe, of every conceivable length and breadth and means, to study and so to determine the limits of human endurance, to uncover the greatest level of duress only, barely, *just* short of homicide and suicide and madness, to know the farthest reaches of ascendency into which the elite could penetrate without the entire scheme collapsing in on them, imploding into non-utility, into uncontrollable anarchy, before their lesser terminally succumb."

Lainy, in whispered awe:

"Imagine the *suffering*... imagine the greed founding its root...."

Lainy drifted away, drifted into trying to imagine the depth of such suffering and the depth of its causal greed, trying to imagine the unimaginable with eyes closed, breath gasping, heart racing....

Abruptly Rob seized her and embraced her and held her... *"what else is there? What else can there be?"* as other thoughts lay in wait, coruscating in the dark, of insatiable need to expunge all that is Allman's.

Chapter 31.

Ben Rob stood by the grand window-wall of the back office at the apex of the Liberty Spire, fixated on the scene playing-out in the streets and alleyways far below, a sea of forms undulating in dimmest light. He stood in the dark listening to the outcry rising silently up from the people milling in the dark below, rendering alive memories that augured what would be.

A subdued murmuring rose up in the front office and morphed to distraction as the door flew open with DeCeeve's rapacious laughter in its wake, catapulting Rob back into the here and now.

DeCeeve slithered up alongside Rob, blathering-on about his—"no, *our*," he corrected, in feint of magnanimity, deigning to share 'his' triumph with Rob—"imminent victory over that has-been President Kurb."

DeCeeve's prattle served only to drift Rob away, he absently nodding and fast oblivious to DeCeeve and his rambling self-idolatry, as sight and sound of The Rafford swept him ….

The Rafford was saturated with Panther King emotion as everyone, everywhere, lived and breathed real and imagined issues confronting reason and conviction and evasion:

"King is victim because he will not pander to the elite!"

"King failed The Rafford and is rightfully indicted!"

And darker whispers:

"King fell victim to the established elite because he seeks to establish a *just* elite!"

Versus:

"King is victim to the established elite because he seeks to establish his *own* elite!"

The issue now was whether the proceedings would be open and public—*"as it must need be,"* the King faction declared—or closed and private—*"clandestine,"* the King faction decried, even as Dean Ivry determined the proceedings would be closed… "so to be free of populist coercion."

The first was posed as requisite for honest debate, the latter purported needful to avert politicizing a forthright review of facts.

Crowds, ever present and ever growing, cloistered around platforms erected on which to pontificate above the students from both directions, amid ever-scarcer calm and reason and ever more fulminant rage and provocative, coiling threat.

At this juncture, King was to be barred from attending the convocation, amid platitudes that the determination would be fair and objective—"to be mediated by independent observers."

Lainy and Rob debated to exhaustion:

"No one's saying who the observers will be!"

"No one's saying what the standard of judgment will be!"

"How can anyone base judgment on opinion polls and innuendo without cold facts and objective standards?"

"How can 'they' expect anyone to respect or tolerate any decision they proclaim?"

Rob and Lainy considered King's rhetoric:

"The only rational and reasonable decision is to side with me! Any other decision, even *in*decision—*especially* indecision—reflects servile fear of the reigning elite! We need a new elite that reflects the new *reality*! We must not be interdicted and suborned by the hoary elite and their archaic, conniving ethic!"

One afternoon, as Rob wandered The Rafford in his all too often restless meanderings, he stepped into the student center… and blundered into King.

King sat alone at a table in the dark of late twilight, sitting ever-more alone as opinion drifted steadily, stolidly against him—'not worthy of being in The Rafford', 'here only as grudging courtesy to those everyone *knows* cannot rise to The Rafford standard,' and so on and on ad nauseam.

King, sitting alone in the dim light, recognized Rob as he approached, and began in softest, barely audible voice:

"Dean Ivry intends to—*will*—expel me. His money and his machine pound the ineluctable drumbeat that I'm not, was never, can never be *of* The Rafford, can never rise to the ineffable quality that is 'The Rafford'."

King eyed Rob closely as the other Rob stopped, stared at King without immediate recognition, King continuing firmly, fixing gaze on Rob:

"I'm not the first victim of such political machinations, and as long as there are people like *you*—who bend the knee to Ivry and to such as Ivry—I won't be the last. There'll never be a last."

King stared at Rob and with dull, defeated eyes descended into consuming silence.

Rob suddenly recognized King, and struggled for something with which to console.

"Even bitter enemies deserve some least measure of compassion for their defeated rival—and King's no enemy and he's no rival, just defeated."

Rob mulled for a moment, drew up a chair, broke the stillness, offered kindly:

"The *secrecy* of it is the most telling," Rob ventured, not bothering to defend or excuse or explain himself:

"We have the right, no, the responsibility, no—the *obligation*—to be fully apprised of the facts and deliberations."

King looked accusingly at Rob, gently admonishing:

"You know: Not reaching a decision *is* a decision. Taking no action *is* action. And those are things that you and those like you have already done. Your indecision and your inaction support Dean Ivry and support him buoyantly and exuberantly. You and yours are everything Ivry could wish for—for turning your back."

"No, I have *not* turned my back."

Rob spoke with dredged calmness even as he raged at being pigeonholed and dismissed and condemned—*"and damned"*—but held to equably firm tone and look:

"How should I decide without facts and without dispassionate, disinterested analysis? But you are right about one thing: Not reaching a decision *is* a decision, and sometimes the worst action is *in*action. So—I've decided."

Then and there, Rob realized his decision:

"I'm not *sure*—but I want to help. Tell me how to help."

Even this small step was *commitment*—and Rob loathed commitment, especially on precarious ground.

"Commitment rivets thought and time and action to some 'thing,' any 'thing,' threatening the very core of autonomy and freedom and peace of mind. But... what price peace of mind? At any and all cost?"

Rob shuddered under such commitment and wondered if Panther King understood that he wasn't committing himself to helping King but only to understanding how he *might* help, and wondered how to articulate the nuance—*"deception?"*—and commit to at least deciding *if* to help. Then he realized:

"Lainy would know."

Rob reeled under epiphany:

"Whatever Lainy says should be... should be."

Rob paused in frozen silence mulling the revelation, as Panther King looked on unaware of the decisive moment of that moment.

Panther King stared at Rob, finally muttering:

"Fair enough," to Rob's offer asking how he might help.

Then King stood, and simply turned his back and walked away.

As he reached the door a small group of his supporters burst through the door and engulfed him, loud and agitated—*"desolate and frantic,"* Rob reflected.

They all began yammering at once and it took King a long moment to quiet and calm them enough to extract their story. Rob could hear only their voices, now hushed and intense, their words indecipherable murmurings. In brief minutes they quieted and, at King's orchestration, filed silently out the door.

King stood alone, staring at the ground at his feet until, about to walk out, he turned and stepped quietly back to Rob, still seated at the table, watching. Rob felt King's eyes shrouded as he muttered stonily:

"Time chose for you—and circumstances reduced you to a traitor, reduced you to just one more 'enemy.' Your indecision abdicated your decision, your inaction *was* your action."

Then he turned and walked away.

Someone, maybe Lainy herself, tossed a stack of papers through the door, striking the floor with thudding finality. Rob sat listlessly staring at the stack of newspapers, then came alive and stepped quickly to the papers and eased one out, the latest edition of *The Sentient*.

"Noon!"

The word flared up at him, accusing him, and Rob understood King had been right.

Rob skimmed the article knowing what it would say, and wondered how he'd live with it, live it down. He knew his indecision, his inaction, would never rise to overtly heavy burden but still it would endure as a perpetual undercurrent, plaguing, never healed or forgotten... *"or forgiven."*

Thought streamed in turbulent eddies, not enough to disrupt but enough to disturb, keep ever ignited.

"Trivial or not, there are in our past what need be and should be forgiven—and what should not. It remains only for us to learn which, and to manage to live with it."

"Tried, judged—expelled!" read the byline, anticipating the announcement of verdict.

Rob ruminated as he read:

"Expelled... by greed and fear and—me. By me and all the multitudes of me and mine."

Rob set the paper gently back onto the stack, and walked out into the waiting dark.

Without warning nose and mouth were clamped firmly shut and with it air and, overlong and finally, consciousness. He hardly noticed the fists and feet and weapons pounding him as struggled for breath before the dark fully descended and relieved, soothed and promised. In waning thought: *"Panther King is not to blame,"* reached him across the gulf.

"Then who, why?" ushered-in the welcome dark.

With a final kick to the head, he not feeling and they regretting his not feeling, they grudgingly relented and walked leisurely away, even still unsatisfied, unfulfilled.

"Why hurry, no hurry—let this vanishingly small triumph linger amid the unutterable loss," thought as 'they' melted into the dark.

In dream of softest touch, an ever-gentle caress for him that woke him to her. He watched Lainy's terrified eyes for a long moment as she clutched him and held him and rocked him and whispered agonized prayer for him, and for herself for him.

Through dawning awareness he watched her, fascinated by her, such fear and worry for him filling her as she stroked him and dabbed blood from him and searched his eyes for assurance he'd be, beneath it all, okay.

He strained, managed to raise head to touch lips to her, held the moment's bliss as long as he was able, so to tell her, assure her, of more than just his well-being, small matter beside hers.

She eased him up and steadied him as she bent under his weight, all-gratitude to be bent under his weight. Together they hobbled further into the dark, he wondering how she'd found him here, like this—and realized his assailants must have dragged him here, for this, for *her*, their gesture to her, in highest regard and near-worship of her, *that* their regard for her, and reserve judgment of what she could possibly be doing with him and the likes of him.

"And what had I done to deserve… her." How little he cared for what he'd done to deserve, now, the rest of it.

Lainy spoke softly of King's expulsion and of the massive demonstration planned for noon the next day, today.

Rob struggled to clear mind amid rage and hate ready-built in him, already full-formed in him, at this senseless and brutal and cowardly affront.

"He's got no right to expect *anything* from me!" Rob growled, not strength enough to scream it as it deserved.

"He could argue and he could hope be he's got no right to *expect* anything from me or *anyone*!" Rage battled reason, he struggling to bridge their uncompromising breach.

"In just a few minutes King's shown what he is and what he stands for..." as Rob's voice trailed to silence under brooding thought, itself struggling to calm rage and hate, recognizing from some now dispassion that: *"it isn't, cannot be, his fault, this... not his way."*

In answer, Lainy kept silent, so fully knowing him, allowing him to deliberate to truth through his outrage.

"Sometimes silence is the only possible answer, stronger than words," she knew he'd understand.

Lainy let the silence linger, awaiting Rob himself to breach it, reason it out, answer it himself.

Still raging, its immolation only slowly subsiding, Rob muttered:

"I should get involved, get behind *Ivry*, speak against King."

Lainy heard the words but saw and heard still clearer and louder his own repudiation of them, it lying thick in his eyes and voice even as he spoke the words, as *she* gave voice to him:

"This is not King's doing," spoken with conviction, certitude beyond doubt. She would cleanse his doubt too.

She continued:

"This... is not his way. *This*... is not *in* King."

They glanced at each other, and she again spoke for him:

"This... is Allman."

She spoke the words with absolute assurance—and no proof. She felt guilt well up, accusing and convicting with no proof but her own loathing, even still knowing: *"What proof needed?"*

Each struggled to put voice to the sanctimony of certitude without least proof and only the *feel* of it proof enough.

"What more needed?" each thought it.

"Yes—more is needed," each mourned it.

Lainy heard his thoughts:

"Why do—I—always have to be fair?" lament heavy in eyes that he and Lainy were too few to be the only ones feeling the need to be scrupulously faithful to honesty and fairness.

Aloud: "Just my *doubt* should be enough to smash Allman's face—why do I have to be victim of injustice *and* of justice? I can't even *want* to smash his face, not knowing for sure that he's to blame," he pleaded.

Lainy smiled despite herself, knowing he damned fairness while struggling to fairness. He saw her smile, understood her smile, and couldn't draw himself from smiling back and then fiercely pressing lips to her. How could he not, that feeling for her stronger than anything else of him, even now.

Lainy said what both knew:

"You *know* King had nothing to do with this. You *know*: It's not *him*. It's not *in* him."

Both understood the corollary: *"It's Allman. It's fully and fully rapaciously... in Allman."*

They both understood, too, they needed proof before even *thought* of righteous retribution—*"no, of justice,"* a word to beguile and to soothe, the updated opiate of the masses, rife for renewed oppression and repression.

"Vengeance in the guise of justice," both mourned being suborned by rage and outrage.

"Forget about the police—they'd never take a stand against Allman." Somehow they were sure of that, too, without least silt of proof.

"*So* we suffer under the boot heels of arrogance and condescension and contempt and self-idolatry," and both kept silent about whose.

"So too, we suffer under the boot heels of The Rafford—and of far beyond," adding: "And under the boot heels of the horde, of the herd."

By noon the mall fronting the administration building was an undulating sea milling and brooding confronting a tense line of riot police set on taunting, tempting display.

Dean Ivry was just mounting the platform, taking his time taking his place in front of the microphone, turning to confront the clamor welling to a deafening thunder amid leering and jeering, contemning rage at him—and he silently at them, *"with trace smile on his lips,"* Lainy and Rob swore they saw.

Ivry began his speech even as the raging mass denied him voice but, after prolonged caterwauling, the raging gradually subdued enough for Ivry to finally be heard:

"...and so I cannot deny *you*, all of *you*—the heart and *soul* of The Rafford, the very essence and *raison d'étre* of The Rafford—the definitive voice in the disposition of Panther King. Headlines to the contrary: King has NOT been judged. Final decision has NOT been rendered. King's disposition STILL REMAINS—to be decided by YOU!"

The crowd reacted with stunned silence—then with hesitant, growling watchfulness wary of unknown deception and threat, their feral outrage held barely under tenuous constraint. They heard his repeated assurances and only slowly settled into sullen disquiet, their rage subverted to skeptical, restive milling.

Ivry stepped briskly but unhurriedly off the platform, leaving the crowd bewildered and searching for an outlet to their harbored suspicions and circumvented, frustrated savagery.

As Lainy and Rob watched Ivry saunter by, they imagined, or saw, more than a trace of smile play across Ivry's eyes, and imagined they heard his thoughts:

"Flourish a bit of half-truth and non-lie alongside a bit of wishful thinking steeped in half-promise and even such pretenders as these, of The Rafford, could be turned—on each other and, especially, on themselves."

Both Lainy and Rob heard the whisper in Ivry's silence:

"In half-truths and promises are they bridled and so, neutered."

'He' lilts ever slightly forward into his vermillion borderland—how can he not—and falls fully into his shadowland.

He is witness to a vast, undulating sea of skulls, of blinded orbs riveted above silenced screams submerged in shadow reaching at him, lurching to him, clawing for him.

He is drawn nearer... nearer... finally reaches the shadow of skeletal fingers and claws—and feels himself rent and shorn of every worn and wan comfort, torn from the remnant of feeble, cosseting aura, and propelled and submerged into this, his vermillion shadowland.

He stares and cannot but stare, nothing more to do or be done, now, and so stares into the heart of shadow aware of pivoting, here and now on the verge of plunging, headlong into its depths. He is less than faded stain in this, his sea of shadow.

Lurching, clawing shadow stretches out beyond imagining as his former, vanishingly faded aura of receding memory fades, and is... gone.

How else to know what stalks him and reaches for him in shadow but to face shadow? Abandon faded memory—now is for staring, unflinching, into the heart of shadow.

Chapter 32.

Dean Ivry stepped languidly off the platform in a leisure of arrogance, allotting to his wake a silence transfigured into a steady drone of murmuring voices guardedly pacified at this concession, illusion, of incipient victory: the promise to them *they* will be decisive in King's judgment and disposition.

The dense line of riot police tediously calmed and dispersed the crowd... "okay now, it's all over now, move along now, nothing to see now..." as the crowd gradually thinned and melted away.

Abruptly, a din from the platform ground through the quiet of the fading crowd and what eyes remained turned back and glanced up and watched Panther King storm the platform with scarcely checked outrage burning his face. They saw him grope after the microphone and finally manage to confront the waning crowd in a thin, distant bleating—*"weak and whiney,"* Lainy and Rob thought—assailing the now dead microphone.

King raged with white-knuckle ferocity straining to resurrect life out of the dead microphone, now a repulsive organism scornful and sneering in his hand, needing to be smothered and obliterated and so he slammed the dead thing to the ground with scarcely a whispered clatter as call-to-arms to the scattering audience, his fiery outrage rendered farce perpetrated on a guileless audience in wildly failing travesty. The few remaining eyes riveted on this spectacle of incarnate impotence saw King diminished and shamed before their eyes.

After a moment's confused bustling a bullhorn clumsily found its way to King's hand and he struggled to unleash thunder in his voice, but only hoarse cry found its way to ears and faces even now turning away as only distant, plaintive pleading issued out that bullhorn:

"People! PEOPLE!" in reedy squawk, the crowd dead to him.

King screamed all strength and purpose into that bullhorn... to people faded and lost to him.

"Do NOT allow yourselves to be *deceived* by Ivry's lies and manipulations!" forlorn, hallowed words impotently bellowed on the deaf and blind.

King paused, all hope that his words would reach and resonate and penetrate minds and hearts slipping away, stripped away.

"PEOPLE! Do NOT be conned and duped by Ivry's slogans and bromides! Do not allow yourselves to sway yourselves, to beguile yourselves into believing that anything of *real* justice has been achieved here, like this, by him and by the likes of him!"

Voice of desperation pleaded against minds drawing, drawn, closed under simmering apathy derived of comfort and contentment and blandishments assuring that 'nothing has been decided' and that 'King's disposition remains in *your* hands!'

"You *must not* allow Ivry to confuse the issues and to confuse *you*! People... *people*... PEOPLE! Don't let Ivry blunt you and steal you from the certain *urgency* of the issues facing you right here, right now! *YOU* must give *voice* to The Rafford! You cannot—*must not!*—allow apathy and lethargy and the blandishments of the administration mollify you and rob you of your inalienable right to steer The Rafford to *real* equality and to *real* opportunity and to real *justice* for you the people and for *all* the people—for YOU and for *YOUR* future! You *must not* allow Ivry and the likes of Ivry to *rob you* of your *FUTURE*!"

Someone yelled out:

"You mean *YOUR* future!" to hoots and caterwauls and raucous laughter flaming at him from among the dissolving silt.

King, visibly shaken, soldiered on:

"I will *not* allow Ivry and those like Ivry to cheat us of our *rights*! I will *not* stand idly by! I must—I *will*—take *action*! But only *together* can we hope that *we* control our future! *We* must act and we must *all* act and we must act NOW!"

King glared at the backs of people drifting away, already drifted away, lost to him.

259

Lainy and Rob watched King shudder and cringe, then cry out:

"You damned, stupid *brats*! If *you* cannot do what must be done—*I will!*"

With that King slammed the bullhorn to the ground in a thunderous shower of debris and stormed off the platform to an infestation of jeers and derision and laughter.

Lainy clutched Rob's hand, pressed herself to him, wondered what, exactly, she'd just witnessed and what, exactly, it meant and what, exactly, she'd write in her column.

Rob returned her grasp with every bit equal need, and the two ambled away, dazed by the spectacle they'd witnessed, brooding quietly over what it meant not just for the here and now, for Panther King, but, as King had put it, 'for your *future*,' whatever *that* meant.

The two returned to their place—together, *that* their place. The chores of the day finally done, they were now ready and anxious for the silence and the dark, for each to soothe and comfort and assure and reassure the other, knowing there is no greater reassurance than in each other in the silence and the dark, and now they had time and state to consider the day....

In pitch dark and absolute silence sudden and urgent *demand* pounded and bellowed at their door, shattering them awake. They held each other in bewildered half-sleep as they roused themselves fully awake.

The pounding and shouting at the door was *demand*, and so Rob hurriedly eased out of bed, fumbled housecoat over himself, and tiptoed to the door to listen for the reality behind the door. He heard near-silent breathing and shielded mutterings across the gossamer fabric of the door, what substance that door to this thunderous demand on the door.

Then fists pounded on other doors all down the hallway and now again on the other side of their door, with peremptory orders ordained across a half-dozen doors to: 'OPEN! *POLICE!*'

Rob hesitated, listened to the sound of metal-on-metal and of hands manipulating tools working the lock and doorknob and furtively he reached for the lock and unlocked and opened the door.

The door slammed bodily against Rob and Rob fell back as a large man tramped into the little apartment and into Rob with flash in hand dazzling and blinding, the mass of the great man obliterating nearly every inch of the hallway behind him.

The great mass demanded instant obedience and *obeisance* from any and all who might least contrive to stand in his way. Behind the hulking form another man, far smaller in stature but far greater in bulk of power and control, edged past and confronted Rob.

Lainy materialized at Rob's side and transformed the man's belligerence into quiet, steely threat as the two faced him down together.

Then the smaller/greater man paused, assessed the shape of things, smiled treacly, and with infinite softness intoned solicitously:

"I'm so sorry to… intrude on… the two of you."

With smile of fatuously transparent warmth, the man hunted down the precise word and tone and glare to exact only what he wanted of them, nothing more—nothing less.

"When did you… ah…" again a moment's pause to conjure the precise voice and look… "last see Panther King?"

Lainy stood silent, judged Rob to speak for them. Rob raised brows, shrugged shoulders, and gestured mildly with arms and hands that 'no, we haven't seen him, why do you ask?'

A shadow passed across the small man's eyes and all pretense to cordiality instantly shifted to rough-idled threat and then back to softness and thin warmth. Pointed finger thrust ungently into Rob's chest with each word, he snarled in quiet, imminent threat:

"You… seen… Panther… King?"

The man inspected Rob, studied the bruises coloring Rob's face, jabbed a finger ungently to one especially darkened bruise and repeated, gouging finger into bruise with each word:

"I… said… 'You… seen… Panther… King?'"

Rob pulled back, scowled through clenched teeth, and quickly muttered:

"No," shaking head once to reinforce the word.

ar grey

The big man standing behind the smaller/greater other slid deftly past the smaller man and, with movement too fast to evade, gripped Rob by the throat and lifted Rob to tiptoe, and ungently squeezed, ungently insisting sputtering breath from Rob, now struggling for breath let alone voice.

The smaller/greater man smiled thinly, invisibly caused the larger man to relent just a bit, allowing Rob breath to intone:

"No—last I saw of King he was storming off a platform this afternoon."

Rob couldn't snuff the rage out of his eyes but managed to struggle outrage out of his voice, what use, what good, exposing outrage for this, to… this.

The big man stepped back into shadow at invisible signal from his smaller clone, who offered a half-smile and quiet apology for his associate's 'diligence,' then breathed, in barely audible whisper:

"That's all I'm asking. No need for… this," hand sweeping across them. "Just doing my job. I'm sure you understand. If *you* were in trouble… or your little sweetheart here," eyeing Lainy with a trace, deft touch of salacious threat, "you'd pee-in-your-pants… ah… be very happy… for me to be doing my job. And you would surely-as-Hell be wanting me to do my job with utmost… ah… diligence, just as I'm doing here and now."

Leer of wan smile was all gesture of apology the smaller man offered for interrupting their… 'sleep,' with hint of lewd wink and lurid smile intended not as salacious provocation but as slumbering threat.

The man stared into Rob's eyes in feint of power to examine Rob's thoughts and feelings and intent, then gestured an imperceptible nod back to his men, for them to withdraw, and slowly turned his back and ambled away.

Rob quietly eased the door shut, the onrush of silence and darkness leaving a surreal sense of it all having been a dream, but for them standing there at the door.

Rob pressed against Lainy and held her and felt her return his hold with every bit the same need. They stood by the door holding each other, the silence and the dark enveloping

262

them, cosseting them, until thought and feeling quieted enough to allow them to slip back into bed and cling to each other again, to deliberate on their manifold gratitudes for not having been molested more than they'd been, slight as they'd been.

Neither was sure of having slept at all when a barely audible tapping intruded into the silence and the dark. Barely louder, the sound reached for them again, seeming to cry out for them in softest whisper in the dark.

The sound insisted, then a quiet rustling in the dark revealed Rob again tearing himself from Lainy and slipping on his robe and stepping to the door through the otherwise silent dark. Each repetition of tapping grew barely louder, each plea fractionally more urgent.

Whispered ever-quietly through the door, Rob heard desperation whispering:

"Rob—open. *Please*, Rob… open. *Please… open!*"

The whisper withheld any trace identity, but Rob recognized King's voice whispering through the door.

A bare moment's hesitation and Rob silently opened the door, barely wide enough for a blinding shard of dim hallway light and King to slip through, and the dark enfolded, cosseted again as Rob heard Lainy stir, don robe, draw near to Rob, and hold him, affirming his decision to open the door.

In hushed tones urgent with need, King whispered:

"Don't switch on the light! Don't let a *thing* look like anything but the same and *just* the same and *nothing* going on here!"

The door's lock clicked shut ever-quietly as the two whispered… Rob's calm detachment alternating with King's panicked, desperate fear. The stench of King's fear was manifest ghoul pervading the room, embodiment of panicked breath and pounding heart and wild eyes standing beside them in the dark.

"But—why? *Who?*" breathed with instant recognition that King was in hiding from far more than just the police.

Rob and Lainy ushered King to sit in the overstuffed chair beside their bed, the two sitting on the edge of their bed to hear him out, struggling to be honest and fair in hearing him out.

ar grey

So King began.

Chapter 33.

Rob stared out the vast panoramic window that was the back wall of the back office high in the Freedom Spire, staring down at the mass agglutinating and milling and seething outside, far below him.

The silence and the dark abruptly exploded into raucous laughter and garish light as Deceeve intruded on Rob's calm and quiet, announcing his own imminent ascension to the Presidency and declaring President Kurb's impending concession.

A thrill of triumph charged through Rob at this impending fruition, finally and at long last.

"And with it—dread and fear and abject misery at having reached so near this culmination and all it augurs."

The image assaulted him: *"Deceeve ascending to his throne—and the vast to suffer the ensuing privation of greeds."*

He allowed mind to wander, as ever inclined when DeCeeve opened mouth… *"to spout smarmy self-adoration and self-idolatry, inherent to his kind, beguiling with deception and self-deception and self-righteous sanctimony spouting platitudes in the name of Goodness while flaunting vanity and greed behind their false-gods in guise of humility and beneficence and piety."*

As DeCeeve frothed on and on, Rob allowed, couldn't help but allow, mind to wander, to reflect back to long ago days with Lainy, and King—and Allman….

Rob found himself sitting in the dark with his Lainy, roused in thought that *"as she is mine, I am hers"*… while setting King to sit atop the overstuffed chair beside their bed, King struggling to calm as he recounted how he came, now, to be sitting there beside them with the two grappling to hear him out and to hear him out honestly and fairly, they battling to suppress their misconceptions and preconceptions, understanding those as the munificent 'gifts' of hate and rage and greed and outrage, their bare edges radiant with cavernous bias and bigotry:

"Since when does anyone care about honesty and fairness?" aware of their own limitations flailing against those self-same 'gifts,' the two reflecting as one mind.

King began in quietest voice, so sound of his words would not risk alerting too acutely those stalking him in shadows of the dark, lurking for him amid his words:

"I was off-campus. I left as soon as my... speech"—the word broken, revealing near-overwhelming sense of betrayal barely tethered, at having been assailed in mid-speech by a crowd newly and inexplicably hostile and animate against him—"right after Ivry's emollient sop. I got back to campus hours ago... but when I drove by Main Gait... security"—again his voice broke, wallowing in magnitudes of writhing disillusion—"security felt... different... something about it, about the whole... scene... felt of... inimical *threat*. How can I describe what I... *felt?*"

He paused amid his stuttered narrative searching for words, besieged by frantic thought and word to convey sense of how those security guards were, somehow... different, then shuddered and pressed on:

"There was something different, something malevolent, something *foul* about the whole landscape, and them. They seemed... agitated, hyper-vigilant, malevolent... as if expecting some preternatural *something* to tear into them at any moment."

King struggled to convey the *feel* of the setting, of the guards, of their vigilance... *"vigilantes,"* silence whispered:

"Their eyes were waiting for *me*... scrutinizing every *thing*, every *one*, forcing them to stop, be inspected, as I drove by."

"I felt a drumbeat in my head—the way they *looked* as I slowed, about to turn into the gait, then didn't. They were looking for me like looking for a *dead* man."

King broke off, abandoned trying to convey the full sense of those moments, then continued on:

"So I drove on to South Gait... but *they* didn't seem right either, that same vigilance, like renegade vigilantes, like I never saw in them before," his look struggling to convey the full depths of the scene.

"They were expecting something, something... bad."

Not able to convey the full sense of that immensity, he finally settled for simplest look and word.

"It didn't seem right... something in their *eyes*! So I drove past them, too, figured to go to some off-campus buddies of mine."

"Then I noticed the headlights behind me—*staying* behind me no matter how slow or fast I went or how I turned this way or that with random turns to see, just to see, if they kept behind me or not. And I got this awful *feeling*..." pause for breath:

"That's when I knew it was bad, real bad, worse than I'd ever dreamt it could be, worse than any nightmare's ever been, for me. But I never dreamed it could be like... this."

King's voice struggled as he re-lived his panic and fear, the very same that had filled him then, and he floundered for strength that wasn't there, hoping that pretense would materialize it to reality, then whispered harshly guttural:

"I thought it was just in my head, just the pressure of the past weeks playing in my head, just tricks in my head. But inside I knew it was real. Even greatest imagination and worst delusion can't rise to reality."

He stared through the dark *willing* the vision and the feel of those moments into Rob and Lainy, so they could understand some least glimmer of those moments:

"I drove in random patterns, turning this way and that, without direction, and finally the headlights were gone. And how is it headlights were right behind me one minute and then not, and no one else—at all—on the road?"

He answered himself: "How else."

Resignation soaked his voice... of *others* watching, who didn't need headlights trained on him.

"I gradually drove closer to the house of some buddies of mine... my 'safe house.' What did I know? I drove in random patterns—they *must've* been *random*!—but when I got to that street and that house they were already *there*! It must've been *them*! I could see them sitting in two cars parked near the house, obvious, too obvious—to be sure I *knew* they were there watching, waiting, for me."

His voice trailed to silence as panic rose in him, thoughts racing over what he'd thought to do, had done, no choice in doing.

"What in Hell do they care if I knew or not, that they were watching for me, waiting for me?"

"To put the scare into me," he answered himself, wondering, near-silent:

"Who in Hell am *I* that they should care in the least if I'm scared or not, know or not? Who in Hell cares what *I* think and feel—I already in Hell, knowing it or not."

Images of Ivry reared, and still King wondered:

"Why should anyone care in the least what I think and feel? But somebody sure as Hell does. And I know damn well it isn't *Ivry* who cares. Why should *he* care? He's got me right where he wants me... down and out and to my very soul. But..." he paused, "if not him... *who*? And *why*? For *this*?" He gestured around himself, at overstuffed chair and room and world.

Silence was his reply.

Rob stared through the dark, searched to see the eyes that went with the voice, feeling the voice overtaken with fear, wondering what King had done to inherit that fear, realizing it wasn't *King* who'd earned that fear, he being just the effigy of... something else.

King continued, voice still low, near silence, but now harsher, more terrified even than before, at images rearing:

"I slowed, saw the men in those cars as I drove past, thought maybe it *was* all just in my head, they not so much as glancing my way as I passed by. Even so, I made senseless turns 'round random corners onto random streets and random alleys and finally I pulled over, switched off my headlights, to see, just to be see. I thought maybe it really was all just in my head... or they'd given it up, I not worth their time or effort to bother with, why bother with *me*? After all, who am *I*?"

268

"But deep down I knew it *was* me they wanted, but—what could they possibly want with *me*? Who am *I* that they should bother with *me*? Then… headlights again. And as I drove off this time, they were sticking right to me, bare inches behind me, and I knew they were after *me*—though Goodness knows why. Why *me*? Who am *I*?" the thought echoing in his head.

He shuddered, quiet for a long moment, finally resumed, fear stuttering his whisper:

"F-f-flashing red lights b-b-behind me," he paused, calmed marginally, breathed deeply, continued:

"I slowed, stopped, glad they were only pullin' me over and not jammin' me up on that street. I watched in my rear-view mirror… two men steppin' out of their car, walkin' slowly up to me… and *that's* when I got this real bad feeling fillin' me up, pourin' all over me."

Through the dark, in the silence between words, Rob saw King sitting there beside him, staring into the dark, seeing it all, alive again in the dark. Then he continued, breathing word:

"Maybe it was the way they walked or the way they held themselves as they walked or the look in their eyes even though it was too far and too dark for me to see their eyes, but somehow, somehow… I knew what they were gonna do. I *knew*… without least shadow of doubt. I knew… I *understood*!"

"It took me less than half-a-heartbeat to decide, and I waited till they were almost to me, almost right *on* me, so they'd have to take time, have to run back to their car, before they could start after me… and *that's* when I slammed that pedal to the floor and rammed that pedal to the floorboard and I peeled out of there with my tires *screamin'* me out of there—and there I was, sitting in my car, watching it all play out, watching *myself* like I was watching some movie or some god-awful play—it wasn't me at all, just some actor performing on some god-awful stage, getting fear poured into him and sweat drained out of him."

"I crushed that gas pedal hard as I could and with all my strength I prayed it was hard enough and I started swerving and weaving all over the road 'cause I *knew* what they were gonna do—just what they did."

"I was no more'n two feet gone when *thunder* cracked and *lightning* flashed and I saw their *minds* drilling into me—and they were blazing away at me as I watched them in my rear-view mirror with their lightning blinding me and their thunder deafening me as they shattered my rear windshield and flattened my tire and as I watched those men take dead-aim at me and squeeze their rounds off at me fast as they could and only by some miracle of dearest Goodness I got as far as to get here, now, telling you this, telling someone, *anyone*, the God-awful truth. And I thank dearest, most-wonderful Goodness that He, She—*Goodness*—took me in hand to someone who'd *listen*... or at least make a show of listening."

All three wondered how it was that King had gotten this far, why they'd let King get this far, as far as to here, now, to tell of this, swear to this.

Lainy and Rob felt King's eyes, lost in the dark, reflecting the sound of his thoughts:

"And only Goodness knows if even these two here, sitting here now, listening to me now... are listening at all."

The silence was absolute, and Rob and Lainy both understood: he and his circumstance and his wounds and his words couldn't be too bad, not imminently life-threatening... or he wouldn't have made it this far, to be here and now, both understanding it was only *just* short of being even worse.

With quiet calm and self-assurance that surprised even her, Lainy whispered:

"Where."

It wasn't question but pronouncement... telling King she, they, *were* listening—and willing, even yearning, to help.

Her tone was not lost on King, and in the dark they could *feel* his relief and his gratitude, that his trust had been well placed.

"I stopped one left side of my back, up by my shoulder. I can't feel too good with my hand, can't use my arm too good, but can still move use my fingers and hand some. Funny, though—it don't hurt bad as I always thought it would, always imagined it would. Funny, ain't it."

270

King's voice was vacant awe of what time and circumstance do—thinking about what's funny, and what's not.

Lainy and Rob led King through the dark and into the bathroom, sat him on the toilet near the sink, pointedly in a room without windows, where a light could be switched on with the door shut tight and no one could see or know.

All silent, Rob and Lainy stepped from the room leaving King entombed in silence and the dark, entrapped by thoughts screaming imminent betrayal, struggling against rage and panic suffusing him in every second that passed. Then he heard whispering and readied to fight or bolt, not sure which begged most, which *needed*, as more of him readied to scream foulest curses or fight with last breath, and then he… just … stopped.

He heard *her* voice, angels' sweetest, softest whispers, of summer breeze warming the cracking cold of all that surrounded, engulfed, him. And he cursed himself to think he could ever curse her, this Lainy, or her Rob.

She bent near, whispering all softness and gentleness, to settle him, just before switching on the light, whispering assurance with her sound and her nearness, and Rob's alongside.

King found himself relaxing, even against all will, under such assurance, guarantee, as nothing else ever had or could.

"Who could know what it's like? Only living it can anyone even begin to know," King breathed, struggled to imbue them with some least awareness of what it was like, for him.

Lainy startled herself with her calm as she worked silently to clean, best she could, the small, gaping wound at back of left shoulder, tending him, with Rob's help, with singular competence, her signature, *theirs*… and here, now, with soap and water, with clean handkerchief and stray necktie as dressing and sling, with soothing whisper as emollient and anesthetic, beyond anything of any drug or salve.

"No exit wound at front, bullet lodged somewhere in your shoulder, will remain in you, for now." Lainy's assessment, accurate as any surgeon's, and thoughts

271

lingering… *"for now and for ever,"* shuddering to augur his future.

But as they felt King begin to relax under their touch, they felt him tighten again, heard his fear and desolation renewed in his whisper, and they switched off the light and listened to him speak under cosseting shield of the dark.

"Now I *know*: You can be sure of nothing and no one…" and was about to add 'on absolutely nothing and on absolutely no one,' but *their* presence, Lainy's and Rob's, halted that notion, proved it just as absolutely wrong.

Then King continued, quietest voice, harsh and broken:

"I got away, somehow. How? Goodness knows, 'cause I sure don't."

And they all thought, knew: They *let* him get away. How else.

"I'm not good at this cops'n'robbers thing, you know, or don't… but I'm *not*. I never been in *any* kind of trouble with the law—not *any*!"

Sensing lingering doubt in their silence, King reiterated in shrill-whisper insistence:

"I *never* had *any* trouble with the law! Not *ever*! I always been clean and straight with the law! Law's all we got, little as it is, separating us from mindless mobs, from chattel and less. What choice *but* Law, corrupted as it is?"

He sighed, surrendering, imagining their disbelief even as they assured and re-assured him they fully believed him and fully believed *in* him.

"Honestly," they insisted, but understood—what use insistence when credence and trust had eroded to nothing in him.

Lainy spoke for Rob too:

"We believe you," declaration clear: *"Who else will?"*

Rob whispered to King:

"You can be sure of nothing and no one—except Lainy."   King felt the veneration in Rob's voice for Lainy, and was stilled—for now—remarking on Rob's adoration, adulation, of Lainy, as clear as anything could be. Then King continued, still in hushed voice:

"I rounded a turn, slowed to a stop, jumped out of the car and ducked into an alley and ran, best I could, my blood draining and dripping, a neon roadmap to where I was running. But my trail of blood didn't lead them, it didn't have to—they knew. No need to follow *knowing* where I was headed. How else were they there, waiting."

King eyed Rob and Lainy through the dark, thoughts furtive and hidden, then he continued softly:

"I ducked into every shadow, *became* shadow, and finally wound my way to within sight of that 'safe-house' I was betting on, where I knew I'd be safe, for a time."

"I watched that street, the one between me and what I thought sure was salvation, at least for a time. No one was out, no one was about, all was deathly still."

King paused at resurrected thought, of complicit, ephemeral joy, then continued:

"Finally, I scrounged enough nerve to cross that street sure at any moment I'd get a bullet in the back but—no bullet. I just waltzed-on over to my buddies' apartment…" eyes flailing in the dark:

"But no sooner do I show my face than one of my 'buddies' glances at my bloodied shoulder, hardly even a look, and clacks me a pity over squinting eyes and tells me: 'Cops are sure to look for you here—take yourself over to some buddies of ours'—people I didn't know, couldn't trust… not like I trusted these guys. Then I got to wondering… 'what's *really* going on? My buddies turning me out like this, making a show of being afraid for me, afraid for *me*, that the cops'd show up any minute, searching me out?'"

"'You'll be safe there,' they told me, swore to me, *swore!*… to be sure *that's* where I would go, cause… 'that's where you'll be *safe.*' They swore: 'Cops'd never think to look for you *there.*' They *swore* it to me!"

King strained through the dark, to look Lainy and Rob in the eye, failed, quietly continued:

"But I didn't know the place and I didn't know the people there and I didn't know how—*why*—my buddies could turn me out like that, send me away like that, to who and to what and to where I didn't know and couldn't trust and what was *with* that? And if I couldn't be sure of *them*... how could I be sure of anyone or anything?"

King paused for breath, flinched at implications:

"And then I couldn't think anymore... I couldn't *think*! And what was I to do if I couldn't *think*?"

King shut eyes, took deep breath, hunted out calm and smallest vestige of reason in the dark, then spoke again, in hushed, guttural sound:

"My 'buddies,'" and he let out a near-silent half-cry, stifling it to silence in the dark, so no one would hear, so *he* wouldn't hear:

"My 'buddies' told me to get going and to get going *now* 'cause that place those other folks were at was a mile or two out and I had to get away and get away *now* before the cops could get to crawling all over searching me out. I told my 'buddies' I got hit and got hit hard and it hurt and I couldn't feel my arm and I felt weak and sick and had to rest but they were already telling me I couldn't be bad-hit and had to man-up and had to get out and had to get out *now*... as they eased me out and shouldered me out and *threw* me out the door!"

King silenced, re-lived still again nightmare hardly past, that won't ever pass:

"I was hurt and hurting all over and I could barely walk let alone run as pain shot through my arm and through *me* with every move I took. I forced my mind to stop, to forget the bad and to remember the good and I swear, I *swear*—I started laughin'! I started laughin' and thought I'd laugh right out of my head, it was so funny, so damn *funny*—forget the bad? Remember the good?"

King suppressed genuine laughter that hung in his eyes and melted on his lips and threatened to howl in the dark, only despair shutting him up.

Through the dark, Lainy and Rob could feel his thoughts: *"In all my life... what 'good' have I had?"*

King continued, in that same defiled, guttural whisper:

"Goodness *knows* and only Goodness knows *how*—but I did it! I *did* it! I scrounged up all strength and... it was enough! And then I was *glad* to be going and glad to be out, cause—who the Hell wants to be with *them*? Who the Hell wants to be with wraiths and specters like *them*—that couldn't be right and couldn't be trusted? And I thought: 'Thank Goodness for making them real, for showing their *real* selves to me!'"

He quieted to silence as the impact of that cascade sank in, as gratitude—*"of all things... gratitude!"*—welled in him:

"I forced my mind to stop, to think, to—*hope!*"

King turned to stare at Rob and Lainy through the dark, fear and rage dampened to incredulity:

"I turned to hope... *that*, not religion, the opiate of the desolate, of the desperate: I could wiggle my fingers a bit, now. I could feel, even move, my arm a bit, now. I could breathe more easily, now. The bleeding had stopped and I could walk and even run a little, now. And I could bear the pain a little, now—and I near laughed aloud at all I had, the so-much I had, for which to be wholly grateful. And best of all: I could *think* a little, now."

King stared, saw it there in the dark, such munificence:

"And I thanked Goodness and prayed to Goodness and surely and fully meant all gratitude to Goodness and swore to Goodness that someday I would pay her back for her vast wealth of kindness and generosity to me this day, if she lets me live long enough... 'cause *that's* when I realized where to go."

With that he looked Lainy and Rob full in the eye through the absolute of the dark and thanked Goodness in that silence in the dark:

"I walked in shadow and took the shape of shadow and *became* shadow as I struggled to make it here, to *you*—and as I wound my way her I agonized, dreaded to make sense of it all. I'd freeze and shrivel and disappear into myself at every sound and sight and thought that trespassed me, with every sound and sight of car or man or cat or rat or the devil itself. It took me *hours*... but I kept my head and made my way—to you," guttural whisper in the dark, full gratitude to Lainy and Rob in the dark.

"But before I could bring myself to here I had to know, had to be sure, to be absolutely *sure*—if my 'buddies' had told me true, or not. I had to *know*! How else to *know*? So I made my way to where my 'buddies' had told me to go."

"I finally made my way there... and waited. And waited. Crouching low, I hid in shadow and *was* shadow—too spent and too exhausted to move, needing just to breathe... and think and dream and pray, a little, just a little, for all I dared."

He paused, wondered:

"I don't know why I hid there so long—so much longer than pain and exhaustion demanded and far longer than I thought I needed. But... I waited."

King stared into the dark, re-living:

"The street and the pavement were all clear, and other shadows were calling to me, beckoning to me... to hide out in *them*, to make *them* sanctuary. So many shadows called out to me, some at the street, some across the street, some leading right up *to* that house, to where my 'buddies' had sent me. And I thought how wonderful those shadows were, like true and faithful friends, when I had no others. But I stayed where I was, in that one shadow where I was... cosseting me and caressing me and shielding me and *proving* itself to me. I don't know why I stayed right were I was for all that longest time. Then I started thinking *clearly*... like never before."

He startled at that—*"like never before"*—and continued:

"I found myself not so much thinking as *listening*... to thoughts inside my head—as if *I* wasn't thinking but was just listening-in on someone *else* thinking, inside my head. But just who, for Goodness sake, could that *be*, thinking inside my head?"

King shuddered in the dark, resumed guttural whisper:

"Those thoughts told me how strange it was, how it made no sense, and asked me questions I couldn't answer: 'How'd your 'buddies' know so much about it? How'd they know right where to send you? Why'd they rush you out and throw you out like they did?' Then I understood."

King threw Lainy and Rob an invisible, knowing look:

"Those thoughts explained it all to me, clear and calm and kind as kind can be: 'Would *you* send *your* buddy off like that, with no kind word and no warmth and no hope and just rush you out and throw you out the door, hurling you from one cold threat straight into the jaws of another, even worse for all its unknowns, and offer not comfort or sanctuary but *illusion*?'"

Panther King paused, wiped sweat and fear beaded on brow, shivered ever faintly, stared into Rob and Lainy through the dark, pleading cold, harsh whisper:

"And then I got this… *feeling*," whispered, this more horrific than the moment before:

"I couldn't put my finger on it but I felt as if that shadow, the one I was even then crouched and cowering in, was my last and only sanctuary in all the world—in all existence!"

King stared into Lainy and Rob, compelled his vision *into* them, for them to understand some least of it:

"That shadow was my last and final and only friend and sanctuary from all that I'd always fought and loathed and cursed all my life. And all of those things, all that hate and rage and evil that prowled for me all my life, were at that instant massing against me just outside my shadow. And all those other shadows, beckoning and calling to me, were illusion and worse than illusion—the incarnation of all that stood against me and against all that was fair and honest and good in this life… and my shadow was all I had left. Then I looked all up and down that street and across that street, at all the shadows calling to me and singing for me, from all around and all over me, and that… *feeling*… rose up in me so *strong*, so fully *alive* and—I swear… those shadows *came alive*! I felt their hunger—for *me*! And I knew: If I stepped one step outside my shadow, I'd be damned."

He paused, caught a shard of breath, continued:

"I couldn't move, couldn't breathe, couldn't *think*! All I could do was shrink deeper into my shadow. *That* was all I had! And as time dragged on I begged and finally *prayed* for death to take me, once and for all, and have done with it."

King stared into the dark, lived it again in the dark, and with inconsolable wonder, whispered:

"Then Goodness intervened."

'He' girds himself and reaches, stretches through his vanishingly thin veneer of peace and comfort, of palest vanishing aura enfolding him, and is torn and shorn from frailest illusion—and finds himself fully enveloped in his veneer of shadowland.

Now he is fully engulfed within the shadow of vermillion borderland, the last ember of his vanishing aura now mournfully, disconsolately abandoned, the feel of it now less than memory, less even than lingering desolation, his last and only comfort dissipated, and here, now, he was mired: an endless sea stretching beyond awareness... of sightless orbs and silenced mouths riveted in skeletal faces sobbing, wailing, screaming out for him, he suborn and submerged within shadowland, confronting the boundless dark awaiting—him.

Sight and sound and thought and dream twist and churn and transform vast unknowns into kaleidoscopic haze of might-have-beens and could-have-beens and should-have-beens until, finally, they transform into being and into inevitable being—and morph into the inexorable will-have-beens whose nature and character and meaning elude and escape all but the vaguest traces of insights and understandings within which all he could do is wonder "why?" and above all: "why me?" and pray for some least comprehension of whispers in silence and portents in the dark.

Chapter 34.

 Rob and Lainy sat on the edge of their bed, arms draping each other in the dark. King, resting on the chair facing them, his wounds neatly dressed, resumed his story in near-silent whisper against the dread and fear haunting and hunting him:

 "I couldn't move or think or breathe—all I could do was cower in my shadow, cling and clutch at that last and final vestige of shelter, as near-eternity inched by me, even as I begged and prayed for death to overtake me, to just take me, to have it over and done with once and for all."

 He quieted to silence as he stared into the dark, seeing it all there in the dark. Then he suddenly looked up, light shining in his eyes, and in doleful, quietest voice:

 "Then Heaven intervened."

 He paused an ever long moment awed by the sight and sound and thought and feel of all that floated in the dark for him, of that moment:

 "A miracle of Heaven tore me from my tomb!"

 Wild eyes staring through the dark to where Lainy and Rob sat, he whispered:

 "And it happened so fast, it all happened so *fast*...."

 King stared into the dark, mesmerized by contrasts, lips moving to near-silent words:

 "That eternity of being hunted transformed in an instant, unveiled my life from what it was to what it is become."

 He stared into the dark mesmerized by all he saw in the dark: "And I didn't even see him 'til he was standing right over me."

 Living the vision, his guttural whisper continued:

"There was only blackness all around me—*us*—under that moonless, starless sky. Not even a glimmer of city-glow greyed the dark that bound us."

"His steps were slow, each so very labored. With his head bent low and his shoulders hunched high and his hands buried deep in his pockets, he sludged along with the slowest steps I ever saw taken, and..." again he stared, seeing it all there in the dark, staring in wonderment for all it was and all it meant:

"And he... just walked right *up* to me! He hadn't seen me at all but had just... found himself... standing above me, standing right over me. And then he looked me straight in the eye and I sat there frozen and couldn't move from the spot where I was crouched and cringing and frozen."

"He got to where I was and he just happened by some miracle of existence to glance down right to where I was and he saw me cringing there, quailing and shivering and huddled deep inside myself, cowering in my shadow as I struggled to draw still deeper and as far deep down as I could get into the farthest, blackest reaches of my farthest, blackest shadow. And when he saw me like that he got this look in his eye and he froze, for just that slightest bit of time he froze... startled?... by the sight of human terror crouched in the gutter by the garbage in the street inside the darkest shadow in the dark. He looked me straight in the eye, looked right *into* me, and he saw terror *alive* in me, just as plain as I saw him. He looked at me and he stared at me and he sickened at sight of me... crouched and cowered in the gutter in the dark. And *revulsion* swept through him, flooded him—then hate and rage and *outrage*... seeing me cringed and cornered, a rat cowed and cowering in a darkest corner of the dark. And then and there I saw *it* grip and take him, right there and then in the shadow in the dark."

"In that instant—in that fraction of an instant—my eyes met his and his met mine and we saw *into* each other right then and right there in that miserable corner of the dark."

King hissed the whisper, awe in that whisper:

"I saw *into* him—and he saw into *me*!"

A long moment passed as King re-lived that moment, stunned by all that transpires in the blink of an eye, then:

"I saw the endlessness of *his* despair filling him and overflowing him and gouging at his eyes."

A sudden rush of words spilt from King:

"Then a blinding river of light caught him and held him and ripped him from the dark not half a heartbeat from where I knelt and prayed and cowered in the dark. I saw broiling hate and rage and *outrage* burning through his eyes, but *sadness* overwhelmed it all, and in all my life I never saw such *sadness* overwhelm it all… and I saw his eyes fill evermore with sadness—seeing me cowed in prayer in that shadow in the dark."

Again King paused under lingering silence, seeing it all alive in the dark:

"He looked at me and looked into me and saw *me* through his eyes—and he flashed a crying-smile for me through faithful, loving eyes. He offered his smile to me and *so* told me why—then swung around to face that light as thunder echoed down:

'FREEZE!' the voice thundered down from heaven."

"FREEZE! DROP TO YOUR FACE! *DROP… TO… YOUR… FACE!*"

"He turned full-face to that shard of streaming light under that thunder-rearing voice—then turned full face to me and… *smiled*! He smiled down on me—*for* me—with the saddest eyes I ever saw as *Goodness* held him there, lingered him for me, whispering all there was of me—and all there was of him. And right there and then he knew all I was—and all that he would do… and had yet still to do, nothing else to do, nothing else would do."

"We were caught and held in an ageless breath of time, and in that sliver we both knew we were caught. We sighed a breath of whispered groans as he saw all of me and I saw all of him, all there was of him… and all there ever would be."

"I saw his every thought and dream screaming in his eyes—and knew how much he did *not* want to do what he would do, nothing else would do. What had to *be* flooded and *still*, deep inside his eyes, he had a smile for me—that he could do this thing for me."

"I knew he'd never surrender, never drop to his face, his eyes screaming into me, *for* me: 'I worked and dreamed to do more than just to work and dream: to redeem those trampled-under by their lives, and here now is my chance to be more than I am—even just as helpless as those I dreamed to help... but here now is my chance to be more than I am!"

King stared living memory into Lainy and Rob:

"How strange it is to see all of a man in a single moment's glance."

King was silent, adrift in vision of the thing.

"Then—everything *snapped*!"

"Time snapped and space jolted and everything happened and happened so fast—and then it all was over, over and done and gone. In a moment too fast for thought or breath it was over and it was done. The moment rushed at me and flooded me as I knelt and prayed and cowered in the dark, and then it all was... over. Everything was over and... done."

"In the blink of an eye and the space of a breath, fear and hope pitied us and released us and he jerked his hands from his pockets and sprang to life and raced down that street and in that space of time only silence and his footsteps were alive—footsteps faded to silence in the dark."

"Then lightning flashed and thunder crashed as they hunted him in the dark—and found him out and lay him down, spent and lifeless in a pool of crimson gleaming in the dark."

"The thing lay still and silent in the gutter in the dark, grim-eyed satisfaction reveling in its eyes—for all he'd done and *had* to do, done so awfully well."

King stared *satisfaction* into Rob and Lainy in the dark, through eyes lying cold and silent in a gutter in the dark:

"He never dropped to his face in the gutter in the dark."

A moment's respite, and again in deepest whisper:

"I crouched in my shadow for near eternity not knowing if I was caution or coward incarnate. Shadows on that darkest, lifeless street remained unchanging landscape of terror in my eyes, until... shadows rose to life. Graceful, cautious shadows flowed up into view, to gloat over their virtue's trophy staring up out of darkened, deadened eyes—of certitude mixed with sadness, of final moments rendering not just life but *exultation* for what he'd done and done so well. I stared at lifeless eyes lying silent on that street, and saw no shred of terror there of the kind that lorded me. And as I watched those shadows worming through the night, I saw them sneer derision at that lifeless piece of life, I only seeing how great a man he'd been—and who would ever know."

King turned eyes to Lainy and Rob, saw only shadows in the dark:

"I wish I could have known him. I wish I could have stopped him. I wish I could have saved him—but knew that I could not. I know I could not have done what he had done for me, and suffer how to feel—that a better man than I gave his life for me."

King turned eyes to heaven, whispering:

"And a better man than I—should not have died for me."

King was torn by simplest brutality:

"I didn't care and didn't care *enough* and all I was… was grateful—that he'd been a better man than me. And as I watched those shadow-vermin crawling up to him, I saw my chance and took my chance and stole myself away, and realized: even still, after death, he was *still* a better man than me… shielding me from filth and worm creeping on two legs so near to where I knelt and cringed, praying in a shadow in the dark."

"I dissolved into backstreets and alleyways and rooftops and made my way through the terrors and doubts impaling me. And what I wanted most to know was *how* in this living Hell called life had my people—*my people!*—been turned to prey against me. My blood ran colder than my dearest savior's eyes to think how *easily* my brothers and sisters had been twisted 'round against me—easier than cleaving life from my dearest savior's eyes. And how quick and easy it is to rend my shards of peace, and next would be *my* corpse lying cold and sightless under worm-rotted egos in the gutter, in the darkest corner of the dark."

King's voice faded to silence as he whispered:

"I burned to know by whose mind had my people turned on me. And if those brothers and sisters are lost to me then… everything is lost."

King stared into the dark:

"You see: My safe-house and my people were only known to *me*. I trusted them completely—and now there's nothing left to trust. Something *evil's* hard at work, and hard at work on *me*… because I'm innocent, had done *nothing* worth all this. Whoever, *what*ever, is behind all this knows full well I'm innocent of crime: My people *knew* I'm innocent of crime and were somehow made *not* to know—or just made not to care… or made too afraid to care. And imagine what *power* caused all *this* to come alive…."

King staggered to silence at thought of such power… "as gods and kings must know:"

"Lost in labyrinths of fear and doubt there is no room for 'why,' as I found myself alive, and knocking on your door. I don't know how or why, but I found myself standing here, knocking on your door."

Lainy and Rob glanced at each other with but a single thought:

"Once he'd been so proud and strong under highest hope and dream—now bent and lost and wandering, alone in darkest shadow in the silent, fading dark."

Chapter 35.

Rob stared through the vast panoramic window that was the back wall of the back office at the heights of the Liberty Spire, staring out over the vast crowd massed and amassing below, lost in thought of what would follow next from the culmination of their agitated milling. He struggled to erase the nagging doubt eroding him, of the inevitable and all-to-soon next, unfolding on the streets and alleyways below.

The door flew open and repugnant laughter and *DeCeeve* filled the room, assaulting and defiling the silence and the dark as Rob cringed under visions of the next, of what he and that *thing* DeCeeve had invited in, Rob clinging to remain oblivious and insensate to cause and effect knowing *he*, himself, the cause and DeCeeve and his breed, self-idolaters, just one among the effects, the least of those effects, the spare dawn of those effects. Rob struggled inwardly to deny complicity… *"no, genesis, of all that happens next and… how to expunge what happens next."*

"If I remain hidden and unknown in a shadow in the dark—can that exonerate?" The answer self-evident:

"No, even despite any greatest ends that might—that will!—follow," Rob's thought remaining cloaked in struggle for certitude amid precarious uncertainty of all that is foreshadowed.

DeCeeve's grating prattle droned on as Rob struggled vainly to ignore—*"no, erase"*—DeCeeve and his corrosions and the burden of his own culpability for DeCeeve and his corrosions, and Rob found himself drifted back:

Light edged into the dark, shepherded out the dark as it ushered-in the gentle sounds of life awakening, *"re-awakening,"* Rob managed sleepily. Beside him, Lainy turned in deep sleep, draped arm over him, claimed ownership of him, and Rob celebrated her claim, felt renewed under *her* cause and effect.

"*My well-being is her motive and intent,*" he was sure, fully as his for her, and so celebrated her intent, silent whisper exposing him:

"*Whatever her intent,*" such was his trust in her, she unaware of the path she'd chosen for him, he allowing, abetting, *propelling* himself into her choice for him with perilous joy.

The Rafford night melted into a Rafford day and Rob braced for the inevitable return of all that a Rafford day augurs. Here and now it was police, Rob absently wondering aloud to his now-alert Lainy, realizing he wondered aloud only the outermost edge of his thoughts:

"How soon will ordinary, law-abiding people fear and dread and damn the police and the very mention and thought of the police—*thought* police?"

Rob shuddered, recalling prosecutions and convictions for *thought*, revealed by one's internet searches, as one example: the courts divining future crime by one's internet searches, adjudging as *res ipsa loquitur*—the thing itself speaks—and so needs no other proof and is, of itself, proof of inevitable crime.

Rob considered aloud, to receive Lainy's judgment:

"What conditions generate inevitable crime? To what degree of desperation must people need be driven, in their masses, to be so provoked—to allow themselves to be so provoked—into taking to the streets and falling to murderous action against relentless oppression? Can tyranny ever anticipate the inevitable rewards—the *consequences*—of their oppression? Does the one percent wait *knowingly*—and leave the grim consequences to some future generation?"

Rob tried to quiet veiled thought—"*thoroughly hidden from Lainy,*" his guilt compounded by the dark intimations of his silence to Lainy—"*that I will be found guilty of procreating the people's murderous actions... simply by awarding the oppressors all they ask and demand. I will be found fully guilty, there is no doubt, and adjudged fully deserving of that guilt— and the righteous, justified ends be damned... as I will be.*"

Aloud to Lainy:

"Is a speaker culpable if his speech triggers a frenzy of murderous action? Where lie the lines between free-speech and hate-speech and mass-murder-provoking speech?"

And more:

"What reckoning is heaped upon the unknown provocateurs of the murderous throughout history—those who provoked the Mao's and the Marx's and all their madness? And who are the amassed—hidden and shrouded in the shadows of the dark—who acted on the dictates of those so provoked?"

"What power the Hitlers and the Maos without the great unknown masses who abetted and executed their whim and command?"

He tried to silence thought, settled for quieting thought:

"How could I silence my disquiet, ever immanent to me, with King—and Dean Ivry—intruding into my every thought? May they both find peace, deserved or not, even if only Ivry is the one resting-in-peace... so far."

He wondered aloud to Lainy about the manifold privations suffered by ordinary, law-abiding people:

"To where does their privation lead? To humility and frugality—or to outrage and rampage?"

He considered his own privations... *"so petty beside the vast numbers who've been ground down and ground under by the smirking duplicity harbored by the one percent,"* and wondered:

"Is my motive—or my delusion of it, that I am working to the ultimate benefit of the ninety-nine percent more even than to the usurpation of that one percent—borne of humility or of outrage? Do I aspire to liberate the oppressed or to tyrannize the oppressors? Which motive ascends?"

He knew, understood fully, his outrage—*"and that of the ninety-nine percent"*—and understood, as fully, the precarious and perilous risk he contemplated... *"as the agency unleashing that outrage,"* the edge of remorse already baring fangs.

Rob wondered, all-silent to Lainy:

"Why does humility subordinate to outrage rather than outrage subordinating to humility? When humility reigns,

peaceful solutions burnish. When outrage ascends, reason flees and rampage flourishes—so why do we succumb to outrage, why do we allow ourselves outrage?"

The answer was blindingly clear:

"How else but through outrage can we ever hope for change, for justice—when humility is derided by those who hoard the power to deride?"

Of course he understood its corollary:

"Whose justice should we hope for?" as silent whispers cry out in deafening cacophony of self-righteous certitude: *"'mine,' no 'Mine,' no 'ONLY MINE is true Holy Justice!'"*

Rob's thoughts ran on:

"Still, I pray for at least some small share of clemency and forgiveness for those few among the one percent who victimize and gouge the ordinary people"—as the words *'for they know not what they do'* whispered silently through him.

Rob wondered at the justice of wishing pity and compassion for the *un*deserving—*"whether the likes of Dean Ivry or of King, who can attest to their being un-deserving? Should—I—judge who is un-deserving, even of least clemency?"* Aware of King's likely providence, sooner rather than later, of finding himself keeping Ivry company in the hereafter:

"Mindless forgiveness undermines what we need most cherish: just reward and impartial punishment—the essence of 'an eye for an eye'," as thoughts of the self-righteous flitted through, proffering sanctimonious forgiveness of transgressions they have not the least right or grounds to forgive.

He shut away thought of what is and what is not 'fair,' and of who should and should not measure what is 'fair.'

"What do our judges and law-makers know about 'fairness,' so many having been bought and paid-for by the moneyed one percent..." not even a question, as thought ravaged... *"their laws crafted by and for the exclusive benefit of plutocrats and kleptocrats, under whose grinding privations we now labor."*

He deliberated:

"Only an infinitely dispassionate judge could decide who is—and who is not—deserving, and what they deserve. But we could—should—be doing so far more and far better than we do, what we do hardly even a pretense of what should be done."

His reflections reached out to King, *"utterly abandoned and desperately interred in our vanishingly small, precarious sanctuary... utterly but for Lainy and, for her, me as well,"* and Rob wondered whether King deserved abandonment above deserving sanctuary.

Rob thought back to the previous night—*"hearing King's near-silent knocking on our door, urgent and desperate, stooped and steeped in the dark—and seeing him on opening the door, worn and bloodied and abject, hardly daring even to whisper his need in supplication to strangers, fully supine to the unknowable reaction of strangers and the terrifyingly perilous consequences of supplicating desperately to strangers."*

Rob studied his memory of King's *look* as Lainy and he cracked open their door to him: *"gaunt, eyes haunted, lips praying silent whisper, cheek gouged, ear lacerated, one hand stained with blood"*—his own, Lainy and Rob had needed to assure themselves—*"presenting in torn and filthy shirt and jacket, eyes the look of prey fleeing desperately for life, for what little of life remained to him."*

Rob had thought to ask Lainy's permission *before* allowing King entry into their tiny sanctuary, then had thought better of it—*"time fleeing,"* recalling his thought—and had opened the door, barely wide enough to let King slip in before furtively but silently shutting the door... but that only after catching a glimpse from Lainy confirming her full support to letting him in—*'ask questions later,'* acknowledged silently.

"Appearances could—no, do—deceive," but he'd reserve judgment of King, no matter the all-too likelihood of judging harshly—*"and maybe even damning."* But Rob had been confident enough that King would do him—and infinitely more importantly, Lainy—no harm.

He knew Lainy would think just as he did, *"so much the same we are,"* and smiled at how much the same they are.

He recalled stepping back ever lightly, to allow King entry, and recalled Lainy's instant and full comprehension, she already moving silently to their little kitchen, for soap and water and makeshift bandages and all else she anticipated he'd need, knowing he'd be in need, and of a lot more than just soap and water and dressings, seeing the look in his eye and the trembling of his fingers and his every slightest movement.

King's immediate physical and emotional state assured, safe and shielded for now, Rob and Lainy waited patiently for King to confess to them whatever and all he deemed in need of confessing, seeing in his eyes and manner and every movement his urgent need of confessing as penitent to Confessor.

"As if I, or Lainy, could ever be his Confessors," that simply beyond pretension.

To King's silence they remained silent until, finally, Lainy took courage and responsibility and broke the silence, auguring the needs of impending moments, and began:

"We've got to get ready," both understanding her meaning... *"for the police."* Inevitable.

"Everything's got to look like 'business as usual,' or we're sunk, for what you," eyes to King, "did—*or* not—to deserve being hunted, and for us... harboring you."

Her sound and look were limned with apology for even least considering what King might have done to deserve this predation. But, too, was her sound and look full with unabashed realization and no starry-eyed defiance against what simply *is*.

"There is no room for starry-eyed idealism, not in this or any real world," thoughts of its brutality rendering her mute for a long moment, contemplating what future there might be— *"will be... and won't"*—for him, and for her and her Rob. At long last, she shrugged off precarious, perilous meanderings and tore herself back to the matter at hand.

She led King to the bathroom, to lie flat in the tub, feet under the spigot, and then assiduously overlaid him with a white sheet, tucked-in from head to toe and all around, allowing him spare scope for breath. She shook-in bath soap, swiveled the selector to 'shower,' and turned the knob—the shower springing to life, raining down water nearly too hot to touch, filling the tub with opaque bubbles and the room with impenetrable steam.

Then… the wait.

After a brief/prolonged wait, barely three hours, it was as they knew it would be: the rap on the door followed in quick succession by pounding, then insistent demand, then full and unquestioned command over the door and over anyone and everyone on the other side of the door: *"Open… or we'll break it down!"*

Lainy glanced at Rob, tried to smile encouragement, and abruptly slipped her nightshirt over her head, holding it in front of her, barley concealing her, the gesture meant for Rob, knowing King was in no position to see any of her, secreted as he was beneath sheet and dense steam with only nose and mouth above water beneath sheet, and silently assuring Rob she'd never have anything to hide from him, ever.

The pounding on the door ceased and a heavy rustle of metal on metal at the door's lock signaled imminent violation.

Rob nodded curtly to Lainy, tried to smile with a confidence both knew wasn't there, knowing there was nothing to smile about—except for the two of them being together, even here like this, *that* worth smiling about, and Rob stepped to the apartment door, leaving the bathroom door ajar.

Rob stepped to the door shouting 'coming' as the door was thrown wide, revealing a troupe of large, rough-looking men crowding and shouldering into the tiny apartment.

For a moment Rob thought he'd laugh out loud, struggled to suppress laughter, as men filled the apartment with their number and mass, hardly able to move in the tight constraint of the tiny apartment, Rob and Lainy vanishingly tiny drops of pristine water held against this torrential flood of rough and coarse, what possible threat two drops against such flood.

With military precision they filled the room and took the room and flooded through every room, all three diminutive rooms, tiny kitchenette the second, bathroom the third… the latter filled with dense steam and sound of a running shower.

One man, their headman, stood apart, stood firm within the space of the apartment doorway.

A small scream issued from the bathroom and Rob moved to vault in, halted in his tracks at first step by a second man, restraining Rob, hardly exerting himself as he inspected Rob. His eyes narrowed to the third man, checking the bathroom and shower. The command, the headman, from his vantage at the apartment doorway, clearly in control and in command, accustomed less to immediate obedience than to instant subservience, glared at Rob as he rapped his walking stick on the floor twice, to alert Rob against any insolence or resistance to his lightest will and whim, the great knob of his walking stick held in a grip that Rob was sure could be as instantly deadly.

Rob watched impotently as the third man, inside the bathroom, swept open the shower curtain, taking an overlong look at Lainy, standing in the shower, making a show of covering herself with arms and hands. Of an invisible signal from the headman, the third abruptly drew the shower curtain closed and stepped away.

The headman stepped casually into the tiny apartment, stood commandingly surveilling all, silently scrutinizing every detail of its content and substance. Leisurely, imperiously, he silently shut the apartment door behind him and stood in full and absolute command over all existence within that tiny apartment.

Rob was struck by the casual, leisure authority commanded by the man, possessed of absolute and definitive dominion over all that existed in that tiny apartment, expecting and receiving without least effort or demand or delay instant submission and abject obeisance to his least whim and command.

"The air of fully righteous justice," Rob understood. *"For such a man, there does not exist even the concept of 'self'-righteous, his whim and command incontrovertibly righteous in and of itself,"* and Rob marveled at the prickling dread ignited by such absolute certitude of righteous dominion over all.

"Even his superiors tread warily in his presence," Rob was sure, did not doubt in the least.

"What must the feel of such absolute command be like," he shuddered, without least envy over the magnitudes of responsibility of such unimaginable power.

"But then, such men hardly care about responsibility," trying to imagine the thorough disregard proffered by that one percent, possessing very near such unassailable command, derived of overarching wealth and power, wielded over politics and policy and law, relished over their diminutive lesser, the remaining ninety-nine percent.

Rob shrugged away distracting thought and returned to the room and to the moment.

From the shower, a small cry of outrage as the third man, at invisible command from his superior, returned to the bathroom and two-fingered Lainy out of the shower and into the mist-shrouded air, she struggling with towel, to clutch it to her, barely covering her, the man now not so much as noticing her as he drew the shower curtain fully open to peer in and inspect.

Rob's heart pounded harder than the fists earlier pounding on the apartment door, as he watched Lainy lunge at the man, dive at him, struggling to throw him into the tub under her own righteous reckoning *just* as he was about to peer into the tub, she exerting all strength to propel the man into the tub, face contorted with the effort, quietly grunting outrage through clenched teeth as she dove at him with all strength, he looking mildly amused, standing immobile to Lainy's full effort.

With smooth and casual and expert movement, the man shunted Lainy aside and sent her sprawling to the floor, towel flailing and she groping after it, he hardly glancing after her, not least interested in her, about to peer into the tub. But he'd glanced over his shoulder to *Command*, and with signal too subtle for Rob to catch, Command signaled the man out, the subordinate instantly leaving, and leaving the bathroom door wide with Lainy sprawled on the floor frenetically draping her towel around her.

With movements as casual and relaxed as any could be, the men filed out of the tiny apartment, melting away under command too subtle for Rob to perceive, as Command sat himself down on the over-stuffed chair beside the bed, eyeing Rob dismissively, then frowning lightly as he reconsidered his dismissal of this... boy.

The man spoke with unnatural calm, but seemed sincere in casting an ever gentle, even paternal face to Rob and, then, to Lainy, now in bathrobe approaching Rob. *Command* waited for Lainy to compose herself as she made her way to Rob's side, she engaged in wistful solidarity with Rob, sitting ever-close to him, a spectacle the man appeared to find somehow surreal and vaguely cheerless, witnessing what Rob was sure the man considered pretense of intimacy, alien and affected, *"likely never having known even remotely what Lainy and I know of,"* the thought pitifully sad, *"tragic,"* in silent, unbidden thought.

The man spoke disarmingly, gently and sparingly, fully sparing them the brunt of his full-frontal roughness, likely common to his everyday blunt-brutality, revealing something deeper of him, of shadow tenderness to this youngest couple despite their likely feigned attachment:

"I am looking for a dangerous—a *very* dangerous—man. He's believed to have viciously, sadistically, tortured and murdered a man a short time ago. *You*, Ben Rob," he paused, an appraising eye holding Rob and Lainy pinioned, "have met with the murderer very recently."

The man paused, inspected Lainy and Rob for any least betrayal of look or posture, of pallor of skin or pattern of breath or any errant betrayal, invisibly marking them through firm denial. He continued mildly, observing everything, missing nothing:

"As such you yourselves are suspect to complicity. I *know* both of you," eyes pinning Rob, then nod to Lainy, "accept your responsibilities, your legal and *moral* obligations, as most-honest brokers of our social order and of our laws. I *know* you both will be honestly and immediately forthcoming should any news avail itself to you—as your acquaintances and compatriots have done and continue to do. It a grievous crime, otherwise."

The man stopped expectantly, eyes drilling into Rob's, then Lainy's. He sustained his glare and his silence, waited for their next, expected Rob to say next what *had* to be said next.

In a flash of insight so brief it came and went without word or image, Rob understood he had no choice but to reply, and struggled for words to say which would not perjure him, soil his integrity, taint his vanity… or Lainy's. But in that very moment's insight came the words to say and he blessed Goodness for her kindness, then wondered to what length people—*he*—would go… to preserve the illusion of personal integrity, of feigning to himself more even than to the world the lofty heights of his integrity.

Before speaking, Rob recalled arguing with Allman about truth and illusion… and deceptions of truth, especially to *self*-deception, and shuddered, what else here and now, as he recalled:

"To withhold truth and to still believe you are truthful is the ultimate vanity and the ultimate deception: self-deception. Self-deception ushers in the definitive and inexorable corrosion of justice and righteousness."

The thought flashed through Rob's mind that Allman had been right, fully right, and Rob wondered just who and what Allman was, *is*, as Rob replied to the expectation put to him, hoping not to evade but to *avoid*, even knowing he cannot elude, Rob answering without, he hoped, noticeable pause:

"I take my obligations seriously. I would not obstruct justice."

Rob returned the other's stare fully, aware his own sorely lacked the other's conviction—*"mindless conviction,"* he judged, aware he judged the other too harshly, likely unjustly.

Rob struggled to justify thoughts intruding, beguiling:

"There are greater truths than simple truth," thought whispered, wondering him where rests that vermillion shadowland between righteousness and self-righteousness.

The man ground his stare first into Rob, then into Lainy, with neither credence nor trust in anything they might voice, and with an unnatural calm, hypnotic quiet to eye and voice, rasped:

"Be warned: some freedoms are allowed great latitude. Others... none. Liberties can never be limitless, must always be controlled... and your freedoms," eyeing Lainy and Rob knowingly, under some undisclosed certitude, "hang by the finest thread, a thread of *my* tolerance. Justice *will* prevail, one way or the other—at *my* forbearance and, I most sincerely pray, not to your everlasting regret."

But his eyes were soft, more even than his voice, and Rob took it to mean the man understood, genuinely understood, not just the circumstance but *them*. Still, Rob's thoughts screamed silently:

"Justice? Whose justice? Yours? Your overlord's? No, yours is not justice... it's law, just Law."

And in silent whisper, maybe even to himself:

"No, MY justice will prevail!" the words whispering Rob's absolute conviction in evermore insistent whisper, inescapable even if unuttered, if unuttered even to himself.

"Yes, justice WILL prevail—at MY forbearance!" Rob hardly auguring the thought before the thought cringed him.

To Lainy's and Rob's silence, the man gestured a barely discernable movement of chin and eye above grim smile... toward the bathroom door, still wide open, still with shower steaming opacity through the room. Then he stood, turned his back, and ambled leisurely out the door with all the time in the world.

'He' is engulfed within his vermillion shadowland witness to the feel of fear and dread and hate and rage as he'd never known, could not comprehend... as the pedestrian masses gaze up to him in this, his most-superficial heaven, listing precariously above them, hardly a hair's breadth above them, as scornful overlords, in their tentative, tenuous ascendance, strut and preen contempt dismissively and derisively and contemptuously from above, staring them all down.

The amassed see no end to their need and so, now, coil to hurl themselves up alongside their overlords—to fling them, and themselves, out into the awaiting dark, the dark ever patient just beyond the vermillion shadowland of their specious illusion of sanctuary.

He rouses amid the boundless concatenations laid before him, laid at his feet in this, his vermillion shadowland. He screams to have and to be as he'd earned, and now—is granted what he'd earned:

Wave on wave of sightless orbs above silenced mouths interred within skeletal faces ebb and flow and rise and crash against his feet in rising tide, rising to overflow and smother him, and these of the amassed—and every bit, too, of their sneering, preening overlords—caught as one in the maelstrom.

This great phantasm is unleashed on him and he is battered and torn by its savage onslaught, submerged under its blinded brutality, drowned under images and sounds and thoughts and very feel of their outrage, here and now fully and finally untethered, leveled fully and finally against him.

He is crushed beneath the residue of half-forgotten hope and dream, of abandoned honesty and fairness and dispassion, as all of it and all of them wash over him and sweep him away.

Through shadow atop shadow now remain only what and how to understand this and, above all, how to transform them, how to deliver them, from preconception and misconception and hate and rage and the inexhaustible, self-righteous greed that leads them all, here and now, to this. And here and now they search for still more, anything more, of deliverance, deserved or not.

Glaring blindly, screaming silently, they wash over him and grip him and tear him under outrage—only the least of it rising at him from outside him.

He struggles to regain semblance of reason and calm, struggles to right himself, wonders if he has earned the right to least consolation or comfort—witnesses his dream clawing for understanding, to be judged reasonable and defensible and justified, as his dream lists him to obliteration and oblivion.

Nothing is recognizable of him now but a skeletal remnant of misbegotten hope and dream, corruptions of his own greed and arrogance, and he wonders limply why 'this'

his need: to render himself back to what he is and has been—
empty.

Chapter 36.

No sooner had the detective strolled out the apartment door than Rob rushed to lock the door while Lainy ran frantically to the shower to switch off the steaming torrent. Sweeping the sheet off King she eased him up out of the water, a half-drowned rat… *"lost and abandoned and thoroughly alone, even for us,"* that last a mournful sop to this fleeting brotherhood.

The three sat for a long moment in complete silence once King had dried, recovered embers of calm, and after furtive whispers apprised King of the moments just past, what to say in the wake of such moments.

"Indicted as murderer."

Each fought to *not* look the other in the eye, fearful of meaning and intent communed in the look of an eye or curve of lip too readily, or willfully, misconstrued.

Sighing from the endless well of unimaginable mire, King struggled to calm, failed, tried again, and again, finally accepted middling success under simple terms:

"I am no murderer," sound more than word exhorting credence of innocence.

As if that statement satisfied all, King lapsed back to silence, not daring to look his saviors in the eye and they not daring to look him in the eye, fearing sight would nullify sound.

King glanced up as their crushing silence fed his fear and dread, no longer room for rage, those welling and threatening more than he could tame, rendering him faded and shriveled to tenuous mirage, the brutality and finality of murder settling in him alongside the arbitrariness of justice, what justice, baffling behind veils of lies, what else, nothing else, to explain such judgment, and only remained 'why,' alien and inscrutable.

Rob finally broke the back of consuming silence by switching-on overloud music and quietly speaking with measured calm of what they already knew, where else to begin, whispers barely audible even with head and ears bent to hear:

"We've got to keep you here until the heat eases, until the feverish manhunt subsides, at least a bit. The police will be back. No doubt. None at all. The only question being when— and then, *after*, to spirit you away...."

He stopped at that, no word or thought to where, more crying even than how.

Lainy caught Rob's eye, motioned to King, whispered:

"We can't be too quiet for too long, they'll suspect. We've got to make some noise, move around a bit, at least a little bit."

She rose, strode to the small space that was kitchenette, and began puttering with pots and pans as Rob joined her in a ritual of preparing to cook, what more natural and innocent.

King heard quiet murmur of conversation amid the overloud music, and waited anxiously. And waited. Shifting nervously on his seat, he glanced furtively about the room, edging deeper into something he'd never before encountered, having always been so sure, so confident, never having known need, not of anything or of anyone but himself, the rest always falling into place as unalterable law of the universe, of existence. And here, now, this... struggling to a calm eluding his greatest will.

King watched Lainy and Rob walk to and then circle around the overstuffed chair on which he himself now sat. He watched the two eyeing the chair, feeling of it, checking underneath it, quietly rapping at the wood supporting the seat cushion, exchanging glances, nodding, smiling thinly... for him, he realized. He smiled still more wanly, understanding.

The work was slow and tedious, having to be done silently so to not rouse the suspicion of unseen listeners, no doubt of unseen listeners, all the while struggling to sustain the 'normal' ambience of quiet conversation, of occasional laughter, of other noises relevant to ordinary living and not to furtive, hidden ploys and evasions and constructs.

All three worked tirelessly until the work was done. Then, only then, they rested, and preened uncertainly over their cleverness and workmanship, never for a moment sure of their goal: King's safe keeping.

The chair had been disemboweled and reassembled, to all outward appearances having been totally unmolested... for concealment.

They'd built a sturdy casing beneath the seat-cushion of the chair... where a man could be secreted from vigilant eyes.

King would need lie on his back, face wrenched to one side and no space to so much as turn his head, his head right at the seat's edge, his legs bent up at the hip and splayed behind the seat-back, space enough, barely, to breathe but rendered blind and scarcely more than deaf within the confines of the casing.

King stared at the result grim-faced and panic-eyed, knowing to be grateful and to express gratitude to the two for assembling his... tomb.

"Better such a tomb than one in which to be permanently interred, this at least transient," whispered assurance with nothing assured, King's 'I hope and pray' lost even in his own mind.

King plied himself into the casing, quickly emerged, managed a reedy smile of grim satisfaction for having disappeared within the confines of the chair without apparent trace, if only for a moment.

Preparations complete, no sign of tampering revealed... "at least to us," understanding: a trained eye would see more than they could ever hope to.

Rob and Lainy reasoned aloud, each supplementing, augmenting, the other:

"If they suspect—and they *will* suspect—they'll check this apartment and everything in it with minute exactitude, expediently as possible."

They glanced at one another for a long moment nodding grimly, King staring, then Rob clenched fist around invisible knob of razor-sharp blade and stabbed one quick, sharp jab into the back cushion of the chair, whispering:

"With that stiletto of his," meaning the detective's walking stick, why else grip it so firmly and expertly, a murderous weapon, tool, what else could it be.

Rob saw the look in King's eye on hearing their deliberations, and rushed to soothe, assure:

"It'll be through the middle of the back cushion, where your heart would be if you were seated in the chair, or seated behind the back cushion... to check if you're hidden in the chair. The solid board beneath the seat-cushion will protect you should they decide to jab there, unlikely as it is."

Lainy struggled to suppress the 'I hope and pray,' knowing they all struggled to the same, she and Rob more even than King, that being the way of them, little doubting the wooden seat-support would hardly stand up to a stiletto wielded by expert hand.

"At least in this," Lainy whispered, "the odds are with you more than any other I can imagine... and later, the odds will be even better," the 'I hope and pray' still and silent in the dark.

In early evening, after settling King inside his vault and triple-checking that no telltale signs betrayed him—*"us,"* Rob and Lainy understood as well—the two strolled out the door.

"It wouldn't do to have us permanently ensconced in our apartment, too suspicious, we've got to act—*be*—'normal.'" They all knew it and *so* King acquiesced to secrete himself in his tomb.

/

Lainy and Rob strolled, to all outward appearance they hoped, carefree and casual, deluding themselves they succeeded. They refrained from furtive looks over shoulders, afraid to glimpse the watchers, sure there were watchers.

They strolled arm-in-arm, hand-in-hand, as always, quiet, as always, ambling leisurely, for all the world carefree and natural. And so they were, in this, each other.

The evening was cool and clear and full with life flitting and scampering around them, they understanding the wonder of life proceeding without least regard of them.

Lainy remarked, with a smile and quiet laugh:

"It's funny."

She stood in her tracks, contemplating the notion.

Rob was silent, waited to hear, would always await her.

"When people pass by, the birds up and fly away at their least approach. But…" she laughed ever quietly, squeezing to Rob still closer, shying a bit from her notion, "but when *we* reach near… it's as if they knew, could *feel*, our love for them."

The ensuing silence was warmth between them.

They stepped into the student union with arms still intertwined and stepped quietly to a table on which lay a stack of The Sentient, the headline instantly gripping them:

"MURDER"

They flinched as the word lunged for them, furtively glancing around to see if anyone noticed their manner and reaction—no one, it seemed. But who could know, aware that watchers scrutinized their every move and *that* no delusion, even if unseen.

They withdrew to the darkest, quietest, farthest corner of the great atrium—as always, no different for this than for any other, for simple privacy and intimacy, in farthest, darkest corners of the opulent luxury of intimacy and privacy at little cost, hardly any cost but for whisperers of cynics and gossipmongers and slyest slanderers. Lainy and Rob cared precious little—but still more than nothing, that being life—of that and of those.

They sat and their knees touched and their thighs brushed and their arms lay intertwined as they shared the paper, Lainy reading softly to her Rob. Then, whisper of quiet horror:

"What mind could have *done* such a thing?" awe thick in her voice at a thing beyond understanding, reading quietly:

"…King's fingerprints found on bloodied letter-opener… blood matches Dean Ivry's… witnesses heard heated argument... clear and compelling... means, motive and opportunity... most intense manhunt in local memory...."

Another article, Lainy read in hoarse whisper:

"...Ivry... tortured, mutilated, murdered... cause of death final stab through eye... Panther King sought for suspected ritual mutilation-murder... political agitator well-known to authorities... militant extremist with history of violence and severe mental illness... psychopath... sociopath..." and on and on in grimmest detail.

Lainy paused, fought nerve, hunted calm, continued, now reading from an editorial, not hers:

"...not only must Panther King himself suffer the fullest extent of Law but so too must any and all who—*at this very moment*—abet and sustain the Beast within secreted sanctuary. They who shield the Beast must know—from scratches on skin to bloodstained hand to wild-eyes and wilder mind—of his irrefutable and incontestable and unpardonable guilt and so they too must share his justice to the fullest extent of Law. They who avert eyes and shut minds perpetuate such abhorrent crime and so *must* be as severely held to account as King himself. They *must* surrender their charge if they have any smallest hope of mitigating their guilt... and that only if they do so *now*."

"I admit I *myself* was once blinded and misguided in supporting Panther King. Now I face my misguided judgment and so fully admit: *I was wrong!*... and now throw all my resources and The Power Fraternity itself behind every effort to bring the murderer Panther King *and* his abettors to the fullest justice of Law, and pray it is full enough to expunge such atrocity from humanity."

Lainy drew-in a breath as she read the signature: "TJ Allman."

Lainy looked at Rob:

"Signed in his own hand."

It was, they both knew, singular, to have the signature rather than the printed name appended to an editorial.

"This is Allman's message... to us," they silently understood, shuddering at cascading implications.

After a moment, they drew each other out of the Student Union building clutching each other, and the paper for King to read.

Once well outside, Lainy asked the question lancing both their minds:

"Could we be *wrong?*"

"Could King *have* done it?"

Incredulity scored Lainy's eyes at both thoughts:

"Is he a sociopath, a deranged and sadistic *murderer*— and we so very misjudging?"

Her eyes were wide, reflected both their greatest fear, that they were, in fact, harboring such a creature in their sanctuary, the only place existing anywhere in which they had assured *themselves* peace and sanctuary, or deluded themselves into so believing, and now imperiling that drawn hope.

Rob felt her turmoil every bit as his own and tried to soothe her, and himself, with softly calming whisper, with voice and touch more than word and conviction:

"It just doesn't... *feel*... right. And you feel it too."

He was sure she did, she seeing more of existence than he could hope to, he knew.

"It just doesn't feel... *right*. You saw him, you heard him. Does he strike you as a vicious sociopath, a sadistic murderer? Can he so thoroughly suborn us... of *that?*"

Lainy sighed and snuggled closer to her Rob, held him still more tightly to her:

"Yes. But how can we be *sure?*"

And in forlorn despair:

"It's so hard to *know*. How can we *know?* How can we be *sure*... of *anything?*"

A half-moment's hesitation, with finality in word and look:

"How can we be sure... of *Allman*."

Their words faded to silence as both fully apprehended:

"Reversed—it makes perfect sense. But only in reverse: Allman the sadistic sociopath, King the victim more even than Ivry. It makes perfect sense, wallows in perfect character, imbued with the sound of truth."

Rob assured Lainy of one thing more as he turned to her and held her and soothed her with look and sound more than word:

"It's okay not to know. It's okay to be wrong. Even in this," as he prayed being wrong wouldn't get *themselves* hurt, or worse—only Lainy.

It struck Lainy:

"The writing goose-steps to thoroughly and virulently demonize King, and just the other day Allman was spouting self-righteous tribute about King and his rights and the justice of his calling. Now Allman's reviling and defiling King... according him no trial and no jury and no appeal and no slightest doubt to his guilt. Allman's anointed *himself* judge, jury—and executioner."

"The sound of truth," both recognized it, both wondered how duplicitous and mendacious such sound could be, too often is.

"Allman wants everyone to doubt even the *possibility* of King's innocence. Allman wants us to doubt not him but *ourselves* if we least question King's guilt—or Allman's authority."

Lainy's voice trailed to silence as both wondered at the truth *behind* Allman:

"Just who—what—lurks behind 'Allman'?"

Quietly, she wondered aloud for them both:

"Unless this has nothing to do with guilt or innocence but has only to do with the politics of casting circumstance to achieve a goal: Ivry erased—King devoured."

Suspicion dawned that Ivry had now been definitively eliminated... *"as rival? As threat?"* And so too, King.

Buried in her words they heard the sound of truth, and only 'why,' what *for*, lingered unanswered.

The question haunted the two as they walked, locked arm in arm, side by side, cosseted by the dark.

Finally, from Rob:

"Who would profit from this? King is worse than dead, sentenced to what's left of his life, whether caught and tried and convicted or running and hiding and cowering—for what little remains of his life. Who profits from that?"

Lainy: "Allman."

The word rolled off her tongue, incantation of unearthly wraith, the word rife with dark treachery and darker intent, a haunting, slithering corruption lurking in the dark, the word—*Allman*—possessed of sinister life all its own.

Compassion personified, in the form of Lainy, lamented:

"Even this atrocity against Ivry is as nothing to that against King... and all we can offer King is pity—and to prolong his misery for the pathetically little longer that we can."

They walked quietly, spare words lingering:

"Whatever happened that day, however it happened, one thing's sure: King's already been judged... and found guilty—and condemned to the worst possible sentence: to life, to suffer calumny and withered dream, to enduring oblivion."

"If King hadn't run and hid—he'd have fought and died. Only knowing *why* remains to him—and even that will surely be denied him."

/

The detective, a squat, powerful man, stood in the doorway of a residence hall apartment, a shadow in the dark, recollecting an image: a girl faintly screaming, rushing to cover herself, clawing at the man he'd ordered to inspect the room and... the shower.

The subordinate he'd commanded into the room had glanced at him for orders... now all eyes on memory, on the scene resurrected in memory—orders issued to his subordinate, imperceptible to all else, to relinquish the search.

"What need search when the finding is perfectly clear. What need see to confirm, confirmation derived from the commotion, from the misdirection of faint scream, no further evidence warranted."

The detective remembered his subordinate's look and took pride in that look, calm dispassion of a subordinate simply awaiting orders—any orders, whatever ordered.

The detective considered that… *"whatever ordered"*… and wondered to what degree the 'whatever' extended, how far would subordinates go to please, to curry.

He smiled a trace curve of lip—*"as it should be,"* not challenging the dark harbored in doubt, of a too-willing subordinate, not daring to consider at too long a length: *"too willing… to what?"*

He ignored implication with rational pretension:
"I would order him only to the Law."

But doubt lingered, silent in the dark, if a time should reach him when the Law is rendered subordinate to… something else.

He loved simple truths, pure and beautiful and sacrosanct. His subordinate had obeyed instantly, unquestioningly—*"as he should."* And for that too, only a wan smile, dread clinging with death-grip to the coattail of fulfillment.

The detective conjured the image, resurrected the scene: the glimpse he'd had of a half-closed bathroom door and a curtained, steaming shower. Of course. No doubt. None. Not then, not now.

"Res ipsa loquitur—the thing itself speaks," silent whisper affirming ancient teachings.

With movement too subtle to notice, the detective coaxed open Lainy and Rob's apartment door and slipped from the dark of hallway into the dark of imminent revelation—dark for the cascade of consequence always immanent to revelation.

Memory kindled detail and the exact position of every *thing* in the diminutive apartment, its exact nature and place and purpose and—all attention now abruptly riveted to an over-stuffed chair. Where else, how else.

He glided through the dark, silent apparition, motionless but for stealth of legs and feet and eyes and mind stirring, seeing everything, matching memory to this, now newly revealed reality. He flicked-on a finger-sized beam of light, penlight resting in quiet grip of one hand, the other occupying knobbed walking stick, fingers caressing the knob as a heartless lover does, less for love than utility.

He stepped soundlessly through the apartment, regarded the overstuffed chair, its placement in the room, how it listed in its corner. He compared resurrected memory to this reality, instantly spied the contrast and… smiled. He smiled a trace, grim smile, a trace broader than before, notwithstanding insight, thorough understanding, of centers of gravity and of what that shift tells of, portends, and of the unassailable heights of Law… and understanding its limit, every *thing* has its limits, after all.

He didn't need to but nonetheless, for the rigors of thoroughness, stepped into the bathroom, contemplated the shower, then to the hamper, lifted the lid, peered in, regarded an assortment of soiled fabric, one still-soaked through and… three towels.

His lips shed their grim smile, transformed to grimace: confirmation of what he was already fully certain, and now… no evading decision no matter his greatest urge to evade decision.

He strolled leisurely, no rush this, to the stereo, rummaged through mp3 lists, selected quiet classical, *that* for this, then back to grim smile… and overstuffed chair.

Every detail, risen fully alive in the reality of memory, compared itself to every detail fully revealed in *this* reality, confronted here and now.

He backed smoothly away from the chair, circled it with slow, measured step, drew nearer, very near, near enough to stroke the fabric of the chair and whisper comforting words shielded under soft, musical composition… certain of being heard and understood by no one but the cowed and hidden.

He whispered forlorn truth, only *that* for this:

"I am above suspicion," he confided to the chair.

"What I say *is* believed unquestioned. What do I care about cake and having my cake and eating it too… when those in dire need have no cake, nor bread, and lie in helpless want, cowed and hidden. What do I care for the first… or the second?"

He left unsaid: *"still, I care,"* wondering if *so* he'd been blessed, or cursed, and if *so* he should bless or curse himself.

He fully understood that he cared, having finally relinquished his need to know why, to understand *why*.

"Enough that I care…" he whispered, and *so* allowed it be known to this chair, that he cared, establishing it simply by doing what he would do, *"no need words, for this."*

"Even for this, the so little I do, will do, is enough, must be enough, and maybe too much," recognizing to what he was condemning the… chair.

He whispered softest, kindest words to the… chair:

"There is worse than unjust punishment for crime: punishment for no crime, and worse still, for another's."

To the chair:

"You must remain perfectly still and silent," he counseled the chair, drawing to softest voice and gentlest tone and quietest manner as he leaned just so, caressing the fabric of the chair tenderly, as true lovers do, reaching heart and mind to the overstuffed chair and its nestled ward.

"So little is left to be done and now nothing more to be done—by me, for you."

He exerted all will to *not* weep silent tears in the dark for this… chair.

He counseled the chair in softest, dearest tones:

"Don't respond to me, don't reveal yourself to me, not in *any* way. Make no sign you exist at all… so I may overlook you, so I cannot *know* you exist here, now, like this"—and all silent: *"even as I know and cannot help but know, cannot NOT know."*

Of self-corrosive lament and half-soaring pride, silent whisper in the dark sought to comfort:

"It is what I am, it is my essence. Who am I to deny what I am, all that I am and was born to."

He gripped the knob of his walking stick, unsheathed the hidden, hardened steel, and rammed it through the heart of the chair's seat-back, trembling to see the blade, to witness whether emerging red and wet or clean and dry, and grim joy to see it perforate the seat-back and emerge—clean and dry, as he'd known it would be, prayed it would be.

So he taught: "Take nothing for granted, nothing in the least: even the list of a chair... determines."

He stared through the seat cushion of the chair, saw a vision there as starkly evident as any dream in its dreaming: a face with sweat beaded on forehead and limbs strained to immobility, teeth clenched in grim despair, eyes fading in the dark under dread more even than fear—this the least of his fear, even barely fathoming his own dread.

The detective listened raptly to the dread harbored in cowed and hidden eyes, wondering, wishing to know:

"Who are you, harbored secret in the dark, who has buried this one here, here and now cowed and hidden from me, secret in a chair?" And speaking quiet whisper to that one:

"What is it you want?" and the detective could not help but reply to his own quiet whisper:

"We, all of us—even you, cowed and hidden here— work for ourselves. No matter what we do or think we do: We labor for ourselves... for self-preservation, for sanctimony, for love, for god and country. We *do* for and only for ourselves— all else is illusion, delusion, *self*-delusion, that we work for any one else or anything more."

/

Later that night, three figures huddled in the dark, music sounding not-softly, to drown furtive, desolate whisperings:

"I swear to you! I *swear*—I had *nothing* to do with Ivry's death!"

If eye and tone could impart gospel truth, here was incontrovertible proof, truth beyond doubt.

King continued:

"He... Allman... told me to work it out with Ivry, defuse the impasse, calm the frenzy—*compromise*."

King's eyes shone in the dark, lips quivering as thought raged, what to say, what to *not* say, to convince beyond any illusion of vaguest shadow of smallest doubt.

"I thought: I could repeat a course or two—that's what Allman told me Ivry would settle for. Allman would see to it that I'd get good grades, more than enough to replace the failing ones I'd gotten—which I swear were politically motivated! I *always* got good grades before this!" forcing calm on himself, continuing:

"In exchange... I'd have to tone down my rhetoric, ease-up on damning the administration, relent, a bit, on how they're exploiting us..." he eyed Lainy and Rob, added, "exploiting *all* of us," then continued: "They exploit the electorate, you know, should know, by constraining membership to the elite, to the brokers in this country."

Seeing incredulity fill Lainy and Rob, King asserted:

"Of *course* you're skeptics, who wouldn't be? I only know what I know from what I've found doing my 'homework,' my *real* homework—which our *media* should be doing with us and *for* us! Damn their souls, pandering to the plutocrats and kleptocrats...."

King calmed himself, continued:

"Allman told me it was all set: Ivry'd already agreed to it and all I needed was to meet with him finalize the deal and shake hands on it face to face, eye to eye. But when I got there...."

King's voice broke, fingers trembled, sweat beaded brow as he struggled to right himself, managed a bare truce:

"I went over to Ivry's office, just like Allman told me to, nine o'clock *sharp*. Allman insisted it be *exactly* nine pm *sharp* and *'Don't be late!'* he commanded. So I wasn't late. I was a little early, in fact. And right away, from the first second—I knew it would be bad. I should've known it would be bad!"

King paused, groped to recover himself:

"When I got there, the door stood a little bit open, and pitch dark inside the office."

He silenced as the scene unfolded in memory.

"I knocked anyway, called out 'anybody there?' but only dead quiet in the dark."

A wild look of suppressed hysteria etched his eyes, he struggling to recapture himself:

"I was gonna leave—I should've left! *I should have left!* But I didn't. I went in. What did I know? How was I to *know*? I should have *known*!"

Again he paused, saw it alive:

"As soon's I stepped into that office there was a sudden explosion of pain and that… that *sound*… a dull thump, like a coconut getting smashed…" feeling it, hearing it all again, the feel and sound of his head being smashed-in.

"Next thing I knew I was on the floor and all whirling in my head… and blood on my hands, and splattered over my face and on my clothes—look! *Look!*" as if looking would prove him innocent.

He grabbed Lainy's hand and brought it to the back of his head, treading her fingertips over the crusted fissure on his scalp… "could I have done that to *myself?*"

To Lainy's flaring distress, King instantly relinquished his grip on her hand, his eyes dull, cold, what use such pitiful relic, shallow proof to retrieve and shelter stolen dream and life.

"Don't you *see?* What good is 'proof' to a walking *dead* man? I'm a walking *dead man!*"

His voice edged to hysteria, to fever pitch under frantic eye and quivering lip, and Rob flew to calm him, to salve him, seeing King flame to madness as dread and despair overwhelmed rage and hope and prayer limned in desolate panic.

Rob pressed himself against King, face-to-face, eye-to-eye, as he clapped a hand over King's mouth and set lips to King's ear with desperate urgings whispered to King's ear:

"Shut up! Shut UP—use your brain, man! You're lost if you don't… use… your… brain!"

The desperate urgency in Rob's eye and voice tempered King, subdued him for that moment, and King collapsed, head fallen to knees, and he covered face in hands breathing "*help me!*" in barely audible whisper, and finally moaning silent "*help me*" to anyone and to no one—who could help, after all.

Minutes of quiet whisperings transmuted to hours and finally Lainy whispered for them all:

313

"I can't see you getting a fair deal… and if you turn up—you'll turn up dead."

They all thought it: *"Grim truth, detest truth, what else is there but truth."*

Her voice, full with pity and lament, simply said what needed to be said, what simply was.

More silence, and finally, still from Lainy:

"If what you say is true…" she was interrupted by King's frantic eyes and whisper "If? *IF?*" to which Lainy placed a calming hand on his and he quieted, understanding her.

"There's *power* behind it. After all—*your own people turned on you!*" whisper of quiet fervor in manifest truth.

"I can think of only one way for you: you've got to hide out for a while, for a long while, for—the rest of your life."

She didn't add: *"for what's left to your life."* What need.

"You'll stay here till the heat eases up, at least enough to spirit you away. You've got to hide out—here—until heat and memory fade a little, at least a little, so *you* could fade away and get away, to…."

She didn't finish, couldn't finish, no idea where he could fade *to*. And with boundless, impotent apology:

"That's all we can *do*. There's nothing more we can do," her eyes mournful prayer for the vanishingly little they could do.

Chapter 37.

Ben Rob faced the panorama displayed through the great window wall of the back office high in the Liberty Spire, staring out, down, over the vast crowd massed and amassing below—*"packed beyond withstanding, strained on verge, roiled to tearing itself apart, writhing to and fro, caged Beast seething, coiling, primed...."*

Ben Rob roused from his fugue and, facing that great vista outside and below, turned mind's eye to watch that selfsame scene in *him*, microcosm in *him*—*"caged animal coiling, straining, on verge of..."*—but conflagration in him willed itself manifest not in his own outward violence but through inner workings, seething to this massed and amassing below.

"Through them I will wreak justice," whisper haunted, *"vastly more than vengeance: Justice!"* and in silent whisper: *"My justice—who else's?"* as images of Allman and the machine *behind* Allman prowled invidiously, insidiously.

He silenced whispers... *"intent on revealing me—to me,"* and refused their taunt and contempt and shame.

The front office suddenly lit with DeCeeve's loud outburst, crass and repugnant, ripping into the silence and the dark, violating yet again, flaring Rob's outrage still whiter hot, barely contained violence in him burning, demanding.

"Have you *seen* that crowd out there? Can you *feel* it?"

DeCeeve glared at Rob through panic-eyes and scarcely hidden, tremulous voice not knowing if to blame Rob or the amassing dissenters or that other, that hidden other, that shadow puppeteer lurking always and ever behind and within DeCeeve's own every thought and whisper.

Rob shrugged invisibly, *"who cares now about hidden shadow and who is to blame,"* knowing full well:

"*I am to blame—and thank,*" and he prayed that gratitude be the end result, cringing that damnation will all likely be, thought and dream haunting, of being contemned as just another, just the latest, of history's most reviled, judgment here and now resting, waiting, ever vigilant and ever patient.

/

Amid errant and vague, imagined light of earliest day, only the dark was clear as Panther King's voice, far away, small and resonantly afraid, rasped whisper through the phone:

"Allman."

The phone had rung out of the dark, receiver lifted to a distant whisper '*Allman*', sound near-empty but for all the word held, the concept *Allman* more portent than sound or name, rasped from inside the phone:

"Allman." The sound distant, strangled, drained.

A brusque, dismissive voice sneered reply to that whisper, fully aware of source and complexion of such whisper:

"Of course."

Sound and word compelled meaning, retained silence:

"*So dim of you not to have known all along: It's I to whom you must turn, now, at this, for this, with no where else to turn and no one else to turn to.*"

King's voice was desolate plea:

"Why'd you do that thing to Panther King."

It was statement of fact with no question or wonder to it, whispered through the remnant of that voice, laden of exhaustion and abject defeat and willing, yearning surrender, implacable conclusion to relentless flaying of will and hope.

A quiet laugh, near-hidden and flauntingly *not* hidden, from Allman, at this paltry rendition of cleverness and guile that the speaker was not, in fact, pathetically, ridiculously, clearly Panther King himself speaking, beseeching some all-important need—the reply: "What 'thing' is that?" a contemptuous artifice implicit in the sound of Allman's voice, manifest without need even to hint at asking, the truth of it looming impudent and heedless of King and of what little

316

remained of King, of life and pride, sumptuously flaunted in King's face, by Allman, in understated clarion pronouncement, catastrophic and wrenching for King, triumphant gore and glory for Allman… *"just as it should be, as Goodness Graced it be and would always be for me and for my ascendance over King and all the Kings of this world—and they are ALL Kings,"* hidden in the almighty triumph of Allman's voice, exactly as expected and ordained.

A change then, of this spiraling tone of certitude, and Allman's voice transformed to consummate, politic, emollient, embodiment of humility—in word and only in word, not deigning voice to tow—now pleading King to patience over events onrushing, beyond anything anyone, hinting even Allman himself, could otherwise have anticipated and interdicted.

The new words with old voice were apparition, ruse derived of deep understanding of King and of those like King, of King's circumstance and of King's desperate need and, so, of utility for some smallest sop from Allman to face-save King's ignoble annihilation, some sheerest fig-leaf, transparent veil, to lend to some smallest vestige, residue, of integrity and self-esteem and validation.

Allman: "I had no choice. My support for King was absolute—and he betrayed me."

Prolonged silence, then, finally:

King: "I—he—*never* betrayed you!"

Allman, feigning: "There was nothing I could do. King knew I was putting *myself* on the line for him when I arranged his meet with Ivry—and King betrayed me. There was nothing I could do. When he took Ivry's life he very nearly took my own—my career, my future, my *life*. There was nothing I could do. I *had* to renounce King—for what he did and for what he proved to be. There was nothing I could do."

The silence that followed was absolute, and Allman waited crushingly-silent on the inevitable, with long practice and finely honed mastery, luxuriating in the onrush of triumph climaxing on and on through King's long and labored silence.

King, finally accepting unalloyed and miserable shame and defeat, bleated in hoarse, rasping whisper, all that was left to him:

"He is *innocent!*" implication unsaid: *"You— betrayed—me! Who else."* The last was resignation to blinding reality, for the moment abstaining pretense, even to himself, of Allman's insidious perfidy—but: What recourse? None.

Again, absolute silence, now still more prolonged, as Allman waited on King to surrender his last, miserable shard.

Finally, King again, still, with nothing more to say or be said, simply rasped again, for want of something, anything, of greater substance: "*You* betrayed *him!*" muttered through dying embers of voice and self.

Allman allowed King a smallest relent, and replied in cool, calm voice:

"Only the *murderer* could say, *know*, with such absolute conviction, that King is innocent. So—*you* are the murderer. *You* betrayed Panther King."

The effort King exerted to claw out speech was palpable through the plastic and wire of the phone, unmistakable, like nothing else. Allman *knew*, with absolute certainty derived of long-practiced experience, having heard just the same in word and tone and shame from so many others just, exactly, like King, that King had now fully ripened to final, decisive submission.

King hissed through the phone: "I am *not* the murderer! I am NOT a *murderer!*"

Allman heard King exclaim it, scream it with all will and every effort, barely managing a hoarse whisper through empty, guttural drawl in open and shameless display of exhaustion and fear and decisive surrender.

Allman knew to keep silent, to allow King this.

"I was tried and judged and executed—by *you!*"

Allman plied his genius through voice honed to smooth perfection of spellbinding salve:

"I couldn't bring myself to believe it of you, *you* of all people, in whom I had and still have *absolute* trust and faith. But when you didn't step forward and surrender yourself to scrutiny and the rule of law, everyone didn't just think you guilty but *knew* you guilty. I as well. And whoever hid you and told you to stay hidden—he, she, *they*—are the guilty… of condemning you and damning you. I held out for you as long as I could and far longer than anyone else, longer even than I should have. Those *others*, who hid you and kept you hidden and kept you looking guilty as sin, *they* betrayed you, *they* sold you out, *they* condemned—*damned*—you."

"Now is the time" thought whispered to Allman, of gut instinct and long practice, to utter his final incantation, feeling King's desolation crested, King now fully ready to leap at this last and only hope, not daring this final crumb of hope slip by:

"Every shred of evidence pointed to you—there was nothing I could do." Practiced pause: "But, *now*…."

Allman left the rest unsaid, waited for King to want it, to need it, to be ecstatic-relief and bliss to seize upon it, before all would be lost and too late: *That or nothing—ever again."*

The silence was absolute, seemed endless, and finally King exhorted, pleaded, with dead eyes and deader voice incarnate through the phone:

"*Help me*…." voiced through whisper so weak and distant as more emptiness than silence, hardly voice at all, trailing to less than sound in King's voice.

Now Allman readied his final stroke, speaking calmly and decisively, with spellbinding smoothness:

"Tell me you're innocent—I'll believe you, and make others believe too. All you need now is to come home, come back—to me."

The lure and seduction were irresistible:

"Tell no one, not *any* one—especially not *them*—that you're returning home, to me. There's no one you can trust. *I*— am the last and only you can trust, can ever trust."

The shade, that remnant that was Panther King, melted into the dark, exhausted and terrified and wholly alone. Beneath awareness he understood… his will, his life, had been torn from him, was lost to him, only this parched and pathetic remnant was left to him… as benediction to Allman.

The shadow that was Panther King faded, dissipated, remanded permanently under Allman in the silence and the dark.

'He' gazes down at the remnant of the amassed, draped and listless and torn and strewn beyond the horizon, of sightless eyes imbedded in skeletal orbs, of wave after wave of their remnant, and he struggles to gouge some least exultation, some least residue of fulfillment from boundless regret and immeasurable remorse, all that is left to him, of him, in this residue of peace and silence in the dark.

He lifts eyes up to the heavens, seemingly a hair's breadth above this here and now, where such as he, those least notable of all, had believed they'd earned and deserved their portion of bliss and sanctuary and riches through their endless endeavors to be more than they are. Now those heavens too are, simply, gone, dissipated, and he and those execrable like him are remanded and abandoned to the silence in the dark.

No shard of memory remains here, now, as witness to such works as once were his pride, pretensions to aspiring for the greater good, and now he stands mute and doleful wondering how to uncover, recover, the path from pretension to redemption.

He squints through hungry eyes urging to see above, to some least glimpse above, to witness firsthand the transcendent heavens hidden from him, certain they must loom somewhere near, just a bit higher than he could hope to reach, which he'd so longed to reach, had been so desperate to reach—but he glimpses only echoes of the dark, and bemoans:

"Who am I, how can I, least hope to deserve such promise, let alone deliver that promise for the greater good?"

He is irretrievably certain how vanishingly pale is awareness, his or anyone's, realizing only now that there is, must be, some indefinable time, thought, impulse—something— between what was and what will be, immanent within what is, inherent between each 'now' lingering in him that might promise a least glimpse of those transcendent heavens.

"Intentions mean, must mean, something, some least thing, as some least means by which I and those like me might be granted pity and pardon and passage. Only 'how' remains veiled behind sanctimonies of illusion and self-delusion.

He recalls awakening, so short a time ago, to how empty he'd been, had always been, and only now wakes to a trace glimmer of what he must otherwise endure being... stranded and empty as time and sense grind on, he grudging both for not abandoning and ending and finally sparing him.

Still... ever slowly, ever gradually, he witnesses glimmers surfacing up from out of that sea of empty hope lying bent and broken and shattered and scattered, endlessly flowing out from his endeavors. He feels more than sees embers of new awareness slowly rising up under new hope and renewed prayer for a dawn within which to reach some least glimmer of genuine understanding leached out of genuine contrition:

"Only for having been empty could I, now, begin a newfound inspiration, with renewed clarity, with forethought under new awareness limned behind greatest vigilance underpinning all intentions."

"And now," he smiles thinly, at long last understanding: "'Now' remains to be seen."

Chapter 38.

Rob sat in the silence and the dark, contemplating:

"How often do we deliberate amid rational awareness—and how often are we simply interred under primitive reflex, rising to provocations, swept aside by circumstance... which fully controls, we unable to control even ourselves...."

/

Rob sat in the front passenger seat of the town car, beside his young woman, his driver and shield, just one among his manifold beauteous people. He thought to turn to her, felt urged to regard her, to stare into blazing pulchritude of flowing hair and piercing eyes and smoothest skin and most-delicate hands and sharpest wit and keenest intellect and fullest insight shaped and guided by him, all of her fashioned first and foremost for planning, deliberating, dreaming... and only lastly for touching and stroking and loving, by someone—*"but not me."*

He wondered at that last, whether lament or simple, honest understanding of his assiduous fidelity to his calling.

He absently wondered—*'why not me?'*—and reflexively refused his urgency to turn to her now, to stare at her fully, at all of her, to take her and feast on her and devour her, and of that, least of all the sight and scent and feel of her, urging to plunge not into her presence but into her essence.

He shrugged off primal, self-absorbed listings and turned to face manifest reality, the reality of the dark awaiting him just beyond the car's door. He reverted to contemplating why he sat here, now, in the front passenger seat of this town car:

"I will be seen as not thoroughly 'of the people' if I sit in back, 'Lord' chauffeured by the 'Lesser.'"

He smiled a thin crease of lip:

"Let the sanctimonious self-idolaters, the notables ascended and gathered here in this grand home, cluck tongues and roll eyes. Let them exchange sneers and knowing glances of contempt and derision of me, insinuating and leering at perceived, ostentatiously covert intent, with my beauteous. Let them defile me as shameless lecher and self-promoter, self-adulating pretender, flaunting self-effacement, affectation of humility personified, perched beside the 'lesser,' my driver, whose real purpose they whisper is base and tawdry. Let them natter that I am too pretentiously humble and let them contemn me... 'for not knowing any better than to sit beside my lesser, my driver, rather than in his proper place in the back seat, being served and serviced by the 'lesser', for whatever puerile purpose.' Maybe I am all that, and maybe much, much worse."

With eyes gently shut, thought transmogrified and he envisioned the mighty and ascendant gathered here in this fine home, of one of their finest, this audience on verge of being newly seeded with revelation, *"awaiting my least whim and command: I am not to be served but—worshipped."*

He envisioned their hopes and prayers... *"to deliver them to as yet unimagined heights of triumph and ascendance, orders of magnitude beyond even this grotesque opulence."*

"They await me as their deliverer and I... am shamed even to imagine such delusion and self-delusion as I am about to allow myself to perpetrate here and now. I sit here convinced of their hopes and prayers for deliverance to never-before imagined heights of ascendance... as I sit here in the dark contemplating their imminent humbling, beyond their worst nightmare, only just beyond the horizon of their vision."

The thought, the *full* sense of it, was a distant, hazy, tentative pall... growing palpably nearer, inescapably:

"I understand the dreams and prayers of the ascendant gathered here, now, to hear and see of me. It is unalterable that they... will... themselves here, to so hear and see of me, so voraciously urged to adulate me and genuflect to me... for all my promise."

He thought it, prayed it be free of even trace hubris:

"It is the inevitable consequence of the grasping greed of those gathered here—to see and to hear and to receive of all they see promised in me... for them. I am met as their imminent deliverer into untold riches and power and pride and sanctity the likes of which they cannot imagine but of which they are certain beyond all doubt they more than fully deserve, to catapult them towering above and transcendent over anything even remotely witnessed in the past, the very least of all they fully deserve and to which they have almightily been born."

Rob recoiled at his own greed and rapacity and self-idolatry, inherent in this interpretation—portent—of those gathered here. He re-focused on the silence and the dark, concentrated on seeing nothing, struggled to think of nothing—and prayed this elusive moment's simple peace and quiet, here and now, seated in the front passenger seat of this grand town car beside his beauteous driver, would endure, somehow survive this moment and each and every newly-created moment, aware that the realization of such prayer could exist only in fantasy, in a realm beyond any possible reality except, maybe, in the unimaginable bliss of the hereafter and, so... *"pray for the hereafter—peace is not for the likes of me in this existence."*

He wondered if his self-deprecation was genuine or simply a pretended humility, and smiled grimly:

"Such is the power of will, reifying the impossible, the unimaginable—that I am humble and pristine."

He laughed silent lament under shame of his arrogance and ascendance, real or imagined, that he could materialize any sort of peace or understanding for himself let alone for any other:

"We genuinely welcome peace only when all else fails us and we are thoroughly spent."

He opened his eyes amid the embers of silence and welcomed-in the engulfing dark. His driver understood, was thoroughly aware of the need for silence now, so her silence too engulfed him, all-welcomed, urgently needed. She, as all his beauteous acolytes, understood *need*.

"I'd fashioned my beauteous with as much, or as pathetically little, of such understanding as I could impart to them, for them, of the vanishingly little that I possess of such understanding."

"Impart for *them*… not for me, not for *my* self but for *theirs*!"

He mouthed the thought struggling to convince himself, despairing of convincing himself, of its truth, wondering how much was genuine and how much arrogance and hubris deeply buried under guise of truth.

"How much is simple truth, understanding my lowly and vulgar hubris, and how much is a pretention to humility? And how to decipher and who would decipher its reality?"

He felt empty—*"how else to feel when all I'd worked toward lists into the meaningless and purposeless and irrelevant, sitting here in this town car beside my beauteous, one among my manifold acolytes, and even of all I'd worked toward this far, this the least of my pernicious malevolence."*

"How could I not feel empty," not question but lament.

"No, not empty… full—of myself," he despaired. *"And that,"* he shuddered dolefully, *"empty."*

He stared into the dark reviling himself his arrogance—or the humble truth—*"that I could be, could will myself to be, lord over lords, I, the lowest of the low, and for all that am ordained to dispense the just and righteous future."*

He breathed-in the silence and the dark for a long, luxuriant moment languishing in the moment, contemplating the quiet terror of what lay in wait—*"of betrayal and self-betrayal concealed in the silence and the dark, as an infant frightens himself with some horrific imagining and dwells in fascinated terror so deep it blots out reality, renders reality itself imagined, blotting out all dream and memory of softest skin and warmest breast and sweetest milk and coziest bed and soporific scent of lilac nestled within caressing curves of doting mother just before sleep overtakes and soothes and blesses with oblivion. Even the eldest and wisest among us, just as the newest-born, are too steeped in ignorance and denial and self-delusion and simple, cavernous greed to understand the diversity and ephemera of the reality of need. The imagined terror of defeat and the imagined joy of triumph sustain our ignorance and denial of the reality of need... as the zealots among us exploit to the fullest, ever wantonly and fully shamelessly, anyone and everyone who succumbs to them or least resists them."*

The trance dissolved into the reality of the silence and the dark—he, seated in front passenger seat of town car beside his beauteous driver, she in punctilious evening attire topped in chauffeur cap, encumbered by being—or fully honored to be—shadow to him, to enshroud him in the image of adoration and veneration and, so, of incipient, sweeping power.

His driver knew, now, to step out of the silence and step fully into the dark, to circle the car, to open wide his door, and to stand aside, stiffly erect, ready to step briskly after him as he himself emerges from the silence and steps fully into the dark—*"I emerging not fully dead and not fully alive but extant in the dream-fugue of the nightmare of my own creation"*—and then follow him into the dark as his blindly-faithful guardian, just one among beauteous angels existing to inure him against the confines of this existence, of his reality... *"of the impending and inevitable future ordained of my design."*

"Existence is the aggregate of what we are created from and of what we create because of our collective histories and self-glorifying intentions. Existence flows out of the cascade of impenetrable consequence—by way of how we act and how we react amid that cascade of consequence flowing all around us, at times uplifting and at times casting down, even as so vastly many of us preen in our illusion of mastery. So we are generated by this world, this existence, into which we are thrust and compelled, first through no fault and then through every fault of our own."

/

Rob sat in the front passenger seat of his town car, his beauteous young woman, his driver and shield, now standing by his fully opened door. She was attired in extravagant evening gown—with chauffeur cap crowning her. He shut his eyes gently—and materialized Lainy beside him, warm and alive beside him, holding him, gracing him, he peering into her eyes, luxuriating in her lips, listing nearer to her, ever nearer, her breath at his, as he, even now… edges back, turns away.

He realized Lainy had seen it, had always seen it, and had looked past it, for her own sake, and his—he edging back, turning away—much as he denied it to her almost as much as he denied it to himself, he listing away from her for *need* too seductive, too demanding, too overpowering from which to turn away. He clawed at remembering her, her eyes, her lips, *her*, she scintillating in the dark, bathed in the dark, this dark finer than any light, this of her to fill his memory of her….

He turns to his Lainy ever softly, in deepest lament:
"I've got to—go."
He can't look at her as his lips shape that final word, the word slipping past silent cry as he holds her and breathes of her one last time, their future reduced, now, to silence in the dark.
"And what of now?" he thinks to ask.
"In the span of life and of all time, what is one year before we are re-joined? Or two? Or…."
Silent whispers strive to console:
"In the blink of an eye such time ends. From our dotage we gaze back and suddenly… it is over. As if only first beginning, we look back and suddenly see our time is… over."
"It's not enough, it can never be enough!"
He wonders if Lainy feels as he does, watching her eyes in the dark, praying 'yes,' then wondering about prayer.
He recalls their words to each other, a chimera of hidden silence in the dark amid ruminations:
"And what now?"
"Now… nothing. Now, only the future is anything."
"No. Only 'now' is anything." So alike in thought and feeling there is no difference in who says what to whom.
He recalls memory to the fore:
They step back from each other, no matter the hurt, no matter the harm, and one long, last hold and lingering look before she turns slowly away, walks silently away, each wondering when, if, the next hold would be, each wondering

327

how, where, could go the hours and the days and the years...
now no longer with each other.

He is silence as he watches her eyes and holds her
close and listens to far away whispers in the dark, and wonders
how to convey to her, fully convey to her, of *need*:

*"I've got to—can do nothing less and with all that I
am—stop Allman and all that is Allman's from rendering the
world... uninhabitable,"* the only word that comes to mind.

He wonders about impossibilities, of convincing any
one—*Lainy*—beyond least doubt, of *need*, and strives to *will*
his need into her:

*"Allman and all that is Allman's... is driven to render
the world uninhabitable to compassioned, reasoned minds.
How can I but intercede with all I am."*

He labors over how to convey passionate truth to her,
most passionate. Forlorn thought whispers his need, all-silent:

*"How impossible... to impart the irresistible command
of irrevocable need."*

His silence is all she'd needed.

They stare into each other eye-to-eye, breath-to-breath,
with no thought left to 'what if'—what if they, *he*, could will
himself to overcome *need* in him, owning him wholly.

He takes her and holds her and stares into her eyes,
seeing past her eyes, seeing *her*, then pulls back ever slightly,
to look at her again, to press into himself and to fully possess
that image of *her*... *"nothing more left of her, all that is left of
her."*

All silent, she turns and walks away.

*"She turned and walked away—and I just watch her
walk away."*

He thinks to deny it, expunge it, command it, and
finally beseeches—of himself:

"I could have stopped her!"

Grim thought hunts him, trembles him with rage and
outrage... *"that I didn't try, I didn't want... even to try."*

The silence and the dark flows in her wake, hearing in
the silence and the dark his own whispers augur:

*"You command me: "Relinquish her." You command
me: "Abandon her." You command me: "Turn your back... on*

her, on them... on every man and every woman and every child ever born and still to be born."

He stares into darkest eyes, his own reflected back on him from hers... *"revealing me and heralding me with untold misery and immeasurable anguish and—maybe—triumphant deliverance and supernal redemption."*

He labors to understand:

"And through it all and for it all... You damn me for it all," his prayer of lament beseeching to *deserve* redemption.

He sees himself aflame in a gaunt and dreamless world, of darkest nightmare riven in vacant orbs impaled on skeletal faces and, too, sees himself—maybe—shepherding-in the dawn.

Here and now he is ready to alight on the way, and to light the way, and usher-in the dark and, maybe, the emerging, brilliantly dazzling dawn—filled with penetrating hate and singular joy, one and the other and both together, by virtue of what he is and by what he is commanded. He wonders who, what, commands him and where such commandment leads— *"and of what use 'why.'"*

"And through it all and for it all they—You—curse ME for it all! Still, better cursed for trying than blessed for never having tried."

He shudders at that last:

"And am I to be held to account for all their sufferings? And if I chance to rouse them and raise them up, should I care if I'm reviled—or revered?"

He shudders to know: *"Yes and... yes."*

He considers, sweeps aside:

"And who will know, and who will care."

He puts off damning himself:

"Can a people better themselves when those they choose to plead their cause plead only for themselves? Can a people better themselves by kneeling to plutocrats and kleptocrats they themselves elect to rule them?"

He understands, prays he understands:

"Wrenching the people out of their pall is left to me, remains for me and for those like me"—as silence whispers

irreducible truth and repugnance: *"and who is like me?"* That not question but damnation.

He struggles against the repugnance of hubris, thinking he and only he could gouge and scrape the people out from their brume and misery:

"Who has stepped in to believe in them and release them?" images of Allman and all that is Allman's towers to full view in their vast, unfettered kinds and numbers—*"they and their horde, pretense personified to being 'of and for the people' in the sanctimony of 'for the greater good,' grasp under the boundless, shameless greed of self-adulation and self-idolatry."*

He shudders under the enormity of pretensions and deceptions—especially his own.

/

Rob sat in the front-passenger seat of the town car beside his beauteous driver, one among his shield and vanguard, peering into the dark seeing, aspiring to see, praying to see, the future awaiting him. He regarded this one future among the blindingly many, this clearest of all: he, bearing the rigid bounties springing of being the essence of patience, knew this future to be of his construction, of his design... his *creation....*

He faced the vast panoramic window of a back wall of a back office of some exalted structure rising up to the heavens, looming above the masses milling and churning below him, standing amid his hubris, that they were not simply below where he stood but were below *him.*

"And so, I am guilty, and more, as any and all those I despise and damn, and abominate the thought: I am as they are, I am of their kind... and worse, beyond even their depth and breadth. Who am I to arrogate the future," as whispers taunt under overarching hubris, or truth: *"but far better mine than theirs."*

He shuddered at that last, arrogating the future *he* would create as being ordained brighter and higher and more righteous than any other could possibly be.

Rob struggled to shake the portent of his hubris, of his urgings to control, no command, no *ordain* the future—and succeeded only in pallid pantomime of the humility he craved... and found himself again and still, standing in the back-office of the towering Spire, lost in thought even as distraction groped to corrupt the sheet of images floating in the dark before him— DeCeeve rambling on, fully immersed as ever within his vast greed and flourishing self-adulation, the hallmark of his kind—*"and mine,"* silent lamentation, silent whisper in the dark.

"Some things do not change: DeCeeve and his kind sermonize, impaled within the full faith and vainglory of their self-idolatry—and the people hang on their every word as if of prophecy, blinding themselves to the self-evident: that he and his ilk are nothing more than the sons and daughters of those endless incarnations of shameless hubris and untethered greed."

Rob meditated on the vast numbers of smarmy martinets coveting that same primacy and supremacy... *"even if in smallest measure,"* and was mystified how humanity and civilization had managed to get even this far under such privation.

Rob mused at images of people clothed expansively, gemmed opulently, milling and flaunting and posing, all shamelessly, casually, groping through imperious persona and thoroughly veiled desperation to be esteemed and desired and revered, vacuously opining empty erudition from their blind, alien landscapes, pronouncing on a world from which they are as far removed as any alien could be—*"what do such as they and their kind know... of the people. And how can people fall so thoroughly under them?"* Inscrutable, beyond understanding.

Rob understood the murk, this moneyed elite... and reviled himself for being certain he understood them thoroughly:

"The elite hunger to bend society to their own image 'for the greater good,' and construct a barest, most simpering endurance, most bare survival, for the people, for 'the greater good'—for their own greater good."

"The elite convince each other and themselves that only so can 'the greater good' manifest at all. And more: The elite contrive that the people be grateful—no, worshipful—for the people's own vanishingly spare existence. And the elite wage holy war against any and all who work toward egalitarian principles, in all good conscience... their conscience... believing they must—for 'the greater good.' Only remains is to indelibly carve their fortunes and their futures into the fabric of this and every conceivable future—by still further diminishing and debasing 'the people.' How else to guarantee the unfettered, eternal, cavernous preeminence of the elite?"

Rob breathed deeply, aware of this risk, struggled to rise out of his fugue: to avert desecrating the elite even as the elite themselves desecrate the people—*"to keep myself from perpetuating on the elite what the elite perpetrate against the people. So easy and simple a thing to do... undermine the elite by subverting them, in turn, into the simpering cowed."*

"The thoughts and urgings of the elite are the transparent occupations and pre-occupations of their class and of their kind, how can I fault the elite for being true to themselves? How can I fault the elite for being, simply, what they are and what they were born to: base animals wracked by arrogance and hypocrisy and, above all, sanctimonious greed? So were they conceived and reared fully to believe," and with silent whispers: *"as are most all of us, as I am myself, to the fullest bounds of our endowments."*

Rob struggled to absolve himself: *"I am being realistic, not righteous, not self-righteous, in auguring and effecting the demise of the elite,"* and then loathed himself for the risk he was willing, even urging to take: *"that I could transcend my own, native greeds and compulsions and so could constrain myself from doing to the elite as the elite have done, are doing, will do, to 'the people'"*—as portent stretched clawing fingers at his throat.

"The elite preen and strut as I penetrate them with their own greeds and plunge them into the depths of their own self-idolatry. They are chattel at my hand and one day soon they will waken to the abomination of knowing themselves."

Rob was suddenly repulsed by his own repugnance of the elite, *"do they deserve such repugnance? They are only being true to themselves, as any base animal—as am I myself."*

He battled against himself, floundering for that vermillion shadowland looming somewhere in the dark, suspended between damning the elite un-justly and fully justly—and woke to DeCeeve expounding a soliloquy of self-idolatry.

Rob wondered why he should be so repelled by his repugnance of DeCeeve and his kind, as he witnessed this repugnance embodied here in his face, personified in DeCeeve.

"This harlequin marionette preaches my platform—believing it his! The depth of DeCeeve's self-deception, rooted in unfettered greed and self-idolatry, is staggering... and even still I feel dirtied by my own overarching pride in this, the earliest incantation of my harvest—with DeCeeve droning on, not knowing enough to quake in anticipation of being imminently set-upon by 'the people,' without least clue of what fully awaits."

DeCeeve: "I don't have to tell *you* where I've got President Kurb!"

DeCeeve's smile was repulsive gloat as he flourished grand self-importance and absolute triumph fully credited to himself—as Rob strained against self-loathing for the horror standing before him: *"the horror I created!"*

DeCeeve droned on, now raging as he nodded toward the people crowding the front office:

"They're scared, you know!"

He laughed chillingly:

"They're scared of that mob down there," nodding at the enormity gathered in the streets and alleyways below.

"Who'd have thought so many people, such vast numbers, would actually show up to protest what is only for their own good, for their *own* greater good? The fools! The very people who *should* be supporting us have turned ugly and against us, and now our people are scared to walk out the door, scared of the people out there, scared the people will stalk them and snatch away their diamond rings and platinum chains and gold watches and precious drippings, scared those people will trail them home and steal away their treasures and ravage their wives and sons and daughters and *them!*"

DeCeeve peeled repulsive laughter as thought pierced Rob:

"And so I've got to reckon with this homunculus, this corrosion to sight and sound and mind, for what I am and for what I've done—he... the embodiment of MY sins!"

Revulsion swept him—of himself. Then he steadied himself, fought to regain some semblance of equilibrium, to regain a bit of calm and of reason, and reminded himself that his *intent* had been, still is, worthy, and he fought to convince himself:

"After all—it's for the greater good!" and struggled to absolve himself:

"The benefits ARE worth their sufferings—the ends DO justify the means!"

Thought preyed on him as he augured the cost, images agonizing, extolling *"for the people!"* in boundless hypocrisy, justifying his means and lionizing his ends with platitudes and clichés, fully aware:

"Only when it's in-your-face, only when it's staring the elite full in the eye, only when the elite see it, feel it, LIVE it for themselves—those privations the elite had leveled against 'the people' for all these countless ages—only then can the elite even begin to understand the crying need for change."

"And only then will I understand the exorbitant precariousness of 'the ends' and the full-form anguish risked by 'the means,' through which I'll deliver those ends."

Rob cringed under his feint 'for the people' as he clawed for the words within which to veil his lies, groping to justify what he'd set into motion, fallen under the weight of the struggle to understand, to fully apprehend, just how lofty those 'ends' must be and just how gentle those 'means' must be for the ends ever to justify the means he was setting into motion.

/

Rob sat in the town-car beside his beauteous driver in a fugue of portent as portent skirted clawing tendrils round his throat....

Rob gaped stonily through the panoramic window-wall overlooking anarchy fulminating in the streets and alleyways below, struck mute and rigid by the sight, unbelieving, struggling amid boundless shame and overarching pride poised between guilt and glory, until gnawing remorse erupted and seized him:

"The worst of all nightmares will triumph—until, if ever, the new dawn emblazons the dark."

That, as DeCeeve burst into the room bleating hysteria:

"I can't get *away*! They're swarming *all around us*!"

Rage overtook Rob at this homunculus yammering terror in his face, DeCeeve not recognizing his own complicity and guilt. DeCeeve lurched at Rob, stared him eye-to-eye, bleating:

"You did this!"

Rob slumped under rage and vanity drained dry under absurdity smiling invisibly at him—*"now... he accords me credit"*—staggering under the enormity of that truth, finally and far too late filling DeCeeve with comprehension, and Rob could only breathe:

"Yes."

The sound carried realms past enduring....

A telephone buzzed softly for Rob, as he stood high in the back office of the Liberty Spire. He eased the phone from its dock, lifted it to ear, listened as he eyed DeCeeve, standing impotently by under terror roiling him.

Rob eased the phone back into its cradle, eyed DeCeeve another instant, then quietly announced:

"A mob is swarming the atrium."

Rob, thinly grim, unsure if this invasion boded for good or ill, pondered the nature of 'good,' adding:

"They've blocked the elevators and are storming up the front stairways... you'd better duck out the emergency stairs," and, seeing indecision in DeCeeve, commanded: *"Now."*

DeCeeve wavered for another instant, spun around to rush off, then paused, seeing Rob stand firm:

"And you?" DeCeeve's eyes revealed all of him:

"This of him reflects not concern for me but simply another tactic: to see which way I run, where I run... to follow—or not."

To this fleeting thought, Rob reviled himself still and again, imputing base motive to simple look and tone.

"Still—I know I'm right," and he shamed himself punishingly, to be so sure.

To DeCeeve:

"Go! *Now!*"

And in hardly audible whisper:

"It's your best and only hope."

Rob watched DeCeeve waver for another brief instant, watched him surmise that Rob was ever-likely correct and, for whatever mystifying reason, remained standing firm even as he wished DeCeeve safely escaped.

Silently, to DeCeeve's back, Rob lamented, wondered what he lamented, knew only that the sense overwhelmed: the need, now, to lament... for DeCeeve, not for himself: *"I... am lost beyond the reach of lament."*

Rob turned to the vast panorama-window, stared out, down, to the sweeping flow of a vast and infinitesimal fraction of humanity flooding into the Liberty Spire, sweeping in, rising up—*"for me,"* and felt relief flood him... *"to be targeted, as I've fully earned, finally in their sights."*

Rob stood facing the window and the dark beyond, the dark held at bay by glass and thinnest shadowland cleaved from his other, darker self, the one to which he'd surrendered long ago... *"with Lainy as my witness,"* envisaged amid deepest lament and shame, even still unable to reconcile surrendering her, aching to be with her and to scrounge back the years without her, even still steadfastly defiant... *"that 'the people' and 'the greater good' should rightfully have been—*

maybe," its rearing ambivalence tearing at him— *"subordinated to Lainy."*

Rob stood his ground and patiently welcomed-in the amassed. No rush, this.

A near-distant clamor, now louder, and louder still, approached, now suborn by a rumbling outcry as his door burst open.

The amassed fulminated into his sanctuary there in the back office of the Liberty Spire in a crescendo of outraged faces, of women and men near-fully unleashed. The horde surged through the doorway, filled the back office—and held itself at bay on seeing him, heaving and undulating at sight of him, only his thinnest presence lodged between them and simply one more trifling atrocity.

They stood amassed against him glaring rhythmic threat, confronting Rob staring them down, standing rigid against their *intent* etched in piercing eyes and gnarled lips and white-balled fists raging against him, diminutive stilled figure standing up to them, standing against them with only *defiance* denying them.

The horde jammed into the back office and—froze.

Rob clung to the silence and the dark as he faced the amassed, his back now to all he held most dear—the silence and the dark awaiting him just beyond the sheet of glass at his back, the coveted silence and the dark waiting patiently only *just* beyond reach behind him, into which he'd joyously leap, so to be, again and finally, one with all he wanted and needed… the silence and the dark.

Now there was nothing for him but to face the clamoring Beast—*"conceived and borne and endowed by me!"*—ebbing and flowing at his reach, backing away and surging nearer into that vanishingly scant distance between them, their hunger for him palpable, he within so easy reach of them, so easy prey to them—*"what holds them suspended lay beyond fathoming."*

The clamor abruptly stilled to silence as Rob heard the rustle of one now materialized among them, suddenly imbedded within them, a presence awing them to silence now stepping from within them, they parting like the sea to usher-in one who need only step ever-gently and the horde parting like the sea.

A demure, diminutive figure slipped silently into a hallowed emptiness, a gilded treasure shepherded-in to their fore under reverent silence, their hearts and minds entombed here and now by this slightest figurine presented against that which stood alone and unbending against their full will and intent.

The horde held back, rage abruptly aborted, staring, now silent, behind eyes and lips and fists held in deepest fount of adoration, adulation, outrage held beyond enduring all the years building and roiling to now, now held still and silent in the dark, all eyes fixed and rapt on this beauteous apparition materialized among them.

Rob stood his ground, no rush, this, as the diminutive seraph materialized among the amassed to stand against him.

He stared, amazed, to witness so diminutive a form rise up from the amassed to stand so inviolable against him.

And then he saw, and time and breath abandoned.

She scanned the room, eyes settling on the solitary figure confronting her, daring to stand against her, her eyes settling to his face, staring into his eyes... and then she saw.

Lainy froze in mid-intent, mute and senseless for that briefest instant, staring into the solitary figure confronting her.

Then she recognized, realized, and suddenly all fell clear. She saw, and recognized, who confronted her, who dared stand up to her, who stood against her, here and now, like this.

And suddenly, everything fell clear.

In that instant hate and rage and outrage vaporized, replaced by dawning understanding.

"This can't be," thought shot through her in that half-instant, *"so—is not."*

"Then—what?"

"Then..." realization dawned, understanding staggered.

Seeing her, Rob could no longer contain himself and buried face in hands and crumpled into himself kneeling to the floor at her feet, for all he'd done and would do, for all he was and would be—how could he, such as he, face her, such as her.

Silence filled and seized the room as the amassed stared transfixed at two figures facing each other in the dark.

Finally, slowly, she took a hesitant step nearer the figure crumpled to the floor at her feet.

She stepped near, nearer, reached tremulous fingers to him, guided him up to face her, to look her in the eye, to face her eye-to-eye and breath-to-breath and, finally and at long last, all was clear:

"Finally, we are as we'd always known we would be."

Silence flooded the dark around them as they fell into each other and pressed into each other and melded into each other as the congregation witnessed them light up the dark.

/

Rob sat in silence in the front passenger seat of the town car, beside his beauteous driver. For a long moment he stared into the dark peering into the portent of his own creation looming in the dark before him, incipient life and future patiently awaiting him.

His beauteous driver stepped from the car, walked smartly around to his door, and stood aside as she swung the door wide for him.

Rob peered into the silence and the dark, witnessed images of gaunt cravings crying-out to him, *for* him, in their need and in their greed—and, most of all, in his own.

Of silent whisper:

"Who are you to arrogate self-righteous conceit for this moment, even if—especially if—you so deserve."

He shuddered, returned to himself, knew to resolve for himself, here and now, to step into the dark—or not.

§

www.ingramcontent.com/pod-product-compliance
Lightning Source LLC
Chambersburg PA
CBHW062020170626
46813CB00001B/234